1824

# LOGAN

# LOGAN

*by*
*Duane L. Petersen*

**Published 2006 by:**

D&D Books
P.O. Box 458
Cascade, Idaho 83611
USA


**ISBN 0-9763421-5-4**


Cover Photo and Design by Don Dopf, Cambridge Litho, Inc., in cooperation with Earl Nelson

**Printed in the United States of America**

# CHAPTER 1

The Rafter T Ranch was a large cattle operation on the western slopes of the Rocky Mountains and was one of the first ranches settled in this area. Hugh Davis, a Texas cattleman, was looking for greener pastures when he first rode through the area. He had left his folks' big ranch in Texas looking for a place of his own. He wanted to get away from the dry desert country where he had grown up. An old friend of his father had spent many years traveling the Rocky Mountains as a trapper and scout for the army. He always told of the clear rivers and the tall green grass in the mountain meadows. These stories caused Hugh to want to see this country. All these stories made him dream of homesteading and starting his own ranch. He was in his middle forties and had a wife and son. The Texas ranch was owned by his parents and their three sons who were all still living and working there. All three sons were married. Each one would inherit a share of the place when the folks died. Hugh decided he wanted no part of sharing a ranch. He wanted one of his own. When he informed his family of his plan, they told him he was crazy to leave. "I'm going to sign over any share I've earned on this ranch and I want to leave as soon as possible."

Hugh's wife really didn't like the idea. "I'm not going to travel all over this country while you look for a place to build this ranch you're dreaming about."

She moved back to El Paso to live with her folks who were well off. Her family was in the banking business. They never figured out what their daughter had seen in a cowboy from west Texas. Hugh had met Helen while he was in El Paso delivering cattle from the ranch. With a short courtship he'd talked her into marrying him. They had one son, Hugh Jr., who was fifteen when Hugh headed for the Rocky Mountains. Hugh Jr. stayed with his mother to further his education. It would be seven years before Hugh saw his son again.

The second year after Hugh left Texas he settled on a homestead on the place which was now the Rafter T. It was the largest ranch in the area. He wrote for his wife to join him. He told her by letter he would meet her in Denver. This would be half way between El Paso and the new ranch. Later, when he got her answer back, he found out she had filed for divorce and it had been granted. It seems her family had a friend who was a judge. She filed on grounds of desertion. The judge granted the divorce.

When Hugh found out he was no longer a married man, he turned the rest of his life into developing one of the finest ranches west of the Rocky Mountains.

When Hugh first left Texas on his trip north, he had met up with a young man by the name of Ted McTier. McTier was from Tennessee and was looking for a better life. He had been raised by a family of dirt farmers trying to raise crops on ground that was worthless. Ted had earned enough money working in a small sawmill to buy a horse and a saddle. The horse and saddle were both in poor shape, but to Ted they were his treasures. Now he could leave Tennessee and head west looking for that better life.

Hugh was camping one night by a small creek. While cooking supper he heard a horse approaching. It was almost dark. Hugh moved his rifle close in case the rider was not friendly.

The rider hailed the camp, "I'm friendly and just looking for someone to talk to."

Hugh chuckled when he heard this, "Come on in, just keep your hands in sight." A tall skinny kid sitting on a horse that looked like it was on its last legs rode into camp.

Hugh nodded, "Why don't you step down. I'll throw another couple slices of bacon on to cook and we'll eat. The name is Hugh Davis."

The lad stuck out his hand, "I'm Ted McTier, from Tennessee. I'm heading west to look for work." As Ted unsaddled the skinny old horse, Hugh noticed that all he could see for firearms was an old cap and ball rifle. Ted moved over to the fire carrying a sack. "I got some bacon I could add to the supper." Out of the bag came a few other items, mostly salt and some dried jerky and a coffee pot and frying pan.

Hugh decided that was why this kid was so skinny. He was about to starve himself to death and did not know it. Hugh took the bacon and sliced off a few slices and added them to the skillet he had on the fire. Hugh had a pan of biscuits he had baked the night before to add to the supper.

As they ate Hugh asked, "How come you left Tennessee?"

"My folks are dry land farmers and I just wanted away from that dirt farm. Where are you headed?" Hugh chuckled at the question.

"The reason I'm asking I thought maybe I could ride along with you for a few days." Hugh nodded, "We'll see."

After supper Hugh rolled out his bed roll. He watched as Ted untied a long coat from behind his saddle and rolled out his saddle blanket. This was all this kid had for a bed. Hugh looked over at this lean skinny kid. "Ted, I'd be glad to have your company on the trail for awhile," and with that went to sleep.

They finished off the bacon the next morning. While saddling up, Hugh nodded off to the west. "There's a small town about half a day's ride north of here. We can pick up more supplies there."

"Mr. Davis, I don't have any money."

Hugh grinned, "How did you make it this far with no money?"

"I'd stop by any ranch or farm and offer work for supplies. Sometimes I got run off without getting paid for my work except maybe for a meal. I built a chicken coop for a lady a couple weeks ago. She had given me the bacon and a few other supplies. I run out of powder for my rifle so I haven't been able to shoot any meat for a week or more."

Hugh shook his head and thought to himself, "This is one tough kid, and he'll make someone a good hand." As they neared the small settlement, Hugh asked, "Ted, would you be interested in working for me? I'm traveling around looking for the right place and when I find it I'll start building a new ranch. When I find the right place I'll need a good hand to help me."

Ted just looked at him, "Do you really mean what you just said?"

Hugh nodded, "I really do. But I expect hard work when we find this place." This was the way Ted McTier became Hugh Davis's right hand man.

When they rode up to the trading post store, Hugh spotted a sign down the street that read, "Boarding House." Hugh stepped down off his horse and motioned for Ted to join him. As he entered the store, he was surprised how well stocked the place was. There were two men behind the counter. One moved down the counter to wait on Hugh. Hugh looked back toward the door. Ted was still outside looking in. Hugh motioned for him to come on in. Hugh turned to the clerk, "I need some clothes for this kid and we'll need some boots."

Hugh winked at Ted, "I'll take these clothes out of your wages."

Hugh started stocking up on supplies for the trail. "How about we leave these supplies here until we're ready to leave?"

The clerk nodded, "You bet. We'll put them in the store room."

"Now we've got our supplies, where can we buy a horse?"

The clerk laughed, "I can help you on that too. My partner and I have taken in some horses in trade for supplies. Some are pretty good stock."

The clerk motioned to follow him out the back door. Hugh could see a house across a small opening with corrals and a barn. They walked over to the corral with a couple dozen horses. Hugh climbed up where he could see better and could see some good horses in the bunch.

He motioned to a tall bay horse, "What's the price on the bay?"

"Fifty dollars and I'll throw in a saddle."

Hugh nodded, roped the horse and led him back to the store.

The clerk opened the door to a storage shed, "Pick out the saddle you want."

There was at least twenty saddles of all shapes and condition along the back wall.

Hugh nodded toward the pile, "Ted, pick out a good one and get a good blanket."

Hugh walked back into the store. He noticed a rack of used guns on the back wall.

The clerk nodded over toward the rifles. "Take your pick on a rifle and I'll toss in two boxes of shells."

Hugh picked out a Springfield trap door 45-70 and a scabbard. After Hugh paid for everything, the clerk asked, "Where're you fellows headed?"

"West, I'm looking for some land for a cattle ranch," Hugh motioned up the street. "Is that boarding down the street there open for one night stays?"

The clerk nodded, "Sure is. The lady running the place put on some mighty good grub and plenty of it."

Hugh laughed, "If that's the case, I hope my new hand don't founder himself."

At the boarding house the lady showed them their room and added, "Supper is at six sharp."

"It's four o'clock now. We'll have time to clean up and get you into those new clothes," Hugh smiled at his new hand.

The lady running the place walked back from the kitchen, "I've got a tub in my wash room out back. The water is still hot in the tank. If you want, you can leave your clothes. I'll wash them tonight and you can have them back come morning."

Hugh grinned, "Lady you got a deal."

Hugh smiled to himself. He didn't think Ted had ever seen a tub before, but once in it he was all smiles. With the new clothes on, Ted was strutting around like a rooster.

"We'll just throw these clothes away if that's alright with you, Ted."

Ted looked over at Hugh, "I'd really like to keep the pants; Ma made them for me."

When Hugh and Ted entered the dining room, there were only four people for supper." The food was good. Ted had two helpings of everything, then later on had a piece of berry pie.

As they walked out, the lady winked at Hugh, "Now, that boy was hungry."

As they got into bed that night, Hugh remembered something he had forgotten. Ted did not have a good bedroll.

After eating a big breakfast, Hugh and Ted stopped by the store to load up. Hugh went back into the store and picked up a bedroll for Ted.

The clerk stepped out on the porch while they were mounting. "Take that north trail west of here and that'll take you over the crest of the Rockies. If you do go that way, don't waste any time because these mountain passes close early each fall. It's now into late summer and in the high country it'll be freezing at night."

The clerk had given good directions and the trail was easy to follow. They traveled steady for about three weeks and now they were above timberline. The country was rocky and bare. All day as they moved west, the wind was getting stronger.

Hugh looked over at Ted, "I think we're heading into a storm. We'd better start looking for a sheltered place out of the wind."

By evening the wind was almost too strong to stay on the horses. Hugh had earlier spotted a valley down below the trail. They were now trying to find a way down to it before it got dark. As soon as they rode into the timber, the wind died down and they started looking for a camping spot. Hugh spied a good place in a thick grove of trees with good grass for the stock. It was still light enough to see when Hugh saw Ted pull his rifle and move into the trees. He heard a shot and before long Ted walked into camp carrying a young buck deer over his shoulder.

With a good fire going and meat and coffee cooking, they saw the first snowflakes drifting down on them.

It was a cold night, but with wood everywhere, they'd stay warm. At first light Hugh and Ted were surprised at how deep the snow was around camp. It was almost knee deep and was still snowing. Not as hard as last night but it was still coming down.

After breakfast Hugh told Ted, "We'd better head down off this mountain before the snow gets too deep for the horses."

Hugh followed the creek down through the meadow and then on down the canyon. This canyon was wide and pretty good traveling for the horses and by noon the snow was not as deep. They were dropping in elevation real fast and that night they found a place to camp. It was raining lightly. While Hugh was staking the horses out to graze, Ted started cooking supper. They were filling their plates when a voice from the trees hailed the camp. Hugh said, "Ride on in, supper's on."

Out of the trees appeared a man with a full beard and wearing all leather clothes. He was leading three pack horses, all with big packs. He stepped down, "The name is Dave Bowman."

"You're welcome to fill a plate and join us. I'm Hugh Davis and this young fellow is Ted McTier."

The old trapper laughed, "I'll take you up on that offer as soon as I unload my horses."

As he moved off, Hugh nodded to Ted. "I think this fellow might be what we've been looking for. He may know which way we can travel to find that place I'm looking for."

Dave walked up to the fire carrying a plate and a cup. From under his arm he pulled out a small jug. "This will take off the chill," and offered it to Hugh.

"It's a good after dinner drink, or before dinner, whichever you prefer."

Hugh poured a small amount in his coffee and passed the jug to Ted.

Ted took a small drink and smiled, I do believe this man carries some good whiskey."

As Dave filled his plate, he turned to Ted, "I'd say from that drawl of yours, you've probably drank some mighty fine whiskey in those Tennessee hills."

Hugh laughed, "I think maybe this fellow knows where you came from."

6

After the chores were all done Hugh asked Dave. "How long have you been in this area?"

Dave thought a minute, "I've been trapping in the area for about ten years. I'm headed back to my cabin up on the mountain to spend the winter trapping. When I get the horses unloaded at the cabin, I'll take them back to my other place about twenty miles down river from here. They'll winter out down there and the feed is good this year."

Hugh asked, "How come they don't drift away from the place?"

Dave grinned, "I usually block the main trail out and the only other way is up into the snow country."

Hugh added, " Dave, what I'm looking for is a place to build a good cattle ranch."

Dave nodded, "Come spring, I'll show you some country you might really like. It's too late in the year now to be trying to travel around this country. Where do you and Ted figure to hold up for the winter?"

Hugh shrugged, "I really haven't given that much thought. Being in country that is controlled by winter snowfall is new to me. In Texas snow isn't a traveling problem," he laughed.

Old Dave nodded. "You'd be smart to find a good valley down along the river and build a small cabin for the winter."

As the evening passed, Hugh learned a great deal about the area from this old trapper. They banked up the fire and rolled out their bedrolls. When Hugh woke up he could see Dave building up the fire.

Dave saw Hugh move, I'll cook breakfast. I owe you boys for that supper last night."

Hugh could smell venison cooking. He looked over at Ted who was now awake, "I think we're in for a mighty fine breakfast."

Hugh was surprised when he saw a Dutch oven next to the fire. When the meat was done, Dave brought out hot biscuits from the oven.

After finishing a great meal, Dave turned to Hugh, "I've got a deal you might be interested in. You fellows need a place to winter and my cabin down river will be empty. If you'll help me move my supplies up to my winter cabin, I'll take you down to get settled in the river cabin. Usually I move my supplies to the winter cabin, then return the horses to the river cabin. Then when I get ready to go up for the winter I have to walk."

"One winter I tried to keep one horse with me at the high cabin. He almost starved by spring. I cut willows for him to eat and finally I was able

7

to pack a trail down to the river so he could find feed. Since then I've walk back up from the lower place. If you boys help me now, then when its time for me to move up for the winter, you boys can help there too. We'll take horses up until the snow gets deep then I can walk from there and you fellows can take my horse back with you."

Hugh nodded, "I think that's a very fair deal for me and Ted. We'll do it."

After breaking camp, Hugh left their pack horses and headed up the mountain with Dave. Dave nodded, "We'll be back here in camp before dark. Your horses will be fine here." As they were mounting up, Ted motioned to a herd of deer across the river.

He looked over at Dave, "If you don't need me to help, I think I'll get us some meat for the winter."

Dave nodded, "Good idea. Hugh and I'll get along fine. We'll see you come evening."

Ted grinned, "It's cool enough now the meat wouldn't spoil and I'll jerk part of it for later use." As Hugh and Dave were heading up the mountain, they heard three shots back toward camp.

Dave smiled, "Can that Tennessee boy shoot like most of those mountain boys do?"

"So far since we've been together Ted always has meat for us and I haven't ever heard him shoot twice yet."

Old Dave nodded, "I grew up in those Tennessee hills. I learned at a young age, to shoot well was necessary to survive."

Hugh was surprised when Dave stopped, "Well, we're here."

All Hugh could see was tall trees. Dave grinned and motioned to some willows along a small creek. Then Hugh saw the cabin; it was almost hidden.

Hugh laughed, "I'd ridden right by this cabin without ever seeing it".

Dave grinned, "I kinda hid it a little. I didn't want too much company."

Hugh was again surprised at how well the cabin was built. There was a rock fireplace on one end and a bunk along one wall. A small table made from a log and one chair completed the furniture. They put all the supplies in a cellar under the cabin. There was a trap door in the cabin floor with a ladder leading into the cellar. There was an outside door in from the bottom of the cabin.

Dave said, "Come winter this lower door is covered with snow." When they finished packing the supplies into the cellar, Dave closed up the lower door. He barred it from the inside with three cross bars.

Hugh laughed, "I guess you don't want anyone breaking in here."

Dave smiled, "I only use this door when loading in supplies once a year." Hugh followed Dave up the ladder leading upstairs to the main cabin. When Dave moved the table over the trap door, it was no longer visible. Dave closed the door to the cabin. "One more chore and we'll be ready to head down the mountain."

Dave moved to the side of the cabin where the cellar door was. He moved some logs over the opening and covered them with brush. Then he brushed away their tracks and all signs of the door was gone.

As they headed back down the trail, much of the snow that fell the day before was gone, except in the shady places. "It's a little early for the snow to stay on. I always try to move my supplies right after the first snow. One time the first snow stayed on and I had a hard time getting my camp stocked for winter."

As they rode into the camp, there was meat everywhere. Ted was busy boning out the three deer he had got. He was roasting their supper over the fire. He had one drying rack set up and had it loaded with cut strips making jerky.

Hugh and Dave walked up to the fire after unsaddling their horses. Dave nodded to Hugh, "This young fellow would make somebody a good wife."

Ted turned toward them, "For that, go get your own meat for supper."

The coffee pot was on so they all sat down and enjoyed a cup. "I'm through with the boning. I'll finish with the meat when we get to Dave's cabin. I've got the hides already salted and rolled up. I'll work on them while we're snowed in this winter."

After breakfast they loaded all the meat on the pack horses and headed down the trail. Hugh could only smile when they arrived at Dave's main cabin. This was a beautiful valley with good grass and plenty of water. Dave had been watching Hugh. "I thought you might like it here."

Ted, like Hugh, replied, " I've never seen a place like this before."

They unpacked the horses. Dave walked over to show Ted the meat house. "You can hang the deer in here."

When they finished unpacking Dave's supplies, it was getting along toward dark. "Come morning I'll show you where to store your supplies."

The cabin had two rooms and a covered porch. There was a cookstove

9

and a fireplace in the biggest room. The other room had four bunks along the walls and a table in the middle of the floor. Dave started a fire in the cookstove and rolled out biscuits from his sour dough starter. Like many old timers, he kept the starter in his flour bin. After a good meal, Dave brought out another jug and they spiced up their coffee.

Hugh asked, "Where can we buy supplies for the winter?"

"There's a trading post down river about twenty miles. They're well stocked with about everything a person could want. I need to make one more trip there before heading up to trap. We'll go down there the day after tomorrow, if that is okay with you. We'll spend the night and then head back up here the next day."

Dave laughed, "Besides that, they make mighty fine moonshine if you boys need a winter supply."

Ted and Hugh looked at each other. "We could use some snake bite medicine, besides we might catch cold and need the medicine."

Ted and Hugh spent the next day getting settled in for the winter. There was a good barn behind the cabin with a good sized tack room for all their gear. Hugh decided to hobble his pack horses until they got use to this being home.

Dave told Hugh, "My horses never leave the valley and I think yours will stay." They were up early the morning they headed for what Dave called the Sutter Creek Trading Post. It was a sunny but cool ride downriver. Hugh was again surprised when they rode into the trading post. It was almost a small town, a hotel with a café, saddle shop, blacksmith shop, and a saloon. The trading post itself was a big building. Inside it was a real well stocked store. Hugh was trying to remember if he had ever seen such a place.

Ted smiled, "I've never seen a store this big."

As they started filling their order, Hugh was watching the prices. He commented to Dave, "These prices seem very fair."

Dave nodded, "The family that owns this place freight their own goods in. They've always been cheaper than any post around." Hugh paid for the supplies they had purchased then made arrangements to leave them until morning when they were ready to head back. With the shopping done, they decided on a drink, then to find a place to spend the night. They found a room in the hotel with three cots in one room. After stowing their gear, they went looking for something to eat. With supper over, they headed back to the saloon for a night cap.

Hugh and Ted had one drink, "We're heading to the room."

"I think I'll stick around for a while to catch up on all the local gossip."

The next morning with the horses all loaded, they headed back up toward Dave's cabin. It was a cool morning with clouds starting to form in the south. Dave was looking at the sky, "It looks like we've got a storm coming. I think tomorrow I'll have you take me up to the winter cabin."

As they rounded a ridge, they heard a shot close by and a small bunch of deer came running past them. When the deer saw the riders, they turned back up the hill. Dave had pulled his rifle and downed the big buck with the bunch. It was a running shot and a good hit, and when the animal hit the ground, it never moved. Dave rode over and got down to cut the animal's throat. Hugh spotted a rider coming down off the ridge toward them. When the rider stopped in front of them, Dave looked up, "It's not like you to miss, Lottie."

Both Hugh and Ted were surprised when they heard the name Lottie.

The gal had swung down and walked over to where Dave was kneeling by the deer. "We'll dress out the deer and load it up behind you. How's your dad doing?" Dave asked the girl while they dressed out the deer.

She shook her head, "Not good."

Dave introduced her to Hugh and Ted. "Lottie and her dad will be your closest neighbor this winter." As Lottie was mounting her horse, Dave looked up at her. "Do you need any supplies?"

She nodded, "We're out of salt and low on flour. I really need some coffee to keep Dad happy. I've got a few skins stretched but I don't like leaving Dad to go to the trading post."

"I'll have one of these fellows deliver the supplies over to you tomorrow."

She just nodded her head and rode off.

Dave told the other two as they rode along. "Lottie's old man broke his leg a year ago and it just won't heal up. The girl's mother had died on the trail out here during child birth and the baby died too."

Dave looked over at Hugh, "I'd appreciate it if you two would kinda keep an eye on their place this winter."

They both nodded, "We'll make a point of doing that."

The next morning a cold wind was blowing and Dave started packing his gear. "It's time for me to move." While Hugh and Dave were getting ready to head up the mountain, Ted prepared to be the one to deliver the sup-

11

plies to Lottie and her dad.

Dave drew a map on the ground. "This is where we shot the deer yesterday. You follow that ridge over into the next little valley and you'll spot their cabin." Hugh had noticed Dave had included a few 45-70 cartridges in the pack for Ted to deliver. Dave nodded when he saw Hugh watching him. "That shot yesterday sounded pretty weak. I think old Ike is getting low on powder and is loading his rounds too light for Lottie to hit anything. Lottie is normally a good shot."

"Ted, if you get a chance, pass her this small bag without Ike seeing it. It's new primers and some fresh powder and a few bullets."

The weather was getting colder as Hugh and Dave worked their way up the mountain. Dave told Hugh as they rode along, "If you don't mind maybe you should head back down the trail tonight after we get unloaded. If this storm does hit, you might have a rough time in the morning getting off the mountain."

Hugh nodded. "I think that's a good idea. I'll at least get back down to the river before I camp."

Ted rode out right after the other two had left for the mountain cabin. He was trying to find all the landmarks Dave had told him about. Then he saw smoke coming out of the trees down below. As he rode closer he could see some corrals and a lean-to built for a barn. He was almost to the corrals before he finally saw the cabin.

A dog was barking and the door of the cabin open. Lottie stepped out. She recognized him and waved, "Come in. I've got a fresh stew cooking."

Ted unloaded the pack Dave had made up and headed for the cabin. He handed her the smaller sack, "The coffee is in there."

She laughed, "Dad, did you hear that?"

It was dark in the cabin with only one small window for light. Lottie stepped over to a chair in the corner, "Ted, this is my dad, Ike."

By then Ted's eyes were adjusting to the light and he could see a tall man sitting there. Ike held out his hand; they shook. Ted could tell by the grip this was a very sick man. He didn't have any color and he was just skin and bones. "Dad, Ted is one of the men staying at Dave's cabin for the winter." He nodded.

"Lottie, did you have enough hides to pay for these supplies he brought?"

She looked over at him and nodded, "Dave told me that my furs would cover everything."

Ted knew she was telling her dad that so she could keep what Ted had brought. This sick old man was not going to take anything without paying for it.

"I'll take the furs back with me," said Ted.

When the coffee boiled, Lottie poured them all a cup. Ted could see the grin on the old man's face as he sipped his first cup.

With his stomach full of stew, Ted stood up, "I'd better head for home before this storm sets in."

Lottie put on her coat, "I'll get those furs for you."

Ted shook hands with Ike, "I'll stop by again to visit."

Outside Ted told Lottie, "You can keep the hides."

She shook her head, "You take them so Dad won't be asking questions. Besides, Dave needs something for all the supplies he sent."

As Ted finished tying down the furs, he handed Lottie the other sack Dave had sent over. She looked into the sack and smiled. Then she went into the lean-to and came back with a small leather pouch, "I'll trade you."

Ted laughed. He could tell by the feel of the pouch it contained empty cartridges.

With Dave up in the mountain cabin, Hugh and Ted had a routine set up around the place. The winter was passing rather quickly. Ted made weekly trips up to see Lottie. Then one night he did not come home. Hugh rode over the next day and found out that Ike had died. Ted was digging a grave when Hugh arrived and Hugh helped him finish it. They laid Ike to rest with Hugh saying a prayer before they covered him up.

As Hugh looked around the place, he could see that Lottie had nothing to live on except what they brought her. The cabin was in real poor condition. Hugh took Ted aside, "We're going to move Lottie up with us until spring."

Hugh walked over to Lottie, "Why don't you put together a pack of your belongings. You're going home with us for now." Lottie broke down and cried. They gathered the horses, and with the dog along, moved Lottie over to Dave's cabin. With some moving bunks around and making a blanket wal,l they got Lottie settled. The best part of this was that Lottie could really cook when she had supplies to work with. Hugh made a trip into the trading post to let them know about Ike's passing and where Lottie was living until spring. On his way back he stopped by to look over Ike's old place. He

13

wanted to see if the wagon he'd seen earlier was worth fixing. It was a well made wagon. Crossing the plains had taken it's toll, but Hugh thought it would be worth fixing up. Lottie had four good work horses to pull it.

The snow was leaving and the days were getting warmer. Ted and Hugh finished building the cabin for Lottie and now she had her own place. One night just before supper a figure could be seen crossing the meadow toward the cabin.

Lottie was the first to recognize Dave. "It's Dave," and ran out to meet him. Dave was happy to hear about the two men making Lottie move over with them after Ike died.

"How come you're down from the mountains so early?" asked Lottie.

Dave grinned, "I got tired of my own cooking. Besides it's getting too warm and the hides aren't any good anyway. The snow's melting real fast. I think next week we'll go up and bring down my winter's catch."

"When we get that done, we'll be ready to start looking for that ranch you want."

Two weeks later Hugh, Dave and Ted had everything moved down from the upper cabin. Ted had brought Lottie's wagon over earlier and had it ready to hit the trail whenever she was ready.

One evening after supper they were making plans to head out when Ted and Lottie announced, "We've got something to discuss with the both of you. We want to get married. Then I can go with you three to look for Hugh's ranch," Lottie grinned.

"Finding a preacher may be a problem unless one had moved to the trading post during the winter. I'm going to take my furs into the trading post tomorrow and I'll check for you while I'm there."

Hugh grinned, "Dave, I think this wedding party will join you on your trip tomorrow."

"Good, we'll liven up the place and have a big party."

When they told the people at the trading post they needed a preacher to perform a wedding, the clerk shook his head, "There's not a preacher anywhere around these parts."

The clerk's wife spoke up, "I can solve this problem real quick. We'll have my husband say the words. Then we'll get everyone present to sign a statement stating they were present when Ted and Lottie said their vows."

Ted and Lottie laughed, "Let's do it now."

With everybody crowded around, Ted and Lottie were married that evening. A big supper was cooked by the few ladies at the trading post. A jug was found and the wedding supper was a great success.

The following week the group headed up over the pass leading to the western slope of the Rocky Mountains. They had left the wagon at the trading post along with the teams. "We'll be back for them once we find the place I'm looking for," Hugh told the trading post owners.

It was their fifth night on the trail and as they were eating supper Dave smiled. "I think tomorrow you will see your new home, Hugh."

Hugh nodded, "I've already seen country I never knew even existed ."

"Well tomorrow we'll see the best country I have ever traveled through," Dave assured them.

The next morning they broke over a ridge and before them lay a long valley with a creek running the full length. Dave motioned, "This is the place I think you will like. The creek is called Sheep Creek. Early trappers could always find big horn sheep up at the headwaters of this creek, so came the name."

Ted laughed ,"That's a good name for a creek running through a cattle ranch."

Hugh just sat there not saying a word as his eyes roamed the beautiful valley.

Lottie motioned toward Hugh, "I believe we're home."

As they rode up along the creek, Dave motioned off up the valley. "There is a small homestead up the valley about a mile at the mouth of Deer Creek."

As they moved up toward Deer Creek, they could smell wood smoke. Dave turned and rode up the creek a short ways. Across a small opening they could see buildings. There was a house, a small cabin with a barn and two other outbuildings. When they rode into the yard, they were greeted by a tall gray haired man with an old calvary hat on his head. "Dave, it's good to see you again."

As they dismounted, a lady came out of the house dressed in bib overalls. When she spotted Lottie she waved. "Lass, you are the first white woman I've seen in a year. All you folks come in and I'll make coffee."

The couple were Joe and Elsie Philips, and they called this place the Bar P ranch. They knew Dave from his trips through the area so he introduced everyone.

Dave told the Philips, "I brought you and Elsie some new neighbors."

Joe and Elsie were full of questions and before long it was evening. Elsie jumped up. "I'll fix you some supper."

Hugh nodded, "Only if you'll let us furnish the grub. Lottie, get into our packs and get the grub."

Elsie grinned, "We are getting low on flour, sugar and coffee. Joe's been planning a trip to Gold Field for supplies."

Dave explained. "Gold Field is a small town a day and half's ride from here."

"We've got a good supply of all three items and we'll share them with you," Lottie said looking over at Hugh. He nodded.

After supper it was still day light. Hugh and Dave mounted up to look over the area before dark. Dave told Hugh, "I know a spot that I think will be a great place for a building spot." It was dark as they both rode back into the Bar P yard. Ted walked out to help put away the horses.

"Ted, I've found where I want the ranch headquarter buildings," Hugh smiled.

"We usually have a hired hand, but he had quit this spring. So Lottie why don't you and Ted use that cabin for the night?" Elsie told the young couple.

Hugh and Dave made their beds in the loft of the barn. Hugh was up at first light and helped Joe with the morning chores. He was full of questions about the area and where Joe's boundaries were.

Joe smiled, "I'll ride with you after breakfast and show you what I claimed." After breakfast the men all saddled up and headed out. Joe and Hugh then turned to Ted.

"Ted, you go with Dave to see the place where I want the buildings. I want your ideas on where you think we should start building."

It was about noon when they all met at the new ranch location. They were all putting their ideas together on where the building locations should be.

Joe motioned, "I think we have company coming." Down the valley came a light wagon with Elsie driving.

Lottie jumped down. "This is a beautiful spot." The women had brought lunch.

# CHAPTER 2

For the next week Hugh drew plans. "Ted you're going to be the master builder here. This is what I have in mind," as he and Ted looked over his drawings.

"Dave and I are leaving tomorrow. I need to hire some men and Dave can then lead them back here with more supplies. We'll go to the trading post and get the wagon and team. I'll load it with all the supplies I can get on it. I'll need to buy another wagon or find some freighter to haul more supplies for us."

Ted nodded, "Good, I'll get started a list of tools and supplies we'll need. Lottie is adding to her list to help feed the extra men."

Hugh drew Ted aside that night. "Ted, after I get the supplies headed this way, I'm going to travel on south looking for some stock. I may not be back before fall, but you keep on building. I'll get credit for you at Sutter's Trading Post so you can keep supply wagons moving back and forth until the snows stop them."

Ted noticed that Hugh was carrying a pouch in his belt when they walked out alone to talk. He handed it to Ted. "This will keep you in supplies and wages to pay any men I hire. I think you should find a place tonight to hide this. When you hide it, you probably should let Lottie know where it is. You never know about the men you hire. If they'll be honest and if they think you have money, it could be bad."

Ted nodded. "If you don't mind, I'm not even going to tell Lottie about the money. It'll be safer for her if I don't tell her where the money is, in case we do have trouble."

"I guess you're probably right, Ted."

Ted thought for a minute. "If something happens to me while you're gone, it will be forty paces north of the spring."

Hugh nodded and they headed back to join the others.

Work on the ranch went along well and three of the four men Hugh had hired were good men. The fourth rode off the second week saying he did not care for manual labor. Ted paid the man off in supplies so he didn't need to use any of the coins. Joe Philips decided he wanted to work to make a little extra money. Ted put him in charge of building a fence around a horse pasture. He also had Joe build a small corral near where they planned to build a barn before winter. One evening when everyone was washing up for supper, they noticed a dust on the ridge above the ranch. As they were starting to eat, a small horse herd could be seen coming out of the trees. There were three riders, and as they got closer, two of the riders held the horses away from the group while the third person rode up.

"My name is Yates. I'm suppose to deliver these horses to a Ted McTier."

Ted walked over to the rider, "I'm Ted McTier." Ted motioned to the pasture. "You can turn them loose in there and then come join us for supper."

When the three walked to the fire, Yates introduced his wife and son who was maybe ten years old.

Elsie, who was helping Lottie with supper, hurried over to welcome Mrs. Yates.

As they were eating Ted asked, "How far did you have to travel with these horses?"

"We met Hugh Davis at the Sutters Trading Post while we were there trying to trade horses for supplies," Yate's answered. "Hugh told me he needed some stock, and he'd buy the lot if I'd deliver them to his ranch."

Yates smiled, "I told him I had some good horses at my ranch south of the trading post. If he'd ride along, we could go look at them. Hugh spent the night with us and we made a deal for these twelve horses to be delivered to this ranch."

After supper, the Yates spent the night and headed for home the next morning.

Two more men showed up to work. One handed Ted a letter from Hugh. "This fellow told us we could find work here."

Ted motioned for them to sit. "If you're hungry, Lottie will fix you some grub while I read this letter you brought." Ted opened the letter. Hugh wrote he was looking for cattle and not to worry if he didn't show up before winter set in. If it got too late to make it back over the mountain, he'd see them come spring.

Dave would show up from time to time and help. He usually brought in fresh meat whenever he did appear. Ted decided he'd better send two wagons back to the trading post to stock up on winter supplies. "Dave, how about you taking these wagons back to Sutter's for a load of winter supplies?"

Dave nodded. "I need to check on my place anyway. I'll be glad to make the trip."

One evening after the crew had gone back to their new bunkhouse, Lottie walked over and sat down on Ted's knee. She grinned, "I'm going to need some help feeding this crew with the baby coming."

Ted almost dumped her off his lap. "Are you sure about the baby?"

Lottie nodded, "Yes, we're going to be parents. Elsie can help me some, but she needs to start canning and getting their supplies ready for winter too."

"Joe's going to go over to Gold Field next week with a pack string. I'll have him try to find you some help." Ted had asked Joe if he could get supplies easier at Gold Field before he sent Dave to the trading post.

"The trail to Gold Field from this side is too narrow and steep for wagons.

Joe returned from Gold Field. He brought with him a dark haired lady dressed in men's clothes. Joe and Elsie both knew her. Her name was Rose Miller and she was a widow. Her husband had been killed last spring while working in one of the stamp mills. They had a small place near Gold Field. Rose, with her husband gone, was not able to work the place alone, so she sold it. She had been working in the boarding house where Joe spent the night. He mentioned to her, "Rose, do you know where I can find someone looking for work, mainly feeding a crew on a ranch?"

She smiled, "Joe, when I finish these supper dishes, I'll be around to talk to you. I want to know a little more about it. I might decide I want the job." After talking it over with Joe, Rose quit her job in the boarding house and packed her bags.

Lottie hit it off with Rose right from the start. With these two hitting it off so well, Ted was back to full time work on building a ranch. When Dave returned with the supply wagons, he brought two letters from Hugh that had come to the trading post. From the letters Ted found out they would not see

Hugh until next spring. He was returning to Texas on business. Then he would head back north looking for stock. The second letter was to let Ted know where he would be spending the winter.

Dave told Ted, "I'm heading back to the cabin to get ready for another trapping season."

Ted nodded, "I'm going to miss you around here. We'll be looking for you come spring."

As Dave was packing up the next morning to leave, he motioned to Ted, "I forgot to tell you that you'll have some visitors before it snows. Little Bear and his tribe always pass this way on their way to the winter camp."

Ted's ears perked up, "You mean Indians?"

Dave laughed, "Yes, they are a small group from the Shoshone Tribe. Little Bear is their leader and he's friendly to whites. Some of the younger bucks will try to steal a horse or two, but otherwise you shouldn't have any trouble. They'll camp on the creek down below Joe and Elsie's place. Joe's a good friend of Little Bear. He'll introduce you then everything will be okay for you and the crew. You might want to pass the word to the new men not to start shooting when they see the Indians coming into the valley."

Ted waved as Dave rode away, "Thanks for the warning about Little Bear."

In about a week Joe rode up one morning with four Indians. He introduce Little Bear and three of his sons. Little Bear was dressed all in skins with an old calvary hat. The boys were wearing leggings and a breech cloth and no shirts. Little Bear was a well built man of what Ted guessed to be in his early forties, maybe younger. He shook Ted's hand and in broken English introduced his sons. The youngest looked to be ten or twelve years old. Joe motioned to Little Bear, "He'd like to trade a couple horses off if you have anything to trade."

Ted nodded. "I've got two horses that I'd be interested in trading. They're in the small pasture." Joe nodded and motioned Little Bear to follow him.

Little Bear sent one of the boys back to their camp for the Indian ponies he wanted to trade. Little Bear looked over the two horses. "What else you trade?"

Ted looked over at Joe and he was just grinning. Ted nodded, "I'll wait until the boy brings back your horses before I'll make any trade."

Ted was surprised when he saw the horses Little Bear wanted to trade.

20

They were two well built young fillies and Ted really liked their looks.

Ted looked over at Little Bear, "Why do you want to trade good young breeding stock."

Little Bear grunted, "All foals born last year were females. I need some work stock for packing my people to winter camp."

Ted grinned "What do you want besides the two horses?"

Little Bear motioned three more horses.

Ted nodded, "I have a couple more I could trade, but I don't really want to part with them." Ted noticed that the oldest son was carrying an old muzzle loading rifle. This gave him an idea for trading material. He still had the old muzzle loading rifle he had brought from Tennessee and Lottie had her dad's old muzzle loader. Ted smiled, "Little Bear, I've got something in the new tack room you might like."

Ted had put all their extra gear in this building to make more room in the main cabin. Ted walked out carrying the old rifle. He could see he really had Little Bear thinking. This had a bigger bore than the one Little Bear's son was carrying.

Little Bear nodded, "I want to shoot it to make sure it works."

Ted had some caps, powder and balls with him when he motioned for Little Bear to follow him. They walked away from the buildings to a knoll. Ted loaded the rifle and handed it to Little Bear. When he fired at a stump, the recoil really surprised him; he stood there staring at the rifle.

Joe spoke up, "Little Bear, that's a big bore rifle. You're just not use to that big a caliber."

Little Bear nodded, "I shoot it once more." He fired again at the stump, "We'll trade if you have more balls and powder."

Ted nodded, "I've got a few more balls and I'll also throw in the mold." With the trade made, Little Bear rode off.

Joe stayed to talk with Ted, "You just made a friend for life. Your stock is safe and come spring he'll be stopping by on his way back to the mountains. You better start thinking of something else to trade come spring."

It was getting dark one evening in January when Rose woke Ted. "You take the wagon and go get Elsie." He started to ask questions when she shoved him out of bed, "I mean now."

Elsie grabbed her coat when Ted told her what Rose said. Elsie grabbed his arm, "Let's go," and was already in the wagon before Ted could close the door. That night Logan Ike McTier made his appearance into the

21

world. Mother and son were doing well. Rose and Elsie were worried about the new father. He was walking around in a daze and they were afraid he might hurt himself.

Ted had put Joe in charge of cutting some hay from the lower meadow. They would need hay for the work horses that they would be using every day this winter. The other stock, Joe told him, "They'll get along good finding feed. In the five years that Elsie and I've lived up here, our horses had survived real well. I've always cut hay for the milk cows, but usually we don't use it all by spring."

Joe told Ted about packing in a mower the second year he lived here. A wagon train on the trail to Oregon had trouble and many of them had turned back. One fellow, as he turned back, had dumped a mower that wasn't assembled along the trail. Joe had heard about it and went looking for it. He followed the route until he found it and decided he would try to pack it home. He had just come down with horses. With help from a friend at the trading post and a borrowed wagon, he hauled it to the trading post. "While I was trying to figure out how to get it home, I had many offers from others to buy it. Other men had saw it along the trail but didn't realize what it was. The local blacksmith had taken in a wagon on a bill and asked Joe if he wanted to buy it to haul the mower home. I hired two boys to help me get the wagon up to Sheep Creek Valley and from there on it was easy going to the ranch. When I drove into the yard after this trip, Elsie met me with all kinds of questions. I'd brought Elsie something a little extra so I was in good standing."

When Joe had mentioned he had a mower, Ted shook his head, "I've never seen one." When Joe headed for the meadow the first morning, the entire crew was there watching. It worked well and it didn't take long before the haying was done.

The winter was mild and Ted's crew could work almost every day outside. The days it was storming they could work inside on the buildings. The barn needed stalls and hay mangers and feed boxes. The main house was done except for cabinets and furniture. The first thing built had been a cook shack and bunkhouse combined. The foreman's quarters was the next building to be finished. The main house was really the last to be started. They had built a big barn, a granary, blacksmith shop and a big cellar was dug in the bank behind the cook shack. They had dug the post holes and buried the corral posts before the ground froze. Now a crew was back in the hills cutting poles. They were going to cut poles and posts so next summer they could fence a big share of the meadow to keep the cattle off the hay ground.

The grass was green when Little Bear and his people showed up one evening. Ted and Lottie were sitting on the porch that evening when Little Bear and his youngest son rode up.

Little Bear was carrying the rifle, "I need more balls and caps. Do you have any I can trade for?"

Lottie was listening to this, "I'll go look through my dad's pack to see if there are any caps." When Lottie came back, she was carrying a pouch with caps and a small bar of lead.

Ted counted out twenty-four caps, "There is enough lead for maybe that many balls."

Little Bear pulled a pack from his horse. When he unfolded it, he offered Ted and Lottie each a pair of moccasins. They were decorated with beads in the shape of an eagle on Ted's and a deer on Lottie's. Little Bear nodded toward Logan in his crib. "I heard of you having a new son," and he pulled out a pair of leggings.

Lottie started laughing at the short legs. Little Bear grinned, "He wear them next year." Ted thanked Little Bear for the presents. "The next time we go to the trading post I'll get you more caps and powder and lead."

Little Bear nodded, "Do you know when you'll be going?"

"Three weeks at the most."

Little Bear grinned, "I'll stop by later and pick up the supplies," and with that rode off. The next morning Little Bear and his people were going up the mountain when Ted and the crew started working.

It was June when Dave showed up one afternoon with gifts for the new one in the family. He also brought Lottie a gift from the people at the trading post. "Brought you a message from Hugh. He says to tell you the cattle will be here in about two weeks. I heard at the trading post that a herd of cattle was headed this way so I rode out to see if it was Hugh's herd. Hugh has his son with him and he says he's going to stay up here. He looks just like Hugh and seems to love this country or what he's seen of it."

Hugh came riding in one evening just before dark. Ted first saw him sitting on his horse on the ridge above looking over the buildings. When he stepped down in front of Ted's cabin, he just stuck out his hand not saying anything.

Lottie had walked out carrying Logan. This brought a grin to his face. "I can never, ever repay you two for what you have built here."

He walked up to Lottie, "Can I hold the lad?"

Lottie laughed, "You can't hold the lad, but you can hold Logan."

Hugh lifted him from his mother's arms, "This kid is going to be a big man when he grows up." Hugh followed Lottie into the cabin while Ted went to put his horse away. When Ted got back, Hugh told them while he ate where he had been and why he was away so long.

"Dave probably told you I've got Hugh Jr. with me now. He wants to be called Henry which is his middle name. He was nineteen this spring and has been good help on the drive. While I was in Texas, I heard that my ex-wife was really sick in El Paso, so I headed there. When I got there, she was on her death bed so I went to see her."

She recognized me and asked me to take our son away with me. She told me that she did not want him raised around her family. She whispered she had made a mistake listening to her parents. "I should have stayed with you and helped find that new ranch for us," she whispered to me.

"I told her about this place and of its beauty. She died the next day. Before her death, she had talked to both Henry and me about what she wanted. After the funeral, Henry told his grandmother he was leaving with me. She made all kinds of threats but soon found her grandson had a mind of his own. My former father-in-law had died the previous winter and the bank was now being operated by an uncle of Henry's. When the father died, his will was divided between his two children and his wife. Henry's mother had inherited some ranch land north of El Paso and some cash. Her brother and their mother inherited the bank and all the buildings in El Paso. Henry, being the only child, inherited all his mother's wealth. I've made Henry a full partner in the cattle I bought, and he's half owner of the ranch."

The next day cattle began to appear and by evening the whole herd was on the ranch. Ted had told Hugh about good grazing in the foothills. For the next week cattle were cut into smaller herds and scattered over the land claimed by Hugh. Young Henry was busy trying to see the country he now called home. Ted took part of his builders from the ranch and built some line cabins away from the main ranch for line riders to live in. Young Henry was eager to work and was a good manager of men.

During the fall roundup, Joe started not feeling well. Elsie told Ted, "I need to take him out to see a doctor. The mine at Gold Field had a company

24

doctor and they let him have a private practice on the side."

Hugh sent one of the wranglers with Elsie when she took Joe over to see the doctor. They were gone about a week when Elsie and the wrangler came back without Joe. Elsie told them, "Joe's heart is bad and he needs to get a lot of rest if he wants to live. Hugh, Joe wanted me to ask you if you'll buy our place?"

Hugh nodded. "I'll pay whatever you two think it's worth."

Elsie smiled, "We already have a price set," and told him what they figured it was worth.

Hugh nodded, "That sounds like a fair price; it's a deal."

Elsie smiled and shook Hugh's hand. "We're going to spend the winter in Gold Field. Come spring if Joe is feeling better can we come back and stay at the ranch for awhile?"

Hugh nodded. "You can stay as long as you want anytime."

Ted and the wrangler helped move Elsie over to Gold Field the following week. While they were getting Elsie and Joe into a cabin Elsie had rented, Dave showed up.

Dave had known Elsie and Joe longer than anyone around. "I was shocked when I heard Joe was sick." Dave turned to Ted, "You two can head on home. I'll stay and help Elsie get settled."

With Hugh back on the ranch, Ted could spend more time getting the ranch ready for the coming winter. Joe had taught one of the ranch hands to operate the mower last fall so the haying went on even with Joe gone. Henry was everywhere trying to learn all he could about the ranch operation. As Hugh rode the mountain valleys, he found more and more good summer graze. He could see bringing in more cattle in a few years as the country settled and the market increased.

One evening he was talking to Lottie and Ted, "When I buy more cattle and head for here, I'm going to need a brand. How does the Rafter T sound? Before Ted or Lottie could answer, Hugh went on. "It's the brand I want on my cattle. I had the irons made by a blacksmith in a town along the trail up here. Ted, we'll need to brand the cattle that's already here too."

Ted nodded, "We'll get started the first chance we get."

Dave came riding into the ranch about a week after Ted had seen him in Gold Field. He brought news that would turn out being a big asset to the ranch in later years. "Two brothers from back east were traveling through on a wagon train and liked the country along the river south of here. They're

25

the Benton brothers, and they have their wives and four children with them. They've found land they like and are starting a town along the river. They've already got the store building up and a hotel is being built along with four other businesses. It's only a day's ride or less from here and will make getting supplies a lot easier. A wagon can make the trip now and with a little work it could be a good road. They're calling the town Benton. The valley south of there is good farm ground. I heard people are starting to build homes and filing on homesteads on that ground."

Hugh smiled. "This will be good for the ranch. Now we'll have a local market for our beef. I think I'll ride down there and make myself known and see what the store has for supplies."

"Lottie, you and Rose make a list of what you'll be needing for the coming winter. Ted, why don't you figure up some supplies we'll need for the ranch. Maybe I can impress them with a big order," Hugh laughed.

As Hugh rode into the new town, he was surprised at how much was already open for business. He could see a livery stable and blacksmith shop, an eating place, laundry, hotel and two saloons; one was just being built. There was a barber shop with a new sign saying hot baths. The Benton general store was a big building. Hugh walked in and found it to be well stocked. The man behind the counter introduced himself as Ed Benton.

"I'm Hugh Davis. I own the Rafter T Ranch up the valley."

Ed nodded, "We've heard there was a big ranch north of town. My brother James and I have been planning a trip up to the ranch to let you know we were in business."

Hugh pulled out his list from the ranch, "What can you do with this?"

Ed laughed and called his brother from the store room out back. "Mr. Davis, this is my brother and partner, James," and he handed James the list.

James grinned, "This will be the biggest order we've ever filled. We can cover almost all of it."

Hugh asked, "Is there anyone running a freight outfit here yet?"

Ed shook his head. "Not yet, but we have our own wagons and will deliver these supplies."

"Sounds good; I'm spending the night in town. I'll settle up with you in the morning." As he walked out, he noticed a sign in the window advertising horses for sale. Hugh turned back toward the Benton brothers, "Where do I find this person with the horses for sale?"

Ed said, "Their name's Wilson; they just moved into the area. They've got some good Morgan horses for sale. Their ranch is about ten miles south in the foothills. When they left the notice in the window, they said they would check back once a week for messages."

Hugh nodded and walked up toward the hotel to get a room for the night. After a good supper in the hotel dining room, Hugh headed for the saloon across the street for a nightcap. The bar was mostly empty. Hugh struck up a conversation with the bartender. Hugh spent an hour listening to the bartender talk about all the new people moving into the area. He had one last drink and headed back to his room. As Hugh laid in bed, he started thinking that he had timed it just right to find the ranch. With all the people moving in and the new town, they would have a supply point close by.

The next morning Hugh paid the Benton brothers for the supplies and delivery of the goods to the ranch the following week. Hugh told Ed, "I'll send a fellow down from the ranch to lead your wagons up river to the ranch." Hugh was hoping Dave was still at the ranch so he could send him down.

When Hugh paid the bill in full, Ed smiled, "If you need a little time to pay for supplies, we can carry you for a time."

Hugh nodded, "Thanks for the offer. There may be a time when I'll need the credit, but not this time."

When Hugh got back up to the ranch, Dave was still there. "How about going into Benton and lead a supply wagon up here?"

Dave grinned, "I'll leave now and spend a night in town with you paying the bill."

When the wagons got into the ranch and unloaded the supplies, Hugh was happy with the order.

The teamster on the lead wagon told Ted, "You know with a little more work the road between town and the ranch would be good road to travel."

That night at supper Hugh told both Ted and Lottie. "You two should make a trip into Benton before winter just to get acquainted."

Lottie laughed, "Sounds good to me. Did they say anything about a doctor moving into town?"

"Yeah they did. The bartender said there was suppose to be a doctor moving in before winter. Why you asking Lottie? Are you or Logan sickly?"

"No, we're fine but with another baby coming it would be nice to have a doctor close." "Rose is good help but I would feel better with a doctor."

27

Hugh must have looked funny when she said she was going to have another child because Ted started laughing.

Hugh looked over at Ted, "Hugh, she's been waddling around lately, and if you'd notice, that isn't her normal speed." About then Logan came through the house at full speed with Rose right on his tail. His short legs were still going when Rose scooped him up.

Rose laughed, "When you get out the wash tub, he's gone; this kid hates taking a bath."

Hugh laughed, "Give that kid another year and you'll never catch him, Rose."

Dave headed back for Gold Field to see how Joe and Elsie were getting along. Before he left he told Lottie, "I'm going to try to talk them into moving to my main place by the Sutter Trading Post. The weather is a lot better down there and that way my cabin won't be setting empty all winter."

Ted, who had been listening added, "If that don't work, see if they'll move to Benton. If they'll do that, we'll have a cabin built for them before it snows."

Dave nodded. "I'll pass the word along."

Henry decided to ride over to Gold Field with Dave. He'd bring back Joe and Elsie's answer of what they were going to do. Henry was planning on leaving in a couple of weeks to head back to Texas.

He told Hugh, "I got a letter the other day saying someone wants to buy my land I inherited down there."

Hugh smiled and winked at Lottie. "I also think there might be a young lady down there that Henry wants to bring back to the ranch."

When Lottie heard this she grinned. "Good for you Henry. We need another woman around here."

Ted sent a rider one morning into Benton to see if the doctor had moved there yet. Lottie was getting close to her due date. Ted told the rider, "If the doctor is there, bring him back to check Lottie over."

The next evening two riders were seen coming up the valley, and Ted recognized one of them as the rider he had sent to Benton.

When they dismounted, the rider introduced the stranger. "Ted, this is Dr. McCrea." He was a middle-aged man with a little gray hair around the edges.

Lottie was in the kitchen when Ted told her, "We've got a visitor here to see you." He had not told Lottie about sending the rider to Benton. Ted was not too sure how she was going to act when she met the doctor.

Lottie walked out. "Lottie, this is Doctor McCrea." She started laughing. "I think my husband is worrying over nothing. I feel fine."

The doctor grinned, "As long as I'm already here, I'd like to examine you anyway." Lottie grinned and motioned toward the bedroom.

When the doctor and Lottie walked back to join the others, they both were grinning at Ted.

"This lady is in fine condition. I believe the baby will be here before another day."

Ted was awakened by a nudge in the ribs a little after midnight. "You'd better go get Rose up. The time is here." Ted dressed and headed for the room at the cookhouse to wake Rose. Doctor McCrea had also spent the night, so Ted went to the guest room in the big house to wake him.

Just before daybreak, Rose came out of the bedroom grinning. "Ted, you're the father of a healthy baby girl; mother and daughter are doing fine. I'm going to the cook shack to cook the crew their breakfast."

Ted was later joined by the doctor. "Why don't you go in and see your new daughter?"

Lottie was sitting up in bed with a smile on her face. "Do you want to hold your new baby girl?"

Ted shook his head. "You know I hate to hold new babies. They're too small for my big hands to handle."

"Ted, I'd like to name her Rebecca after my mother."

Ted nodded, "That's a fine name."

Life was back to normal after the new child was born and the winter months passed by real fast. Green grass was showing along the river when a buggy came bouncing into the ranch one sunny afternoon. As Ted and Hugh looked out from where they were shoeing a team, they recognized Henry driving the buggy. Next to him on the seat was a dark haired young lady. They stopped in front of the house. When Hugh and Ted walked up to the buggy, Henry looked at his dad, I would like you to meet your new daughter-in-law, Becky."

Hugh, with a grin, walked over and offered his hand to help her down from the buggy.

With a laugh, she gave him a big hug, "What, no kiss for the bride?"

Hugh grinned, AI don't know if an old fella like me can stand that but I'll give her a try." About then Lottie, carrying Rebecca, came out of the house to meet the newlyweds.

Henry grinned, pointing to the baby, "When did all this happen?"

While Lottie was telling about Rebecca joining the family, down from the cook shack came Rose trying to slow down Logan.

"Becky, now you'll meet the terror of the Rafter T Ranch." As Logan came running up, Henry scooped him up. "This is Logan."

After Rose was introduced to Becky, she announced, "I got hot donuts and coffee at the cook house."

Becky looked at Henry, "For hot donuts, I'll forget unpacking." As they all sat around the table, Henry and Becky filled them in on their trip north.

"I can't believe all the new buildings in Benton," Henry added.

Hugh looked over at Henry. "You and Becky will move into the main house. I added a room to the tack shed and that'll be my home for the time being."

Henry shook his head, "You don't need to move; there's plenty of room in the main house." Hugh grinned, "I do believe I'm still one of the owners of this place and I'm happy in my new room. Besides, it's closer to the cook house and I can sneak in for a midnight snack."

Hugh was watching the sun go down from the back porch of his new quarters. The high peaks of the Rocky Mountains were visible from here, with their snow capped peaks. This view was his. He knew he owned one of the most beautiful ranches in the west. He could thank Dave for finding this place. His main hope was it would stay in the Davis family forever. Henry was here now with his new wife. There were sure to be children to keep this ranch in the family for many generations. This view was his life, and as it got dark, he was still sitting there thinking about how lucky he was. He had a foreman who had made his life helping Hugh develop this place. Ted and Lottie could have staked a homestead of their own but chose to stay with him. He had made a will and kept those two in it. When he died, the Phillips place would belong to Ted and Lottie. This would be a small payment for their friendship over these years. Hugh had told Henry of his decision to will the Phillips place to Ted and Lottie. Henry agreed it was small payment for their years building the Rafter T. Hugh finally got up from his chair and headed inside to bed. The family had fought him about living out here in his room attached to the tack shed. Lottie and Rose had helped him fix up the room; in fact, it was two rooms now. There was a good size room with a stove and small kitchen in case he wanted to eat without going to the cookhouse. In the same room was his favorite chair and table and some extra chairs for company. The other room was his bedroom. It was small but held a double bed and a dresser. He was happy with this place. Henry still thought that it was not right for the owner of the ranch to have such small quarters. Rose made a point to clean the place once a week and change his bedding.

"I don't need a mother hen looking after me," he'd tell her. She just ignored him.

Hugh, as he crawled into bed, was thinking, "I should just marry that woman."

The next few years the Rafter T grew in size. Henry and Becky had a new daughter. They named her Alice, and she was the apple of Grandpa Hugh's eye. Ted and Lottie had another girl, and just this spring another son was born to them. The girl they named Mary and the boy was John. Lottie kept saying that was the last one. Logan was a ten-year-old now and a big lad for his age. Old Dave was building a cabin up at timber line, a two-hour ride from the ranch. His health was getting poor and he wanted to be closer to Ted, Hugh, and the ranch. Logan had his own horse now and spent much of his time with Dave or out riding with the crew. Lottie was making arrangements for the two older kids to stay part of the winter in Benton going to school. Joe and Elsie had moved from Gold Field when they found out Dr. McCrea had settled in Benton. Joe's health was about the same but he couldn't do physical labor. Elsie was working around town to help with the needs they had. Joe was making horse hair hackamores, reins, and rawhide lariats. This business was picking up after people saw his work. Lottie had made a deal with them to board Logan and Rebecca and send them to school. Logan was not liking this very well but Rebecca really liked school. Joe was able to keep Logan in line and made sure he was busy when not in school. Logan had always liked the Phillips and that was one reason Lottie asked them to board them. Lottie and Ted paid them to board the kids plus Ted kept them stocked with fresh meat from the ranch. Logan would talk Joe into letting him use his rifle and he also brought in game for the family.

The two McTier kids went to school four months a year during the winter months. The school in Benton was growing and it was thought before long they would need another teacher and a bigger building. The local ranchers were glad to have a place to educate their children so they banded together to build a new school for the town. Elsie and Joe became foster parents to many ranch children whose parents lived on outlying farms and ranches. Ted was a driving force to make sure his kids had the chance to read and write. He never had any schooling except what his mother had taught him. His mother had made sure he could write his name and could read some. His older sister had taught him some arithmetic so he could do some figures. With the new school building, they formed a local school board made up of six members. Henry was put on it representing the ranchers. It was decided to have two three-month school terms each year. Three months in the fall and three in the early spring. This was to keep children home during the worst part of the winter. For the kids that boarded in town, winter was not a problem. This plan also helped the children that lived close enough to town to travel back and forth each day. Logan did not care for this new discussion. Logan thought school was a waste of time and ruined his days with Dave.

When Logan was sixteen, he had finished the eighth grade and that ended his schooling. Ted put him to work full-time as a cowhand and he also started getting paid.

Hugh thought they should pay him rider's wages but Ted said no. As long as he's getting fed and his clothes washed by his mother he only got half pay.

Logan had started to argue. Ted told him, "I'll pay you full wages, but if I do, you'll pay your mother board and room or move to the bunkhouse."

Lottie did not like this deal Ted was offering Logan, but she stayed out of the discussion between her husband and son. Logan decided that for now he would leave it the way it was and take half pay. It was a long summer but he still managed to spend weekends with Dave.

# CHAPTER 3

It was a cool day and a coat felt good. You could tell fall was here and summer was leaving. Four riders were coming up the valley at a slow pace and laughter could be heard. These men were cowhands from the Rafter T Ranch on their way back from delivering a hundred head of steers to the railroad siding at Benton. They had delivered the cattle on Friday. Ted told them they could spend Saturday in town. This was Sunday afternoon and they were talking about the weekend in town. A couple of them had somewhat of a hangover from too much partying. Three of the men were old hands on the Rafter T. The fourth was the sixteen-year-old Logan. He had grown up around these cowboys from the Rafter T and they considered him as one of them. This was the first time he had been on the crew delivering cattle to Benton and got to spend the weekend with them. Always before, Ted had been along and he and Logan would head home after delivering the stock.

All the laughter was about Logan winning a new Winchester Model 73 rifle at a shooting contest. Logan was known for his shooting ability with a rifle. He had been taught to shoot by his old buddy, Dave. Dave was the last of the men that had trapped this country long before it was settled. He had hunted buffalo for the hides, scouted at one time for the Army chasing Indians. Now he was living out his years in a small cabin at timber line above the ranch. Hugh had talked Dave into trapping and killing predators when the first cattle were brought into this valley. In the years following, Hugh told his riders to let Dave know if they were having a problem with predators. As time passed, Dave's age was catching up with him and he needed a place to call home.

Hugh always liked the old trapper. "Dave, we'll build you a cabin on the ranch whenever you're ready." Dave found a spot up near the timber line in a small meadow with a small creek for water. He started building his own cabin. When Hugh found out, he sent a crew from the ranch to help Dave. They built a cabin with a barn and woodshed all connected . He was still able to take care of himself, but someone from the ranch usually checked on him quite often.    Logan, as a small boy, spent all the time he could with Dave.

Logan's mother use to say, "Whenever Logan is home, he's just visiting."

Dave had given Logan an old cap and ball rifle when he was real young. The only way Logan could shoot it was when he could find something to prop up the barrel.  Dave would load it and send Logan out to get meat for supper.  If Logan didn't get anything, Dave would make his supper with no meat.

"I want to learn to load my own rifle so I can have more than one shot," Logan complained.

Dave shook his head, "You don't need more than one shot to kill supper."  This went on until Logan was always able to bring in meat with just one shot.  By this time Logan was getting bigger and could hold up the long barrel rifle without a prop.

When Logan was about twelve, Dave decided he needed a better rifle and gave him a Sharps 45-90.  The first time Logan shot it the recoil of the rifle knocked him on his butt.  Dave was watching and laughed until he was in tears.  As time passed, Logan, with Dave's coaching, could shoot better than anyone on the ranch.  Logan carried that old Sharps with him everywhere he went.  About every year they would have shooting matches during celebrations in town and Logan began to win many prizes.  He would shoot against the men from the area and his reputation began to grow.  Soon he had a hard time getting anyone to shoot against him.

On this trip to Benton with the cattle, a firearms salesman was trying to find someone to shoot against him in a contest.  "I'll give a brand new Winchester 73 to anyone who can out shoot me."

The older three riders from the Rafter T told the salesman, "We've got a friend who'll be glad to shoot against you."  A few men in Benton also had signed up for the contest, and when Logan showed up, those that knew him backed out.  There were some new people in Benton that had never seen Logan shoot and they stayed in the contest.

When Logan walked up with his old Sharps, the salesman grinned, "You're too young to shoot with this group."

The crowd started yelling, "Maybe you got this contest fixed and you're scared to shoot against a kid."

Finally the salesman scowled, "If he's got the entry fee, he can shoot."

The hands from the Rafter T loaned Logan the money he needed for the fee. In a very short time Logan was the only shooter still in the contest, besides the salesman. They kept shooting at one hundred yards and neither one ever missed.

Someone in the crowd hollered, "Move back another couple hundred yards." Logan and the salesman moved back. The salesman shot first at the new distance and was just off the target. Logan shot and hit the target dead center. The crowd went wild.

The salesman shouted. "We'll shoot another shot to see who wins."

The crowd yelled, "Logan has already won fair and square."

When the salesman presented Logan with his new rifle, the crowd yelled. "Logan shoot at that same target with that new rifle." Logan stepped back to where the line had been and fired three rounds at the target.

One of the crowd retrieved the target, "Look, Logan hit it all three times dead center."

The local saddle maker moved over to Logan, "Stop by my store this afternoon. I've got a scabbard for your new rifle."

When Logan tried to pay for the scabbard, the saddle maker laughed. "Logan, it's free! That shooting you did today was mighty fine. Beating that cocky salesman was worth twice the price of the scabbard."

Logan, now with a rifle on both sides of his saddle, was what the riders were laughing about as they rode up the valley.

Jay Miller, the oldest of the four riders that day, grinned at Logan, "What's your dad going to say about the new rifle?"

Logan shrugged, "I figure Dad will say it's okay for me to keep it."

"What are you going to do with the old Sharps," asked Jay.

"I'll keep it for all my long shots."

The new 73 Winchester was 44-40 caliber and Logan knew it did not have the range the old Sharps did. The Winchester would shoot a lot faster, but the Sharps had more knock down power. When the four rode into the ranch that afternoon, it was a warm and sunny fall day. Most everybody at the ranch was sitting around enjoying the sun. Ted and Lottie were sitting on the front porch when they rode in. All four stopped by to say hello before heading for the barn. Logan pulled the new rifle from the scabbard and stepped down. "Look what I won in Benton."

Jay spoke up, " Logan won that rifle in a shooting contest with a gun dealer in Benton."

Ted looked the rifle over. "I've been hearing about this new Winchester and this is the first one I've seen."

Logan put the rifle back in the scabbard. I'm going to ride up and show it to Dave."

As Logan mounted his horse, Lottie looked up at her son, "Are you going to be back for supper?"

"Mom, you know Dave; it'll depend on what mood he is in. If he likes the new rifle, he'll want to shoot it. Then he'll want to talk for hours about guns and how it was when he first came to this country."

Ted smiled, "If he's lonesome, you could spend the night and eat breakfast with him."

Logan laughed, "I can handle that," and rode off.

Dave was all taken with the new rifle. "I still prefer the old Sharps for my type shooting." They went up behind the cabin where Dave had targets set up. Logan had spent many an hour here shooting under the watchful eye of old Dave. Dave's eyesight was still pretty good and he shot the new rifle real well.

As he handed it back to Logan, he said, "I could get to like that rifle."

Logan cooked supper and they talked way into the night.

After breakfast Logan washed the dishes and put on his coat. "Dave, I'd better get back down to the ranch and catch up with the crew or Dad will be docking my wages."

When he rode over the ridge and looked down on the buildings, he could see dust over at the corrals where they broke horses. As he rode up, Jay Hillman, one of the newer hands, was doing his best to stay aboard a young three-year-old gelding that was trying real hard to lose him. Jay finally got the upper hand and the colt stopped bucking. Jay rode him around the corral a few more times before he stepped down. As Jay walked back to where the other men were sitting on the corral poles he declared, "I'm getting too damn old for this."

They were bringing in another horse and one of the other riders was getting his gear ready. It took three men to hold the horse while he saddled it. Then as soon as the rider was in the saddle they turned the horse loose. This rider was not as lucky as Jay. He was soon eating dust. They caught the horse and the same rider stepped back aboard, this time with better results. Ted and Hugh had walked up to observe.

Hugh looked over at Logan, "Are you going to try your luck breaking one of these horses?"

Ted just shrugged his shoulders when Logan looked his way. Ted knew this was not the first bucking horse Logan had ever been on. He knew about all the small rodeos Logan and his friends had gone to every chance they got. Logan went over and took his saddle off the horse he had ridden that morning. While the men held the colt, he saddled up. When he nodded his head, the three men jumped back to turn the colt loose. Logan was strong enough and would not let the colt have its head to really buck hard. It was not long before he was riding the young horse around the corral. The crew was kidding him, "How come you didn't let that colt buck?"

Hugh came to his rescue. "I agree with Logan's way. Why let the horse buck you off if you can keep from it?"

These horses they were breaking were some of the stock that would winter over in Clearwater Basin. Hugh had purchased some winter range over the mountain from the home place a couple years earlier. The elevation was lower and they usually had open winters with no snow. Since Henry moved to the ranch, Hugh had started raising horses along with the cattle. The market for good horses was getting better all the time, and with the Clearwater Basin purchase, they could winter them out. They now had a herd of seventy-five mares and colts along with other young stock too young to sell. These horses they were rough breaking now would be sold next spring.

The only house over on Clearwater was a sod house built by a fellow who had homesteaded the ground. Hugh had a new line cabin built, but the other buildings were in good shape. There was a barn, woodshed, blacksmith shop with a tack room on the end and a good set of corrals. There was a cellar and a good spring near the new cabin. The homesteader had planted some fruit trees that were producing each year. This would be the third winter to have horses in Clearwater Basin. The previous years Harry Winslow had moved up here from the ranch to keep the horses on the right range. Harry had worked for the Rafter T for about ten years and looked forward each year to wintering in the basin. The biggest reason to have someone over there each year was to keep predators away from the young stock. The first year they had lost some colts to wolves and mountain lions. There were also a few bears that were hard on stock in the spring. The bears were real bad on newborn colts. Harry had broken his leg this spring during roundup and the leg was not healing right. Ted had figured all summer that Harry would still be able to spend the winter in the basin. Now it was clear he was not going to be able to do it. Ted was looking to find someone else to send up there. None of the crew at the ranch wanted to spend the winter alone.

Ted and Hugh were discussing this during the break at the horse corral. Logan was listening. "How about sending me up there for the winter?"

Hugh and Ted both grinned at him. "We need an experienced rider to send up there."

The other hands, after listening, encouraged Logan into volunteering.

"Logan you couldn't stand living alone all winter up there," they kidded him. "The way you eat, Hugh would not be able to pack enough supplies up there to last you all winter. Besides who would do the cooking?"

"I know how to cook and I can do the job," Logan answered with a grin.

Ted laughed. "You fellas need to get back to work. I'll find someone to go to the basin." That afternoon Dave showed up at the corrals to watch the men break horses. Logan was telling Dave about the job at the basin.

"Dad and Hugh won't even consider me doing it."

Dave just grinned. "Are you sure you could handle it?"

Logan nodded "I know I can, if they'll give me a chance."

Dave grinned at his young partner. "I'll think on it. Maybe I can talk Ted into letting you go."

That night Logan ate supper with the crew. After supper little brother John came running down from the house. "Logan, Dad wants to see you."

Little John thought his big brother was just about perfect. He was always with him whenever Logan was working near the ranch. When they got to the house, Ted and Lottie and Dave were sitting on the front porch drinking coffee.

Logan sat down on the railing. Lottie asked, "Do you want some coffee?" Logan shook his head.

"Logan, your mother and I both think you're too young to spend the winter in the basin. Dave here insists you can handle the job and I should let you go. If I do this it'll keep you busy for the winter," Ted added with a grin.

"It's true, I don't have enough work here for you unless I lay off one of the older hands. When you were going to school in town, we didn't have this problem. If you really want the job in the basin, we will start moving you up there next week."

Logan grinned, "I can handle this job. All I need is a chance to prove

38

it."

Lottie looked at her oldest. "Logan, are you sure you can spend the winter by yourself?" Logan grabbed his mother's hands. "Mom, I can handle this."

The next morning Ted gave Logan a list. "This is what Harry usually took with him in the previous winters. You go over the list, and if you need something different, add it on to the list."

Old Dave walked up and Logan read him the list. "Is there anything I should add to this list?"

Dave nodded, "I'd take more powder and caps so you can reload shells. Knowing you, you will be shooting a lot more than Harry ever did. Take some extra money along so you can buy extra supplies down at the trading post at Kilgore."

Logan took his list down to the cook shack. Rose started filling out the list from the cook house supplies.

She put her arm around his neck. "Logan, from what you know about cooking, you'll be a real skinny runt by spring."

Logan put his arm around her. "Do you want to move up and cook for me?"

Rose pushed him away. "No way would I spend a winter with you snowed in."

Dave found Ted in the blacksmith shop. "I'd like to go along when Logan moves up to the basin and help him get settled."

It was a long day's ride to the Basin. Hugh went with them the morning they headed up there. They had eight horses packing supplies that morning. Hugh had sacked up some grain for the horses during the winter and that took three pack animals. Harry usually kept two horses at the cabin and used grain along with hay to keep them in good shape. Each summer a small crew went up and cut the small hay meadow and filled the barn. This had been a good year and they had more hay than would fit in the barn. The crew had built a pole fence around the small stack outside. It was almost dark when they arrived at the basin cabin. While Hugh and Logan unpacked the animals Dave started supper. After supper they all hit the sack. It had been a long day.

After breakfast the next morning, they started getting Logan settled in for the winter. They put most of the supplies in the cellar and the grain in a big feed box in the tack room. The fellow that homesteaded this place had really been a good craftsman. The cellar was built like a fort and was well ventilated and there were shelves along both sides. The barn was small but well built.

While Dave and Logan were setting up the cabin, Hugh told them, "I want to look over the winter range," and rode off. It was almost dark before Hugh rode back to the cabin.

"The winter feed looks good but I saw a pack of wolves near the hot springs a ridge over. There's also a good bit of bear sign along the edge of the timber."

Old Dave started laughing. " Hugh, I think Logan was just the man for taking care of problems like that."

As they were eating supper, Hugh told Logan, "I'll pay five dollars for wolf ears."

Dave spoke up, "Logan, you can also sell the hides down at Kilgore. If these wolves are the same ones from last winter, they will soon learn how far you can shoot."

Harry just had an old 45-70 carbine with not much range. Logan brought his new 73 Winchester plus the old Sharps with him.

Hugh saddled up the next morning to head back to the ranch. "You'll have the rest of the week to get to know the country. We'll bring up horses next week."

Dave nodded, "I'm going to stay and show Logan the country and make a short trip down to see my old friend Jerry at the trading post." Logan and Dave rode the fifteen miles to Kilgore the next day and Dave introduced Logan to Jerry Crawford, the owner of the trading post. Dave told Logan, "The first time I stopped by here this trading post was the only building here. Now there are maybe twenty buildings and a few other businesses, a saloon, eating place with rooms out back, blacksmith shop and livery."

The trading post was a well stocked place. Logan bought some brass for the Sharps and some more powder.

Jerry told Logan, "I'll buy any furs you want to bring in."

Dave looked over at Logan, "It's getting late so let's spend the night in comfort and we'll have a few drinks with Jerry."

Jerry had a bar along the back wall of the trading post. So they did not have to go over to the saloon. While Dave and Jerry were swapping stories, Logan walked around the store looking. Jerry called over to Logan, "Supper's on." As Logan walked back to the bar, he saw an old colored fellow set a big pot on the counter. He came back with bowls and fresh bread and started filling the bowls with stew. Logan took a bowl and after the first bite knew this fellow could cook. It was real spicy, and Logan had never tasted anything like it.

Dave looked over at Logan. "This is why I wanted to spend the night. Old Bayou can really cook." As the old fellow started to walk back to the kitchen, Dave asked, "Bayou, grab a bowl and join us." The old fellow looked over at Jerry who nodded and handed him a bowl.

Every time Logan refilled his bowl Old Bayou would grin and shake his head. "Logan do you always eat like this?"

Dave laughed. "He sure does."

As they rode back the next day, Dave showed Logan where the ranch lines were and where the best feed was. It was good wintering area and they saw a lot of game. Dave stayed until the horses showed up and decided to ride back over the mountain with the riders. As Dave was saddling up, Logan began to wonder how this winter would go. Dave told Logan, "You ride down at least once a month to the trading post to let Jerry know you're alright. If you need help, let Jerry know and he can send a message for you to the ranch. It'll take over a week but the stage will get it to Benton."

With a wave Dave and the crew were gone. Logan was on his own.

The first week it stormed almost every day and the pass to the ranch was closed by snow. It was clear one morning so Logan saddled up to go see to the horses. Most of the mares in this herd had spent winters here before and knew the layout, such as where they could find protection during a storm and where the water holes were. As Logan rode into a small valley just below the cabin, he crossed a fresh mountain lion track and decided to follow it for awhile. As he rode out of the canyon, he saw about ten mares and they were looking into the willows along the creek. Logan finally saw what had the horses stirred up. It was the cat he had been following. The cat was creeping along the creek trying to get close to the mares. Logan pulled out the Sharps and found a good rest to lean against and got settled to get a good shot at the cat. The mares were starting to move out to the middle of the meadow. Logan figured the cat would try to attack now before the horses got too far out. Logan was ready and when the cat moved out into the open he shot. The mares took off. Logan watched the cat and it did not move. As he started to move, something caught his eye below him in the rocks. As he watched, another cat was moving along really slow watching horses racing across the meadow. Logan waited, and when he had the shot he wanted, he fired and down went the cat.

The first shot had been a long one but this second shot he could have used the Winchester. Both cats were dead and now Logan had the job of skinning them. When he finished, he rolled them in a tarp he had behind the saddle. He decided that since it was not far back to the cabin he could just drag them behind the horse. With the snow cover they should slide easy and not hurt the tarp. When he got back to the cabin, he hung both hides in the tack room. Logan saddled the other horse and headed back down to find the rest of the horses. By afternoon the snow was melting wherever the sun was shining on it. The horses looked good and he found a few coyote tracks, but nothing that would harm a horse. That night before dark he worked on the two hides to trim them up.

Logan decided on another morning to ride over along the north boundary before checking on the stock. As he rode along looking at everything, a rifle shot in the distance drew his attention. He headed toward the river to see if he could find the shooter. As Logan topped a rise he could see some elk on the other side of the river. About then another shot broke the winter silence. Logan could see dirt fly up way short of the elk as they moved away. Finally, Logan spotted the shooters. It looked from this distance like two young boys dressed in skins. As Logan watched, a third person appeared leading the horses. The person leading the horses was smaller than the other two. It looked like they were trying to get some meat and the rifle was too under powered for that long of a shot. Logan watched as two other elk appeared along the river. The boy with the rifle dropped down to his knees to get a good rest before he fired. This shot also fell way short. The elk were looking up at the hill where the shooter was hiding. Logan pulled his Sharps out and decided to help the boys get some meat. This was going to be a long shot, right over the three riders' heads. Logan drew down on the bull, and when he fired, the animal dropped. He stepped out where the three boys below him could see who had shot. They started to run for their horses when Logan hollered at them. They stopped and Logan mounted his horse and headed over to them. As Logan got closer, he saw they were Indians. Dave had taught Logan some sign language, but Logan had never tried to use it. He motioned he was friendly. He could tell they were about ready to run. He was trying to tell them he had shot the elk for them. Logan tried everything he could think of to make them understand.

Finally, the smallest of the three asked in broken English, "Why are you giving us the meat?"

Logan started laughing and finally the others smiled at him. "You fellows are sure making it hard for me to give this meat away."

What happened next had all of them laughing. The one that spoke English pulled off her hat and down fell two long braids. The talker was a girl. Logan grinned, "I'm sorry, I didn't know you were a girl."

"My name is Little Feather and these two boys are my older brothers. We're from a small band living along Smoke River a few miles from here. We're from the Shoshone tribe. Our father is Hawk and he is the leader of our group. My brothers here are Little Hawk and Running Wolf."

Logan nodded, "I live just over the ridge. My job is watching over the horses wintering there."

Little Feather nodded, "We know where you live. You killed two mountain lions. We watch you shoot great distance."

As Logan turned to leave, he stopped. "If you need meat again, come to the cabin and I'll hunt with you."

Logan had been in bed about two hours one cold night when he was awakened by a horse walking near the cabin. He was sure it was a horse with shoes. He could hear the metal on the frozen ground. He was dressing when he heard something hit the ground. He grabbed his rifle and opened the door. As he started around the cabin, a horse was standing there. There was the body of a man laying next to the cabin and he was not moving. As Logan moved the horse over so he could get to the body, he noticed the second horse. As he rolled the body over, he felt under the coat to see if he was alive. He was warm. Logan could feel him breathing real slow. Logan picked him up and took him into the cabin and laid him on a bunk. He took off the man's coat and covered him with a blanket. He went back outside and led the two horses to the barn. He unsaddled the one horse and took the pack off the other one. These were two fine horses. He could tell they were worn out. He gave each one some grain and put some hay in the manger for them. As he walked back into the cabin, he lit a lantern so he could see better. As he turned to the bunk, he could see the man's eyes were open and watching him. Logan set the lantern down, "How are you feeling?"

He just shook his head, "I'm really thirsty. I haven't had anything to eat for two days."

Logan built up the fire and put a pot of water on the stove. He held a cup of water so the stranger could drink, and after a few sips, he laid back and closed his eyes. Logan decided he had a real sick man on his hands. Or he was hurt somewhere that did not show. As Logan was pulling off the man's boots, he noticed the two tied down holsters. Logan loosened the gun belt, and when he pulled it off, two Colts were in those holsters. As Logan hung it on the wall, he could see this was a well used outfit and well cared for. As dawn appeared, Logan went out to take care of the horses. The spring had a good flow and usually did not freeze solid. He led the stranger's horses out and let them drink. In the light he could see these were two well bred horses.

When Logan returned to the cabin, his visitor was awake again. Logan smiled, "I fed and watered your horses."

Logan filled a bowl with the stew he had in a pot on the stove. He propped the man up and fed him some stew. The fellow whispered, "This stew is good."

Logan got about half the bowl down him before he dozed off again. It had started snowing so Logan decided he would not ride out that morning to check the horses.

Logan was stirring up the fire when he heard a voice say, AI could use a cup of that coffee I smell."

Logan filled a cup and sat down on the bunk. "You look a lot better this morning. You even have some color in your cheeks."

He looked at Logan, "My name is Claire Matthews."

"I'm Logan McTier. This is a line cabin for the Rafter T Ranch and I'm spending the winter watching over a herd of horses."

Clair nodded, "I was riding north and I couldn't get over the pass because of snow. I'd been wandering around lost for two days when I spotted the horse herd. I knew then there had to be someone close by. That was the last thing I remembered until the horse stopped by the cabin. When I tried to dismount, I must have blacked out."

Logan gave him some more stew. By now Clair could feed himself. That afternoon the snow let up and Logan walked out to look around. The sun was trying to break through the clouds. As Logan stood there, he could hear a wolf howl off over the ridge. He saddled up and walked back to the cabin for his rifles. "I can hear wolves howling over the ridge. I'm going to ride out to look over the horse herd."

"Why are you taking two rifles?"

Logan grinned, "One for close and one for far off."

When Logan topped the ridge, he could see the wolves trying to separate the horses. He rode down a draw keeping out of sight until he got closer. As he came out of the draw, two wolves were close, trying to down a yearling. Logan stepped down, pulled the Winchester, kneeled down and dropped both wolves with two shots. The wolves in the pack had stopped chasing the horses and were looking back to where the two dead wolves lay. Logan pulled down and shot the one nearest to him. He got one more shot but only wounded the second one. He went back to his horse for the Sharps. The remainder of the pack had stopped on a ridge across from Logan. It was going to be a long shot to get any more of them. As he watched them, he picked out the leader of the remaining five wolves. It was a big gray that was pacing back and forth. Logan drew a bead on him. When he fired, the big gray went down. The others took off over the hill out of sight. As Logan rode among the horses, he noticed they were still looking into the willows along the small creek. He rode over and spotted what they were scared of. The wolf he had wounded was trying to hide in the willows. Logan finished it off with a head shot. Then he rode up toward the last one he had shot. He was just about there when he heard another shot from over the ridge. It was followed by another shot. Logan stopped by the dead wolf. When he looked up, he saw two riders riding his way. When they got closer, Logan recognized Running Wolf and an older man. Then a third rider came into view and he recognized Little Feather.

When she rode up, she introduced her father, Hawk. "We heard the shooting and over the ridge came four wolves toward us. Running Wolf shot two of them."

Logan nodded, "There's four more besides this one down in the little valley. If you can use the hides, you can have them. I only want the ears."

Hawk said something to Little Feather in their own tongue. "My father asks why you don't want the hides?"

Logan grinned, "I only get paid for wolves by the ears I turn in."

"We'll take all the hides and my father thanks you for them."

Hawk again spoke to Little Feather. She turned to Logan. "Father asks why you carry two rifles?"

Logan laughed, "Tell him I carry one for close shots and one for long shots. I could just carry the Sharps, but when I'm close the Winchester gives me many shots without reloading." When she told her father Logan's answer, he nodded and rode off. About then Logan heard another shot way off.

Little Feather nodded, "That will be Little Hawk and his cousin. They were after those last two wolves."

As Logan rode back to the cabin, he decided that was pretty easy money. He'd made fifty dollars that day.

That evening Logan told Claire about the wolves. Claire smiled, "You must be good with those rifles. I'm curious why don't you carry a pistol?"

Logan shrugged, "I generally don't need one."

Claire went over to his pack and brought out another gun belt with a single action Colt in the holster. He handed it to Logan, "Buckle that on."

Logan put on the belt while Claire emptied the pistol. Claire tied the string below the holster to Logan's leg. Claire put the pistol back into the holster. He moved over and sat down on the bunk. "Now draw the pistol as fast as you can and cock it, but don't pull the trigger."

Logan tried a few times and each time he became faster. Claire started giving him tips on his motion, and before long, a grin came to Claire's face. "With a little practice, you could do right well, that is if you can hit anything when you fire it. Now try it with the pistol just stuck in your belt." Claire just nodded and laid back on the bed.

Later after they had eaten supper, Claire looked over at Logan. I'm going to teach you the art of shooting that pistol tomorrow."

Logan looked at Claire, "Why are you so concerned about teaching me how to handle a six gun?"

Claire only shrugged, "You need to handle a six gun if you're going to live in this country. The man who relies on only a rifle for protection usually ends up dead."

The next morning Logan saddled up to check on the horses and told Claire, "I'll be back at noon."

When Logan rode back into the yard, Claire was sitting in the sun along side the cabin. Logan put his horse away, and when he got back to the cabin, Claire handed him the gun belt. "Now we'll see if you can hit anything."

Logan noticed that a block of wood had been placed a ways from the cabin to use as a target. Claire nodded toward the block, "Try a few shots."

Logan hit the block four out of five shots. Claire grinned, "You've shot a pistol before I can see."

Logan grinned back, AI just told you I don't carry one. I didn't say anything about not shooting one. Most of the crew carries a side arm but I've always just carried a rifle."

Claire nodded. "Okay, let's see if you can draw and shoot and still hit the block." Before Logan had been aiming the pistol. Now Claire said, "Shoot from the hip."

The first shot hit half way to the block and the second shot was over the block. Claire stepped up along side Logan. "Like this," and from his belt a pistol appeared. Three shots hit the block dead center.

Logan had never seen anyone draw and shoot like that.

Claire stepped back, "Now you hit the block."

As the afternoon drew on, Logan was getting better, and finally Claire nodded, "That's enough for one day."

That night Claire took from his pack a reloading kit and loaded all the rounds they had shot that afternoon. As they were laying in their bunks that night, Claire said, "Logan, you're faster right now than most men I know. How old are you?"

"I'll turn seventeen this month."

Claire did not say anything for awhile. I'll teach you all I know about gun fighting. What you do with this knowledge is up to you." With that, Claire rolled over and went to sleep.

Logan lay awake wondering where Claire had come from and who he really was.

The next morning while waiting for the coffee to boil, Logan asked Claire, "Where did you ride in from?"

Claire smiled, "I have covered most of the west from Texas to California and north to the Montana Territory. I left home at a very young age when my stepfather threw me out of the house. When he married my mother, he told her he would raise me as one of his kids. Well, as soon as they were married, he started beating on both of us. I was twelve when he came home one night drunk and was beating on my mother. I told him to stop then he started on me. He threw me out the door with only the clothes on my back and no shoes. I was pretty beat up and was bloody from one end to the other. I made it to the barn and climbed up into the hay mow to try to keep warm. I could still hear him in the house shouting and hitting my mother. I remembered a shotgun he kept in the tack room for shooting hawks around the chicken coop. I climbed down and found the shotgun; it was loaded. I pushed open the door to the house. My step dad was standing over my mother kicking her, yelling to get him some supper. When he heard

47

the door close, he turned and saw the shotgun. He lunged to grab the barrel; I pulled both triggers. The recoil of that old shotgun almost tore my shoulder off and I lit in the corner in a pile. It about half knocked me out, but I finally got to my feet and walked over to my mother. She wasn't moving. I tried to wake her up but I finally saw she wasn't breathing. I found my shoes in the bedroom and ran down the road a half mile to our nearest neighbors. The neighbor hooked up a team and we headed back for our house. When the neighbor got to my mother, he told me she was dead. He sent one of his sons for the sheriff and the doctor in town. When I looked over at my step dad, I could see the shotgun blast had almost cut him in two. The neighbor covered him up and said he would stay with me until the law got there."

"I told the sheriff what had happened. He told me I'd have to come to town with him. In town the doctor looked me over to see if I had any broken bones from the beating. We buried my mother the next day."

The sheriff took me aside after the funeral. He said, "You'll have to sell the place to pay the bills and the cost of burying your mother and her husband."

"I told him I didn't have any relatives that I knew of, when he asked me where I could go."

"Then I'll have to take you to a children's home over at the county seat."

"That night he let me stay in the jail and left the door unlocked. I waited until the town was dark, then stole grub from the jail and a pistol from the sheriff's desk. The sheriff's horse was in the barn behind the jail so I took it and rode off."

"I knew I had better cover a lot of ground because come morning there would be a posse after me. Just before dawn the wind started blowing and you could see lightning coming my way. There was a slicker on the back of the saddle so I put it on and soon the storm hit. I had kept the horse at a good pace all night so I knew I had a lead on any posse. The hard thunderstorm would wipe out any tracks behind me. It was clearing by then and I found a horse pasture with some good riding stock and traded horses. I made one more horse swap before I found a place to rest. I knew I had covered many miles during this ride. I found any work I could along the trail and headed for Texas."

"The next five years I stayed alive by working at a job in a saloon. The owner paid me well. My job was cleaning up each morning and I brought him his meals during long card games. He ran a poker game as many hours a day as he could find players. Everyone said he ran a very straight game. I don't remember very many shootings over cards. I learned to play poker from him and he also taught me to shoot. I guess the story from there to now is I'm a gambler and some refer to me as a gunfighter. I have killed too many men but they all drew first. Except when I shot my step dad, and that was in anger. I don't like being called a gunfighter, but there isn't much I can do about that."

As they finished breakfast, Logan asked. "How come the law wasn't after you for stealing the sheriff's horse?"

Claire laughed, "That's a story in itself."

Logan grinned, "I want to hear about it."

"I was going on eighteen when I quit the job working in the saloon. I'd earned enough to buy myself a horse and all the rigging to go with it. I decided I was going to go back and settle up with the sheriff even if it meant jail time. When I rode back into that town, nobody recognized me. I walked into the sheriff's office and the man sitting at the desk wasn't the same man I'd stole the horse from. When he asked me what he could do for me, I told him I was looking for the sheriff that had been there eight years ago."

"Do you mean Sheriff Brown?"

"I thought that was the sheriff's name but I was only twelve when this all happened. So I nodded it was."

"Sheriff Brown was shot about five years ago. He's been confined to his house ever since. The wound didn't healed right. The only way he can get around is by using crutches."

"When I asked where Sheriff Brown lived, he said he would take me there."

Claire grinned, "I really didn't want this fellow along when I talked to the man who's horse I had stolen. When we arrived at the old man's house, the man went in first to see if the former sheriff wanted visitors. When I walked in, I was surprised at how much the former sheriff had aged."

"The old fellow looked up at me and asked me if he should know me. I told him my name is Claire Matthews."

The old sheriff stared for awhile then started laughing, "Why in the world did you come back here?"

"I told him I wanted to make things right with him on stealing his horse.

You were square with me but I didn't want any part of the children's home."

The old sheriff smiled, "Call me Lafe. Claire you don't owe me or anyone in this town a thing. I got my horse back from the rancher where you changed horses. That rancher later got his horse back and I heard later that the other horse you traded for in the night was found in the same pasture six months later."

"I told him I was glad to hear I wasn't wanted and could ride on."

When I started to leave, Old Lafe asked me, "How fast are you with that tied down six gun?"

"I just told him, 'I can hold my own'."

During all this story telling, Logan kept thinking about the life this man had led. He wore good clothes and had good horses and still he was a gambler with a fast gun. With the sunburned face and western clothes, he could pass as a cowhand or rancher. What made him different was the tied down double holsters on his hips. He also had a belly gun in his belt. Logan found it the night he packed him into the cabin.

Logan was taken by this gentle man that was, from all signs, very well educated. Maybe not from formal schooling but from life in general. He could both read and write very well and seemed fast with figures. Logan figured that came with him being a gambler.

Logan went about his chores each day. Sometimes Claire would join him if the wind was not blowing. Every time Claire went out in the wind he would cough all night and at times Logan thought he was going to choke to death. Claire made Logan practice each day. On sunny days he would sit in the sun beside the cabin and watch him shoot. One day, water was dripping off the cabin roof and hitting a pail under the eve.

Claire grinned at Logan, "Face the target and the next time a rain drop hits the pail, draw and hit the pail."

When Logan heard the drop hit the pail, he drew and fired. Logan jumped as a second shot hit the target a split second after his shot. As Logan spun around, Claire was reloading his left pistol. When he finished, he walked back into the cabin without saying a word. Logan walked in behind him and sat down at the table to clean his pistol.

"Logan, you are as fast as anyone I've ever known. I hope you use that gift you have in good faith."

As the weeks went on, Logan could tell Claire was getting worse. "I think I should ride down to the trading post and try to get to a doctor up here."

"I'm happy here. I'd like to be buried on the little hill just above the barn. There isn't anything a doctor can do for me and I just wanted to die with a friend close by. My biggest fear has been to die along some trail with no one around."

That night Claire opened his saddle bag and handed Logan some papers. When Logan opened them he found it was Claire's will.

"I'm leaving all I own to you."

"Why me? Don't you have someone else, somewhere?"

Claire just grinned, "No one but you."

Spring was getting close in the hills. Green grass was appearing on the south slopes. Logan had killed a few more mountain lions. He had not seen a wolf since he and Hawk's family had cleaned out the pack. The horse herd had come through the winter in good shape. Logan had shot a couple more elk for Little Hawk and Running Wolf. With Claire with him at the cabin, the winter had gone by quickly. It would be another month before the pass would be open and Logan could take the horses home.

Claire was having a bad day. "Logan help me outside so I can sit in the sun."

Logan could tell by his color that Claire was not going to last much longer. That night when Claire was lying in his bunk, he asked Logan to come sit close by. He started telling Logan about being a gun fighter and things to watch for.

"Logan, never shoot to just wound a person. If you're in a gun fight, shoot to kill. If you don't, that same man will probably end up shooting you later from ambush."

Claire was having a hard time breathing. Logan added a rolled up blanket under his head, "Lay back and rest for a spell."

Claire had a slight grin come to his drawn face. "If I rest now, I may never wake up again." He looked up at Logan.

"Whatever you do, for my sake, stay on the right side of the law." Claire reached over and grasped Logan's hand, "I'll rest for a while."

Logan covered him up and moved over to his own bunk. When Logan woke it was almost daylight. He looked over toward Claire's bunk and he knew he was dead. Logan moved over to check and his body was already cold. He must have died right after they quit talking.

After he had his morning coffee, Logan went to the barn for his shovel.

He headed up on the ridge where Claire said he wanted to be buried. With the warmer days, the ground had started to thaw out and it was easy digging. It was almost noon before Logan had the grave as deep as he wanted. Logan wished he had some lumber to build a casket. Claire had told him he wanted to be buried wrapped in his blanket and slicker. As Logan started back for the cabin, he saw Running Wolf and Little Feather coming up the trail.

"We were over on the next ridge hunting and saw you digging on the hill," Little Feather said as they rode up. "I told Running Wolf someone has died and you were digging a grave."

"Thanks for coming. I'll need help carrying Claire up to the grave."

They lowered Claire into the grave and Logan read a few verses from the Bible Claire carried in his saddle bag.

Logan thanked his two friends for their help. "I can finish covering the grave."

Little Feather stepped forward. She tossed a small buckskin bag on the body and then said a few words in her native tongue. She looked up at Logan. "The bag contents will help your friend on his way into the spirit world."

Running Wolf took the shovel from Logan. "We'll take turns covering the grave." Logan and Running Wolf placed rocks on the grave so animals couldn't dig up the body.

As they walked back down to the cabin, Logan told them, "I have gifts for you from Claire." He gave Running Wolf Claire's rifle with extra rounds of ammunition. He went in and got Claire's cooking gear and his knife and gave that to Little Feather. He knew the small pot and skillet and knife would be something Little Feather could use.

Little Feather smiled, "We thank you for the gifts. We need to be heading for home before it gets dark."

As they rode off, Logan could already feel the loneliness in the passing of his new friend. Logan decided the next morning to ride down to Kilgore to see Jerry. While there maybe someone would cut his hair. Logan changed the stirrups on Claire's saddle to fit his long legs and saddle up one of Claire's horses. Logan put a note on the cabin door telling where he had gone. This horse he was riding really had a good traveling gait and he made good time getting to Kilgore.

When he walked into the trading post, Jerry looked up. "Well, Logan, I see you survived the winter."

Logan laughed, "It has passed pretty fast and so far the horses are doing good."

He tossed the wolf ears on the counter. "I killed more but I gave them to the Indians along with the cougar hides."

Jerry nodded, "Hawk has been in. He said you had been killing some meat for them. He was really impressed on how far your rifle could shoot."

Logan laughed, "I was lucky on some of the shots they saw me shoot."

Jerry nodded, "From what I hear, I think you don't miss very often."

"Jerry, is there anyone here that could cut my hair?"

Jerry nodded, "I do most of the hair cutting in town."

"I either need it cut or learn how to braid it. I figure I'll look better with it cut."

Jerry grinned, "I know one little Indian girl that would be glad to braid your hair. Come on I'll show you where you can take a bath. When you're finished, I'll cut your hair."

Logan had brought along extra clothes hoping to get a bath while he was down there. With a fresh hair cut and a hot bath Logan felt like a new man. He drank a beer with Jerry while Old Bayou fixed their supper. Logan had noticed two whiskered men sitting at a table in the back of the bar all afternoon. They would holler for Jerry to bring them a bottle every once in a while and were getting louder as the evening wore on.

Jerry motioned to Logan, "Bayou says supper's on. Come on back and we'll eat."

One of the men drinking hollered, "You gonna feed us too?"

Jerry turned to them, "The café is just down the street if you want something to eat." When Jerry sat down at the table to eat, his chair was close to the doorway so he could watch the two men.

"I wish those two would get full of whiskey and move on. I don't trust either one of them. They rode in last night and have been drinking ever since. They say they're trappers but they don't have any gear with them except a couple big bore buffalo rifles."

Jerry looked over to Logan, "I'll fix a bunk in back for you tonight. They saw me pay you for the wolf ears. I think they'll try to get that money, so watch your back when they're around." Logan nodded.

The next morning Logan paid Jerry for the few supplies he needed and was about to leave when the two trappers walked in.

They looked over at Logan, "Is that sorrel horse outside yours?"

Logan nodded, "Why are you wanting to know?"

"Well, we think we'd like to buy him from you," the oldest one said.

Logan laughed. "I'm sorry but that horse isn't for sale."

The two men started to spread out in front of Logan. "In that case we'll just take him."

Jerry started to move behind the bar. "You stay put," the older of the two growled.

Logan smiled as the one on his left pushed his coat back to clear his holstered pistol. Logan had been watching the eyes of the one doing most of the talking. When he saw him wink at his partner, Logan was ready. They both went for their guns at the same time.

Logan's draw was fast and his first bullet hit the older fellow before his gun ever cleared his holster. Logan moved to the side and fired his second shot at the other man as he was raising his gun. His shot went into the floor. Logan had beat them both with ease. Logan looked over at Jerry, who was just staring at him.

"My god, you beat them both."

He walked over and rolled them over. "They're both shot through the heart."

Logan was reloading his gun when the door flew open and two out of breath men ran into the store. Logan spun around and leveled the pistol. They both threw up their hands.

"Logan, they're both friends of mine," Jerry hollered. Then he introduce the blacksmith and the owner of the gun shop.

The café owner looked at the dead bodies. "I knew somebody was going to die before those two left town. They ate at my place last night and refused to pay for the food. Then they told me if I didn't like it, to get a gun."

Jerry told them what happened. Logan looked over at Jerry, "I'd like to keep this quiet if that's possible."

The three business owners smiled at Logan. "We don't need to advertise that those two were ever in Kilgore except for a short while. We'll bury them and let the nearest lawman know they died while trying to rob the trading post."

"I don't like having you lie for me, but I don't want my folks to know I've shot two men."

"You don't have to worry about the story getting out," they assured him. About then more people started showing up. Jerry told them the two had tried to rob the place. Nobody really questioned who shot them.

One fellow motioned toward the bodies, "I'm just glad they're dead before they shot somebody here in town."

Later, after everyone had left, Jerry sent a couple men to dig two graves. "Logan, do you want these two big rifles?" asked Jerry.

"I'll take them but I want to pay for them."

Jerry shook his head, "You take them and that will be the end of this matter between you and me."

Logan tied the rifles behind his saddle and then shook Jerry's hand, "I'll stop by again before I leave." He mounted the sorrel horse and headed back to the cabin. He worked around the cabin the next morning and during the afternoon checked on the horses. He started bunching them up and moving them closer to the cabin. Logan figured any day he would see the riders coming from the ranch to get them. As he rode back toward the cabin, he could see two riders coming over the next ridge. When they got closer, he recognized Little Hawk and Running Wolf. When they rode up, it was a little hard talking to them without Little Feather to translate. With a little sign language and understanding some words, Logan was able to communicate with them.

"We're getting ready to move our camp back toward the mountains for the summer," they told him. "We rode over to tell you we were leaving."

Logan motioned for them to follow him to the cabin. He went inside the cabin and brought out the rifles Jerry had given him. Logan handed one to Little Hawk, "This is for you," and handed him the second one. "You give this one to Hawk, your father."

He turned to Running Wolf. "I've already given you Claire's rifle."

Running Wolf nodded and held up the rifle. "I've already killed a deer with it," Logan said to Little Hawk, "Now you can shoot a long way and kill the elk."

As they rode off, Little Wolf was still waving the rifle over his head and thanking Logan.

Logan went back gathering horses the next morning and later had them headed for the cabin pasture. When he rode out where he could see the cabin that afternoon, he noticed horses in the corral and smoke coming from the chimney. Old Dave was sitting in front of the cabin as Logan rode up.

He grinned, "Boy, I do believe you survived the winter pretty good."

Logan swung down and shook hands with this old friend of his. About then the other two riders walked out to see Logan. Dave grinned, "They've got supper cooking so I'll help you put your horse away."

As they walked to the barn, Dave asked, "Who's buried up on the ridge?"

Logan motioned to the two saddle horses in the pasture. "It's a long story but now I own those two horses and I have a bill of sale for them. I'll tell you and the other riders all about it over supper."

When Logan finished the story after supper, old Dave nodded. AI remember Claire Matthews. He was a very fast gun but he really had to be pushed to get him to draw. He was a fair gambler and as far as I know he was never wanted by the law."

Later after the two riders went out for a smoke, Logan read Dave the will Claire had made out.

Dave grinned, "You must have treated the guy good to have him leave you everything he had." Logan reached in his gear and pulled out a poke and tossed it to Dave.

Dave felt the weight of it. "How much is in it?"

Logan grinned, "A little over two thousand dollars."

Old Dave just whistled, "That's quite a sum to inherit."

When the two riders walked back inside, Logan changed the subject. He decided everybody didn't need to know about the gold coins.

Dave left early the second morning to see if the pass had melted enough for them to take the mares and colts through. Usually, in years before, once tracks were made over the pass, it would melt out real quick with the warm weather.

"I want to make sure it's okay before we head out with the horses." Logan spent the day putting stuff away in the cabin and packing all his gear for the trip home. With the good cellar built in the hill behind the cabin, they could leave many supplies for the next winter. As Logan was packing up, he was thinking about spending next winter here if his dad would agree. He was thinking of things he would bring different from what he had brought this year.

It was a little after noon when Dave rode in. "We'll move out come morning."

The trip home was real good and the young colts had no trouble following their mothers over the pass in the snow. As they hit the home range above Dave's cabin, they just turned the horses loose.

The two riders told Logan, "We'll stay the night with Dave and move the horses to their summer range tomorrow."

Dave grinned, "Lad, you had better head for home to let your mother know you survived the winter. Lottie has let Ted know quite often during the winter that she did not approve of her oldest son spending the winter in a line cabin all by himself."

Logan waved and headed on down the trail toward the home ranch. He was riding one of his new horses, with a pack on the other one, plus the other two horses he had taken up with him last fall. As he rode into the ranch yard, he was greeted by the whole family.

He swung down from his saddle and his mother grabbed him, "It's about time you got here." She gave him a big hug.

Ted offered his hand, "You must have learned to cook; you have grown some."

Hugh and Henry were both there and Hugh laughed, "Lottie, I told you this boy could take care of himself."

Logan and Ted headed for the barn to put his stock away. Ted looked at the two sorrel horses. "Where'd they come from?"

"It's a long story, and when we get back to the house, I'll tell you the whole story."

Lottie cleared away the table and everyone at the ranch was sitting around drinking coffee waiting for Logan to tell about his winter in the basin. When he finished his story, Hugh was the first to speak.

"I spent some time around Claire Matthews during my time in Texas. I saw him shoot two men after a poker game had broke up. These two followed him out of the saloon and demanded their money back. They accused him of cheating because he had won their money so quick. Matthews told them they shouldn't play poker because they both were poor players. They both went for their guns and neither one cleared leather before they were dead. That man was pure hell with six guns."

Logan showed the will to them and also the bill of sale for the two horses. Hugh nodded, "Logan, I think you should ride in and record this will and bill of sale and tell the sheriff the story. I'm taking some cattle into town next week and you can ride along and get it done."

Henry spoke up, "Logan could probably stand a few days in town after a winter in the basin."

With a grin, Hugh added, "I hear all the local girls have been worried about you being alone all winter."

To this Lottie sputtered, "He's too young to be chasing girls."

This brought a big laugh from everyone.

Henry's wife, Becky, added, "Lottie, you better look at your son again."

That evening after everyone had left, Ted, Lottie and Logan were the only ones still up. "Claire left me a good sum of money I didn't mention to the others. I've decided to put it in the bank in Benton under Mom's name and mine. I know I'm too young to sign any legal forms."

Lottie spoke up, "Logan, that's a lot of money you inherited. Why, that's more money than your father and I ever had to our name."

Ted turned to Logan, "What are you going to do with Claire's other gear?"

"I'm going to keep the guns for now and the horses I can use here at the ranch. The other personal belongings I'm going to store in my room for now."

Lottie shook her head, "Logan, why do you want to keep so many guns?"

"They belonged to Claire and I just want to keep them." Lottie just nodded.

Logan looked over at his dad and grinned, "Come next fall if nobody else wants to winter in the basin, I will."

Ted smiled, "That's a long way off and we'll discuss that later."

Logan got back into ranch work and helped Hugh cut out the cattle for the sale in Benton. It was a good day's drive into Benton with the cattle so they left before dawn that morning. They had bunched them down the trail from the ranch. A couple of riders had spent the night keeping them together so when Hugh and the crew arrived the next morning they could move right out. The riders for this trip were Whitey Miller and his little brother, Jerry, and Dave Olson. All three had been with the Rafter T for many years. It was a nice spring day and the herd moved along real well. They moved the herd into the corrals at the slaughter house and the buyer was there to meet them. Hugh and the cattle buyer agreed on price and agreed to meet the next morning at the bank. Hugh motioned to the riders to follow him to the livery stable. After the horses were put away, they headed for the hotel with their gear.

"I'll buy the first drinks," and Hugh tossed Whitey Miller a gold piece to pay for them. "I want everyone to stay sober till after supper. I'm going to buy that later." Hugh then headed for his room.

Logan told Whitey, "I'm headed for the store for some new clothes."

"Do you want a drink first?"

"I think I'll pass. The bartender would probably throw me out before I could even order one."

Whitey laughed, "If you really want a drink, I'll bring one out back. I keep forgetting how old you are."

Logan headed down the street to the store. He was going through the shirts when a voice beside him asked, "Aren't you going to speak?" The voice was Laura Benton. Laura had been in Logan's grade in school. Her father, Ed, was one of the owners of the store. Logan had taken her to a dance once last year before he went to the basin.

Logan laughed, "I'm sorry, Laura. I was so busy trying to find some shirts that'll fit and I didn't see you."

Before she could say more, her father walked up to shake hands with Logan, "Logan, how was your winter in the basin?"

"Well, really it went pretty fast and I enjoyed it."

Logan picked out some shirts and pants and bought a new pair of boots. Laura was at the counter when Logan paid for his purchase. As he started to leave, Laura announced, "The spring dance is a week from Saturday at the school house. They're having a box social during the dance and I'll have a box lunch there."

"I'll make a point to be there. Make sure you mark the box so I will know which one's yours," Logan grinned at her. Laura smiled and handed him his packages.

As he started to leave, her father from the back of the store laughed, "Logan, I think she had that all planned."

The next morning Hugh and Logan were the only ones at breakfast. It seems the other three were in bad shape with hangovers. Hugh looked over at Logan, "Logan, do you want me to go with you to see the sheriff?" Logan nodded.

When they walked into the jail, Sheriff Del Rogers was pouring a cup of coffee. He offered the two visitors a cup and sat down at the desk. "What can I do for you two; you both look serious about something?"

Logan told the whole story about his winter with Claire Matthews. Then he handed Del the papers from Claire.

Sheriff Rogers nodded, "I knew of Claire but I never met him. As far as

I'm concerned everything here is in proper order. Logan, you should either record this will or at least put it in the bank for safe keeping."

Logan and Hugh walked to the bank. Hugh suggested to Logan that leaving the will at the bank would be fine for now.

"Come fall we will be in the capital and you can record it there."

Logan opened an account with the gold he got from Claire and put his mother on the account with him.

When they finished, Hugh suggested that they go eat some lunch.

Logan nodded, "I can't believe the morning has passed so fast."

Hugh announced while they were eating lunch, "I've decided to spend the rest of the day in town. We'll start for home early in the morning." They were about through with lunch when Whitey walked in.

"How soon are we leaving, Hugh?"

"I've decided to spend another night and get an early start come morning. If you boys want, you can spend another night in town or you can head for home now."

Whitey grinned, "We'll stay as long as you tell Ted you let us stay so he won't think we were too drunk to ride home."

Hugh laughed, "You remember this the next time you boys think I'm too tough on you."

Just before the bank closed, Hugh went over to get the money for the cattle they had brought in. He wanted cash to take back to the ranch. They always paid the hands in cash and payday was getting close. Cash was always needed around the ranch and Henry was now handling almost all the bookkeeping. The bank clerk was the only one in the bank when Hugh picked up the money.

The clerk asked, "Do you think this a good idea? We've got more strangers passing through town every day and many of them would do anything for money. There's been some robberies lately and some horses stolen nearby in the last month. With the war just over, many of the returning men are crowding to this area looking to settle. Some of these men are from the border war gangs. They're wanting money anyway they can get it. They could rob you tomorrow while you're riding home."

Hugh laughed, "I'll have four riders with me and I'm sure we won't be bothered." He walked back to the hotel and had the clerk put the money in the hotel safe until morning.

The next morning Hugh and Logan met the other three at the café for breakfast. Whitey and his group were in good shape this morning. Logan and Whitey took the wagon over behind the store and helped Ed Benton load the supplies. Hugh had made arrangements for Ed to meet them early so they could load and get gone at sun up.

Hugh climbed up over the wheel. "I'm driving the wagon for a change," and stepped up into the seat. He had picked up the cash bag as they left the hotel and now had it under the seat.

That morning Logan had belted on a holster on his left hip with another pistol out of sight under his belt with the handle toward his right hand. Hugh had noticed that Logan was wearing a gun but he hadn't seen the belt gun. Whitey had decided to also ride in the seat of the wagon and he and Hugh were talking cattle. Logan was riding alongside of the wagon listening to the two swap stories and the other two men rode behind. They were near the forks of the road that led to the ranch when two riders jumped out of the brush in front of them.

Both had rifles covering the wagon and the other riders. "Pull up and keep your hands in sight the bigger of the two yelled." They both had white bags over their heads with holes cut for their eyes and mouth. The bigger of the two rode up to the wagon.

"I want the cattle money."

Hugh growled. "I'm not carrying any cash from the cattle sale."

The masked rider was getting mad. "Either toss the money over or I'll start shooting men."

The rider next to the wagon had put his rifle in the scabbard and drew his pistol. About then the third rider came out of the brush. He also had a pistol aimed at Hugh and his crew. He was a little behind them and his first words were, "You fellas shed your hardware right now, real slow like." The only guns showing on the riders were rifles except Logan, who had a pistol showing. They all did what the rider wanted then he rode up alongside Hugh and put the pistol barrel against his head.

"I want that cash now old man or you're dead." Hugh slowly reached down under the seat and grabbed the bag. As the road agent reached down for the bag, Hugh jerked the sack off his head. The man dropped both the bag and his gun as his horse jumped sideways.

Hugh yelled. "Say, you're one of the Coulter boys."

The rider who had his horse under control yelled, "Shoot them all; they know who we are." Logan was off to one side and with one clear motion

61

drew his belt pistol. He shot the man next to him. He spun around to see Hugh falling backward at the same time he heard the shot. The man behind Hugh was holding a smoking gun. Logan fired at him. The rider revealed when Hugh jerked off his hood was just clearing his rifle when Logan shot him. Logan jumped off his horse and ran to Hugh, who was trying to get up.

Whitey told Hugh, "Stay down while we see how bad you were hit."

About then they heard a rider racing away from behind the willows. Logan grabbed his rifle from the road where it had landed when they were disarmed. He ran through the willows, and when he topped a small rise, he saw a rider laying low over his horse and riding hard. Logan dropped to one knee and fired. He saw the rider straighten, then fall from the running horse. Jerry Miller had followed Logan through the willows and witnessed the shot. Logan motioned to Jerry.

"Ride out and get that guy, but watch it, he may still be alive."

Logan walked back to where Hugh was. Whitey was binding up his shoulder. Logan turned to the other rider.

"Dave, head for town and get the sheriff and the doctor." Logan helped Whitey move Hugh to a blanket.

Hugh grabbed Logan's arm, "Where in the hell did you have that gun?"

Logan grinned, "In my belt."

Whitey was trying to make sure the bleeding had stopped. Logan walked to the dead men and pulled off the sack hoods.

Whitey motioned, "Those two are Ollie and Thad Coulter. I don't know that third one." Jerry got back from retrieving the rider Logan had shot. "He's wounded, but he'll live."

Jerry looked over at the dead men. "These four are all cousins. I think the one I've got tied to his horse is Willie, but I'm not sure."

Dave was back with the sheriff in record time. About then a light buggy could be seen coming up the road from town at a high speed with more riders behind it. The sheriff looked over the bodies while Dr. McCrea examined Hugh. They loaded Hugh onto Doc's buggy and Doc headed back for town along with a couple of the towns people who had ridden out. Sheriff looked over the bodies. "I know them all and they are all related. That one is Darrel Wilson; he's a cousin from Missouri who had just moved into the area."

As they loaded the bodies, Sheriff Rogers turned to Logan, "You must have had a busy winter with Matthews. Each one of these fellows was shot through the heart except the one who was racing away."

Logan nodded, "Claire did teach me a few things."

The sheriff nodded, "I hope you will also remember how Matthews used his skills."

Logan looked at the sheriff, "I heard that same thing before Claire died."

Whitey spoke up, "If Logan hadn't pulled that gun, we'd all be dead here in the road."

"Sheriff, do you need all of us back in town," asked Logan. "If not I'm going to head them for home." The sheriff just nodded.

"Whitey, we need one rider to go on ahead to tell Ted and Henry what has happened."

Whitey turned to Dave, "You and Jerry bring the wagon; I'll head for the ranch."

Logan walked over and handed the bank bag to Whitey. "Take this to Henry."

The group of riders rode back to Benton with Sheriff Rogers. Everyone was pretty sober about what had happened so close to their town. Ed Benton, who had ridden out with Doc and the others, was riding beside Logan on the road back. "Logan, I'm proud of you and how you stood up to the Coulter boys."

Logan nodded, "If Hugh hadn't pulled Ollie's mask off, maybe everyone would still be alive."

Ed nodded, "I know Hugh dislikes anyone who doesn't earn their keep. These boys were trying to steal from him. Someone trying to rob him of his money and not earning it must have turned Hugh wild mad."

When they rode into town, the walks were crowded with towns people wanting a look at the robbers. When they carried the bodies into the undertakers parlor, one of the crowd recognized the Coulter boys. Logan knew they had a reputation for being on the edge when it came to the law.

Logan rode over to Dr. McCrea's office to see how bad Hugh was. As he walked in, Doc was making Hugh comfortable in bed. Hugh was awake and motioned for Logan to step closer. He grabbed Logan's hand, "I hear you shot them all."

Logan nodded his head and Hugh gripped his hand hard, "You did good, Lad."

Doc stepped over to the bed, "You lay back and get some rest."

Doc motioned for Logan to follow as he walked into the other room. He closed the door and motioned for Logan to sit down. He poured himself a drink and offered Logan one. Logan shook his head no.

Doc nodded, "Hugh's lost a lot of blood. With rest and no infection, he'll be alright. Hugh, for his age, is in good shape and all this will help the healing."

Logan got a room at the hotel and decided he would stay in town until his dad and Henry showed up. He had just finished supper when he saw Ted and Henry riding up the street. Their horses showed they had been ridden hard and needed to be cooled down. Logan waved and they rode over to where he was.

Henry asked, "How's dad? Where is he?"

"He's over at Doc's and he's going to be alright."

Ted and Henry both hurried off toward the doctor's office. Logan took both horses and headed for the livery stable. When Logan got to the livery, the manager told two of the boys working there, "You boys cool both of these horses down before you put them in the barn."

Logan thanked the manager, "We'll settle up tomorrow for the horses," then he headed for the doctor's office.

When Logan walked in, Hugh was sitting up in bed. He looked real peaked and Doc was telling him to lay back down. Henry and Ted both told Hugh, "We'll see you come morning." As they walked out, Sheriff Rogers was waiting on the streets for them.

"How about all of us walk down to the office where we can talk?"

When they got to the office, first thing the sheriff said was, "I'll have to have an inquest on these shootings. I've scheduled it for tomorrow morning at 9:00 am. I've already got the riders from the ranches statements and Logan will have to be at the inquest in person."

Ted, with a worried look asked, "Why does Logan have to be there? Is he being charged in the shooting?"

"Ted, the inquest is to clear Logan of the shootings. It's the law and he needs to have it on record in case someone later would try to charge Logan with murder. I worry about what the Coulter family will do when they get word of the shooting. I've already sent a deputy over to their place to let them know and to find out what we should do with the bodies. I think the best idea will be for Logan to head back to the ranch as soon as the inquest is over. If he's in town when they ride in, I'm sure there will be more shooting. If he's gone, maybe I can talk some sense into them before they go off half cocked."

Ted nodded, "We'll head out first thing after the inquest."

Henry turned to Ted, "I want to stay around for a day or two or until Hugh is out of danger." With this agreed on, the three walked back to the hotel.

Henry had a room for himself and Ted roomed with Logan. When they were alone, Ted told Logan. "Your mother's not taking this very well. I thought for awhile I was going to have to tie her up to keep her from coming with us."

Logan looked at his dad, "You know I didn't have any choice on this. If I hadn't started shooting, they would have killed us in cold blood."

Ted reached over to take his son's arm. "I'm proud of what you did and the fact you were that good with a pistol. I knew you were special with a long gun but I had no idea you were good with a hand gun too."

Logan looked at this father for a moment. "On the hand gun, I had a good teacher. Old Dave taught me to shoot a rifle and Claire Matthews taught me the art of using a pistol. I've had two of the best teachers in the use of firearms. I'll never shoot anyone that isn't trying to kill me. I hope both you and Mom can understand that."

Ted smiled at his son. "I understand that but we may have to work on your mother. I think in the end she'll also understand."

The hearing the next morning only lasted less than an hour and the six-man jury found Logan was justified in shooting. As soon as the meeting was over, Ted and Logan headed back to the ranch. When they rode into the ranch, they were met by Lottie, who hugged her oldest son as soon as he dismounted. She looked at him the way only a mother can. "Are you alright?"

"I'm okay and I'm glad to be home."

Henry arrived back at the ranch the next day and told them Doc wanted to keep Hugh for a few more days.

The Coulters came for their boys and said they would bury them back on their ranch. The sheriff talked to them and they never mentioned Logan at all.

Two weeks went by real fast. One morning Logan told his mother, "I'm going to the dance in Benton Saturday night."

"Who's box lunch are you going to bid on," then laughed when her son blushed.

"Laura will have a nice lunch made for you."

"I might not get the bid on her basket."

"Logan, if you don't, that will be your own fault."

"Ted and I thought about going but since Henry brought Hugh home we've decided to stay with him. With Henry and Becky making that trip to a territorial meeting in Capital City, we didn't want to leave him alone."

Benton had elected Henry to represent the area in statehood for this territory. He was well educated and worked well in a crowd and was really behind this area becoming a state. Logan and three of the young single men from the ranch headed for town early Saturday morning. They all wanted to get haircuts and new clothes for the big dance.

Logan, as he walked out of the house, was stopped by his mother. "Logan, maybe you should leave the gun that's on your hip at home."

"Mom, there won't be any trouble."

As Logan mounted up, Ted walked up. "You boys have a good time, and stay out of trouble."

He looked at Logan. "I hope there is no trouble. If there is, take care of yourself."

Logan walked into the store to buy a new shirt. Laura was behind the counter. "Are you ready for the big dance?"

Logan started to answer when Ed, Laura's dad, walked up. "How's Hugh getting along?" After Ed walked away to wait on customers, Laura was also busy so Logan decided to leave. As he walked toward the door, Laura held up a bright blue ribbon and smiled. As Logan headed for the hotel, he laughed out loud. He'd just figured out what Laura meant; her box lunch would be tied with a blue ribbon.

When the four Rafter T men entered the school that evening, there was a sheriff's deputy checking all guns at the door. Logan was the only one in their group that was armed. He was wearing a dress jacket and in the inside pocket was a double barreled 44 cal. derringer. This jacket had belonged to Claire and the pocket was lined so as to conceal the weapon. Logan felt better by having the gun close. He was feeling like something was going to happen tonight. He was hoping it wouldn't but he had felt very uneasy ever since they'd ridden into town.

The dance hall was full and the music was good. Logan had danced with many of the local girls. He had danced with Laura more than the rest. She was a great dancer. The music stopped and the band leader announced, "Folks, it's time for the auction of the lunch boxes."

Laura's was the sixth box auctioned off and Logan had some competition. It seemed he wasn't the only one that knew which one she had made. Logan walked up to get the box and Laura walked over to stand by him when all of a sudden the crowd went quiet. Logan was tall enough he could see back toward the door. He could see the deputy with his hands up. Three men were standing in the door with their guns drawn and aimed at the crowd. The sheriff, who was in the crowd, started forward and told the three men to leave. The tall dark one standing in the doorway seemed to be the leader.

"Sheriff, you just stand easy. We'll leave as soon as we find Logan McTier. I'm Jess Coulter and I want the man who shot my kinfolk down in cold blood."

Logan stepped out, "I'm Logan McTier."

Jess Coulter spun to look over at Logan. "You're just a kid. I want the man who shot my family."

"I shot the men that were trying to rob Hugh Davis."

Jess grinned, "Then you're about to die, no matter how old you are. Where's your gun?" Logan motioned to the rack by the door.

One of the other men holding his guns on the crowd growled, "Which one is yours?" The man took down the holster and put the pistol in his belt and handed the belt to Logan.

"Strap that on."

Jess motioned Logan toward the door, "Now walk outside real careful like."

The sheriff pushed his way forward. He was hit from behind and knocked to the floor.

Jess Coulter told the fellow who had Logan's pistol, "You get that deputy's sawed off shotgun, and keep this crowd in the dance hall."

The fellow tossed Logan's pistol to the other man and grabbed the shotgun. Logan stepped into the street with Jess Coulter following him. Jess told the other man, "Step up behind our friend here and slip his pistol into the holster."

When the man stepped away, Jess Coulter laughed, "Well kid, how's it feel to know you're about to die?"

Logan turned slowly to look at Jess, "You'll have to answer that question."

Once Jess figured out what Logan had meant, he yelled, "Why you young punk, you're a dead man," and went for his gun.

Logan, with the fluid motion Claire always talked about, drew and fired before Jess Coulter's gun even cleared the holster. The other fellow in the street with Coulter was just staring at Logan.

"You, drop the gun," Logan growled as the fellow dropped the gun into the street.

The man with the shotgun in the doorway was hollering, "Jess, what am I suppose to do with this crowd?"

His back had been to the action in the street and he did not know his partner was dead.

Logan motioned for the man who had just dropped his gun into the street to move to the side. Logan started walking toward the man with the shotgun. He started to turn to see what was happening in the street. "Easy those hammers down and lay down the shotgun on the floor," Logan said in a normal voice.

The man started to spin and raise the double barrel when Logan fired. The shot gun dropped and the man tumbled into the street. All the men in the dance hall came running out to see what had happened.

The lone gunman still standing was staring at the body of Jess Coulter.

The sheriff, who by now was back on his feet, walked up to Logan, "What happened?"

The other man stepped forward about then and grabbed the sheriff. "Jess never even cleared leather."

Sheriff Rogers turned to the deputy who was picking up his shotgun. "Take this one over to the jail and lock him up."

Ed Benton had stepped up beside Logan. "Son, trouble just seems to follow you."

The music started up in the dance hall but nobody seemed interested in the box social or dancing. Couples started moving off toward home. Logan, Ed and Mrs. Benton were the only ones left standing in the street. The sheriff was getting the bodies moved.

Laura came up and put her hand on Logan's arm. "I'm sorry you had to do this."

She was carrying the lunch she had fixed and offered it to Logan.

68

"Maybe you can eat this on your way home."

She smiled and started for home with her parents, leaving Logan standing in the street.

The three Rafter T cowhands walked up to Logan. "Do you want to head home tonight?" They had been in the crowd in the dance hall and had not seen any of the shootings outside.

"I suppose I'd better leave town after I talk to the sheriff. You fellas can stay in the rooms we rented and finish out the weekend before you head home."

"We'd rather just ride home with you. We'll saddle the horses while you walk over and talk to the sheriff."

When Logan walked in, Sheriff Rogers was telling his deputy, "After I leave, lock this door in case some more of the Coulter family shows up."

When he saw Logan, he motioned the deputy to go check on the prisoner. The sheriff's wife was sitting at the desk still in her party dress and the sheriff still had his suit on. He motioned for Logan to sit down.

"Sheriff, if you don't mind, I'd like to head back to the ranch tonight."

Del nodded, "I think that is a good idea, Logan." When Logan heard his friends ride up outside, he stood and headed for the door.

Del shook his head. "Logan, I don't think this problem is over for you and the Coulter family. I think maybe you should stay out of town for awhile and let this cool off."

"No problem."

Mrs. Rogers walked over to him and took his hand. "Logan, I wish they would just let you alone but like the sheriff says, I don't think they will." She looked at him like a mother. "You be careful going home."

As Logan mounted, the sheriff added, "Logan, tell Ted and Hugh I will be out the first chance I get."

It was almost daylight when the four riders got to the ranch and smoke was coming from the cook shack. As they rode by the house, Logan knew his father would be up and hear them. After unsaddling, they headed for the cook shack. Logan saw his dad walking toward them. Logan told the two, "Go ahead. I need to talk to Dad."

Ted looked at Logan. "How come you're home so early?"

"There was some trouble with three of the Coulters that came into the dance hall after me. I ended up shooting two of them and the third one's in jail. The sheriff asked me to stay out of town until things cooled off."

Ted nodded and headed up toward the cook house.  Logan looked toward the house.  His mother was standing on the porch.

"Logan, maybe you should walk down and tell her what happened before she comes up here."

Logan nodded and headed for the house.  He was really dreading this.  When he finished the story, Lottie still had not blinked an eye, only looked at him.  She poured them a cup of coffee, still not saying anything until she sat back down.

"Logan, I think the winter on the mountain maybe caused some of this, but from the start, you grew up too quick.  I've always known we'd lose you here on the ranch once you grew up.  I think the best thing for you is to get away from here for awhile.  Take a pack horse and ride up north and see some country.  If you stay here, more men will come trying to beat you to the draw just because you killed Jess Coulter.  They all won't be Coulter family; they'll be men trying to make a name for themselves."

Logan nodded.  He could not believe his mother was saying this.  He had been thinking about the same thing on the ride home from town last night.  To hear his mother say the same thing was really weird.

Lottie cooked Logan breakfast.  Ted joined them and before they finished, Hugh hobbled in.  They all were talking about Logan's problem when Lottie told them her plan.

Hugh nodded, "I agree with Lottie.  I think the sooner you leave, the better."

It was decided to get Logan on the trail no later than the day after tomorrow.  Logan was wondering to himself where he would head when he left.  He decided he needed to spend one night up with Dave.  Dave knew this country and would give him some ideas of where he should go.

Lottie looked over at her oldest.  "Logan, get your gear ready and make sure your horse is well shod."

Ted interrupted, "I'll take care of shoeing Logan's horses."

"Dad, I want to take both horses that Claire gave me.  I can ride one and pack one and trade off each day."

Hugh had been pretty quiet during all this discussion.  He looked at Logan.  "Son, I think you should leave one of them horses here.  You can take another pack horse.  There's many horse thieves out there looking for horses.  When they see a young kid with two horses like those two, it's going to cause a problem.  I don't doubt you can take care of yourself but why cause a problem you can leave here."

Ted nodded, "Logan, Hugh's right about taking both sorrels on this trip."

Logan nodded. He knew they were only trying to make his trip easier. "I guess you're probably right so I'll take the sorrel with the white stocking leg."

Hugh grinned, "Make the other one that little grey of mine; he's tough and he's been packed before."

Logan started to object when his mother gave him a look and nodded her head yes.

"With the horses settled," Lottie grinned, "I'll fix you up with a trail outfit for cooking and get together the food supplies."

Hugh started outside. He stopped and stepped back inside. "We've got company coming from toward town."

When they rode up, it was Sheriff Rogers and Ed and Laura Benton. While they were all dismounting, Lottie asked, "Did you folks have break-fast?"

Ed nodded, "Laura and I ate early with the sheriff and his wife. I brought Laura along because I've always promised her the next time I rode up here she could ride along."

Laura was walking around the porch looking out over the ranch. "This is more beautiful than anything I've ever seen."

When everybody was settled on the porch, Sheriff Rogers told them, "The towns people are worried after the other night that when Logan is around, trouble would be close by. I agreed with them but for another reason. It'll be gun fighters now showing up to try to beat Logan to gain a reputation. One was already in Benton yesterday. I told him to ride on or spend the night in jail. This was a bluff on my part. I didn't have any grounds to put the man in jail. He left town but I figured he isn't very far away."

"Del," Lottie interrupted, "we've already decided that Logan is leaving this area for a spell."

Ed Benton nodded, "I guess that is probably a good idea. I hate to see Logan being the one that has to move on for awhile, but I agree with the sheriff. This will only get worse. I hope maybe in a year people will forget about Logan and maybe he can move back."

Laura had been listening to all of this. "Why doesn't the law protect him instead of making him leave?"

Before the sheriff could say anything, Logan spoke up. "Laura, there's nothing the sheriff can do to protect me. There'll always be Coulters or people like them who want to settle everything with a gun. I'll stay away for awhile and see if things change."

Logan could tell Laura did not like his answer but she did not say anything.

Ted, who had been at the blacksmith shop putting new shoes on both horses, walked back into the house. "Lottie," Rose said, " Lunch is on for all that want to eat and just out of the oven are cookies for dessert."

Lottie grabbed Ted's arm, "I haven't eaten fresh cookies for a long time so let's go."

Logan walked with Laura, "I'm going to miss seeing you and going to dances together."

"Logan, this isn't fair, you leaving."

After lunch the sheriff and the Bentons were getting ready to head back to town. Lottie had walked out with them to their horses. She could see the tears in Laura's eyes when she said good bye to Logan. Lottie grabbed Laura's hand and whispered, "Don't worry, he'll be back."

There was not much sleep that night for Logan. He laid there staring at the ceiling. His thoughts went to stories Claire had told him about life on the run.

Logan was not the only one not sleeping. Lottie tossed all night. Finally, she got up and headed down to the kitchen. When she got up, she noticed Ted was not in bed. When she got the fire going and put on the coffee pot, she walked out on the porch. Ted was sitting in the old rocking chair staring out over the ranch as dawn was first appearing. Lottie walked up behind him and was rubbing his shoulders. "Lottie, do you think Logan will ever be able to come back here?"

"He'll never work here again, but he may visit, I hope."

Ted nodded. They knew their son's life would never be the same again.

Henry and Becky were still gone so Logan told Hugh to tell them goodbye for him. Logan had told the ranch hands goodbye that morning at breakfast. As Logan was getting ready to mount up, he walked over to where Rebecca, Mary and John were standing and gave Rebecca and Mary a big hug. The younger brother, he shook hands with, "Us McTier boys don't hug, right?" He was kneeling down when he said this. All three grabbed him in a big hug.

He shook hands with Hugh. "I'm sorry this had to happen. If you had-n't shot, we'd all be dead today."

Logan just nodded. He shook hands with his dad and then took his mother in his arms.

"Logan, don't take any chances and stop by sometime."

Lottie turned away and walked into the house so her son wouldn't see her cry.

As Logan reined his horse away, Ted said, "Logan, write your mother once in awhile to let us know where you are."

Logan stayed with Dave that night. "Logan, I hate to see you leave, but after hearing the story, I think it's best. I think I'll ride along with you for a few days, I'll turn back whenever my back starts bothering me."

Dave rode with Logan for two days, but on the third morning he just stayed by the fire while Logan was packing up. Logan knew the day before Dave's back was hurting him. Logan looked over at this old friend. "Dave, do you want me to saddle your horse?"

Dave looked up and shook his head no. Logan poured them another cup of coffee before he washed the pot out and put it in the pack.

Dave motioned for Logan to sit down. Neither said a word for a spell. "Logan, I'm going to spend the day here and rest up before heading home." He looked at this young man he had always considered his adopted son. "Logan, I'm not going to bid you a good bye, instead I'll say until we meet again. You keep your wits about you. Don't do anything stupid with those guns. I don't want to ever see a wanted poster on you."

Logan nodded, walked to his horse, mounted and with a wave rode away. This was the hardest thing Logan had ever done, riding away leaving his old friend sitting there alone.

Dave had suggested Logan head for Placer Butte country on the Clear-water River. There was some mining in this area and there was the small town of Butte City. Logan, for the last week since leaving Dave, had been just looking over the country. He camped one night with a family traveling west looking for what they kept calling their promised land. They were a very religious family and spent the whole evening trying to save Logan. They did not like the guns he carried. But he noticed they did not turn down the meat from a deer he had shot that afternoon. They told Logan they had picked up supplies at a small trading post not a day's ride away. Logan was getting low on some supplies so he decided to ride over that way.

It was evening when Logan rode up to the trading post. It was a long low log building with a small barn connected on the rear. Logan walked into a dimly lit room and had to wait before his eyes became use to the darkness. The owner was a big fellow with a bad leg and he used a crutch to get around.

"Name is Sam Nelson, I own this place. Which direction did you ride in from?"

Logan held out his hand. "I'm Logan," not giving his last name, "I just came in from the south."

"What do you need?" Logan handed him a short list he had made up.

Sam handed it back. "Son, I can't read so you'll have to tell me what you want."

Logan paid for his supplies with a gold piece.

Sam looked up at him, "Are you traveling by yourself?"

Logan nodded. "You look mighty young to be traveling alone. Which direction are you headed?"

"For now I'm just looking over the area. Maybe I'll head up toward Butte City."

Sam nodded, "You're welcome to spend the night if you like. There's only my wife and me here right now. There's a bunk in the tack room and there's no charge."

Logan grinned. "I'd like that, but only if I can pay for the bunk and supper."

When Logan had put his horses away, he walked back into the store. An Indian squaw was behind the counter.

Sam was nowhere in sight and in perfect English the lady smiled and said, "Supper is ready in the kitchen."

Logan followed her into the kitchen. He found Sam already at the table in a big log chair. When the meal was over, Sam motioned for Logan to follow him. "Let's go out back. It's cooler out there. Logan, have you seen any riders the last couple days?"

Logan shook his head. "Only the family that told me about your trading post."

"I've been hearing about a strange family traveling around, and there's been a few people found shot and robbed along the trails. The stage driver mentioned he had heard from the Marshall in Sweetwater that anyone riding this area had better keep a sharp eye out for this family. There's an old man with three sons who they think to be the ones causing trouble. "They're from the back woods of Tennessee. One of the sons was a big lad that's mentally retarded. The other boys seem normal. One's about twenty and the youngest was maybe twelve, if that old. They've got a wagon that they had changed into a big wheel cart and usually have extra horses with them. Some of the robbed victims were badly cut up with a knife and the mental giant always carried a big knife. So far there hasn't been any witnesses, only bodies. You better watch out especially since you're riding such a fine horse."

Logan nodded. "Thanks for the warning, I'll keep a close watch for them."

The next morning Logan left before anybody moved around the trading post. As he topped the ridge, he looked back and smoke was just now coming from the chimney. They were good people. He wondered if Sam was worried about the family he had told Logan about. That afternoon Logan noticed some black clouds pushing his way. He decided he would watch for a grove of trees for a camp site tonight. If those clouds meant a rain storm, the trees would help keep him dry. The wind started just as Logan found a place to camp in a stand of big fir. That night it rained hard, and come morning the creek next to camp was running high. Logan waited that morning until the sun popped through before he headed out. The sun was real hot, and as Logan rode down the small ridge, he started smelling something dead. He saw some birds fly up as he came out into a small meadow. Across the meadow Logan could see some charred timber, and as he rode closer, he could see the remains of a wagon. There was a dead horse near the creek. Next to the burned wagon he saw human remains. The stench was terrible so Logan moved the horses up wind from the wagon. He tied the horses so they could feed and walked back to the wagon. As he got closer, he could see another body and it looked to be a child. Logan heard a movement behind him, he spun and drew at the same time. Before he shot he could see it was a dog tied in the brush. It was trying to get to a water puddle and it looked almost starved. You could see its ribs. Logan first thought maybe he should just put the dog out of his misery. But with those eyes looking at him, he could not do it. He walked over and cut the dog loose. He decided to leave the rope around his neck until he could make friends with him.

Logan started looking for a shovel. In the gear scattered around the camp, he spied another body in the brush. This had been a woman. Somebody had ripped her body apart. It was the worst thing Logan had ever seen and to think this had been done by another human being. Logan decided it had been a crazed two-legged animal. After Logan finished burying the bodies, he walked back to his horses to get away from the smell. He built a fire and put water on to make coffee. The dog had followed Logan and was laying a few feet away. Logan dug through his pack for some jerky and found a couple cold biscuits. He tossed them over to the dog and they were gone before they hardly hit the ground. He dug in deeper and found some bacon that he had not eaten this morning. The dog had crept closer, and Logan held out his hand and soon a cold nose was touching it. He fed him the bacon and slowly pulled his knife and cut the rope from his neck. The neck was raw from where the rope had cut into it. He had some grease his mother had sent for wounds on his horses so he put that on the dog's neck. As he was doing this, he noticed a crease between the ears of the dog. He added some grease to this too. As he looked at it, he decided the people here had shot the dog and just grazed the scull and knocked him out. They must have thought he was dead and left him alone. After having coffee, Logan moved back to where the wagon had been burned. As he looked for tracks, he noticed one person was barefooted. The print was big and the man was heavy according to how deep they sank into the ground. He also found some tracks that were small and some where you could see the person was being dragged. This he could not figure out, unless there was a girl with this wagon and they took her away. As he rummaged through the stuff scattered, he found a Bible, and under the cover was the name of Jesson and what looked to be the first names of the family. He found some dresses that would have been too small for the lady he buried. After looking around, he found tracks of what could have been another wagon or a big wheel cart. The rain had washed many of the tracks away, but Logan found enough to be able to recognize them if he saw them again. Logan put the Bible in his saddle bag and mounted up. He'd done all he could here. As he rode away, he could see the dog laying over by the wagon. He was watching Logan.

Logan stopped. "Come on dog; I can't leave you here." The dog got up and headed for Logan. Logan knew he would not last very long in the condition he was in. They traveled about a mile when Logan looked back to see the dog lying down. He looked plum worn out. Logan rode back, got down and lifted the dog up into the saddle and mounted behind him. He lifted the dog onto his lap as he slid into the seat. This dog was in bad shape. Logan figured with food he would bounce back quickly.

Logan stopped for the night about five miles from the burned wagon. He was not hungry after that mess but knew he should eat. As he was building camp, he noticed the dog was watching something in the brush. He slowly turned and finally saw a rabbit trying to hide in the brush. Logan drew and fired in one fluid motion. As he skinned the rabbit, the dog was really wanting his share. Logan shared the rabbit with him and gave him a couple biscuits. As Logan looked after the horses, the dog's eyes never left him. Logan decided he had a traveling partner from now on.

It was a week later and the dog was back to running alongside Logan and even chasing a rabbit once in awhile. Logan found a place along a creek that was shaded. There was a good pool behind a log jam. There was a rock ledge near the pond with an overhang where Logan put his gear. He stripped off and took a swim and washed a few clothes that needed it. He had supper and was lying on his bedroll when the dog's ears perked up and started growling real deep down. Then Logan could hear the crunch of wagon wheels on the gravel. His gun belt was hanging on a tree limb above him. He was using his saddle for a pillow and in the small scabbard was a short double barrel shotgun. Old Dave had tied that on Logan's saddle the day they left from his cabin. He pulled it and laid it out of sight by his right leg. He had his pistol in his belt but it would be hard to draw it very fast. About then he heard a voice hailing the camp. It was a very southern accent and Logan started looking for other people closing in on camp. He kept telling the dog in a low tone to lay down.

"That coffee sure smells good. How about me having a cup?"

"Come ahead but keep your hands in sight." As they walked into the opening, Logan could see this old man with a long white dirty beard. With him was a big, young giant dressed in bib overalls and barefooted. Around his middle was a belt with a pistol on one side and a huge knife on the other.

The old man nodded toward the horses. "I'd like to trade for those horses you got staked over there."

"They're not for trade or for sale."

The old man laughed. "You're not in any shape to talk terms. I see your guns hanging in the tree."

About then the big giant started to move forward. He was mumbling about it was his turn to kill the next person. The old man grabbed the younger man's arm as he started pulling his pistol. Logan brought up the shotgun from beside his leg and pulled both triggers. He'd seen the look in the old man's eyes when he saw the barrels come in sight. Both men were almost blown over backward with the blast. Logan could hear running feet coming up the creek so he rolled over and pulled the gun from behind his belt. Another young fellow came running through the trees with a rifle in his hands. When he saw Logan, he started to turn the rifle toward Logan. Logan fired twice, both shots knocking the man into the pond. As Logan reached up and got his gun belt, he heard another voice hollering.

"I'm coming Pa." Through the trees came a young boy of maybe twelve or so with a rifle in his hands. He saw Logan; he fired. He hit the tree off to the side of where Logan was standing. Logan shot him as he ran through the creek and he fell in the water. Logan looked around at the four dead men. He heard the dog bark and it headed across the creek at a high run. Logan reloaded his gun and followed the dog. He stayed in the willows along the creek as he moved. A covered cart came into view and Logan could see a girl tied to the wheel with a gag in her mouth. She was mostly naked, and when Logan walked up, she was straining at her tied wrists.

"Hold still. I'm not going to hurt you," as he cut the ropes. The dog bounced into her arms knocking her down. She grabbed him and buried her face in his fur. Logan knew then he had a survivor from the other wagon. He found a dirty coat laying on the seat and covered her with it. The girl kept looking toward the creek. Logan shook his head. "They won't be back. They're all dead."

"There are four of them."

"I know. They're all laying over across the creek."

Logan looked down at her huddled on the ground holding the dog. "Is your last name Jesson?"

She shook her head yes. "My name is Mollie. Where did you find Traveler? He's my dog."

Logan told her of burying her folks and finding the dog tied up and about half dead. The girl kept looking at Logan. "Who are you? Where did you come from?"

"I'm Logan. I was camped across the creek for the night. Are there any clothes in the wagon you could wear?"

"I don't think so."

Logan offered his hand. "Can you walk?" She nodded. She stood up holding the coat to her. Logan led her over to his camp. When she saw the

78

bodies, a small smile appeared on her face.

When she saw the youngest one, she said, "He's the only one that never beat me. He was trying to get from me what the rest of the family had been doing all week when the shooting started. They never would let him near me while they were having their fun with me. When the old man and the other two boys started for your camp, the old man told him to circle around behind your camp. When the three were out of sight, the younger one came back to have his way with me. I was tied to the wagon with the gag in my mouth so I couldn't scream. He was about to get his way when the shooting started. He grabbed his rifle and went running across the creek."

When they got to where Logan's camp was, he told her, "I'll get some of my clothes for you to wear."

It was dark by now. Logan built up the fire so he could see around camp better. Logan found a pair of pants and a shirt that would be way too big but at least she'd be covered. Logan tossed her a towel and a bar of soap. "Why don't you go take a bath in the pond?" She just stood there looking at him.

"I'll start packing these bodies over to the cart while you're in the pool." When he got back on the third trip, she was trying to dry her hair over the fire. She had put on his clothes and had the sleeves and pant legs rolled up. When he picked up the last body, he nodded toward his gear. "If you're hungry, there is food in my pack."

When Logan finished the last of the coffee, he looked over at her. "We need to find a town with a law officer."

Mollie nodded, "We're close to a town called Sweetwater. The day before yesterday they left me with the crazy one and the youngest while the old man and the other one went into town for supplies. I'm sure the town is just a few miles away."

"Why don't you lay down and get some sleep. We'll wait for dawn and maybe I can back track the cart."

When first light appeared, Logan had the team on the cart hooked up and his horses ready to travel. There were three extra horses along with the team for the cart. Logan had two bodies in the cart. The old man and the giant he loaded on two of their horses. He helped Mollie up into the cart seat and then climbed up beside her. It was close to midday when Logan first sighted some buildings and a better road than the trail they had been following.

They traveled down this road about a mile when they met a rider heading toward them. When the fellow rode up, Logan asked, "How far is it to Sweetwater? Is there a sheriff or marshall there?"

The stranger was looking at the bodies on the two horses behind the wagon. Finally, he answered. "You're about a mile from Sweetwater. If you want the sheriff, he lives in the next place you come to. I just rode out from town with him. He was going to have lunch with his wife."

As Logan pulled up to the picket fence in front of a small white house, a man with a badge walked out the door. Logan stepped down and offered his hand. "I'm Logan and I think this girl needs your help."

Logan told the sheriff about finding the girl last night and about the four men who tried to rob him. The sheriff called back to the house and asked his wife to come out. As the sheriff's wife came out, Logan was helping Mollie down from the cart. The sheriff asked his wife to take her inside.

The sheriff looked back at Logan. "Would your last name be McTier by any chance?" Logan looked at the sheriff and he smiled, "My name is Jeff Rogers and Del Rogers, the sheriff in Benton, is my brother. He wrote me a letter about you and told me to keep an eye out for you."

Logan filled the sheriff in on what had happened since he found the burned wagon. The sheriff looked over the bodies. "That shotgun done a job on those two," and he motioned to the bodies on the horses. As they unloaded the bodies from the wagon, he nodded. "This one is only a boy."

Logan nodded, "He was pulling the trigger of that rifle like he knew what he was doing when I shot him."

A boy of about ten came out of the house and the sheriff motioned him to come over to them. He boosted the lad up on the horse that had been standing at the hitch rack when Logan drove up.

"Josh, ride into town and get the doctor, and tell him to bring a wagon from the livery."

After loading the bodies into the wagon from the livery, the sheriff told the driver to take them into town.

In the meantime, Doc had gone in to see the girl. When he came back out, he was shaking his head. "That poor girl has really been worked over. Shooting was too good for those four."

The doctor had brought his own buggy out from town. As he settled in the seat, he looked at the sheriff. "I'll catch up with the livery wagon and see that the bodies were taken care of."

As the doctor drove by Logan, he stopped. "I don't know who you are, but I'm glad you stopped those four."

Logan walked over to his horse and got the Bible that belonged to Mollie's folks. He followed the sheriff into the house. Mollie was in one of the bedrooms lying down. Mrs. Rogers asked Logan, "Can I fix you a plate while the sheriff finishes his lunch?"

Logan grinned, "I'll take you up on that offer."

When they finished eating, Logan turned to Mrs. Rogers. "Thank you very much for the meal. I kinda get tired of my own cooking." Logan handed the Bible to Mrs. Rogers. "I found this when I buried Mollie's family."

She looked at it. "Mollie's not asleep so why don't you take it to her. Besides she wants to see you before you leave."

Logan walked into the room. With her hair all combed and cleaned up, Mollie was a good-looking girl.

She held out her hand and when he took it she squeezed his hand. "Will I ever see you again?"

Logan was at a loss for words and mumbled, "I hope so."

Logan gave her the Bible, and when she saw it, she broke down into tears. "I'll be leaving as soon as the sheriff lets me go."

"Mrs. Rogers washed your clothes I was wearing. They're not dry yet. Can't you wait until morning to leave?" and with that Logan nodded he would.

"I have a favor to ask of you. I hope you will say yes. Will you take Traveler with you? He seems to like you, and if I go back east, I won't be able to take him."

Logan laughed. "We'll make a good traveling pair and I'd be glad to have him along."

Mrs. Rogers walked into the room. "Mollie, you should rest now," and she motioned Logan to follow her. As he went into the other room, he heard Mollie saying, "You promised to stay until tomorrow."

Logan left his pack horse and gear in the sheriff's barn and rode into town with the sheriff who drove the cart.

When they got to his office, there were four of the local businessmen waiting for him. "Who are those dead men that Doc brought in?"

Sheriff Rogers looked at them. "Wait a minute and I'll answer your questions." He told the two deputies standing there, "Take this cart out to

81

the shed behind the office and unload it. I want everything looked at, and if you find anything valuable, record it. All these people that have been killed were robbed before or after they were killed. I'm hoping maybe we can find some idea how many people these four have killed."

The sheriff then walked back to talk to the four businessmen in his office.

Logan looked over at the sheriff. "I'm going to look around town while you're busy with these fellows."

"You stay right here to fill in anything I may miss while telling this story."

After the sheriff finished, the older of the four businessmen looked over at Logan. "You're just a boy and you shoot like that?"

Sheriff Rogers nodded, "I'm thinking maybe him looking so young fooled the robbers into being careless." He made it a point not to mention his brother from Benton had written him about the gun speed.

Logan looked toward the older man. "After burying the people at the burned wagon, I was a little leery of anyone walking into my camp. When I saw the big fellow without shoes carrying that big knife, I figured I had better be ready for trouble."

After the businessmen had left, the sheriff grinned, "What they don't know don't hurt them."

"Logan, can you draw me a map of the location of the burned wagon so I can go up there and look over the place." Logan pointed to the finished map. "I also located the swimming hole so you can look over the place they were killed."

The next morning as Logan saddled up to leave, Mollie came out to see him. "I think there is more to you than you just being lucky when you shot those men. You seem older, but I don't think you're any older than I am." With tears in her eyes, she grabbed his arm. "Logan, I'll never forget first seeing you as you walked up to the wagon that night. You were so sure of yourself. Those men trying to kill you didn't seem to phase you in the least."

Logan, again being lost for words when trying to talk to Mollie, smiled. "It does bother me and I shoot only when my life is threatened. I'm sorry about your folks and wish maybe I could have been there before they were killed. I'll take good care of Traveler and maybe we'll meet again."

Mollie turned and ran back into the house. Sheriff Rogers and his wife both shook hands with Logan and wished him a safe journey. When Logan mounted up, he looked down at the sheriff. "What will happen to Mollie?"

Mrs Rogers spoke up. "We'll make sure she'll be alright before we let her go." With that Logan reined around his horse and headed for the road.

Two weeks later found Logan and Traveler up on the Clearwater River near Placer Butte. For about two days they had been traveling by miners washing gravel in all the small creeks. Logan camped one night with an old prospector. He showed Logan how to pan and what to look for along the creek bed. Logan tried his luck and did find a little color in the pan. The old fellow drew a rough map in the gravel and showed Logan where the big claims were and the location of Butte City. Logan was about a day's ride from Butte City and decided to head that way to get a few supplies and buy a gold pan.

As he rode down the main street in Butte City, he could see new buildings going up, and there were still many tent structures scattered around town. There were people everywhere and the stores were all full. Logan was looking for a place to leave his horse while he shopped around. He noticed a store with a big sign out in front but no line of people trying to get in. The sign was in Chinese written on top with Ling's Store written below in English. Logan reined over and tied his horses in front of this store and walked in. Inside it seemed to be a well-stocked store with full shelves.

A little man with a pigtail stood behind the counter, and in good English asked, "Can I help you find anything?"

Logan told him what supplies he wanted. Then he added, "I also need a gold pan."

The little man laughed, "Have you ever mined for gold before?"

"I spent the night with the old prospector upriver and he showed me a little about panning. So I decided I want a pan in case I find some good gravel."

The little man laughed, "At least you don't figure on being rich by evening."

When Logan walked back to his horses, two men were starting to go through his packs. Logan shifted his packages to his left hand. "Those are my packs so just step away."

They both looked at him and laughed. "Boy, if we want these packs we will take them."

"I hope there's room for you both in hell, because if you don't step back, that's where you're going."

A voice behind Logan asked, "Is there some trouble here?" Logan looked back to see a fellow wearing a star asking the question.

"When I came out of the store these two were going over my gear."

One of the men in the street laughed. "Marshall, these are our horses and they were stolen from our camp about two weeks ago."

Logan turned to the Marshall. "If you'll notice, both horses carry brands and I have a bill of sale for them both."

The man standing behind the one talking was pulling his gun when Logan drew and fired. Logan could only see the shoulder and arm of the man. His bullet almost blew the shooter's arm off at the elbow. The man was just lifting his pistol when Logan shot and his pistol discharged when it hit the ground.

Logan heard the marshall tell the other man, "Unbuckle your gun belt and drop it." The marshall turned to Logan, "What's your name young fellow?"

"I'm Logan McTier," and the marshall nodded.

"I want to talk to you after I get this fellow in jail." A deputy showed up right after the shooting. The marshall told him, "You take that one to the doctor," pointing to the one holding his arm on the ground. "I'll put this one in a cell."

He looked over at Logan. "I'll be right back."

"I'll be right here."

When the marshall walked off, the little Chinaman stepped out onto the street to talk to Logan while he loaded his supplies. He smiled, "You're very good with the gun you carry."

Logan finished putting his gear on the pack horse and turned, "Maybe I was just lucky." The little man just smiled and headed back into the store as the marshall walked up.

"I don't know how you pulled that gun so quick, but you probably saved one or both of us from being shot.'

"I was lucky. I saw that fellow drawing his gun."

The marshall was looking at Logan's horse. "I think I know this horse."

"I have a bill of sale for this horse from Claire Matthews."

The marshall smiled. "I believe you. How did you get one of Claire's horses?"

"I've got them both. He willed them to me before he died."

The marshall nodded. "I spent one winter riding with Claire before I took this job."

Logan then told the marshall about Claire being dead and how he got the horses. "I thought I also recognized the gun rigging you are wearing."

Logan nodded. With that the Marshall chuckled. "Then that wasn't luck when you drew back there."

Logan shrugged his shoulders. "Do I need to stay around town or can I get back on the trail?"

"You can ride whenever you like. Watch your back. Those two have some friends around town."

As Logan worked his way up the main fork of the Clearwater, the miners got thicker. Later that day Logan found a place near the main river without any miners close by so he made camp for the night. There was a small trickle of water from a spring close by so Logan had good fresh water instead of the murky river water. After eating supper, Logan cleaned up the dishes and decided to try his luck at panning. He walked down near the river and filled his pan and went to the river to pan it. When he was done, all he found was one small color in the bottom of the pan. He moved to another area and scooped another pan full. In this pan he found better color so he got another pan from the same location. Some pans were real good, others were almost bare. It was getting dark when Logan and Traveler headed back to camp. Logan was laying in bed when he heard Traveler growling real low. About then he could hear real soft steps on the trail above his camp. Logan pulled one pistol and in a low voice said, "If you don't want to be shot, walk into the light with your hands empty."

Soon Logan could make out a little person coming into the light. When he walked into the full light, Logan could see a Chinaman carrying a big pack.

The fellow had his hands palm forward in front of him. In broken English he said, "No got gun."

Logan motioned for him to drop his hands. "You want some coffee. I think it's still hot."

A look of surprise came over the little man's face. "I would like that."

Logan found his cup and poured the fellow a drink. The Chinaman nodded his thanks. "My name is Lo Lin. I don't speak very good English. I have a mine up on the south fork of the river."

"Why are you sneaking around during the night?"

"I'm trying to get to Butte City to buy supplies. There are men on this trail who made their money killing and robbing the Chinese miners. I hide my gold near my claim and I'm only carrying enough to buy supplies I need. Two men have been watching my claim for a week so I snuck out last night. I'm trying to make it to Butte City before they find me. I hid in the trees all day and saw the same two men riding down the trail toward town."

Logan nodded. "I remembered two men riding by about the time I started making camp."

"Lo Lin, you're welcome to spend the night and come morning I'll take you into Butte City."

The little man with a grin said, "I'll pay you to help me get my supplies back to my claim."

"You've got a deal."

The next morning Logan told Lo Lin, "I've changed my mind. I've decided I'll go after the supplies myself. Lo Lin, how far is it to your claim?"

Lo Lin shrugged. "By horse maybe eight hours."

Logan nodded. "Let's ride back to your claim and I'll leave my gear. Then, I'll ride into Butte City for your supplies."

Lo Lin asked, "Why do you want it that way?"

"Nobody knows me so I can ride in without any trouble and buy your supplies and be back the next day."

Lo Lin nodded. "That's a good idea."

Logan lifted him up behind him on his horse and put his pack on the pack horse. When they got to the cabin, Logan was surprised at the size of the mining operation for one man to operate. They put Logan's gear in the store room. Then Logan made ready to head back down the trail.

Lo Lin handed Logan a poke of gold dust and a folded piece of paper. "This note is for Ling, the store owner. It also has my list of supplies."

As Logan mounted up, the little man asked. "Do you think anyone will stop you?"

Logan grinned, "Only if I want them to."

Lo Lin grinned, "You wait," and up the hill behind the camp he went. Soon Lo Lin appeared carrying two saddle bags and they looked heavy. He handed them to Logan. "You take more gold to Ling's store. You keep one third of the gold if you deliver this to Ling."

Logan grinned, "Don't you think that's too big a share for handling this gold?"

"No, in the past five months they have stolen all my gold. If you make it, that will be my first gold to be banked." Lo Lin held up his hand, "I want the note that I gave you. I'll add this deal to it. I'll be safe here working my mine, and if they come back, I will hide. When you come back and don't see me, just stay here. I will appear."

With that Logan and Traveler headed back to Butte City.

It was getting dark when Logan rode into Butte City. He rode into the alley behind Ling's store. He stayed in the shadows until he was sure nobody was following him. He went up to the back door, and as he went to knock, he noticed someone standing in the shadows by the door. He drew his gun. "Step out where I can see you."

A small Chinese girl stepped from the shadows. "Do you speak English?" She nodded.

"Will you tell Ling I need to see him back here. Tell him it's the man who shot the man in front of his store this morning."

The girl disappeared into the store and soon Ling stepped out in the alley.

"Why do you come to my back door so late?"

Logan handed him the note from Lo Lin. "You have the gold now?"

Logan handed him the saddle bags. Ling motioned Logan to follow him. They walked down the alley to a small barn. As they entered Ling stopped. "You duck down and follow me." They passed through a small door that opened in the wall. They walked down some steep stairs. At the bottom was a big room with tables and gold scales and a big safe. Ling motioned Logan to a chair. Two more Chinese men soon appeared. They helped Ling weigh out the gold Logan had brought. When finished, Ling handed Logan a poke. "This is your share according to the note from Lo Lin."

Logan could tell by the feel this had been a money-making trip for him.

Logan handed it back to Ling. "Can I leave this with you for now?"

Ling nodded. "I'll give you a receipt for it."

They retraced the steps back to the alley behind the store and Logan followed Ling into the store. Inside the girl was waiting on a customer at the front counter. Logan followed Ling into the office in back of the store. Ling made a receipt for Logan.

Logan looked down at it. "Where can I collect this if I need it?"

"Here at the store or in the Chinese Town Bank in the Capital City.

Logan nodded. "If I should get killed, I want this money delivered to

Lottie McTier at the Rafter T Ranch over the Sheep Creek range."

Ling filled out some papers and had Logan sign them. "I would like to get Lo Lin's supplies loaded tonight and camp out up the trail."

"I think you are wise to do this. We'll have the order ready in twenty minutes." Ling rang a small bell next to his desk and two young boys came down the stairs. Ling talked to them in Chinese and handed them the list.

Ling motioned to Logan. "Come, we get you something to eat before you ride out." Logan had noticed a small Chinese café next to the store this morning. He did not know they were connected. He followed Ling through a side door into the café and they walked behind a curtain to a small table. Ling said, "We will eat here."

While they were eating, Ling asked, "How come Lo Lin trusted you with so much gold when he hardly knew you?"

Logan shook his head. "Well, Lo Lin was moving past my camp last night and I invited him to spend the night. When he told me about his troubles, I decided I could get his supplies to him without trouble if he wasn't along. I don't know why Lo Lin decided to trust me with that much gold on the first trip. The one third was Lo Lin's idea. That's being real generous I think."

"You can make big money if you'll bring the gold out for all the Chinese miners. They'll gladly give you a third. That's better for them than getting nothing as it is now. One out of ten Chinese miners ever get to town with their gold right now. There are a bunch of thieves living up at a road house near the summit. The owner is the leader. They rob both white and Chinese but nobody cares if the Chinese are robbed and killed. The owner is a fellow called Tiny Lang. He's got about ten men living up there working for him. He keeps two girls up there to keep his men in camp where he can control them better. He collects from all the miners each week a toll for his protection. They watch each claim to find out what each miner makes each day and charges them accordingly. When a Chinese miner tries to get his gold out, they catch him and beat him the first time and take his gold. The second time they kill him and take over his claim. This has been going on for about six months and there's no law that will go up there and stop it. If you could figure a way of getting more gold out, you'll be able to name your own price. Most of these Chinese miners have fooled the people watching them. They all have big caches of gold."

Logan smiled. "I kinda like the sound of helping them move their gold."

As Logan tied down the last pack, he told Ling, "If I decide to do this, I'll need some different horses and some pack mules."

Ling nodded. "That'll be no problem. If you bring in another load, turn off the main trail at the sign north of town that says Murphy Mine. Ride into the buildings and lead your animals into the upper tunnel of the mine. Inside a short ways you will find a large open area. Put the packs in the mining car, and before you leave, take the hammer and hit the rails behind the car three times. Then ride on out and follow the trail off the end of the dump. It will lead you into town. Then come to the store like you are packing supplies for the mines."

Logan nodded, and with a wave headed down the alley and up the trail to find a place to camp for what was left of the night.

Logan camped close to where he met Lo Lin the night before. Logan took his time the next morning getting packed up. He figured if someone saw him hurrying down the trail they might decide he was trying to hide something. He took his time heading back to Lo Lin's claim. He stopped a few times to pass the time of day with miners working along the creek. As Logan was passing the trail leading to the roadhouse and store, two riders rode up and blocked the trail.

Logan stopped. "What can I do for you?"

He recognized them as the two who were following Lo Lin the other day.

The older one with his hand almost resting on his gun butt asked, "Who are you anyway? Where do you think you're going?"

"I'm just bringing in some supplies for a friend."

"We sell all the supplies these miners need at Lang's store down that trail. Who's this friend you're working for and where is his claim," growled the second fellow.

I really don't think that's any of your business." Logan used his off side spur to make his horse move side ways, and when he turned the horse back, the two men found themselves looking down the barrel of a shotgun. Logan carried it in a scabbard next to his right leg. With the stock cut off at the grip and the barrels shortened, it was easy to miss next to his leg. The two riders both started to rein their horses around.

"Just stay still and drop your gun belts." He motioned with the barrel to dump their guns on the ground. "Now step down off those horses real easy like." Logan threw his leg over the saddle horn and slid off onto the ground still facing them. "Now you boys take off your boots."

They started to argue. About then Logan noticed a bulge under the younger man's coat. Logan stepped across and stuck the shotgun in the fellows gut before the man could move. "Now I'll take the extra gun too. If I find another one on either of you, I will shoot both of you right here and now."

They both sat down and took off their boots. "Now head down the trail you just come up."

"You're a dead man as soon as we get some guns," the younger one growled.

Logan laughed. "You better hope you never find any guns then, because if you try it, you're both going to be very dead."

When they were out of sight, Logan picked up the gun and boots and tied them to the saddles of their horses. He tied the horses behind his pack horse and headed for Lo Lin's cabin.

When he rode up to the cabin, it seemed deserted, so he started unloading the packs. Traveler's ears went up and Logan stepped behind the cabin.

Lo Lin called out, "You have a good watch dog there."

Lo Lin looked at the extra horses. "Did you have trouble with the two men who own those horses?"

"No trouble Lo Lin. I just met them two on the trail."

Lo Lin looked up at Logan. "They'll come looking until they find you."

Logan nodded, "For their sakes I hope they don't."

Logan took the extra horses down the trail a mile or so and tied up their reins and sent them down the trail away from Lang's store. That night while eating Logan told Lo Lin what Ling had said about moving more gold for other Chinese miners.

Lo Lin nodded. "That will be very dangerous as soon as Lang's men find out what you're doing."

Logan nodded. "I can make a few trips before they figure out gold is going out."

Lo Lin smiled. "I'll pass the word to the other miners."

After supper Logan told Lo Lin, "I'm going for a short ride before dark to look the place over."

Logan rode up on the ridge out of sight of the cabin then dismounted and tied his horse where it could feed. He pulled the Sharps from the roll behind the saddle then moved back over the ridge where he could watch Lo

Lin's cabin. He did not have to wait long before he spotted four riders coming down the trail. They all had rifles across their saddles and were looking for tracks on the trail. When they rode up to Lo Lin's cabin, he could hear them holler and tell Lo Lin to step out. The door opened and Lo Lin stepped out. Logan could hear and see them pointing to Logan's pack horse in the corral. Lo Lin was nodding his head yes and motioning down the trail. The fellow in the lead and doing all the talking was the older man Logan had sent walking. Lo Lin started to move back to his cabin door. The man swung his rifle to fire just as Logan's bullet knocked him out of his saddle.

The other three turned to look up the hill. Then another man from the trail hollered. "Shoot that damn Chinaman."

Before any of them could get a shot toward Lo Lin, a second shot came from the hill hitting the one that said to kill the Chinaman. He fell from his horse and the other two men threw up their hands.

Logan called down, "Stay where you are. Toss those rifles over the bank and drop the gun belts. Now move back away from your horses." Logan walked back down the hill to them.

As Logan walked up, the one said, "Hell, it's just a kid." They both looked at Logan as he checked the two men he had shot.

"I told those two this afternoon that if they caused trouble, they'd be dead."

Lo Lin came around the cabin carrying an old muzzle loading shotgun.

Logan laughed, "Lo Lin you pull that trigger and we're all in trouble." Logan walked up to the two men. "I'm going to pack grub in here for anyone who hires me. So you go back and tell Lang to back off."

One of the men shook his head. "Lang's not going to like this."

"Mount up and leave your guns where they are. Lo Lin has asked me to stay here with him. If any of your buddies from the roadhouse bother him, I will be seeing you."

After the riders left, Logan started to go back up the hill to get his horse. Lo Lin grabbed his arm, "You stay here. I'll bring down the horse."

It was dark and Logan was thinking about bed when Lo Lin motioned toward the door. "We have company coming."

He went to the door and in walked three more Chinese miners, at least Logan figured from their looks they were miners. Lo Lin introduced them as neighbors of his that also needed supplies. The four were talking in Chinese and Logan could understand none of it.

91

Lo Lin turned to Logan, "These three speak very little English so I will talk for them." "This is Lin Wa, Sun Lee and Ah Toy, they want you to start moving their gold to Ling's store. They'll pay you the same as I do."

Logan nodded, "I'll need one trip down to get different pack animals. I'll take some gold with me then. I'll leave at dawn if you can get some of their gold ready to go by then."

Sun Lee said in broken English, "I have my gold ready to move now."

Logan told Lo Lin, "You tell them I don't want all their gold in one trip. If they do catch me with the gold, you won't lose everything at one time."

Sun Lee nodded. "I'll be back before dawn with my gold."

Logan was up and had the horses saddled before dawn. Sun Lee showed up with a back pack that was heavy. Sun Lee gave Logan his order for supplies and with a bow turned and hurried back toward his claim. Logan looked toward Lo Lin, "You watch out for some of Lang's crew snooping around."

Logan had noticed another little used trail heading up the mountain and turned off on it. He decided he was going to vary his travel to different trails each time. He would come back to the main trail, but going down he would try to hide his travels. Logan kept to the little used trail until he topped the mountain. He could see the main river below him and miners working the different sand bars. The trail he was following turned back up river and away from the river. Logan started down the mountain picking his way through the trees. Soon he was on a trail next to a creek. He could hear water falling and knew he was close to a mining operation. As he moved on down the creek, he could see a big tent in an opening ahead of him. Two men were shoveling into a sluice box. When they saw him, they both laid down their shovels and picked up rifles that were leaning against a tree. Logan waved, "I'm friendly," and they motioned to come on in. They never offered their names so Logan did not either.

"I'm just passing through and I guess I missed the trail up river. I'm packing supplies to some miners over the ridge."

One of the miners grinned, "That's mainly just Chinese mining over there."

Logan nodded, "That's who I'm packing for."

Logan had packed the pack horse so it looked like it was carrying only a rolled tarp. Inside that roll was the pack sack of Sun Lee's gold. "If you fellows ever need supplies packed, let me know. The name is Logan."

With that he rode off down the trail and along the main river.

It was almost dark by the time Logan turned off the trail and headed for the Murphy Mine. He unloaded the pack and rolled the tarp back like it was and moved down the trail for town. When he tied up out front and entered the Ling store, it was almost empty except for the girl who worked there. When she saw Logan, she walked behind the curtain in back and disappeared. Soon Ling walked into the store. He smiled, "You made good time in from the mine."

Logan nodded, "I need a place to stay tonight and come morning I'll need a good saddle horse and two pack animals."

"Do you want to leave your horses here in town? If so, I have a place for them. You ride down Main Street and you'll see a livery on the left side. They have some rooms behind the livery for the freighter. You can stay there tonight."

"Sounds good. I'll see you in the morning."

As Logan mounted up, Ling looked back at him. "If you like, I'll buy your breakfast in the morning," and motioned to the café beside the store.

Logan had a good night's sleep and even Traveler did not mind the cabin. Logan walked the three blocks to the café with Traveler at his heals. Traveler really did not like town life, but Logan wanted to keep him close. When he arrived at the café, he stepped in to see if Ling was there yet.

Logan did not see him so he walked into the store. The same girl was behind the counter. "Would you have any meat scraps for my dog?"

She smiled, "I'll feed him for you while you and father have breakfast."

Logan was surprised when Traveler followed her.

Ling was watching Logan's expression. "My daughter can do many things with animals." After breakfast Ling and Logan went back into the store. Logan looked out back. There were three horses tied to the hitch rail and his saddle was on the tall grey horse. Ling smiled, "I also own the livery, but not everyone knows that. I have a manager and he is white and we want everyone to think he is the owner. It makes it easier that way. I hope you don't mind we brought your gear along."

Logan noticed his saddle bags were missing. As he turned toward Ling, he added, "You can get them when you go back to the cabin." Logan noticed a small Chinese boy sitting on a horse by the railing. Ling nodded toward him, "This is my son Ling Wa. He will show you where to take your horses. I figured you would want to see where they're being kept. Ling Wa

93

also speaks good English"

Logan picked up his two horses from the livery and followed the boy out of town. About a mile out they turned up a road along a small creek. Soon they came into a meadow with a cabin and barn. As they rode up, an old man walked out of the barn and motioned to bring the horses inside.

He looked over at Logan, "I'm Fred and I run this place for Ling." He kept looking at Logan, "How old are you?"

Logan laughed, "Eighteen," and the old man just shook his head.

"From what I've been hearing, I figured on seeing an wild-eyed gunman instead of a young kid. If you expect to survive packing this gold, I hope you can handle those guns real well."

"I get lucky once in a while."

The old fellow just grunted and tied the horses to the manger. Logan decided his horses were in good hands for now.

When he and Ling Wa got back to the store, his supplies were sitting on the back porch ready to be loaded. As Logan loaded both pack animals, he was thinking about which way to go home. He decided to do what he first figured and stick to the main trail going back to Placer Butte. Ling motioned him to his office. Logan walked back into the store after loading the horses. Ling handed him a receipt. "This is for your share of the gold brought in last night." When Logan looked at the amount, he just shook his head. Ling smiled, "Sun Lee must have really trusted you to send that much the first time."

"I knew that pack was heavy, but nothing like this."

"You're going to be a rich man at a young age if you live that long."

Logan laughed, "I'll do my best to watch out for Lang's crew."

When Logan headed up the trail, he was trying to think the best way to avoid meeting Lang's men. They were mad enough to just shoot him on sight. Logan was thinking maybe he should hide the pack horses and ride on ahead to check out the trail. There were two or three places that would make for a good ambush between here and the pass into the mining area. There were also many places along the trail from the pass down to Lo Lin's cabin to watch out for. Logan found a place where he could leave the horses and ride up the mountain. From there he could see the trail ahead for a few miles. He stayed there and from here he could also see the pack horses on the trail below him. Logan's idea was he had the old Sharps with him, and if anyone tried to steal the pack horses, he could, from here, probably stop them. The trail ahead looked clear so Logan went back and got the pack horses and headed on up the trail. As he neared the pass, he knew he had to pass through one rock outcropping. This would be a good ambush point. He stopped in some trees along the trail to rest the horses in case he needed to make a run for it. Logan noticed Traveler had stayed out on the trail. His ears were up like he was hearing something in the rocks ahead.

Logan tied his horse and the pack horses to the trees. Taking his rifle he started climbing up the ridge behind the rocks. When he got on top, he could hear some horses in the trees below. Logan worked his way over toward the sound. He soon spotted two horses. They were saddled and tied to some willows. He watched for a few minutes but could not see a guard anywhere around. Logan walked over to the horses and with his knife cut the cinches on both saddles. He left a couple strings holding on each one hoping they would hold while the rider mounted. He wanted the cinch to break when the riders were hurrying away. With the cinches cut, Logan worked his way over to the rocks. He slowly worked his way around until he could see two men watching the trail below.

As Logan laid there he heard one of them say, "He should be showing up anytime now." Another voice added, "Remember what Lang said, 'Shoot to kill and don't give him any warning'."

Logan could see the other man nod, and with that, Logan began moving back up the ridge away from the horses. He found a place where he could see both his outfit and the two men.

Logan chuckled to himself, "I guess I'll see if I can give these two would-be road agents a little surprise." He had brought the Winchester and decided to send a few shots to maybe scare the hell out of them. He fired the first shot at the rifle stock of the gunman nearest to him. It was a little lucky his shot hit the stock and pieces really peppered the man holding it. With a shout, he jumped up and headed for the horses. The second man was trying to find the shooter to get a shot. Logan shot and hit the rock near the second man and he got stung with flying rock chips. He jumped up and took off over the ridge chasing his partner. Logan sat for a spell, then saw the two riders hitting the trail going over the pass.

Logan got the horses and headed on up the trail. When he started down the trail after going over the pass, he found a man lying in the trail. As Logan rode up, the man was holding his leg and it looked like maybe it was broken.

He looked up at Logan, "I need help; my leg's broke."

"I'm busy getting these supplies moved. I'll send word to Lang when I get down into the valley."

"Hell, man, I need help now."

"After you shot me from ambush, were you going to help me?"

Logan headed on down the trail and soon came upon the other rider draped over a rock and his head was all bloody. Logan stepped down and found the man was dead. Logan could then see his neck was broken. The horses were no where around so Logan figured they headed for the barn at the roadhouse. Logan saw a rider coming up the trail, so he rode just off the trail and waited.

When the rider rode up, Logan motioned back up the trail, "There's a dead man back up the trail a ways and another one on up the trail with a broken leg. I told the one with the broken leg I'd send help back for him. Being as you're here, you can take care of them." Logan headed on to Lo Lin's cabin without looking back. When he got to Lo Lin's cabin, he found Sun Lee.

Lo Lin grinned, "Sun Lee was afraid you didn't make it through and he'd lost all his gold."

Logan handed Sun Lee a letter from Ling and the receipt for the gold. Logan told Lo Lin, "You two can take the pack horses to Sun Lee's mine and unload them."

When Lo Lin translated this to Sun Lee, he turned back to Logan, "He wants you to go with us."

That night after Logan and Lo Lin got back to the cabin, Lo Lin started supper while Logan cared for the horses. While eating supper, they talked about who also wanted their gold packed out and supplies brought in. Logan was curious when this country would start getting snow. He knew with that pass being that high, snow would come early.

Lo Lin nodded, "We should have one more good month before we have to start thinking of being snowed in."

Logan was wondering what he would do for the winter. He sure was not looking forward to staying up here with Lo Lin.

Logan worked his way down the mountain two days later and had two heavy loaded pack horses. He was trying a new route out of the mining area. This route was steep and he was making very slow time. He needed to rest the horses quite often. He was sure Lang had his men watching all the main trails. It was dark by the time Logan reached the Murphy Mine and unloaded his load. He camped in the hills away from town and did not ride in until about noon the next day. If any of the bunch from Lang's were watching, they would see him come in with an empty pack string. He rode up to Ling's store and tied the horses at the back door. When he walked in, the store was busy so Logan started picking up supplies he needed for himself. Soon Ling appeared and motioned him to the office. Logan gave him his list of supplies. "I think we'll have to have another pack horse for this load."

Ling nodded. "This is really a large order and it'll take awhile to fill it."

"I'll take the horses down to the livery until you're ready to load."

When Logan returned to the store, he told Ling, "It's my turn to buy lunch."

Ling smiled, "I own the café and when I eat it's free, so I'll buy your lunch."

While they were eating Ling asked, "What's your plans for this winter?"

"I'm still thinking about that."

"I have a good idea for you. There are Chinese miners over on the south fork of the Snake that are having the same trouble trying to get their gold to me. I'm the only Chinese banker in this area and most Chinese miners want me to handle their gold. The South Fork area is at a lot lower elevation and the trails stay open all winter. The whites are robbing these miners every time they try to bring gold out. I've already sent a rider into the area checking to see if these miners will trust you to bring out their gold. I'm sure they'll pay the same as you're getting now from the Placer Butte miners."

"Who are the whites that are robbing these miners?"

"I've heard the leader is a good friend of Lang's, or at least he use to work for Lang at one time."

Logan thought for awhile. "I'd be interested in doing that as soon as I finished packing into the Placer Butte."

Logan recognized a couple of the men watching the store as he headed back to the livery for the horses. While at the livery Logan asked the manager. "Do you know anyone who wants to make a quick hundred dollars?"

The old fellow grinned, "Hell, I'd be interested in that myself. What do you have in mind?"

"Well, there's two fellows from Lang's camp in town. I need another

97

person to help me pull an ambush on them when I leave."

The old fellow laughed. "No wonder people leave you alone. I better not get too involved. I'll get you a good man you can trust."

"Tell him to meet me a mile above town in two hours."

When Logan had all three horses loaded, he headed out into the street and headed for the trail. When Logan had gone up the trail about a mile, he saw a fellow sitting on a rock above the trail, his horse tied near by. As Logan rode up, the fellow smiled, "Are you Logan?"

Logan nodded.

"Fred sent me to help you."

Logan then remembered who Fred was. He was the fellow he left his own horses with. The fellow managing the livery, the one at the ranch, and this fellow all were about the same age.

Logan handed him the lead ropes. "You move on up the trail and I'll wait here to see if we're being followed."

Logan found a place where the trail was real narrow. He stretched a rope across about chest high to a rider. He tied the one end and then dropped the rope into the trail and brushed dirt over it. He rode his horse over it and made tracks all around. Then he settled himself down and soon heard horses coming up the trail. When the riders came into view, it was the two he had recognized in town. They were riding along at a good clip. When they got close, Logan fired two quick rounds right behind the back rider. Both men spurred their horse into a run. Logan jerked the rope across the trail tight. The horses, with their heads down running, passed under the rope but the rope caught both riders in the chest. They both hit the ground hard, and before they could recover, Logan was standing over them. One was knocked out. The other was still dizzy when Logan tied his hands. When the other one started to come around, Logan had him tied up too. Logan walked up the trail and found both horses. He tied them both over their saddles and lead them back to where his horse was. Logan moved up the nearby creek to an opening under some large spruce trees. He unbridled both horses and put on halters with good ropes. He tied the horses in the trees out of sight of the trail. By now the two men were wide awake. "Did Lang send you to ambush me?"

"We're not telling you anything."

"Good. When they find your bodies, it'll look like you died a slow death."

As Logan mounted up to leave, they started hollering, "You can't leave us like this." Logan rode over closer. "There is one way you'll live, and that is to tell me what I want to know and then leave the country."

They both were silent until Logan started to ride away. "Okay, what do you want to know?"

"How many more are waiting for me up the trail?"

"There's two more and they're suppose to join us near the pass. Then we were suppose to kill you and get the supplies."

"If you're lying to me, you'll both be dead before the sun sets tomorrow."

They both said together, "We're telling you the truth."

Logan turned to ride away. "Someone will let you loose before night. You won't have any guns, and when you ride away, you better not look back for at least two days. If I ever see you again in this area, I will shoot you on sight."

"You're not going to leave us tied across our saddles?"

"It's safer this way for me." Logan then rode away.

When he caught up with the old fellow leading the pack string, he motioned to pull off the trail and they would rest. Logan built a fire and put on the coffee pot to boil. He unpacked some biscuits and some fried ham he had bought that morning at the café. When the coffee boiled, they had a tasty lunch. As they were eating, Logan asked, "What's your first name or what do they call you?"

"Most people call me Frank. Fred is my brother. The fellow at the livery is Wade and he's our cousin."

Logan laughed, "You have a good family line. You all look alike."

"Back down the trail near the creek where we parted, you'll find two men tied on their horses. You lead them over to the trail below town and turn them loose. They're going to be so stoved up from being tied across the saddles that long, you shouldn't have any trouble turning them loose."

Frank pulled a sawed off twelve gauge shotgun from the saddle boot. "I won't have any trouble from them."

Logan laughed and nodded. As he rode away he thought to himself, "This was probably one fellow who wouldn't hesitate to pull those triggers."

When Logan was a half mile below where the two men he had captured had said they were to meet two other men, he stopped. He moved the pack string up a draw out of sight and tied them where they could feed while he was gone. Logan pulled both pistols and checked the loads and then headed up the trail. He figured he had been lucky the last two times he had tangled with Lang's men. Logan made it a daily custom to practice with the pistols for he knew any day he would need to be fast. Logan spied two horses tied below the trail and two men hunched over a small fire.

As he rode up,one fellow turned to look at him. "It's about time you two showed up." When he realized his mistake, he rolled drawing his pistol. Logan saw the move, drew and fired just as the gunman brought his gun up. The second man had gone for the rifle leaning against the tree when he saw the other man drawing his pistol. The first gunman's shot hit the dirt in front of him as Logan's bullet struck home. Logan, seeing the second man grabbing his rifle sent two quick shots toward the man as he fired his rifle from the hip. Logan felt a jerk on his left arm as he fired the second shot at the rifleman. Logan saw him sag, then turned his attention back to the first gunman. This fellow had not moved. Logan swung down to check both men. The first man he hit just below his chin as he had rolled along the ground. He was dead. Logan walked over to the second man. As Logan bent down, he could see this man had two holes in his chest and was also dead. Logan reloaded his pistol and walked over to the two horses tied below the trail.

Logan finished loading the two dead men and tied their horses along the trail. He then rode back down to get the pack string. When he got back to the dead men along the trail, he tied their horses to the back pack horses and headed on down the trail. Once he got to the forks of the trail leading to Lang's headquarters, he stopped. Logan tied the reins to the saddle horns and with a slap on the rump sent the two horses down the trail towards Lang's camp.

With winter moving in, Logan told Lo Lin, "I'm going out for the winter. I'll be back in the spring."

"Will you take out one more load of gold when you leave?"

"Sure, I'll stay around for a few days while you fellas get together and decide how much you want taken out?"

Logan stayed around Lo Lin's camp most of the day checking over the animals and the pack saddles. Late that afternoon he told Lo Lin, "I'll be back later," and rode back up the trail towards Tiny Lang's road house and store. He rode off the trail and came in the back way through the trees and left his horse in the brush fifty yards from the road house. He watched for awhile and could see that most of Lang's crew were either gone or holed up somewhere besides here. Logan knew he had thinned the crew for Lang this summer but also knew that new men were always moving in. This was known to be a hide out for many wanted men and the law never came up here.

As Logan watched, he saw two men leave the bar and go down to the store then up an outside staircase to the rooms over the store. Logan moved up where he could look in the road house window. Inside he could only see a big man and two girls sitting at a table. He figured the big man was Tiny Lang. The girls were the two he kept around to keep his men happy. Logan moved over to the back door and found it unlocked. He entered and then looked in the kitchen. It was deserted. He moved back and then walked into the bar where Lang and the girls were sitting. They did not hear him walk in. He was almost to the bar before one of the girls saw him.

She whispered to Lang, "We have a visitor," and he swung his chair around. Logan could see he had a shoulder holster under his vest.

Logan had drawn his pistol. "Lang, lay your pistol on the floor and slide it toward me." Lang started to argue but when he saw the look on Logan's face, he slid the gun over. Logan then pulled out a chair and sat down on it with the chair back toward the three. Lang, with a growl in his voice, said, "What do you want?"

Logan grinned, "This was just a social visit. I know you know who I am, so we don't need introductions. I just came to tell you I'll be leaving before long for the winter. I have moved all the gold the Chinamen have stored up. Now you won't gain anything robbing them until they have mined some more. When I get back come spring and if I find the Chinese have been robbed again by you or any of them have been killed, you're a dead man. If this happens, you'll wish you had killed yourself because I will make you suffer before you die."

Lang turned red, "You can't come in here and threaten me in my own place."

Logan grinned and stood up. "Now you've been warned, so come spring, it's up to you if you live or die." As Logan backed toward the door, he thought he could hear movement in the kitchen so he stepped over beside the door. Then he saw the barrel of a shotgun poking through the door. Then a man's head appeared behind it. As the man holding the shotgun moved to see in the room, Logan stuck his pistol in the man's ear. "I'll take that shotgun, real slow like."

The fellow was wearing an apron that was all greasy. Logan figured this was probably the cook. Logan grabbed the shotgun. "Move over with the other three."

Lang was swearing, "Damn you, Charlie. Why didn't you shoot him instead of just handing over the shotgun?" Logan noticed Lang was moving his hand real slow toward the edge of the table where he had been sitting when Logan first walked in.

Logan motioned with his pistol. "All of you move over toward the bar. Now!" The tall, blonde girl was the last to move. As she passed the table, Logan motioned to her. "You stop where you are. Reach under that table and get the gun under there." She reached under real slow like and brought out a derringer in her hand. "Just slide it over toward me." Logan put it in his coat pocket and backed out the door. He was about half way to his horse when he heard Lang hollering for his men at the store.

When Logan got to his horse, he pulled his rifle. The first man was just starting down the stairs at the store when Logan shot the railing next to the fellow's hand. The man stopped and the second man ran into him as the first man started back up the stairs. They both ended up in a pile at the bottom of the stairs; neither one moved.

Logan mounted up and headed back up to the main trail. He rode up to a point where he could see the roadhouse below. Lang was on the porch hollering at the two men at the bottom of the staircase who were now slowly getting up. Logan still had his rifle across the saddle so he brought it up and shot a jug that was hanging next to Lang on the porch. When the jug broke, pieces flew and Lang grabbed his head and dove into the bar. Logan laughed to himself and headed for Lo Lin's. After dark that night, many of the Chinese miners started appearing at Lo Lin's door. They had brought all the gold they wanted moved out.

The next morning Logan just shook his head at all the bags of gold sitting in the floor of Lo Lin's cabin.

After all the miners had left, Lo Lin looked over at Logan. "They brought more gold than I thought they had. This will be one of your biggest trips."

Logan nodded. "I'll leave tonight about midnight."

Logan went out and saddled his horse. "I'm going down toward the roadhouse to see what's going on this morning." He had thought many times last night how lucky he had been yesterday when the cook walked into the

102

room. He could have shot first. Logan knew he had been lucky. Next time he would make sure no one else was around. As Logan was sitting on the trail above the road house, he could see two saddled horses hitched in front of the bar. Logan had decided last night that these were the only two men here with Lang now. Soon the two men walked out with Lang to the porch. Logan could see the men were moving kinda slow from their fall down the staircase. Lang was waving his arms as he talked to the two men. Logan could tell he was mad. Both men mounted and headed down the road toward the main trail. Logan mounted up and moved into the trees to get ahead of the two men. Logan rode up the trail to a narrow place near the pass. He hid his horse in the trees, took his rifle and walked back to the trail. There was a spring here coming out of the bank. Many riders stopped here for a drink of the clear cold water. Logan positioned himself near the spring in the willows. Soon he could hear the two men talking as they rode up the trail.

They stopped at the spring and Logan heard one of them say, "I hope this gent tries moving out today like Lang said. I'll pay him back for this sore leg I got when he knocked me down those stairs."

Logan moved over behind the two. "Just stand still and you'll live for another minute or two."

Both men jumped but neither tried to draw a gun. Logan moved over behind them and tossed their guns into the brush. He checked them over for extra guns. They both carried a small pistol in their belts on their backs. "Now go sit on that rock." He motioned toward it with his pistol. "How much is Lang paying you to shoot me?"

"We're just riding to Butte. We wasn't looking for you."

Logan laughed, "You were just discussing what you were going to do to me as you rode up the trail."

They looked at each other. "Lang offered a thousand dollars and a share of any gold you had with you."

Logan grinned, "Lang really must want me dead to offer you that much. Well, I guess the best thing I can do is hang you two along this trail where other would-be robbers can see you."

They both stared at Logan. "You can't just hang us without a trial. You're not the law."

"What would you two do if you were in my place?"

Neither man said anything for a minute. "You could let us go if we promise to keep riding."

103

"No, you'd probably just double back and still shoot me, if I did that. Well, for now I'll just tie you two up and stash you and your horses up this canyon."

After he tied them up and moved them up into the brush out of sight of the trail, he gagged them so they could not holler to anyone. With that done he rode back toward Lo Lin's cabin.

He told Lo Lin about the two. "I've changed my mind. I'll be heading out as soon as it's dark."

As Logan moved up the trail that night, he had good vision with a half moon and clear sky. When he got to the spring, he tied the pack horses and rode up to where the two were tied up. They were glad to get the gag from their mouths. Logan gave them a drink from his water bag. He tied them both on their horses and headed back to the spring. As Logan neared Butte, he stopped. He rode back to where the two men were behind the pack horses and untied them. "If I ever see you two again I won't hesitate to shoot you both."

They both nodded and spurred their mounts down the trail. Logan waited until they were out of sight then headed up to the mine to unload his packs.

Logan put up the horses when he got to the livery and headed for a cabin to get some sleep. He told Wade who had heard him and walked out to help, "Wake me if Ling shows up looking for me."

Logan woke about noon and headed uptown to see Ling and get something to eat. Logan was sitting at a table in back of the café when Ling joined him.

"You really brought in a load last night." He handed Logan his receipt. Ling looked at Logan for a minute. "Logan, how old are you?"

Logan grinned at his Chinese friend. "I'll be nineteen years old in January." Ling just shook his head.

"Do you realize how much money you have made these last few months?" Ling asked.

Logan shook his head, "I know it's getting to be a big amount."

"Logan, you know you're not even of legal age to be able to sign anything pertaining to the money. I'll work out a way you can still handle your own funds without any legal documents. The way it is right now your mother can draw money from the account. For you to draw out money, you'd need for her to sign for you."

Ling laughed, "We'll make you Chinaman, then use our way of transferring money."

Logan grinned, "I'll leave that up to you. I really don't want my mother to know the amount of this account."

"I can understand that. I'll fix it so you have control of your money in the local Chinese banks."

For the next week Logan spent his time around town and at the cabin behind the livery stable. Traveler was spending all his time over with Wade at the livery. Wade had a way with animals. He had made friends with Traveler the first time they met. Logan had noticed Traveler was getting skinny lately and figured it was from the hard traveling he had been doing following Logan. Logan figured the rest would help them both.

Logan was out at Ling's place checking over his own horses when Frank rode up to pass the time away. "When I left town, Wade told me to tell you Ling wants to see you sometime today." As Logan nodded he walked over and tightened the cinch on his horse.

Frank grinned at him, "Logan, if you ever need some more help, let him know."

"I'll keep that in mind."

Logan left the horse at the livery then headed for the store. As he walked in the store, he saw Ling motion him to his office. Ling closed the door. "Are you ready to get started moving the gold from the South Fork country?"

Logan nodded, "I'm ready anytime the gold's ready." Logan spent the rest of the afternoon with Ling planning the best way to move this gold without a big fight.

"Ling, I think we should do this gold shipment in one big load. I've been thinking that if some of this gang robbing the Chinese on the South Fork are the same men who had worked for Lang, we could have a problem. If these men see me in the area, they'll probably figure out what I'm doing there. Can you talk the miners into going along with that much gold in one shipment? We can probably pull it off with no trouble."

Ling agreed, "I'll send one of my men up there to talk it over with the miners."

"We'll also need to know about how many horses are needed to pack it out."

Ling looked over at his young friend, "How do you figure to get that many horses into the area and not be seen?"

Logan smiled. "I've got a couple different ideas on that!"

"Who's packing the supplies to this area now? We mainly need to know how often they deliver."

"Most of the miners are white and they don't have a regular service. They hire different packers when they need supplies. The Chinese miners each took care of their own supplies. Sometimes they'll double up and two or three miners will hire a packer to make a trip for them."

"How about we start a freighting business up into this area? We could send Frank up to see if he can get some orders from the miners. He could ask them if they'll buy supplies from him if he brings in a pack string. If he can drum up enough interest, we could get a pack string up there without causing anyone to get curious."

Lang smiled, "I like this idea; let's try it if Frank is willing to help."

"Oh, I think Frank will really like this plan."

Logan rode out to the ranch that afternoon to see Frank.

When Logan was through telling Frank about the plan, Frank laughed, "When do I start?"

"We'll meet with Ling tomorrow and get the show on the road."

The next day Ling met them at the cabin Logan used behind the livery. Ling offered, "I can handle all the supplies, and also, any extra orders Frank can get, I'll fill. If Frank wants to take a load of supplies with him and pedal them from camp to camp, I'll bank that too."

After a short discussion, it was decided Frank would make a trip down the river and check out which way he wanted to handle the supplies. Ling told Frank, "Tell the miners the supplies will cost them ten percent over shelf price at the store."

Logan added. "You can show them that it's cheaper than them hiring a packer."

"That's a good way to get the miners to buy his supplies. The more supplies, the more horses it'll take."

Frank grinned at the two partners. "I'll leave tomorrow morning, and I'll be back in about five days."

"I'll stay around town where I can be seen in case I'm being watched," Logan added.

Ling's man, sent into the Chinese camps to see about shipping the gold in one big load, got back the second day after Frank left. The miners were nervous about that much gold in one trip. They decided if Ling thought it would work they would go along with it. They would pay Logan the same percentage as the miners in Placer Butte had paid. They decided it would take about twenty horses to get this load out. Ling told Logan, "I'll have the horses whenever the time comes to head out."

When Frank got back, Ling was surprised at the orders he had picked up. "It looks like this supply order will take maybe ten to twelve horses. How about we load the extra horses with supplies for Frank to pedal along the river?"

It was decided that Logan would go along to take care of the stock and he would dress for the job.

"This way I won't have any close contact with people Frank deals with along the trail, and maybe I won't be recognized."

Frank looked over at Logan. "We'll need one more man to help. I've asked another old friend of mine to help with the pack string. His name is Skinny Miller. He's known by most of the miners along the river and this would help in selling the supplies."

"Does Skinny know about the gold we're going to pick up on the way back."

Frank grinned, "No, I haven't told him that part yet."

Ling and Frank worked out the supplies. They made up a list of supplies Frank thought he could sell besides the orders he already had. Logan spent time out at the ranch helping Fred get the horses ready for the trip. They checked all the shoes because this trail was rocky and hard on unshod horses and mules. Logan moved part of them into town the first night. Fred brought the others in the next morning. They started loading up at dawn the next morning. It was noon before the pack string moved out.

Frank told Logan, "I know of a good base camp where we can keep the extra supplies while Skinny and me deliver the orders."

It was just before dark when they decided to make camp for the night. Logan cooked supper while Skinny and Frank unloaded the pack horses. Frank looked over at Logan. "The base camp I think we should use is up the trail another ten miles."

The next morning they loaded up and headed up the trail with Frank riding lead. Logan was bringing up the rear. The place Frank had picked for a base was an old placer claim that had been mined out and deserted. The main cabin was still in good condition and showed some signs of being used.

Skinny heard Logan asking Frank if he thought the cabin was occupied. He spoke up, "I've been staying here off and on for the last six months."

Logan grinned at Skinny, "That makes me feel better; I guess we can move in."

Logan told Frank, "I'll stay here with the extra supplies; that way I won't be noticed by any of Lang's old crew."

While Skinny was outside watering the stock, Logan told Frank, "I feel like I'm not doing my part."

Frank laughed, "If shooting starts, I figure you'll earn your keep."

Frank and Skinny loaded up the next morning to deliver the orders Frank had taken the week before. Logan stayed around camp most of the morning. Later he saddled up to look over the country around the cabin. He was heading back to the cabin when he noticed some fresh tracks leading up the trail toward the cabin. When he got close to the cabin, he dismounted and led his horse off the trail and around behind the cabin. He could see two horses tied out front, but no one was in sight. As he eased up near the cabin, he could hear voices inside the cabin. He tied his horse and moved around where he could see the front of the cabin. He was about ready to move closer when he heard more horses coming up the trail. Logan moved back in the brush and waited to see who else was on the trail. It was Frank and Skinny. Logan just stayed in the brush and let Frank find out who was in the cabin. Frank hailed the cabin and two men stepped out on to the porch, both wearing tied down colts.

Frank asked, "Can I be of some help to you boys?"

One of the men on the porch growled. "What business is it of yours what we're doing?"

"This is the base camp for me and my partners while we're pedaling supplies to the miners."

The two fellows started to move apart from each other, "I think we'll just take over this business."

Logan had moved out where he could see both men. Frank, so far, had remained real calm. Logan figured he had something in mind in case shooting started. The two men each stepped forward looking at Frank and Skinny. "Now you two just head back down the trail and don't look back."

As Frank started to rein his horse around, Logan stepped from the brush. When they saw him, they both went for their guns. They saw Logan was holding a rifle pointed right at them. The first one started to move. Logan growled, "Just stay put." At the same time, the second man went for his pistol.

Logan fired at the fellow drawing his pistol, and as he turned back, the other gunman was raising his pistol to shoot. Logan's second shot hit him dead center in the chest. Both men were down before Frank ever got his pistol out. Skinny was just staring at Logan.

Frank grinned, "I figured you were here somewhere. Then I was starting to think maybe you wasn't when you stepped out."

Logan nodded, "You were almost right. I've been out looking over the area when I saw the strange tracks on my way back."

Frank looked over at Skinny, "Do you know these fellows?"

"No, but I seen them in a Butte saloon a couple of nights ago. I don't know their names or if they worked for anyone. I only saw them that one time."

They buried both men up behind the cabin in some brush where the graves could not be seen from cabin. Logan looked down at the grave after they finished. "When we get back to Butte, I'll see if Ling thinks we should let the law know about the shooting."

Frank smiled, "Those two started the whole thing and they lost. I say let's forget the whole thing."

When they got back to the cabin, Frank told Logan, "We had a good day. Tomorrow Skinny and me will load up and try to pedal supplies to some of the other miners. I think we might be smart if we moved these supplies tomorrow to another location."

Skinny had been listening. "I know another good place for us to use."

When he explained where it was, Frank nodded his head, "I know that place and it'll work great." Frank drew a map on the ground showing Logan how to find it.

"I'll move up there in the morning as soon as you two leave for mines."

They spent the rest of the afternoon breaking down the supplies for the next day. Skinny started a fire in the stove, "It's my turn cooking supper."

Logan and Frank took care of the horses. When they finished eating supper, they were lying around on the bunks talking about selling the supplies.

Skinny finally got into the conversation. He looked at Logan, "For being just a kid you handle yourself mighty well. Are you by any chance the same young fellow that's been moving gold for the Chinese out of Placer Butte?"

"I'm that fellow."

Skinny looked over at Frank. "You didn't tell me who he was when you hired me."

"I just hired you to help me with a big pack string. Logan is just part of the crew. What I didn't tell you was, he's the boss of this little operation."

Skinny smiled. "Logan how old are you?"

"I'll be nineteen in about three weeks."

This started Frank laughing at the look on Skinny's face. "Skinny, don't feel bad, I didn't know how old he was until just now. Logan, sometime when we have time will you tell me how you came to this country. I think your gun speed and why you're here will be an interesting story."

Skinny looked over at Frank, "How much more didn't you tell me about what we're doing up here with these supplies?"

Frank looked over at Logan before he answered, "We're just selling supplies for now."

Logan stood up, "I'm going out to check on the horses before turning in for the night."

When Frank and Skinny headed out the next morning, Logan's horses were also packed and ready to move out. The map Frank had drawn in the dirt last night showed Logan how he could move to the next place and stay off the main trail. So far nobody knew Logan was part of this supply train, and Logan wanted it to stay that way. Logan had left Traveler with Wade at the livery so people wouldn't recognize Logan when they saw the dog. Lang's crew knew how much Logan relied on the dog to warn him whenever strangers were close. Now Logan wished he had the dog along to scout the trail ahead of him. Logan reached the place Frank had shown him on the map. The buildings were kind of run down but there was a tunnel into the mountain which was dry and a good place for Logan to unload the supplies. After getting everything put away, he found a place with some good grass for the horses.

Logan decided he would keep his horse saddled and close by in case he needed to move out in a hurry. It was late afternoon when Frank and Skinny rode in. Logan noticed most of the supplies were gone and Frank had a grin on his face.

As they dismounted ,Frank smiled "This could be a good business if we decide to keep doing it."

Logan helped them put the horses away. "I've been looking around and it would be easier to sleep in the tunnel rather than try to clean out one of the buildings."

After eating supper, Frank told Logan, "I've got most of the supplies already sold and I'll deliver them come morning. While Skinny was looking after the horses, Logan told Frank, "While you're delivering the supplies tomorrow morning, I'll move over into the Chinese diggings."

Logan knew from Ling where to meet the contact with the Chinese miners. When Logan rode into the placer mine he was met by a big man that Ling had called China Dick. China Dick was the biggest Chinaman Logan had ever seen. He was four inches taller than Logan and must have weighed over three hundred pounds. Logan stepped down from his horse, "I'm Logan." When they shook hands, Logan could not even see his hand in China Dick's big paw.

"They call me China Dick," he said with a big grin on his face. "The miners are ready to bring in their gold whenever you're ready."

"I'd like to be ready to move out about midnight if possible."

China Dick spoke very good English. "We have most of the gold already here and midnight will be no problem."

Frank and Skinny showed up just after noon and Logan told them the plan. "We'll rest the horses now and start loading just after dark."

Frank turned to Skinny with a grin, "I forgot to tell you we're taking gold back on the return trip."

Skinny laughed, "Well, I guess it's too late to back out now."

China Dick furnished the supper. The girls that served them were young. Logan figured maybe they were China Dick's daughters. When the meal was over, they saddled up the horses and China Dick led them over to a building built back into the mountain. This building could only be seen in front view; otherwise, the mountain hid it from all other angles. As they loaded each horse, China Dick had a man weighing each pack. Logan noticed each pack had different markings. As they were loading, Logan could see other men coming into camp with packs on their backs. It was just before midnight when Logan told Frank, "You lead out down the trail and I'll bring up the rear. Skinny, you take up position in the middle of the string."

As Logan was about to mount, China Dick walked up, "I hope you have a safe trip," and held out his hand. "We wouldn't be sending our gold with you, but Ling said to trust you."

Logan mounted and grinned at China Dick, "There'll be a lot of dead men along the trail if we don't make it, including me."

Frank kept up a good pace in the dark and at dawn they were over half way to Butte. Frank pulled off the main trail and waited for Logan to ride up. "What now? Do we go on or stop for the day? The horses are still in good shape, but if we go on, they'll be worn out before we get to Butte. If we rest them today and move out at dark, we'll have fresh horses to make a run for it if needed."

Logan nodded, "We're close to the cabin where we spent the second night coming up. Let's stay there."

They unloaded the gold in an old tunnel across the creek from the main cabin. Logan turned to Frank, "I'll stay here. You two take the horses over to the cabin and unsaddle them. That way if anyone does ride in, you can just say you're heading back to Butte for another load. If they are curious why you're spending a day here instead of traveling on into Butte, tell them you're just resting the horses."

"That's the excuse I figured on passing out."

"That sounded good to me."

Skinny cooked supper for himself and Frank. He filled an extra plate and put it in a Dutch oven he had been heating up. As soon as it was dark, Skinny carried it across the creek to Logan. Logan laughed, "Skinny, I never thought of using a Dutch oven to keep a meal hot while packing it."

Skinny headed back across the creek when they heard riders coming up the creek trail. Logan finished his supper then moved off into the brush and closer to the cabin. He finally got to where he could hear what was being said. He heard Frank say, "We're just resting the horses on our way back from selling all the supplies we packed into the miners."

Logan heard the riders ask, "Have you seen any Chinaman moving around this trail today or yesterday?"

Frank shook his head. "I sold the Chinese miners the last of my supplies, and those are the only ones I've seen the whole trip. Who are you looking for?"

"We've been looking for two white men we just hired to help on a job. We've noticed that the Chinamen seemed to be missing from some of the mines we passed today."

"I still think that kid is somewhere near here trying to move these Chinese miners' gold like he did at Placer Butte," added one of the other riders.

The spokesman for the group turned to Frank, "Have you seen a young kid riding any of these trails?"

"Are you talking about the young guy who brought all the gold out last summer from the claims on Placer Butte?" Frank asked.

All the riders turned to Frank, "Do you know him?"

Frank nodded, "He was pointed out to me last summer in Butte. I saw him in Butte the day we were loading up, but I haven't seen him up here."

Logan was hoping Frank did not talk too much and make them curious about this large pack string.

Logan was thinking about the odds in case the riders did not believe Frank's story. He could see five riders next to the cabin. He had a feeling there were others back along the trail. Frank asked, "Are you the leader of this bunch? Who do you work for?"

"I'm the leader; that's all you need to know."

Frank nodded, "The only reason I asked was to see if you boys want me to bring in your supplies next trip?"

About this time another rider came out of the brush near the horses. "There's nothing back there but empty pack saddles."

Logan could hear another of the crew saying, "Lets head back toward camp. We'll look again tomorrow."

Logan moved out where he could see the cabin and Frank and Skinny. Logan stayed out of sight in case they had left a scout behind. Later Logan worked his way to the cabin and joined Frank and Skinny for coffee. Frank grinned, "I think they bought our story."

Logan nodded, "I'll lead us tonight, and I want an hour's head start. I'm going to make sure they did not post a guard or have an ambush set up the trail to Butte."

"You know, Logan, we can miss all of the wooded areas ahead by using the old trail."

Logan looked over at Frank, "What old trail?"

"When miners first moved into this area, they followed the old Indian trails. Later on they grubbed out the trail through the timber which made a quicker way into Butte. If we use the old trail, it'll bring us into Butte from the north. I don't think anybody would be watching that trail."

"Are you sure that trail is still open?"

Frank nodded, "I think so. The Indians still use it and a few miners who are prospecting on Crystal Mountain. That high area is snowed in now so the trail is unused during the winter."

113

"Can you find this trail in the dark?

Frank nodded, "I'm sure I can."

Logan was surprised how well the pack string moved over the trail in the dark following Frank. Logan was riding the rear again. He had changed his mind about leading when they changed routes. It was breaking dawn as Frank stopped on a ridge above Butte to see how Logan wanted to ride into town.

Logan grinned, "We'll hide the gold in the Murphy Mine for the day." Logan had not told Frank or Skinny about the deal he had with Ling to leave the shipments at the Murphy Mine. Logan had been worried all during the trip about how he was going to get the gold delivered to Ling until Frank changed trails.

When they finished unloading at the mine, Logan told Frank, "You and Skinny take the horses the back way to the ranch. I'll see you both tonight at the cabin behind the livery." After the horses were gone, Logan walked back into the mine and hit the rail with the hammer. He hoped someone was around to hear the signal. As Logan walked out, he thought he heard the padding of feet behind him coming from deep in the mountain. The sound was not being made by boots. Logan knew the sounds of the padded shoes the Chinese wore.

Logan smiled as he mounted up and headed for Butte. Wade was in his office when Logan rode up. Traveler met Logan as he stepped down from the saddle.

After cleaning up, Logan headed uptown for something to eat at Ling's. He was curious as to how much gold they had brought out in that load. Logan took his regular table and before long Ling joined him, "How was the trip?"

"Well, it went well. We had one problem with two men who were set on taking over the supply business. We buried them up behind a cabin, and I wanted to ask you if we should tell the law about it?"

Ling nodded, "I think it best to just keep quiet about the two men you buried. If the law comes around asking questions, then we can tell the story."

When Logan finished eating, he followed Ling back to his office, "This is way more gold than I ever figured those miners would have hidden away. We won't have it weighed and your receipt until evening."

Ling reached in his desk and pulled out a disk type object which was broken in half. It was decorated with Chinese symbols and writing. Ling handed it to Logan, "This is for you to keep, and never lose it. This is your half of the money disk used by Chinese to identify one another in money matters. This will be your identification to any Chinese bank when you tell them who you are. I don't think you still realize how much money you now have. There are other ways of proving who you are, but this disk is the quickest way. The other half of this disk is at the Chinese bank in Capital City in case you ever need money there."

Logan nodded, "Ling, I can only thank you for all the help and the money I've made. I do need some money now to pay Frank and Skinny. I really don't know what to pay them for this last trip. Why don't you give me fifteen hundred dollars in cash. You can deduct that from my share of this last trip."

Ling opened his desk, and from a box, counted out the money for Logan.

As Logan got up Ling asked, "What're your plans for the rest of the winter?"

Logan shrugged, "I think I'll head south for a spell and maybe even visit the folks. I'll be back come spring to help Lo Lin bring out the gold from the miners in Placer Butte. If the miners on the river want my help again, I'll help them too."

Ling shook hands with Logan, "Stop by before you leave town and we'll settle up."

When Logan got back to the cabin behind the livery, Frank and Skinny had made it back. Skinny was uptown but Frank was waiting for Logan.

When Logan walked in Frank grinned, "We pulled it off right under their noses."

Logan nodded, "I think we had a little luck, but I also think we had a good plan."

Logan reached in his pocket and tossed the fifteen hundred dollars on the bed beside Frank. "You can share it with Skinny any way you want; I hired you and he was your hand."

Frank looked at the money. "You pay too well for what we had to do. This is the most money I ever had at one time in my life and it was less than a week's work."

"I made a hell of a lot more than that, and I probably should give you a bigger share."

Frank shook his head, "I'm plumb happy with this, and you're the one they will be hunting when they find the gold is gone. You've pulled their winter's money away from those robbers. Now they'll have to look elsewhere to find someone to rob. I will keep this and consider myself lucky. Come spring if you go back into this business, keep me in mind."

Logan laughed, "I'll buy supper at the hotel, if you'll join me?"

Frank grabbed his hat, "Let's go."

As they walked up the street and started into the hotel, shots rang out in the bar up the street. About then they saw Skinny stumble out the door holding his chest and crumple up in the street. About then two men walked out putting their pistols away.

They were laughing looking down at Skinny, "We'll also kill both of your partners when we see them."

Logan recognized the pair from up on the trail when they rode into the cabin to check out Frank and Skinny. Logan was wearing both guns tonight where they could be seen, one on each hip.

"Frank, step into the hotel." When Frank started to argue, he said, "Now!" Frank stepped into the hotel entrance.

Logan walked up the street where the two gunmen had stopped to light up their cigars. Logan moved closer, then spoke in a tone that got the men's attention real quick, "Turn around real slow."

The two turned to look at who was talking to them, then started laughing. The one who had done all the talking at the cabin spoke up, "This is our lucky day; we also got the pup."

They started moving away from each other.

Logan grinned, "You two might as well stop where you are because the space isn't going to help you."

One of them laughed, "Kid, you're a dead man and don't know it," and started his draw. Both men were laying in the street and neither one had cleared leather. Logan spun around as he heard motion behind him. He saw another fellow clearing leather. Logan stepped sideways as he fired two quick shots. At the same time, he heard a bullet hit the building behind him. The third man was down in the street. The crowd of men from the saloon were trying to get out the door all at one time.

Frank came running up, "Skinny's dead. He was shot four times."

Logan reloaded both pistols as he walked over to Skinny's body. Logan kneeled down at Skinny's body. "He wasn't wearing his gun."

By then a few men from the bar walked up. "Those two men took Skinny's pistol before they shot him."

A man with a star came walking into view with a shotgun cradled in his arms. He looked at the three men laying in the street. The men from the saloon were telling him what they'd seen.

He walked up to Logan, "Are you Logan McTier?"

Logan nodded. The marshall just smiled.

"I figured so. I've seen you around town and heard you were thinning out Lang's crew from the roadhouse while moving the Chinamen's gold. To be that fast and so young it had to be you. I got a letter from Sheriff Jeff Rogers in Sweetwater to keep an eye out for you."

The marshall turned to the crowd, "Some of you fellows pack these three gunmen down to the undertaker's office."

Two men picked up Skinny. Logan turned to the marshall, "I'll pay for Skinny's funeral; he's been working for me this last week."

When everyone had left the street, Logan looked at Frank, "Are you still hungry?"

Frank nodded, "Sure but before we eat I need a big drink."

As they walked into the hotel lobby the manager smiled, "The drinks are on me".

"How about just bring a bottle to the table?" He motioned for them to find a table. Frank poured a big drink and Logan poured a small one then motioned for the hotel manager to join them.

After the toast, the manager smiled, "Your two steaks will be right out. I'm also paying for them. Those three men have terrorized this hotel for a year and never paid me a dime."

As Logan and Frank walked back to the cabin, Logan asked, "Did Skinny have any family close by?"

Frank shook his head, "I don't think so. His wife had died on the wagon train coming out here from back east a few years ago."

Back at the cabin, Frank looked over at Logan, "If all the local marshalls and sheriffs know about you, there must be a story?"

When Logan had finished telling a short version of his life, Frank just whistled. "I was watching as you walked up to those two. I don't think there was a doubt in your mind that they couldn't out draw you. I've seen a few men good with guns in my life but never with the speed you have. I heard from one of the men over at Ling's that you can also shoot that old

117

Sharps a country mile and hit what you were aiming at."

Logan grinned, "Don't believe all those stories."

Logan settled up with Ling the next day and made sure his gear was in good shape so he could head out early the next morning.

As he was packing, Frank walked up, "Do you want some company on your trip south?"

Logan thought for a minute. "If you don't mind a little trouble now and then; it seems to follow me."

Frank grinned, "I'll take my chances."

Logan left his pack horse with Fred at the ranch. "I'll pick him up come spring."

# CHAPTER 4

The next week they traveled south looking over the country as they went. They had stopped at a couple of small settlements for supplies, mostly staying on the main trails heading south. They rode into Sweetwater one evening, and as they passed Sheriff Roger's house, Logan reined in to the hitch rack. As they stepped down, the door of the house opened and Mrs. Rogers walked out to meet them.

She smiled as she walked up to Logan and offered her hand, "Logan, it's good to see you." Logan introduced Frank.

"Will you stay for supper? Jeff is due home at anytime. If you like you can stay in the bunkhouse out by the barn for the night."

"We'll take you up on your offer. It'll be good to sleep under a roof for a change."

As they were putting their horses in the corral, Frank grinned. "I like this where you have lawmen for friends."

After supper the men went out on the porch while Mrs. Rogers did the dishes. Frank and Logan both offered to do the dishes after that great meal. She chased them out onto the porch.

"I'm going to try to see my folks if I can sneak in without being seen," Logan told Jeff.

"I know there's still a few would-be gunmen showing up around Benton. If they're watching the ranch, I don't know."

"Jeff, what ever happened to Mollie, the girl I left with you?"

Mrs. Rogers heard him ask and she came out on the porch.

"Mollie stayed with us for a month and then went to work for the wife of one of the local ranchers. Logan, to Mollie you are her golden knight and she'll never forget you."

This made Logan get a little red in the face. Frank and Jeff got a laugh out of it.

Logan got the shock of his life when Jeff said, "Logan, did you know Hugh Davis is dead?"

"Del wrote me he had died about the same time you were here last year. Del heard it was something to do with his heart. Henry no longer stayed at the ranch much; he lived almost all the time in Capital City. He's to be appointed territorial governor next year. Then after statehood, maybe governor of the state. Your dad is now the main man at the ranch."

This was all a shock to Logan. "Jeff, what do you think my chances of getting in to see the folks are without causing them more trouble?"

Jeff shook his head. "Like I said, Logan, there are still a few riders in and out of Benton looking for you. If they find out you're back in the country, it'll start all over again for your folks." Logan nodded but didn't say anything.

Logan thanked the Rogers the next morning after breakfast for the meals and a bed for the night.

Jeff walked out as the two mounted up to leave. He looked at Logan, "You take care of yourself."

Logan nodded, "I think I'll ride down toward the Rafter T but I probably won't ride in." With a wave they rode off down the trail missing Sweetwater. Frank was listening to Logan tell about how Hugh Davis and his dad, Ted McTier, had first found the Rafter T. When Logan happened to mention Gold Field during the conversation, Frank stopped him.

"Where's this Gold Field?"

Logan looked over at him, "It's a two days ride from here," and he motioned off to the east.

"You know that's the name of a place where my sister once lived. She married a miner and moved up there a few years ago. I never really knew where the place was until now. This is new country to me and I suppose if I'm this close I should see if she still lives there."

"We were all separated when the wagon train that brought the folks out west broke up down along the Snake River. There was a big disagreement about where everyone wanted to go. Some wanted to go on to the Oregon Territory and others wanted to go to California. The folks decided to homestead along the trail and start a trading post. Sis and a younger brother stayed with them. Fred and I headed north looking for a new life. We heard later the Indians burnt the folks' trading post. Later, we found out that the folks and our brother had died in the raid. A few years later Fred was back down in that area and found out our sister survived the raid. Fred looked for her and that's when he found out she had married a miner and was headed for a place called Gold Field."

"If I was you I'd ride over and see if she's still there. I'd ride along but too many people know me there and that's too close to the Rafter T."

Logan and Frank decided to meet in ten days at a small trading post they had passed a week ago north of Sweetwater. After Frank rode off, Logan was alone on the trail. He started to miss having Traveler along. He had left him with Wade at the livery because he knew this would be a hard trip for him. He was a good traveler but he was showing signs of his age. Logan thought the beating he had taken before he'd found him had aged him too. He decided he would be better off if he stayed with Wade. This trip he and Frank were traveling at a good clip. Come spring when he was working out of Placer Butte he'd take Traveler along again.

Logan was getting into country he knew as a boy riding with Old Dave. He really wanted to get a chance to see his folks. But he did not want them in any more danger from men looking for him. It was close to evening and Logan started looking for a camping place. He caught a whiff of smoke and started looking for the source. He spotted smoke in a grove of trees ahead. He started toward it. When he topped a ridge, he was surprised he could see the buildings of the Rafter T. He had not realized he was getting this close to home range.

He hailed the fire as he got close, and then he heard a voice telling him, "Ride in with your hands in sight."

When he rode up to the fire, a man with a rifle stepped out from behind a tree.

"Where did you come from? Where you headed?"

Logan laughed, "I'm just traveling through on my way south. I was figuring on seeing if I could get a meal and a place to sleep at the ranch down there in the valley."

"You won't get any meal at that place," the man with the rifle growled. "They don't let strangers get that close."

"Do you mind if I step down and camp here tonight with you?"

"I was just starting supper, but I really don't have any extra for another plate. My partner will be in soon and I only fixed for two."

Logan reached in his saddle bags and tossed a grub sack toward the fire. "I'd be glad to share." When the fellow saw the extra food, he was all friendly. Logan helped the fellow getting supper and soon heard another horse coming into camp.

A little fellow with two tied down guns dismounted. "Who the hell are you?"

Before Logan could say anything, the man at the fire explained, "This guy has lots of grub with him."

Logan did not trust the little man at all. He made sure to keep him in front of him. The little runt acted like maybe he was a little on the crazy side or something was wrong with him. As they were eating supper, the little gunman told his partner, "I haven't seen a thing all day. I still think we should just ride down and get that woman and force her to tell us where her gunny son is. We've been watching that place for over a month and the son has not shown up yet. I know he's hiding in these hills somewhere and that woman knows where he is," the little man shouted.

Logan just sat there listening and was beginning to figure out the woman the little man referred to was his mother. Finally, Logan asked, "Who are you looking for?"

The fellow at the fire motioned down the valley. "That ranch down there is the Rafter T and the foreman's name is McTier. His son is a young fast gun who got lucky and killed part of the Coulter family. His name is Logan McTier and Luke here wants to kill him to prove he's faster than the kid."

The kid rode away last spring and nobody has seen him. We think he's nearby and staying out of sight. We've been watching the ranch and when he rides in we'll be there to meet him. Luke was run off the ranch by the lady down there with a sawed off shotgun when he tried to get her to tell him where her son was."

The little crazy one was starting to get a weird look and shouted, "I'm riding down in the morning and grabbing that woman."

"If you do that, it'll bring every rider for miles to hunt us down if we harm her." Logan had moved so he was clear if trouble started and he knew it was going to real soon.

The little man spun around to glare at Logan. "You're going along to help or I'll kill you right now."

Logan just looked at the little shouting man and grinned. This really made the gunman mad and he shouted, "Who the hell are you?"

"The name is Logan McTier."

Both men stared for a minute. Then they both went for their guns. Two shots rang out that almost sounded like one. Then one lone shot as the pistol of the little gunman discharged into the ground at his feet. The man by the fire never even cleared leather as he was blown back into the fire. Logan walked over and pulled the man from the fire and smothered the fire in his clothes.

He walked back to the little gunman and said in a voice only Logan heard, "That lady down there is my mother."

Unknown to Logan, the shots had been heard at the ranch. When the word was passed to Ted he nodded. "We'll check it out in the morning."

Three riders from the ranch rode into the grove of trees the next day. They found two bodies laying side by side and covered with a blanket. One rider swung down to look at the bodies. He looked back at the other two. "They're both shot through the heart; that's some shooting."

The riders loaded the pair on their own horses that were tied close by and headed back for the ranch. When Ted looked at the bodies, he recognized the little gunman that Lottie had run off a month ago.

He told the one rider, "Take the bodies into the sheriff in Benton."

As the rider left with the bodies, the other two told Ted, "I'd really like to know who was up there last night. The camp was all cleaned up except for a frying pan. In the grease was a drawing of an ear, like maybe a wolf's ear."

Old Dave who had hobbled his way over to the three men just smiled when he heard about the frying pan as the two riders mounted their horses and rode away. Dave looked at Ted. "The boy was up there and he's well."

Ted was looking up toward the hills. "I think you're probably right. I'll let Lottie know."

Old Dave had fallen on the ice early in the fall and Lottie made him move down to the ranch. She had the crew build him a small cabin close to the main house where she could care for him. He was getting around a little better now but knew he would never make it back to his cabin in the mountains. He was still grinning as he headed back toward his cabin. His foster son was well and this made Dave's day. Lottie had walked out and was watching Dave as he walked toward her.

Ted was also walking toward her. She was looking toward the mountain. "That was Logan last night wasn't it?"

Dave and Ted just looked at her, "A mother always knows when her cub is near," and walked back to the house.

Logan started back up the trail to meet Frank at the trading post. By not going into the ranch, Logan decided he had a few days to kill before Frank would be at the meeting place. He decided to ride toward Gold Field and look that country over. He was known in Gold Field but figured he could stay north in the mining area and not be recognized. There were mines all the way along Beaver Creek which was the largest drainage. When he was small, Dave had taken him through this area a few times. Thinking about his early years, being like a shadow to old Dave, Logan could only remember good times. Dave had taught him so much about how to survive on his own. Today it helped him to stay alive. Tracking people and animals and his ability with a rifle were all things Dave had pressed into him at a young age. Logan grinned when he thought about him leaving the drawing in the frying pan. Dave would understand what the ear drawn in the grease meant.

Logan was riding along a ridge looking down on the different mines when he spotted a horse he recognized. There were some good looking buildings at this mine and it looked real active. Tied at the front of one cabin was Frank's horse. As Logan watched, Frank and an older lady walked out on the porch. Logan watched as the lady gave Frank a big hug. Frank mounted his horse and turned down the trail toward Gold Field. Logan mounted his horse and headed back down the ridge above Frank on the trail. Frank stopped and was rolling a cigarette when Logan gave a whistle from above. He had used this signal once before to get Frank's attention. He was hoping now Frank would recognize it. Frank looked up the ridge and turned his horse. Logan waited on top for Frank to appear. When he topped the ridge Logan rode out to meet him.

Logan told Frank about not getting to see his folks and he was just riding around until it was time for them to meet.

Frank laughed, "Boy, did you save me a long ride to meet you; that lady you saw down there is my sister. She is the cook for that mining outfit. She's about worn out with the work, and her age doesn't help."

Frank went on to tell Logan why she was working here at the mine. It seems her husband, after they moved up here, found this good claim and started to make good money. Well, that lasted for about a year and he started spending more time in town gambling than home mining. The next thing Frank's sister knew, the mine had a new owner and her husband was dead. The story was that he was in a high stake game with some men who had more money to waste than he had to spend. He got further in debt and finally signed over the mine to one of the players for more cash to gamble with. The fellow who loaned this brother-in-law the money told him that he could buy the mine back anytime he had the cash. As the night wore on, he lost all the money and was forced out of the game. He was later found along the trail dead. He had put the rifle barrel in his mouth and pulled the trigger. The sheriff rode out to tell Frank's sister. He told her he could find no reason to believe there was any foul play. The fellow who had loaned the brother-in-law the money was one of the local mine owners. He told the sister she could stay at the cabin as long as she wanted. The new owner sent a miner in to see if the mine was worth working and soon learned it was almost a glory hole. It was the same mine where Frank found his sister working. The owner was paying her real well, but the long hours were about to get her down.

"I was going to ride over and meet you according to plan and tell you I wasn't riding back to Butte with you. I've invited my sister to move back to Butte and live with me and Fred, and she's agreed. Beings that you're here, it saved me many miles of riding."

"I'm glad you found her well. I'll see you back in Butte later on."

"Sis gave the owner notice last night she's quitting. She's going to stay until another cook is found so I don't know for sure when we'll be heading for Butte. I wrote a letter to Fred and want you to deliver it when you get back to Butte."

"I'll do that and you have a safe trip home."

The weather was good so Logan decided it was too early to head back to the mountains. He decided to look over more country. Logan was trying to remember if Mrs. Rogers had said the name of the ranch where Mollie was working. As Logan rode along, he looked over the area he was riding through. He was still trying to remember more about where they said Mollie was working. Finally, he decided he had not paid enough attention when Mrs. Rogers was telling him. He camped that night along a good size creek and with some luck caught a mess of fish for supper. As the supper was cooking, he heard a voice hailing the camp.

Logan answered, "Come on in. Supper is about ready."

An older fellow dressed in ranch hand gear, with no gun on his hip, rode into camp. Logan had placed his rifle close at hand when the voice hailed the camp.

The old fellow dismounted. "I'm Ollie Grey. I ride for the Box Ranch down in the valley. I've been hunting strays all day and was headed back to a line shack over the next ridge when I smelled the smoke from your fire."

125

"If you like trout, you're in luck, cause that's what I'm having. You're welcome to join in."

The old fellow grinned, "I hate my own cooking and I haven't had trout for a long time."

As they ate supper, they discussed about everything a person could think of. Logan happened to mention he was looking for a girl that worked at some ranch in this general area. "I only met her once," but did not mention about how he knew Mollie.

Ollie grinned. "I think I know who you're looking for. It's going to make a couple young cowhands mad. Mollie works over on the Bar 7. She's a housekeeper for the owner's wife. She lived with Sheriff Rogers up in Sweetwater before coming to the Bar 7."

"Well, I guess I have found her then. I think I'll drop by and say hello." "Couple of the local cowhands are trying to court her, and they are having a little trouble over it. They both think she should only see one of them, but she insists they take turns. If you step into the picture, you will really cause a stir."

Logan started laughing. "We hardly know each other but I'd really like to stop by and say hello."

Ollie laughed, "Boy, that's what I'd do if I knew Mollie."

He looked across the fire at Logan. "If you don't mind, I'll just stay here rather than ride on over to the line shack."

"Sure, I'd like the company for the night."

Logan fixed his friend a big breakfast and Ollie asked. "Son, do you always eat like this?"

"No, this is a special occasion. I only cook this way for good company."

They packed up and Logan asked, "Now, how do I get to the Bar 7?"

The old fellow looked at Logan. "You never did say what your name is; are you wanted or something?"

"We spent the night together and I totally forgot to introduce myself." Logan reached for his hand. As they shook he said, "Logan McTier."

The old fellow looked a little funny. "There must be two of you McTiers. I heard stories last summer about a Logan McTier hauling gold for the Chinese up around Placer Butte. He was a gun fighter."

Logan grinned, "I guess if you heard stories about a Mc Tier in Placer Butte, you have the right guy."

126

Ollie shook his head, "You look way too young to have done all the things I've heard."

"You know how stories go. Someone always adds onto them."

As he rode away, Logan could see a smile on the old cowboy's face.

Logan followed Ollie's directions and that afternoon he rode into the yard of the Bar 7. As he rode up to the main house, a couple of young boys came running from around the house with a young lady chasing them. Logan was laughing because those boys were about to get wet. The woman was carrying a pail of water. When she had them cornered, she threw the pail of water on them. While all this was happening, Logan had not noticed but another lady had come out of the house to watch.

The lady spoke before Logan had seen her. "Young man, is there something I can do for you?"

Logan stepped down from his horse. "Yes, can you tell me where I can find Mollie?"

"Why do you want to see Mollie?"

Logan started to explain when he heard his name called. The young lady that had been chasing the boys came running up to him. She threw her arms around him, "Logan, it's you!"

Logan then recognized her. When she stepped back he laughed. "Mollie, I didn't recognize you when you went by chasing those boys."

"I didn't notice you either until I heard you ask for me." She turned to the lady on the porch. "This is the man I told you about who saved me." Then Mollie introduced Logan to Mrs. Lappin, whose husband owned the Bar 7. The two boys, who were now all wet, stood beside Mollie holding on to her skirt looking at Logan. She looked down, "These two keep me busy full time."

Mrs. Lappin smiled and held out her hand. "Please come in for coffee. I'd like for you to stay for supper too. My husband, Jake, will be in before long and he would feel real bad if he didn't get to meet you."

Later, after supper that night, they were sitting on the porch with Jake and Beth.

Mollie was sitting next to Logan. "Where have you been since I last saw you?"

"I spent the summer up near Placer Butte working at different jobs."

When Jake heard him say Placer Butte he asked, "Are you the fellow that's been working for the Chinese in the Placer Butte area?"

"Yes, I hauled freight for them last summer."

Logan could tell Jake wanted to ask more, but with the women present, he dropped the subject. "That's where I'm heading back to now. When I heard Mollie was close by, I wanted to stop and say hello."

She leaned over, "I was afraid I would never see you again and I needed to thank you again for saving me." She started to weep and leaned on Logan's shoulder. "I'll never forget when you walked up to that wagon that night and you had Traveler with you. I was so afraid when I had heard that shooting that they had killed again."

Logan smiled and touched her arm. "That is all over and those four will never harm anyone again. I'm glad I was there and that they tried to rob me. I'd already saw their way of treating people when I buried your parents. I had heard the wagon when they stopped in the trees. When they walked over to try to trade horses, I figured they were the ones. I think when they saw I was young they let down their guard and it cost them. By this time I knew what they had in mind and I was ready for whatever they tried."

Logan smiled, "That's enough about the past. I stopped by the Rogers in Sweetwater and Mrs. Rogers told me you were working at a ranch. I guess they forgot to tell me or I missed remembering the ranches brand. I spent the night with a line rider, Ollie Grey, last night and he knew who you were, so here I am."

Logan turned to Jake, "You have a good looking spread here."

"We're real proud of this spread. We inherited it from Beth's father. He'd homesteaded it and Beth was raised here. I was raised back east and came out west with my aunt to visit and never went back."

"Where were you raised, Logan?"

Logan smiled. "On the Rafter T."

Jake nodded, "I met a Ted McTier once while moving cattle up here from Benton. He was with Hugh Davis when they first founded the Rafter T over twenty years ago."

I've heard a story about how one of the McTier kids moved out at a young age at the request of the local sheriff."

Logan grinned, "I guess you could put it that way, but the truth is it was better for everyone if I left for awhile. After the robbery and I shot those men, it started with family members trying to kill me to get even for killing their kin. Later, it was every gun in the country wanting to shoot me to get the reputation of being a fast gun. Sheriff Del Rogers and my folks talked it over and decided if I left for a spell, things would cool off. As of last week, there's still men trying to get me through my folks at the ranch."

Logan looked over at Mollie, "I think I'd better head up the trail before it gets too dark."

Mrs. Grey looked over at Logan. "You stay the night and get an early start come morning."

Logan shook his head, "Thanks anyway, but I don't want anyone to know I was here. It'll save you problems later on."

The Greys told him, "You're welcome anytime." Logan shook hands with Jake.

Mollie followed Logan out to his horse. Logan had unsaddled the horse before supper and put him on a lead rope so he could eat.

As Logan was saddling up Mollie asked, "What ever happened to Traveler?"

Logan laughed. "He likes to stay with Wade, the man who runs the livery in Butte. Traveler has been my partner ever since I left you at the Rogers'. That dog has saved my bacon a few times when men have tried to ambush me. He's getting older and he aged a lot at the hands of those men who killed your folks. This was going to be a fast trip and I thought it best he stay with Wade. As soon as I head back up into Placer Butte, I'll have him with me." When Logan finished saddling up, he walked over and took Mollie's hands. "You take care. It was great to see you."

Mollie looked up at him. She put her arms around his neck and pulled his head down and gave him a big kiss. She stepped back, "Logan McTier, I will never forget you, and you better stop by anytime you're in this area."

Logan could see the tears in her eyes as she turned and walked back to the house. Logan waved to the Greys and headed down the road.

When he rode into the ranch a few days later, Fred wanted to know where Frank was. Logan pulled out the letter and unsaddled his horse while Fred read it. When he finished he had a big grin on his face. "I never thought we'd ever find her. It'll be great to have her here. I'd better get busy cleaning up the place and fix up a room for her."

At supper Fred told Logan, "The pass to Placer Butte is just now opening. One of the Chinese miners had come out the other day over the snow and said it should be bare in a week. Ling sent word to me that he had freight whenever you got back."

"I've been all week getting the horses ready," Fred added.

Logan nodded. "Good, I'll head into Butte in the morning."

Traveler saw Logan as he rounded the corner. He barked and headed for him. Wade walked out. "I knew that had to be you; that dog never barks."

Logan moved his gear up to the cabin behind the livery while Wade put the horses away. Logan, with Traveler at his heels, walked up town to the Ling store. Ling was in the warehouse when Logan walked into the office. One of the stock boys motioned Logan that way.

Ling shook hands, "You can start whenever you're ready."

Logan and Ling looked over the supplies Ling needed packed into Placer Butte.

Logan nodded, "I'll make it in two trips rather than have to get more horses. I'll be here at dawn to load."

The warehouse crew was ready when Logan rode up the next morning. He was on the trail in half an hour. The trail was bare over the pass but there was snow on both sides of the trail at the summit. As Logan went past the forks leading up to Tiny's place, he could see fresh tracks leading toward the Chinese mines. As Logan rode over the last ridge above Lo Lin's cabin, he heard gun fire below. He tied the pack horses in some brush along the trail and headed down toward the gun fire. When he got to where he could see Lo Lin's cabin, he could see three white men firing from behind the trees above the cabin. They were shooting at the cabin and at someone hidden behind the sluice box below the cabin. There were two people firing from the cabin and one shooting from the sluice box. Logan thought Lo Lin must have had company when these fellows attacked the cabin.

Logan soon heard one of the white men holler down at the cabin, "You in the cabin, give up and throw out the gold or we'll blow up the cabin." About then Logan spotted another white man over on the ridge behind the cabin. As he watched, he could see the man was fixing to throw dynamite down at the cabin. Logan grinned; he laid his rifle across a log to get a good rest for a long shot. There was a sack alongside the man across the draw and Logan could see him take more sticks of dynamite out of it. He pulled down on the sack when he saw the man lighting a cigar. Logan figured when the guy wanted to light the fuse, a cigar would be the easiest way. The fellow picked up the dynamite and Logan could see a fellow below him motioning to throw it. Logan shot just as he was lighting the fuse. There was a huge explosion across the canyon and dirt and rocks were flying everywhere. One rifleman below Logan jumped up and just stared across the canyon at the big hole when a bullet from the cabin cut him down. Logan shot another of the men below him when the fellow tried to run back up the hill. Logan knew he had not killed him and was watching to see if he tried to run again.

The other man from below was hollering, "Don't shoot; I give up!"

Logan hollered down to the cabin," Lo Lin, are you alright?"

Soon the cabin door opened and Logan could see a head peaking up the hill. Logan waved and moved over toward where he had seen the man he shot fall. In the meantime, Logan told the fellow who surrendered, "You start down toward the cabin and your hands better be in the air." The first man, shot by the miners from below, was lying where he fell. Logan could tell he was dead. When Logan could finally see the man he shot, he was holding his leg and trying to wrap a rag around the wound.

As Logan walked up, the guy looked up, "Where in the hell did you come from?"

Logan smiled. He put the man's gun in his belt and checked him over for more weapons before he bent down to look at the leg wound. The bullet had gone through the fleshy part of his thigh just above the knee.

"From the looks of it, it didn't hit a bone. It'll be sore for a long while, but you'll live."

Lo Lin had made his way up the hill and was grinning from ear to ear. "We hoped you would show up before they got our gold."

Logan looked down at the fellow with the bullet hole in his leg. "Where's your horses?" He motioned over the ridge.

"I'll get them," Lo Lin said. Logan waited with the wounded man for Lo Lin to return. Logan looked down the hill. He could see the other miners had the other robber tied to a tree by the cabin. When Lo Lin returned, they helped the wounded man to mount. He was complaining about his leg.

"If you'd rather walk, we can do that too." The fellow quit complaining as they moved down to the cabin.

Logan tied the two would-be robbers in their saddles. He turned to the Chinese miners. "What do you want me to do with these two?"

The Chinese were talking in their native tongue. Logan was grinning to himself at the looks on the two men's faces.

Lo Lin turned, "We will leave that up to you."

Logan looked up to the fellow with the wounded leg, "What was your share of the gold going to be?"

The fellow glared at Logan, "Who the hell are you to be asking questions. Besides, it's none of your business."

Lo Lin called him Logan to get his attention. The fellow that had been talking spun around to look back at Logan. "Are you the Logan McTier that was up here last year?"

Before Logan could answer, the other man laughed. "No way! This is only a kid who probably don't even shave everyday."

Logan looked at the wounded man. "You have two choices, hang or talk. We can hang you in a tree here along the trail and send word for Tiny to come cut you down. Or you can tell me what Tiny sent you here to do and what your cut was going to be." It must have been the look in Logan's eyes that convinced the man to talk.

"Tiny offered us half of what we recovered. We weren't suppose to kill any of them unless we had to."

The Chinese miners had retrieved the body of the man from the hill. They loaded him on a horse. Logan looked across at the hole in the ground above the cabin. He decided there wasn't any use in trying to find any of that robber's body. The two still alive also looked up there. Logan could see they were shocked at what had happened to their partner. Logan walked around in front of the horses. "I'm going to take you back close to the trading post and turn your horses loose."

"What if they head for Butte rather than to Tiny's?"

Logan shrugged, "Either way, I have a message for Tiny. Tell him if he tries this again, I'll gut shoot him. I hope I never see you two again anywhere near this area." He mounted his horse and headed down the trail leading the three horses. Logan turned the horses loose when he got to the forks in the trail, then headed back to get his pack string. After they unloaded the supplies, Logan motioned to Lo Lin.

"I want to load the gold now and get on the trail. I don't figure Tiny has much of a crew up here yet and I want to head out before they start looking for me."

It was full dark when Logan headed back down the trail. After he was over the summit, he headed down toward Butte before he left the trail and hid out in a grove of trees a half mile off the trail. He unloaded the pack horses and staked them out on some green grass on a south slope just below the snow line. He built a small fire and boiled some coffee and fried some bacon he had gotten from Lo Lin. Lo Lin had put some biscuits with the bacon so Logan had a good breakfast. After feeding Traveler, Logan laid back on the pack saddles and closed his eyes. Traveler was lying next to him. Logan knew if anyone was around, Traveler would know it and wake him. It was about noon when Logan was ready again to hit the trail. As he rode down the trail, he met two other riders. They were asking directions to Tiny Lang's place. As they headed on up the trail, Logan was smiling to himself. These were probably two new recruits for Tiny's crew. When they happened to mention to Tiny they met a pack string on the trail to Butte, he would be really unhappy.

When Logan got to the Murphy Mine and unloaded the gold, he went back up the trail so he would come into Butte from the main trail. He dropped the horses off at the livery, then headed up to the cabin to clean up and rest for a spell.

Wade nodded, "I'll wake you if anybody comes nosing around."

It was evening and almost dark when Logan headed up town to eat at Ling's. He was almost finished when Ling walked in to join him.

"You brought in a good haul today."

Logan and Ling discussed the next load. "I want to head out first thing in the morning."

Lo Lin nodded, "I think that two more trips like this last one will about clean out the gold they've mined during the winter."

Logan had brought a note back from Lo Lin to Ling. "The miners needed some mining machinery and some dynamite. I can have the machinery ready for the next trip and it could be packed with no trouble. It's torn apart when it's shipped to me and I'll send it up to them the same way."

Logan nodded, "If the supplies aren't too heavy this trip, I could take some of the dynamite this trip too."

As Logan started to leave, Ling asked, "Did you have any trouble with the last load?"

"Nothing I couldn't handle," and walked off into the night.

Logan was on the trail the next morning just a little after dawn. Ling's crew was ready for him when he got to the store. The supplies were all packed and ready to load. Logan rode with his rifle across the saddle when he neared the summit. This area was the best place for an ambush. He knew Tiny was going to try to get him any way he could. As he rode past the forks leading to the roadhouse, he put the rifle back in the scabbard. When he got to Lo Lin's, Sun Lee was there. He asked in broken English, "Will you take these supplies down to my claim?"

Logan nodded, "Lo Lin, I'll be back to stay the night with you."

Sun Lee had a bigger operation than Lo Lin and had other Chinese working for him.

They unloaded the pack string and Sun Lee said in broken English, "My gold is hidden at Lo Lin's." Logan rode back up the trail to Lo Lin's to let the horses rest.

Lo Lin handed Logan a note. "A girl from the roadhouse brought this message from Tiny while you were down at Sun Lee's."

Logan opened the message and he could tell it was also written by one of the girls. The message said Tiny wanted a meeting with Logan at the roadhouse bar to discuss ending the shootings.

Logan grinned at Lo Lin, "This sounds like a trap to me, but I'll go anyway."

"One of the Chinese miners had been over to the store yesterday and saw the three men from the shootout leave. The wounded one was really having a hard time getting on a horse and the other two wouldn't help him. Tiny was on the porch of the roadhouse yelling at them to never come back. They left by the trail going north out of the basin and not toward Butte."

Logan rode his horse up in the trees behind the roadhouse and tied him out of sight. He watched for awhile before moving toward the buildings. Traveler was moving ahead of Logan and he acted like no one was nearby. When Logan got to the rear of the roadhouse, he peeked in the window and could see Tiny sitting at the end of the bar. One of the girls was at the table in the middle of the room playing with a deck of cards. The other girl was watching out a front window. He heard Tiny ask the girl by the window, "Do you see him yet?" Logan knew he was referring to him.

"When he shows, up I'll let you know." Logan eased over next to the back door and found it opened real easy. With very little sound, Logan walked into the hallway. He moved ahead until he could see into the bar. About then the girl at the table turned toward Logan and saw him.

She grinned at Logan. She turned back toward Tiny and said in a calm voice, "Tiny, I think he's already here."

Tiny spun around on his stool and glared at Logan. "Why can't you use the front door like everyone else?"

Logan walked into the room and found they were the only ones in sight. Tiny was getting his color back. "I'll buy you a drink over here at the bar."

Tiny motioned to a place in front of him. This seemed odd to Logan that he told him where to stand. Logan moved toward the bar and the girl from the window went behind the bar to act as bartender. She set a drink in front of Logan. As she set it down, she winked. Logan did not let on she had winked and moved up to the bar. Tiny raised his glass with his left hand. He was keeping his right under the corner of the bar. This worried Logan but his right hand was resting on the grip of his belly pistol out of sight of Tiny.

Tiny raised his glass. "A toast to stop all this fighting over the Chinese miners' gold." At the same time he said this, Logan saw his right arm moving something under the bar. Logan jumped back as a big explosion shook the whole building and the bar in front of Tiny went flying in small pieces. The whole upper part of Tiny's body just disappeared. The rest landed on the floor. Logan was hit by some of the flying wood from the bar and knocked down. As he jumped to his feet, the girls were just staring at the remains of Tiny's body. One of them started getting sick and ran out the front door.

The other girl looked at Logan. "Well, I guess I'm out of a job now."

Logan looked behind the bar and could see where a shotgun had been mounted. It was aimed to shoot through the bar where he had been standing. Both girls were now in the bar looking at Logan. "What in the hell happened here?"

They looked at each other then told him the story. "Tiny rigged this double barrel shotgun to shoot you while you stood at the bar. He had a pull string under the bar where he always sat. Tiny told us this would be the end of his troubles with you and he could once again rob the miners. When I took the message to Lo Lin's, Tiny went upstairs to take a nap.

The other girl spoke up, "While he was upstairs, I went behind the bar and spiked both barrels with potatoes. When Tiny figured he had you all lined up, he pulled the triggers and the gun blew up."

Logan smiled, "It looks like I owe you two girls my life. As the new owners of this roadhouse and bar, you two can let me be your first customer," Logan grinned at them.

Both girls looked at Logan, "How can we own it?"

Logan shrugged, "I'll swear you two are his only living kin when the law shows up." About this time the fellow who ran the store came sneaking in the door with a scared look on his face.

The girls turned to face him. "Tiny blew himself up while trying to shoot Logan."

This fellow was a very small man and you could always hear Tiny screaming at him in the store. Nobody ever knew how these two had come to be partners.

The little fellow looked at Logan. "What happens to me now?"

Logan looked at the girls and then back at the little man. "That's up to your two new bosses." He then stomped up to the bar where Logan stood. "How come they own the bar now?" Logan decided he would play this along and really find out about this fellow and Tiny's relationship.

Logan shrugged, "I've always heard these girls were part owners with Tiny."

"Well you know, Tiny still owes me one hundred dollars from the sales last winter."

Logan looked over at the girls. "You two should be able to pay the man his winter wages?"

They both nodded. "We could do that."

The little fellow grinned. "I'll be glad to work for you for the same wages I got from Tiny." With this he turned toward the door. "I need to get back to the store, and you know we're getting mighty short on supplies."

After the little man left, one of the girls poured each of them a drink. She lifted her glass to Logan, "I hope you're right when you say we can keep this place. By the way Logan, I'm Rachel, and this is Gail."

Logan laughed, "I hope you can make a business out of this. If you treat those Chinese miners right, you'll get all their business. They'll buy from this store if they know the prices are fair. They really like to gamble. If you would set up tables in here, you could make good money, along with the bar."

Logan stood up, "I will let the law in Butte know what has happened and let them handle it."

Both girls shook hands with Logan. "You're always welcome to stop by anytime and tell your Chinese friends to stop by. We'll deal real fair with them."

Logan loaded up the next morning and had a very quiet trip to Butte. Logan found the sheriff in his office and told him about Tiny getting himself blown up and that the girls were now running the business.

"Well, I guess I'd better head up there now and get their story on what happened."

"If you need me, I'll be at the livery or up in my cabin." Wade was all ears hearing about Tiny trying to shoot Logan and how the girls spiked the shotgun.

Wade grinned, "You're damn lucky those girls spiked that scatter gun; you could have been blown in two."

Logan repeated the story to Ling who just shook his head. "Logan you're really lucky those girls didn't like their boss."

While they were discussing the next load up to the mines, Logan told Ling, "I told the girls if they would deal right, the miners would buy from them."

Ling smiled, "When you get back up there, you make a deal for me to sell the girls all their supplies for the store. I'll keep the prices low where they can still make good money and still give the miners a good deal."

"I'll pass the word."

Logan loaded the next morning and headed back to the mines. When Logan got to the forks above the roadhouse, he decided he would ride in and see how things were going. When he rode up in front of the roadhouse, there were four horses tied out front. When Logan walked in, he was surprised to see Lo Lin and Sun Lee both standing at the bar. The sheriff and another man with a badge were talking to the girls.

When they saw Logan, Gail grinned at him. "I'm buying, what do you want?"

Logan could smell a stew or something coming from the kitchen. "I'd rather have something to eat."

Gail jumped up, "Good, you can be the first customer to eat my cooking."

Everyone else added, "How about us, we'd like to eat too."

The sheriff moved over next to Logan. "From what I hear, you are a lucky man to be alive. I won't press charges against Rachel for spiking the gun. To me this is settled and the girls can have the place."

After eating the stew with fresh biscuits, Logan laughed, "With food like this, you two gals will do alright running this business."

Logan told Lo Lin, "I got your supplies out on the pack string. Where do you want them unloaded?"

Lo Lin smiled, "Me and Sun Lee have made a deal to sell the girls those supplies that you've brought in. This way we miners won't have to worry about storing the food supplies."

Rachel nodded, "We'll sell supplies to the miners at a fair price. When the supplies were put away in the store, Logan put the horses in the pasture out back.

Later in the bar he told the girls about Ling's deal. "You tell Ling we'll take him up on it." Gail smiled at Logan. "Will you be doing our packing?"

A surprised look came from everyone when Logan shook his head no. "I'll find someone to take over for me but my packing days are over for now. With the gold all cleaned up for now and Tiny's gang gone, you won't need me to move gold."

He turned to Gail, "Make out your list and I'll see Ling gets the order. I'll help Ling find a packer who'd like this business. I already have someone in mind. With Lang gone, the new packer won't be robbed every trip."

The next morning when Logan headed back, his pack string was empty and he made good time getting into Butte. Ling nodded, "I'm not surprised that you're through packing supplies and gold. You've done your part; now someone else can take over."

"Frank's back in the area with his sister. I think he might be interested in taking your supply job."

As Ling and Logan talked, Ling opened his desk and took out a paper that had many figures on it. He laid it in front of Logan. "This is the amount of money you have made hauling gold up here."

Logan about choked when he saw the total.

"Logan, you're the richest man in this area right now."

Logan laughed, "In that case I better make sure to buy your supper to-night."

While eating that night Ling asked Logan, "Have you heard your old friend Henry Davis has been appointed Territorial Governor?"

Logan shook his head, "That doesn't surprise me. I always knew Henry really wanted to get into politics and quit ranching."

"I also heard at the same time the Rafter T is for sale."

Logan leaned back in his chair. "I wonder what will happen to my folks. I know Henry is like Old Hugh. Dad was more than just a foreman on that ranch; Henry will look after him. I think I might head down to Capital City to see Henry and find out what my folks are doing."

As Logan got up to leave, Ling grabbed his hand. "Please take care. I'll miss having you around."

"Ling, I'll always consider this my second home and I'll be back someday."

"Logan, you keep the bank disk handy so you can get to your money whenever you need it."

"I'll always have that disk with me or have it stored in a safe place."

Frank stopped by the livery that evening, and Wade and Logan discussed with him the packing job to Placer Butte area.

Logan looked over at his two friends, "I'm heading out tomorrow or the next day so I wish you'd take over the packing job, Frank. You could make a good living and I know Ling will treat you right."

Frank nodded, "I agree, Logan. Ling has already sent word he wants to talk to me."

Wade looked at Logan. "What are you going to do with our dog when you leave?"

Logan shook his head. "I've really noticed during trips this spring into Placer Butte that Traveler is getting older. He needs a good home where he doesn't have to cover so much ground each day. It breaks my heart, but I would like to leave him with you if you will take him."

"You know the answer to that. I'll make sure he's got a good home."

Frank had been hearing all this and added, "Between Wade and me, we'll make sure Traveler has a good life."

Frank rode with Logan out to the ranch to get his own horses. They talked about what Logan had planned. Frank grinned, "I'll really miss you, and if you ever want or need a partner again, send word and I'll be there."

That night Frank, Fred and Logan ate with the brother's sister who was now with them full time. When the meal was over, Logan headed for the bunkhouse. Fred and Frank followed him. Once inside Fred said, "Logan, we're both worried about people trying to back shoot you to gain a reputation. Your gun speed and your dealings with the gang working for Lang have spread all over the country. Once people find out you're traveling about the country, you will start drawing a crowd wherever you go."

Logan nodded. "I've thought about that for awhile, but I can't just go hide, so the next best thing is to ride watching my back side."

# CHAPTER 5

Logan spent the next few days traveling toward Capital City. He stopped in a small town, a day's ride from Capital City and spent two days there. He bought a few new clothes and got his hair cut. He just laid around in peace and quiet where no one knew him. While eating supper one night, he could hear the conversation between two traveling salesmen sitting at the next table. They were headed up to Butte to sell their wares. They were discussing this gunman who packed gold for the Chinese miners. The one drummer said, "I've heard this gunman is just a kid."

The other man shook his head, "I think from what I've heard he's an older man. You know he's a gunman from Texas and he's wanted by the law in many areas besides Texas." Logan smiled and thought it was good that people thought he was an older man. This way nobody even looked his way. Logan paid for his meal and headed down to the local bar for a drink before bed.

Since he had some face whiskers showing lately he was not questioned about his age every time he walked into a bar. Logan had aged in the last year and a half and looked older than his nineteen years. He still looked young but older than nineteen. The bar was not busy. Logan ordered his drink then found a table in the back where he could watch the crowd. Soon the bar filled up. Logan was about ready to leave when two men walked up and asked if they could join him. "We saw you sitting here alone. If you don't mind, we'll join you."

Logan grinned, "Sit right down; I'd enjoy the company."

They ordered a drink for Logan. "Which way are you headed?"

"I'm just riding through and decided to spend a few days resting. Where do you two work?"

"We went in partners and homesteaded a small horse ranch in the breaks west of town. This is our first trip to town in about six months. We've just made a delivery of horses to a buyer here who's buying horses for the army. The man paid us in gold coins, so we finally had enough money to start an

141

account in the local bank. We saved out a few dollars to get a drink or two then go eat a big steak at the hotel dining room. How about you joining us for supper?"

"I would but I just finished a big supper before coming here."

About then three men walked into the bar. The older man was dressed in a suit and the other two men wore twin tied down six shooters. Logan saw the older man motion toward the table where Logan and the two horse ranchers were sitting. Logan moved his chair around so he had a better chance of getting his six gun out should trouble start. The three were moving over toward the table they were sitting at. The older man walked up to the table with a man on each side.

He said in a tone everyone could hear, "These two have stolen horses from me. They sold my horses this afternoon to the army."

"You're a damn liar. We owned them horses," one fellow sitting with Logan yelled. He started to stand when the two men on either side stepped forward and pushed him back down.

The older of the two men growled, "You just listen to the boss and don't call him a liar again."

The older fellow tossed a roll of bills and a piece of paper on the table. "I'm buying you out right now. You just sign the bill of sale and you'll have one day to get out of this valley."

The two horse ranchers just looked at the money. "You can go to hell. We're not signing anything."

As the gunman on the left reached for his pistol, he stopped real quick when he saw Logan's pistol aimed right at his middle.

The older man got red in the face and started yelling, "You stay out of this or I'll chase you out too."

Logan grinned, "I just noticed my two new friends aren't armed, so I think I'll even the odds."

The younger gunman grinned at Logan, "You just signed your own death warrant. When you leave here, I'll find you. We'll show you that you don't mess around butting in where you're not wanted."

The older fellow had calmed down for a minute. "You better take the money and leave or you'll hang as horses thieves."

As the three started to turn away, the older of the two gunmen turned to Logan, "You got a name?"

Logan had put his pistol away. "Logan McTier."

Everyone in the bar heard this and turned toward Logan. Logan then stood and walked over to the older man. "You pick up that money." One of the other gunmen started for the table to pick up the money when Logan stopped him and motioned to the older man. "You go get it." When the fellow picked up the money, Logan stopped him in a very cold voice, "If I ever hear of you bothering these two men again, I will be looking for you."

The three stomped out into the night. Logan turned back to the two horse ranchers. "You two better watch your backs."

The two men were still looking at him when Logan heard a noise behind him and drew as he turned. The youngest of the two gunmen was standing in the door drawing his pistol. Logan fired then moved sideways when he heard a bullet go past him. Then he spotted the older gunman on the staircase with his pistol out. Logan fired twice at him and could see both rounds hit. As he turned to see where the first gunman was, he heard glass breaking in the front window. Logan dropped flat on the floor as buckshot blew a table next to him to pieces. Logan had drawn his second gun. He rolled over and fired three fast shots into the figure standing outside the window with a shotgun. As the fellow was knocked backward from the bullets hitting him, the shotgun blast blew away a light above Logan.

Logan glanced back at the first man he had shot. He had not moved from where he had fallen. People were coming up from the floor and from behind the bar as Logan reloaded both guns. About then a man with a star on his chest came running through the doors. He had a rifle in his hands. He looked at Logan who was sliding a pistol back in his holster. He started toward Logan when the owner of the bar hurried over. "Marshall, this fellow drew in self defense."

After hearing from everyone in the place, the marshall finally was satisfied with what had happened. He laid the rifle on the bar and looked over at his deputy. "Go get the undertaker to move these bodies." He turned to Logan, "So you're McTier. I've always figured you'd be older than I've been hearing. I guess I was wrong."

The two ranchers walked up. Both were grinning and offered Logan their hands, "You just saved our lives tonight!"

The marshall had been looking at the dead men. Then he looked over at Logan, "All three shot through the heart. The three bullets that hit the old man you can cover with a dollar."

The bar owner yelled over all the noise, "Drinks are on the house."

The marshall asked the owner, "How come nobody else drew a gun to help McTier?"

The owner just shook his head, "Hell, Marshall, this all happened in seconds. Nobody else had time to draw a gun."

When the bodies had been moved and Logan finished his drink, he headed back to his room in the hotel. The marshall followed him out. "I'd like to talk to you in the morning before you leave town."

When Logan walked downstairs the next morning, the clerk was staring at him with a funny look on his face. Logan started to ask the fellow what his problem was, when he blurted out, "Are you really Logan McTier?"

Logan nodded, "Why did you want to know who I am?"

The clerk just shook his head, "My sister was one of the girls who now owns a roadhouse and store up near Placer Butte. I got a letter from Gail and she told me about you packing the gold for the Chinese miners. She said her boss tried to kill you and they spiked the shotgun. It blew up and killed him. Gail said you told them the businesses was theirs, and the sheriff told them if Lang did not have any relatives it was okay with him."

Logan grinned, "Those girls saved my life and I hope they do good."

After breakfast in the hotel dining room, Logan headed over to see the marshall. When he walked in, the marshall was cooking his own breakfast in a small kitchen behind his office. "This job don't pay enough for me to eat out all the time, so I cook whenever the money is low." Logan poured a cup of coffee for himself while the marshall ate his meal.

"I'm curious. Who was that old fellow with the two gunmen?"

"Those three came into the area a month or so ago. I've been hearing bad reports on their dealings with small ranchers. It seems they had bluffed and bullied their way into a good herd of horses. They had one shooting north of here and killed an old fellow who was chasing mustang and stole his herd. They claimed they had bought them and had a bill of sale for the herd. Their story was they paid the old fellow in gold coins and figured someone found out and killed him for the gold. It was out of my territory, so I sent word to the new Territorial Ranger headquarters. The new governor had just started a new law enforcement department called the Territorial Rangers, and they're just now getting started."

"I'm hoping maybe this new group will look into that deal. All parties are now dead, but the old fellow had a homestead up near where he was killed. Somebody should try to find if he had any kin somewhere that might

144

want it."

Logan saddled up soon after his visit with the marshall had headed out of town. He decided to go see Henry Davis about how his folks were. He was laughing to himself about Henry being the new governor of the territory. He was wondering what Old Hugh would have thought of that. Logan was going to see if Henry thought he could spend some time at the Rafter T without causing his folks more trouble.

It was two days later when Logan rode into Capital City. This was the biggest place Logan had ever seen. He thought there were too many people for him to stay very long. Logan stopped at the Taylor Livery Stable to get some directions. He found out he was only two blocks from the Territorial Capital building. The livery manager mentioned, "There's a good boarding house just around the corner with clean rooms and good meals."

Logan left the two horses at the livery and headed for the boarding house to get a room. As Logan walked up, he noticed the sign said, "Taylor Boarding House."

Logan laughed when the lady at the boarding house said her husband managed the livery around the corner. "You've got a going business between the two of you."

Logan went up to his room to clean up and change clothes. When he finished, he stopped by the kitchen. "What time should I be back for supper?"

She grinned, "You've got a couple of hours," so he walked back down to the livery to talk to the manager.

"Where's Chinatown located from here?" Logan inquired.

"Now, if you travel down in there, you're asking for trouble. Chinatown starts about eight blocks on the other side of the capital building. The business section is on the same street as the capital."

Logan thanked him and walked out onto the street and headed that way. As he walked by the capital building, he was surprised how small it was. Then on the next block he noticed a big crew working on a building that covered half of that block. He soon came to a building at the start of Chinatown that said "Bank" on the window in English. When he walked in, he was met with many stares from the group inside. As he looked around, he was the only white man in the place. When he walked to the counter, a well dressed man got up from his desk in the back and walked his way.

He held out his hand, "I'm Lu Chung. I'm the bank manager. What can

I do for you?" Logan reached in his pocket and handed the man the disk he had gotten from Ling.

The man stared at Logan for a minute and nodded, "Please follow me." They went into a room behind the desk that Lu Chung had been sitting at. Lu motioned Logan to a chair at a big table in the room. Lu Chung went to another door, knocked and then came back and sat down across the table from Logan. Soon the door opened and an older Chinese man and a young girl came into the room. The girl was carrying a pad with pencil so Logan figured she was a secretary for the old man. Lu Chung spoke to the older man in Chinese and the older man nodded, "Are you Logan McTier?"

"Yes. I just stopped by to see what I have to do to get money from my account?"

The older fellow in broken English smiled, "You already have produced the key to your money and handed the disk back to Logan. How much money do you want to take out?"

"Five hundred dollars should do me for now."

Lu Chung grinned, "With what you have deposited with us I think we can find you five hundred dollars." He motioned to the girl and she left out the side door.

"I know I have a good sum here but I only needed some traveling money for now."

The old man opened the folder the girl had been carrying. "Do you know what your account is?"

Logan shook his head, "Ling gave me some figures but I didn't write them down."

The old man smiled, "You're one of our biggest accounts and you are so young to have so much money. You've earned this helping my countrymen get their gold out. You have risked your life many times. I know you have earned it."

The girl came back with a small coin bag and put it in front of Logan. When she turned back to the older man, she addressed him as Mr. Chung. Logan guessed this must be the manager's father. Logan picked up the bag and put it in his pocket.

"Do I need to sign for this money?"

The old man shook his head., "This is my gift to you for helping my people to keep their gold."

Logan started to protest when Lu Chung added, "This will make my

146

grandfather happy to give you a gift."

Logan looked at Lu Chung, "I was paid real well to bring out that gold."

The old man stood and offered his hand to Logan. "I must go. Thank you again for helping my people."

Logan stood after the old man left, "I also need to be going, but I'll stop in again before I leave town."

When Logan got back to the boarding house, they were just starting to eat.

The livery man looked at Logan. "I was beginning to get worried when you didn't get back from Chinatown."

The other men sitting at the table all looked at Logan. One of them said, "You must really like taking chances to go there by yourself."

"It was all business. I didn't have any trouble."

Logan ate breakfast the next morning then walked down to the livery with the manager. "What time do the offices open at the Capital?"

The livery man frowned, "You sure do travel in strange company. First Chinatown, now the Capital. They open at eight."

Logan looked at the clock on the wall. It was eight-thirty so he headed down toward the capital building. Logan walked into the front lobby and up to a desk where an older man was sitting. The man looked up, "What can I do for you?"

"I'd like to see Henry Davis."

"Do you have a appointment?"

"No."

"I'm sorry but the governor only sees people by appointment." Logan was about to ask if he could leave a note for the governor when he heard his name called from down the hall. He turned to find Henry hurrying down the hall toward him. Logan started to stick out his hand to shake when Henry grabbed him. "Boy are you a sight for sore eyes."

Henry stepped back to get a better look at Logan. "My God, Logan, you've grown up. You look great. What are you doing here?"

"I've stopped by to talk about how the folks are."

Henry turned to the man behind the desk, "Cancel my appointments for this morning," and motioned for Logan to follow him. There was a man standing in the hall with a star on his chest. When Henry and Logan got near, the man asked for Logan's gun. Logan noticed a table full of guns behind the officer.

Henry told the man, "This man can keep his gun as long as he is with me," and headed down the hall. They turned into a nice office with a girl sitting at a desk. "Kate, I want you to meet a very dear friend of mine and my family. This is Logan McTier."

Logan smiled at her as Henry motioned him into another room. "Grab a seat and I'll get us some coffee." When he returned he sat down. "Where have you been and what have you been doing?"

"Well, since leaving the ranch I've been mostly in the Placer Butte area working for the Chinese miners.

Henry's eyes lit up, "Are you the gunman that moved their gold for them?"

"The gunman part I don't know about, but, yes, I did move their gold."

"We've heard stories that the gang working for Tiny Lang was wiped out by you, and now Tiny is dead."

"Tiny kinda done away with himself." He told Henry a short version of what had happened.

"Well, I'll be damned. Well, you probably done us a favor getting rid of Tiny. I suppose you know I'm selling the Rafter T?"

Logan nodded, "I just heard something about it and that's why I'm here."

"I like this job. When we become a state, I would like to move up to be a representative of this state in Washington D. C. I hate losing all that Dad and Ted built, but I can't do both. I'm giving your folks the old Phillips place free and clear. I haven't told them yet."

"Your mother and dad always talked about their first night on Sheep Creek and meeting Joe and Elsie Phillips. I know your mother always loved that place. I have some men rebuilding the house now. It's a small token of what the Davis family owes your folks."

"Who's the new owners of the Rafter T?"

"Well, the deal hasn't gone through yet. It's a group of men from New York that think they want to be western ranchers. They're trying to get me to lower the price, but I've told them I'm going to stand on the price."

"How much are you asking for the place, if I might ask."

Henry named a price.

Logan leaned back in his chair and thought for a minute. "How much have they offered?" When Logan heard the figure he looked over at Henry. "Will you split the difference if I buy it?"

148

"Logan, I'd like nothing better than to sell it to you but I need the money now."

Logan again asked, "Will you split the difference if I buy it?"

Henry looked at Logan, "Where would you get money like that?"

"We'd have to walk down the street about five blocks and I'll pay you off."

Henry leaned back in his chair, "You're serious about this, aren't you?"

Logan nodded, "I didn't move all of that gold for nothing. Those miners gave me one third to move their gold. They made the offer."

Henry looked at Logan, "You have really changed since you left the ranch. Yes, I'll sell you the place, and I'll split the difference with you."

Henry laughed, "Boy, will I have some mad men from New York when they hear I sold the ranch. They were so sure they had me over a barrel and I'd have to sell at their price."

"I have one request and that is to keep my name out of the news about the sale. I'll be on the deed as a partner with my family. I want it recorded as such. I'd like the folks to be the main force in this deal. I want them to be notified about the sale before everyone else hears about it."

Henry nodded, "I'll get the paperwork started this afternoon and we can seal the deal in the morning."

"I'll head down to the bank and let them know what's going on. How do you want the money, cash or gold?"

Henry just shook his head and said with a grin, "Surprise me. We'll make the deal at the Main Capital Bank down the street."

As Logan started to leave, Henry said, "How about you coming to the house tonight for supper."

Logan thought for a minute. "I think it's best if people don't see us together too much. You know too many people want to be the one that shoots Logan McTier."

"Logan, Becky won't stand for an excuse like that, so we'll see you at seven sharp tonight. We live over two blocks on the east side of where the new capital is being built." Logan grinned, "I'll be there at seven sharp."

When Logan walked into the bank, he headed for Lu Chung's desk. When he pulled up a chair, Lu smiled, "You've already spent the five hundred and want more?"

Logan laughed, "No, this time I'm buying a ranch. The Rafter T Ranch. Logan told Lu Chung the amount he needed.

Lu Chung nodded, "It's good you spend your money to buy land. I'll have the money ready in the morning. I'll have Wells Fargo transfer your money to the Capital Bank. We try not to tempt would-be gangs to rob our people while transferring large sums of money. I have no fear you could protect the money," Lu smiled. "There would be shooting and we don't need that in Chinatown."

Logan had been thinking about carrying that much money around as he walked over from Henry's office. "Stop by here in the morning and I'll walk over with you to help with the transfer."

"I need to make arrangements to keep the rest of the money in your bank. I'd like to add one of my family members to the account."

"I'm glad you're trusting us to be your banker. I'll work with whoever you pick from your family." They agreed to meet the next morning at ten and walk over to the Capital Bank together.

Logan went back to the boarding house to change clothes for his supper engagement. He stopped by the kitchen to tell Mrs. Taylor he was eating out.

She smiled, "You've already found a better place to eat. That hurts my feelings."

Logan winked, "I'm eating with the governor tonight."

Mrs. Taylor laughed, "From what my husband tells me, you travel in strange company, so I don't doubt what you say. There's a bathhouse out back and the water's hot if you want to use it for your big night out."

Logan did use the bath and put on the new clothes he had purchased earlier. When he finished, he started to belt on his pistol and then thought about not wearing it. Finally, he decided he would leave the belt and holster here but keep his belly gun. He looked from all angles and couldn't see the bulge under his coat. As he started to leave, he went to his gear and pulled out his derringer and dropped it in his vest pocket. He then put a handful of shells in his pocket. Both guns were the same caliber. When he walked down into the parlor on his way out, both Taylors were sitting in the lobby. Mrs. Taylor smiled, "You really look nice. Maybe you are really going to eat with the governor."

"Why, thank you. I'll really try not to embarrass myself in front of the governor tonight."

"I think there is a lot more to you than meets the eye, besides you being very young,"

Mr. Taylor spoke up. "Do you think it's wise to be unarmed after dark walking these streets?"

"I'll be careful. I'll see you two for breakfast."

When Logan walked up the steps to the house, he was stopped by a man wearing a badge. He looked Logan over. "Are you McTier?" Logan nodded, and the man opened the door and motioned him in.

Inside he was met by an older woman who took his hat. "Please, follow me."

As he walked into the parlor, he heard Henry say, "Becky, our guest is here."

Henry walked over to shake hands. About then Becky appeared and rushed over to give him a big hug. She kissed him on the cheek, then just stood there looking at him.

"Logan, you have changed so much and you look great. I can't get over how much you look like your mother. You have your father's size."

"I'm still in high heaven since Henry told me you bought the ranch; that's really great. I'm having a problem trying to figure out a nineteen year old boy... man," she stammered, "that could have that much money. Henry told me you've been packing gold from the mountains for the Chinese miners and they've paid you real well. Logan, didn't you ever have trouble with people trying to rob you?"

Logan looked over at Henry.

Henry came to the rescue, "Becky, I left out some parts of the story."

Becky looked back at Logan. "Then you did have to use guns to protect yourself."

"Becky, I was hired by the Chinese because they were being robbed and sometimes killed every time they tried to move their gold."

She had a grim look on her face, "I suppose men have died?"

Logan nodded, "Only the ones who were trying to kill me."

Henry spoke up, "Let's talk about where you went when you left the ranch."

Logan told about the areas he had visited but left out all things to do with shootings or other grim parts. Logan heard someone come into the room behind him and the next thing he felt was arms around his neck.

He felt someone kiss his check and whisper in his ear, "Hi, Gunfighter."

When he turned, there stood a good looking young girl with a smile on her face.

151

Logan grinned, "Don't tell me this is the Rafter T tomboy all grown up."

Alice gave him a big hug. "City life has converted me, with a little help from Mom." Becky motioned to follow her into the dining room. Logan had never eaten at such a large table with so many dishes. Alice took the chair beside him. "I'll help you get accustomed to formal dining."

Becky frowned at Alice, "I think Logan can probably take care of himself."

After supper everyone returned to the parlor. Logan stayed standing. "Becky, thank you for the supper. It's getting late and I should head back to my room."

"Henry, I'll see you at the bank at ten."

Becky smiled, "Alice and I will also be there."

Logan was about a block from Henry's when he heard someone from across the street say, "There he is."

Two men came running across the street both pulling guns as they ran. Logan had his coat unbuttoned and drew his pistol as the first bullet hit the building behind him. He shot the man in the lead and jumped to the left as the second man fired. Before he could fire again, Logan shot him.

From the corner of the next building, Logan heard a voice say, "That was good but not good enough."

Logan hit the ground as a roar of a shotgun filled the night. The brush along the sidewalk where Logan had been standing was blown apart Logan fired his last two rounds at the figure by the building. He heard another blast from the shotgun as the man fell. Logan stood up and started to reload when he saw a man approaching him.

The fellow had a pistol in his hand. "I think your gun's empty, McTier, so drop it." Logan had his left hand under his coat getting shells from his pocket when the man said for him to drop his pistol. Logan dropped the pistol in his right hand. When his left hand appeared, it held a cocked derringer. The man had let down the pistol barrel when Logan dropped his pistol. When he saw the derringer, he tried to level it. Logan's first bullet caught him in the chest.

Logan retrieved his pistol and reloaded it. He heard running footsteps coming from all directions. The man from the steps of Henry's building was the first to arrive. He looked at Logan, "You alright?"

Logan nodded, "I guess they wanted my hide."

Before long there were two policemen and a crowd around Logan.

Henry came pushing his way through the crowd and grabbed Logan, "Are you alright?"

Henry looked down at the three men when he heard a person holler, "There's another one over here by the building!"

Logan bent down to look at the man he had shot last and saw a face he recognized from Tiny's gang. It was the brother of the man Logan had blown up at Lo Lin's cabin.

One of the policemen was asking Logan about the shootings when an older man walked up. "I witnessed the whole thing."

Henry called him George and seemed to know him. About then Logan noticed a badge under his coat.

Henry introduced him, "Logan, this is George Bennett, captain of the newly formed Territorial Rangers."

He shook Logan's hand, "You're very cool under fire. That was a fine job of shooting. I've heard stories about you from Henry and also from up in the Butte area. I knew you were suppose to be young and very good with a gun. I never figured for this kind of shooting." About then the man from outside of Henry's building walked up.

George looked at him. "I don't suppose you checked his guns before he entered the Governor's quarters?"

The man turned to Logan, "I didn't see any firearms when he walked up so I never checked him over."

Henry announced, "I'd better get back and report or Becky will be down here next. I'll see you in the morning, Logan."

Henry met Becky and Alice at the steps when he got to the house, "Logan is alright." He motioned them inside.

"Henry, what happened out there," Becky asked.

"Well it seems four fellows were trying to shoot Logan for some reason or another. They're all dead now. I think Logan recognized one of them."

As they were getting into bed, Becky looked at Henry, "So Logan had a gun on him while we were eating tonight."

"Yes, he did. In fact, it seems he had two. If he hadn't, he'd be dead right now."

Becky shuttered, "I don't think Logan will ever be able to have a normal life. His life is already controlled by guns."

Henry nodded his head in agreement as he turned out the light.

The next morning during breakfast Mrs. Taylor asked, "Logan, did you hear about the shooting last night?"

Logan nodded, "I thought maybe that was gun fire," and let it go at that.

When he got ready to go to meet the banker, he wore his gun in plain sight. When he entered the bank, he was met by Lu Chung. "I hear you were attacked last night."

Logan laughed, "How did you know that already?"

Lu smiled, "Very little happens this close to Chinatown that we don't know about. Did you know your attackers?"

Logan nodded, "One I knew from a gunfight at Lo Lin's cabin last year."

"I think you're a marked man now because you helped the Chinese."

Logan shook his head, "No, it all started before I started working for the Chinese."

They walked the few blocks to the Capital City Bank and Logan introduced Lu to Henry and his family.

Lu Chung bowed to all, "I'm honored to meet the governor and his family."

It took about an hour to get all the paperwork signed. The bank said it would be afternoon before all copies were done. Henry told them to bring them to his office. Logan can pick up his copies there. Lu Chung shook hands and departed for his bank.

As they left the bank, a carriage appeared for them. Logan started to walk away then he noticed Becky was in the carriage. "You get in here. We'll let Henry out at his office then you and I are going to have a chat at my house."

Henry started to laugh, then he saw his wife giving him a very cool look. He turned to Logan, "You're on your own. I'm going back to the office."

Becky had coffee brought into the parlor. "Logan, make yourself at home."

"Logan, when I heard that shooting last night, I just knew it involved you. I yelled at Henry to do something. He told me to calm down as he grabbed his coat and ran out. When I heard the awful sound of that shotgun, I was scared they'd killed you. As we waited for word of what happened, my only thoughts were how was I going to tell Lottie you were dead. Logan, I worry about you every time I hear stories about you. Many times Henry

154

doesn't know I'm listening to what people tell him. I know about you saving that girl up in Sweetwater. I don't think Henry even knows about that."

Logan was surprised how much Becky knew about his life since he had left the Rafter T. "Logan, was your mother right when she said you were the one that left the two dead men above the ranch last winter?" Logan nodded.

"Then it was you who drew the wolf's ear in the grease of the frying pan?"

"Yes, I was there. I didn't know Mom guessed it was me. I drew the ear for Dave to see. It was real hard not to go down to see them but I didn't know how many more people were watching the ranch. I've caused them to have too many gun crazy people looking for me at the ranch."

After Logan left Becky, he headed for his meeting with Henry. As he walked toward Henry's office, he was trying to figure out what Becky had meant when she said, "You should take the job they'll offer."

When Logan walked into the Capital, he met George Bennett. As Logan walked down toward Henry's office, George walked with him. He then followed him into Henry's office. Henry motioned to the papers on his desk, "All the paperwork is done on the ranch purchase and I also had them recorded for you."

Logan nodded, "I'll put my copy in the bank in Chinatown. Henry, I don't want a copy of this getting to the ranch before I tell them of the sale."

Henry nodded, "I have an idea how you can deliver it yourself and not cause your folks a problem. George and I have come up with an idea. It's up to you whether you want the job."

Henry said in a very serious tone, "People have already started calling you nothing but a hired gun. We know so far you've shot people who were trying to kill you. I think before long you'll be blamed for a killing. Your picture will start appearing on 'Wanted' posters. A sheriff or marshall trying to make a name for himself will use you to build his career by claiming you've broke the law someway. George and I have an idea we think will keep this from happening. I know you're only nineteen years old. George and I both would like you to sign up for the Territorial Rangers. This way these men trying to kill you to gain reputation will be drawing against a ranger. That's a hanging offense."

Logan looked at the two men and saw they were really trying to solve his problem.

"This will also give the rangers another fast gun. This we're going to need if we hope to tame this area for statehood." Henry added, "If you take this job, we can pin a star on you and you can deliver your paperwork to the ranch yourself."

Henry and George looked at Logan. "You know I kinda like the idea."

Both men stood. Henry was the first to shake Logan's hand.

Henry looked at Logan, "If you're sure about the job, we can swear you in right now." He opened the door and in walked Becky and Alice who had been waiting outside.

Becky hugged him, "Logan, I know you won't be sorry for doing this." Alice smiled and also gave him a kiss on the cheek.

After the badge was pinned on, Henry held up his hand for silence, "This calls for a toast to our newest ranger."

Henry opened the door and called to Kate, his secretary, "Bring in the tray." When Kate walked in, she had a tray with glasses and a bottle of wine.

Logan laughed, "I think I was set up."

After all the toasts, George stood up to leave. "Logan, stop by my office when you're through here," and he stepped out. After George left, Becky and Alice both gave Logan a hug and left.

Henry smiled, "Logan, it'll be awhile before you probably have your own district as a territory ranger. I know you can handle this." Henry offered his hand, "Logan, tell your folks hello for me and Becky. Tell them we'll be up to the Rafter T before long to get the rest of our furniture."

Logan knocked on George's office door and stepped in. George was sitting behind his desk. Across from him was a short, tough-looking fellow. The first thing Logan noticed was the twin pistols. George nodded toward Logan, "Tug, this is your new partner, Logan McTier. Logan, this is Tug Higgins."

They shook and Higgins looked Logan all over. "I've heard some good things about you." Then with a grin he added, "I've also heard things that weren't so nice."

Logan liked the little bowlegged ranger from the start. George sat them both down and outlined what he wanted them to do for the next tour of duty. They would head toward the Rafter T so Logan could deliver his papers and see his folks. "I want you to stop and visit all the law officers in all the towns you pass through and get acquainted. When you get to Benton, Logan, you can go on out to the ranch while Tug visits with Sheriff Rogers. Rogers has been having some trouble with rustlers over in the breaks. Tug can help him look into this while you're over at the Rafter T."

Logan nodded, "When are we leaving?"

Tug looked over at George. "We should be ready to leave tomorrow morning."

George nodded, "Logan, you can go with Tug now and pick out a horse, beings as the territory furnishes the rangers' horses. You can take your horses back to the Rafter T when you head out.

On their way over to the ranger headquarters, Tug explained what he wanted Logan to get from the commissary. "You'll furnish your own saddle, guns and clothing. Most everything else will be furnished by the rangers. There's a basic load for ammunition we carry. Your pistol and rifle must be of the same caliber."

Logan nodded, "I carry my fifty caliber Sharps and load my own shells for it. Tug, I'll be staying at the boarding house tonight. I'll be over here at dawn."

Logan stored his gear in a room that was assigned to him. From now on this would be his home whenever he was in the capital.

Tug gave Logan a lift back to the boarding house in a buggy. Mrs. Taylor had seen Logan from the kitchen as he walked up the steps. When he started for his room, she stepped into the hall. "Logan, supper will be in about fifteen minutes." Logan nodded and went to his room to clean up.

When he walked into the dining room, Mrs. Taylor looked over at him. "Are you a lawman?"

Logan laughed, "Yes, since this afternoon. I'll be checking out real early in the morning so I'll need to settle up my bill tonight."

After everyone else had left the table, Logan had another cup of coffee with the Taylors. Mr. Taylor looked at Logan. "Now, don't take offense to this. Are you the gunman from up Placer Butte way?"

"Well, I did work for the Chinese up there. At times I had used a gun to protect the gold I was packing."

Mr. Taylor nodded, "I know, really it's none of my business, but I just had to ask."

Mrs. Taylor frowned at her husband, "You should mind your own business."

"I'd like to check out my horses about daylight. Is there a night watchman at the livery I should check in with?"

Mr. Taylor shook his head, "I'll walk down with you in the morning. In case something should happen and I sleep in, there's a man on duty to let you have the horses."

Logan paid his bill. "Thank you both for all the help and the good meals."

Mrs. Taylor looked up at Logan as he started up the stairs. "Breakfast will be at five and you've already paid for it."

Logan ate with the Taylors the next morning then walked down to the livery with Mr. Taylor. When he arrived at the ranger headquarters, Tug was packing his gear and had the horse Logan had picked out tied to the hitch rail.

He turned as Logan rode up, "It's always good to know my new partner is on time. You'll find I hate to wait on anyone. Usually, I don't wait," Tug said in a gruff voice that Logan would get use to in days to come.

Logan was riding the new horse when they left the ranger compound. He was leading his own two horses. The sorrel horse he was leading was one of the horses he had inherited from Claire Matthews and the other one was Hugh's. As they rode along Tug looked over at the horses Logan was leading. "If I'm not mistaken, that horse back there used to belong to Claire Matthews, so the stories I've been hearing about you must be true."

Logan smiled, "How did you know what horses belonged to Claire Matthews?"

Tug laughed, "Claire and I shared a cabin one winter down in Texas. I used to watch Claire play cards by the hour and usually he came home a winner. I recall seeing him draw a gun only once. I'll never forget that quick, easy draw."

"A card shark was caught dealing from the bottom of the deck by Claire. When challenged, he tried to shoot Claire with a sleeve derringer. He was way too slow even with the sleeve gun to beat the draw of Matthews."

Tug looked at Logan. "If you learned from him, you could be good too. If you inherited all his guns, you must carry a derringer that Claire kept when he shot the card cheat."

Logan nodded, "I have his forty-four caliber derringer.

The first day out brought them to a small place along the road called Granger where they spent the night. After leaving the horses at the livery, they looked for the Marshall's office. It was next to the general store. The note on the door read, "I'm eating supper at the café across the street."

They found the place, and when they walked in, they spotted the man with a badge sitting at a table talking to the waitress. When she spotted their badges, she must have said something. The fellow turned in a hurry to check them out. He stood and Tug introduced himself and Logan. "I'm Tug Higgins, and this is Logan McTier."

The marshall nodded, "I'm Dave Pence, Marshall of Granger. What brings you two to Granger?"

"We're just passing through. We've got orders to get to know all the lawmen in this area."

The marshall nodded, "Grab a seat and join me for supper." As they were eating, the marshall turned to Logan, "Aren't you pretty young to be carrying a ranger badge?"

Before Logan could answer, Tug spoke up, "He's old enough."

The marshall nodded, "McTier is a familiar name. The foreman for the Rafter T is Ted McTier."

"He's my father."

The Marshall frowned, "Then you're the gunfighter I heard about up in the Placer Butte area."

"I did pack gold for the Chinese up there and at times needed to use a gun." Tug about choked when he heard Logan's answer to the marshall.

The marshall smiled, "I guess the stories I've been hearing aren't right or the rangers wouldn't be pinning a badge on you."

That night they rolled out their bedrolls in the hay mow of the livery.

The next day they started getting into country Logan had known growing up. He started getting a little homesick for the first time since he had left. Tug was looking at new country to him and was glad to have Logan along to point out different points to watch for as they rode through this area. It was mid afternoon when Logan stopped at a fork in the trail. "The Rafter T is about a four-hour ride from here. This other fork will lead you into Benton. You'll make it there in less than four hours. It's a good trail."

Tug had his leg wrapped around the saddle horn rolling a cigarette. He nodded, "Sounds like you know where you're going so I'll head down into Benton to see Sheriff Rogers. I will meet you in two days in Benton. Then we'll continue our swing through the country. If something happens, I'll send word to the ranch. Should you run into trouble, you do the same. If you don't show up in two days, I'll head toward the ranch."

Logan agreed and with a wave headed down the trail for home.

Logan sat on his horse for awhile just looking down on his old home. Many memories were coming back. This was the same place where Hugh and Logan's folks had first seen what would become the Rafter T Ranch. As Logan rode across the hay meadow, he could see someone standing on the porch of the house watching him. When he got closer, he recognized it was Lottie, his mother. When Logan rode up to the porch, he grinned at his mother, "Can a bum get a meal here?"

His mother grabbed him as soon as he swung down from his horse and buried her head in his chest. He could feel her crying. He held her until she stepped back and wiped her eyes with her apron.

About then she saw the star on his vest and smiled, "When did this happen?"

"I'll tell that story while we're all together tonight."

About then Rebecca and Mary came out on the porch. Mary, with a scream, jumped into his arms. Rebecca grabbed his arm and he hugged them both.

Lottie motioned, "Your father is down in the barn helping with a sick colt. John will be in with the crew tonight."

Logan picked up the reins of his horse and led the three toward the barn. He started pulling his saddle off when he heard his name called. He turned to greet his father. They shook hands just as Ted's eye caught the badge. Before he could say anything Logan said, "I'll explain that later."

Logan put the new horse into a stall. "I'll be leaving the other two with you."

Logan could see his other horse in the small pasture behind the house. When the crew started coming into the ranch for supper, John saw him and jumped his horse into a gallop. He bailed off before it stopped and grabbed his brother. Logan laughed, "Little brother, I can't believe how much you've grown in the last two years."

The crew was all standing around shaking hands. About then Logan heard a voice saying, "Young man you better get over here and give me a big hug." Logan turned to see Rose standing on the porch of the cook shack with her hands on her hips.

Logan remembered when he was small and he saw her standing like that it meant he was in trouble. He grabbed her and gave her a big kiss.

"Now Logan, you cut that out!" She pushed him back. "Boy have you grown up but I can still handle you, and don't you forget it!" Logan grinned.

"Where's old Dave?" She motioned to a small cabin out by the spring house. "He's having a hard time seeing things up close. You might have to tell him who you are."

Logan motioned to his dad he was going up to see Dave.

Rose looked over at Logan. "He'll be coming down for supper before long and you make sure he makes it. I usually walk him down but tonight you can help him." Dave heard him walking up the path and was at the door when Logan got there.

The old man was looking his age, and before Logan could say anything, he grabbed Logan's arm, "It's about time you came home for a visit."

"They told me you were having trouble with your eyes. I think you been pulling a fast one on them."

"I can see at a distance pretty good yet but up close I have a problem. I saw you crossing the hay meadow. I could tell it was you just from the way you sit a horse. I also saw the two horses you were leading. If I'm not wrong, that's a badge your wearing. I guess Henry took my suggestion after all."

This really surprised Logan to hear Dave and Henry had discussed him becoming a ranger.

Logan could hear his mother calling his name and could see her on the porch motioning to come eat. He finally figured out what else she wanted when he motioned toward Dave. Logan laughed, "Dave, if I got Mom's message right, you're suppose to eat with the family tonight."

When they got to the house, Lottie greeted Dave with a big hug. She grabbed his arm and placed him at the table.

The rest of the family had many questions, but Logan shook his head. "Wait until after supper then we'll have a long gab session."

After Lottie and the girls cleared the table, everyone sat back down to talk to Logan.

"I'd like to have Rose down here during our talks if someone will run up and get her." Mary jumped up and headed out the door. She was soon back with Rose in tow.

Logan looked at everyone, "I've got something to tell my family and Rose before I start answering any questions."

He walked over and picked up his saddle bags and took out some papers.

As he turned to the table, his mother asked, "Logan, did you know

161

Henry is selling the ranch?"

Logan smiled, "Yes, he told me about the sale and that he's giving you and Dad the Phillips' place."

Ted spoke up, "Are you sure about that?"

"If you two will stop with the chit chat, I have some more important news."

Lottie said, "Logan, losing your home isn't chit chat."

Logan unfolded the papers he had taken from his saddle bags. "First off, you haven't lost your home. In fact, you now own the house you live in." Now everyone's eyes were on Logan. He put the one paper in front of Ted and Lottie, "You're now owners of the Rafter T. This is the deed and we have formed a partnership with me holding the controlling interest."

Lottie looked up at her son, "Logan, we can never pay for a ranch this big."

Logan walked around the table and put his arms around his mother. Then he whispered in her ear, "Mom, it's paid for, free and clear."

She looked at him, "Who's paying for it?"

Logan just stood there for a spell shaking his head and looking at his mother.

Ted laughed, "Finish the whole story Logan; your mother will listen."

Logan told them about going to see Henry at the capital and finding out about the sale. "A group from back east were trying to jew him down on the price. Henry had a price he wanted and they were offering him less. I told him I would buy the Rafter T if he would split the difference on the price from what he was asking and their offer. Henry took me up on the deal."

Logan held up his hand, "Before you all start with the questions about where I got the money. I'm going to tell you."

Logan told them the whole story from the time he left until he arrived that day. He left out many parts that had to do with gun fights. But he told them the complete story about the gold and what the Chinese paid him. The table was completely silent and not even his mother could say anything.

Old Dave started laughing, "I do believe our boy has been busy."

This got everyone talking. Logan looked over at his dad. "Tomorrow we'll decide how we're going to handle this." Ted nodded.

As the evening wore on, the thought of the McTier family now owning the Rafter T was sinking into those involved. Lottie kept saying, "Logan, how much did those miners pay you? It don't seem possible they had that much gold."

It was getting late. Old Dave mumbled, "I'm going up to the cabin."

Lottie motioned to John, "You walk with him."

"Dave, I'll be up and spend the night but I want to stay here for a while yet." Dave nodded to Logan as he walked out.

Lottie started to argue about Logan staying with Dave, but Ted spoke up, "Logan, I think that's a good idea."

After the family had all gone up to bed, Ted, Lottie and Logan had a chance to talk more freely. Logan told them his life would never be like they wanted it to be. "You know as well as I do I'll never be just a rancher. There'll always be that guy with a gun trying to get a reputation by killing Logan McTier. This Territorial Ranger job, I think, will make my life a lot easier. This way many men won't try to draw a lawman into a gun fight. I know now guns will always be a part of my life. By being a ranger maybe I can help make this country safer to live in for everyone. I'll need to head back to town tomorrow. I'm suppose to meet my partner tomorrow in Benton. I won't leave until the afternoon."

Logan had a good talk with Dave who was awake waiting for him when he got to the cabin. The next morning Logan was up at dawn and headed down to have breakfast with his folks. Logan and Ted talked about the ranch and what Logan thought they should do to improve it. Logan also told Ted, "I've got more money for stock to upgrade the herd, so don't worry about buying good breeding stock."

Ted nodded, " I'm glad you want to upgrade the herd. I'll get started on that real soon."

Logan told his folks, "All my money is in the Chinese bank in Capital City. If something happens to me, Lu Chung will work with you there. You and Mom figure how much money you'll need for operating expenses and I'll have that amount transferred to the bank in Benton."

Ted headed off to tell the crew about the change in ownership and to tell them all he would like them to stay on. Lottie told the girls to clean up the kitchen. She motioned for Logan to follow her into the living room. Lottie looked at her son, "Logan you're only nineteen years old and you're already living the life of a man twice your age. You don't have any friends your own age let alone a girl to court. I'd like to have a daughter-in-law someday and maybe grandkids. The way you're going we'll never have any of these things. Logan, you need to slow down your life someway and get to be your own age again."

"Are you going to see Laura Benton while you're in town? You know she's always liked you. When I go into the store she always asks if I've heard from you."

Logan grinned at his mother, "Boy, are you a pest. Yes, I'll try to see her before we leave town."

As Logan was heading to town to meet up with Tug, he thought about how Ted, with John as he grew older, would keep the Rafter T under McTier ownership. Maybe Rebecca and Mary would marry men who would stay on to help run the ranch being as their wives were part owners. Logan knew deep down he would never be a big part of operating the place. His mother was probably right, that for now his life would be a lonesome time. Most women do not want any part of that kind of life.

When Logan rode into Benton, he spotted Tug's horse tied to the hitch rail in front of the sheriff's office. When Logan walked in, Dale Rogers got up from his desk to shake his hand. Logan thought the sheriff had a small smile on his face. "How's the new lawman?"

"Good, Dale. It's good to see you. I've got to know your brother, Del, quite well since I left here."

"Del's written about some of your visits to his area."

Tug walked in the room and said, "Logan, I got us a room over at the hotel with two beds."

Logan replied, "I've got a little business here in town. I'll meet you for supper about six." "You can put your horse in the barn in back of the office."

Dale laughed, "Tug, I'll bet you a dollar he heads for the general store."

"No bets. You know him better than I do."

Logan looked over at Dale, "The whole truth is I'm following orders from Lottie. You know I always do what she says."

Walking down the street a couple people stopped to say hello; some just waved at him. When he walked into Benton General Store, there were only a couple customers at the counter. Ed was waiting on the people. He grinned at Logan and motioned to the back. Logan walked back to the store room. As he entered he almost knocked over a person carrying a big stack of boxes. He grabbed both boxes and the person. When all was calm, he was holding on to Laura.

She looked up and laughed. "You could have told me you were here. I heard yesterday you were out at the ranch. I also heard you're now a Territorial Ranger. I think that badge looks good on you but really I think you're too young to have such a responsibility. We're both the same age. You'll be just twenty years old in January."

Then she grinned, "I guess I shouldn't be preaching to you. You really haven't had much choice in your life in the last few years. Logan, wait here a minute while I go up front to tell Dad we'll be in the kitchen."

She led him back to a small kitchen tucked away amongst the warehouse part of the store. She poured coffee and sat down. "I hear Henry's selling the ranch. What are your folks going to do?"

Logan smiled, "If you can keep a small secret for a few days, I will tell you about that. I don't want this let out until the folks get everything settled. We are the new owners of the Rafter T."

Laura looked at him, "Do you mean the McTier's are the new owners?"

Logan nodded his head, and Laura started laughing. "Boy will this ease Dad's mind. He's been driving us crazy ever since he heard the place was for sale. The Rafter T has always been our biggest customer."

"I suppose you could tell him. If you do tell him, you tell him to let Ted or Lottie break the news to him. Then act like it's news to him."

Laura and Logan spent an hour talking about people they both knew and where they were now.

Finally, Logan asked, "Would you consider going down to the hotel dining room for supper with me?"

Laura looked surprised, "Logan, that would be great."

Logan got up to leave. "I'm going over to the hotel and get settled. I'll pick you up at six thirty."

As they started to leave the kitchen Ed walked in. Laura pressed on Logan's arm. "You tell him about the ranch."

Ed butted in, "Logan, do you know who the new owners are?"

Logan laughed along with Laura, "Ed, I'll tell you if you promise to not let it out until Ted or Mom tell you about it."

Ed looked first at Logan then at his smiling daughter. "Okay, I won't tell."

When Logan told him, his mouth dropped open. "How and when did this happen?"

"Ed, you wait until the folks tell you about it. You better look surprised!"

165

As they walked out, Laura was still laughing at her dad.

That evening he picked up Laura at the store and they walked to the hotel. During supper Logan explained more about the ranch and how he raised the money to buy it. Laura was full of questions, "Are you going to move back to the ranch to live?"

"No, I'm going leave the ranch operation to Dad." Logan could see by the look in her eyes that she was very unhappy about him saying he was leaving the ranch operation as it is.

"Laura, what are you going to do? At one time you wanted to go on to school to be a teacher."

Laura nodded, "I'm still thinking of that. Then maybe come back and teach school here in Benton or close by. I've been seeing a fellow from down on the river. He helps his father run a sawmill. I like him and my folks think he's alright. He's mentioned maybe we should get married. I told him I'd think on it. I'm not rushing into that yet. I want to finish school first."

They talked a little after supper. While he walked her to her folks home a couple blocks from the store, Logan said, "I wish things had worked out differently, but that's all in the past now." Laura just nodded her head.

After seeing her home, Logan stopped by the jail to see if Tug was still there. He had already gone back to the hotel. Tug was sitting in the lobby talking to the manager when Logan walked in. "I'm going into the bar for a night cap; do you want to join me, Logan?" While they were nursing their drinks, Tug looked over at his new partner. "How about we leave at eight or so in the morning?"

# CHAPTER 6

After breakfast Tug and Logan headed for the jail. Logan motioned to Tug, "I'll saddle the horses while you talk to the sheriff." When Logan finished loading their gear, he tied the horses out back and went in through the back door of the jail. He walked over and poured a cup of coffee while Tug and the sheriff were going over some 'Wanted' posters. As he stood at the window, he could see most of Main Street including the bank. Four riders were dismounting across the street from the bank. As Logan watched, he recognized three of the riders. They were men from Lang's old crew from Placer Butte. They were talking and kept looking at the bank. Finally, one of them grabbed the reins of all four horses and turned down the alley between the buildings. The other three crossed over to the sidewalk near the bank. Logan turned to Dale, "Does the bank here carry much cash on hand?"

Dale looked up. "At times they have lots of cash on hand. Like now when the ranchers are selling stock. The payroll for the mines at Gold Field usually comes through here and is picked up by a courier from the mine. It being close to the end of the month, that money will be over there too. Why are you asking?"

"I think it's about to be robbed."

Both Tug and Dale hurried over to the window. "I know three of the men standing in front of the bank. The fourth man just led their horses down the alley. As they watched they saw the fourth man riding one horse and leading three across the street two blocks from where the three men stood.

Tug said, "He's probably going to be at the back door of the bank when they make their break after getting the money."

Dale nodded, "Let's see if we can break this up before it goes too far."

"Logan and me will cross down the street from where the rider crossed over and cover the back of the bank."

"Okay, I'll cross in front of the general store like I'm just going to the store to get some supplies."

167

The three men in front of the bank now were walking in the front door. Logan and Tug hurried out the back door of the jail and mounted their horses. They headed down the alley away from the bank. When they turned up Main Street, they slowed to a walk and rode across the street. Logan jumped off his horse and started walking toward the bank as Tug, leading his horse, rode up the alley. When Tug got even with the back of the bank, the fellow with the horses was watching him but Tug did not see a gun. Tug tipped his hat to the fellow, "Good morning," and kept on riding.

Logan had made it to the building next to the bank without the fellow seeing him. The fellow was too busy watching Tug riding down the alley. Tug turned up the next alley and quickly dismounted and started sneaking back toward the bank. Tug made it back to the building on the other side of the bank from Logan. Both Logan and Tug heard a gun shot coming from inside the building. The fellow with the horse started to swing up on his horse, and when he did, he turned his back on Tug. Tug rushed forward and hit the fellow on the head with the butt of his pistol. He grabbed him and dragged him up against the building. Tug grabbed the reins of the fellow's horse and tied them to the saddle horn then hit the horse with his hat on the rump. The horse spun and headed up the alley followed by the other three on a high run. About then three men came busting out the back door with their faces covered.

"Where in the hell is that kid?"

The next thing they heard was Tug, "You boys move real slow like and drop those pistols. Now turn around real slow like."

The one closest to Tug spun his pistol up when Tug fired. The bank robber crumpled up and hit the ground.

The other two started to draw when a voice behind them said, "Don't be foolish; just drop your guns now." The guns fell. "Now move back real slow and turn around real slow."

When they turned they both recognized Logan. "McTier, what the hell are you doing here?"

" I thought by now you three would know you're not cut out to be outlaws." About then they both saw the badge on his chest. "You can go to hell, McTier."

The one Tug had shot was dead. The one he had clubbed was just now beginning to stir. Logan jerked him to his feet. He was still pretty groggy. Sheriff Rogers and Ed Benton came out the back door with guns drawn. Ed was carrying a sawed off shotgun. Logan could see he was ready for action. Seeing everything under control, the sheriff picked up the bank bags the robbers had dropped. Tug looked over toward him, "What was that shot inside?"

Ed nodded toward Dale. "One of the men saw the sheriff outside the door of the bank and took a shot at him. Everyone inside is okay."

They locked up the three men. The undertaker picked up the dead man. Tug looked at the sheriff. "This town is too wild for us. I think we'll head out."

Logan had retrieved their horses and was talking to Ed in front of the jail when Tug walked out. "Well kid, let's ride."

With a wave Tug and Logan left Benton. They headed on to visit all the towns in the area.

When they were a few miles from town, Tug looked over at Logan. "You did real well back there. I was mad as hell when Bennett told me I was to wet nurse a new recruit on this trip. Now I'm thinking you and me might make a good team. If you're half as fast as they say, I figure my back is well covered."

Logan just grinned, "I figure I can still learn from an older ranger the finer points of being a law officer."

Tug looked over at him, "Oh, go soak your head."

"I got a message from Bennett when I first arrived in Benton telling us to check with the marshall in Clover."

"Do you know anything of that town?"

Logan shook his head, "I've heard of it, but never been there. I do remember, right after the town started, that the Rafter T sold them some beef cattle. I think Ted delivered the beef, but I don't remember him saying much except it was a new town. There's a couple pretty good mines in the mountain above town I've heard."

"I think some homesteaders are in the valley now and a few small ranches, according to the message I got from George. It seems they're having trouble with a bunch of rustlers. There's also a feud between the homesteaders and the small ranchers. Each side is accusing the others of rustling. The marshall has no power outside of town. There's no sheriff in the area yet, so we're suppose to take charge until the governor appoints a sheriff."

"I think it'll take almost two days to get there unless they have built a different road to get there."

"Dale Rogers told me to figure a day and half ride. I figure if we ride until almost dark tonight and then head out early in the morning we should get into the area early tomorrow afternoon. I'd like to scout the area before we ride into town."

It was just getting dark when they found a good camping place near a small creek with good feed for the horses. Logan fixed supper while Tug took care of the horses. When they finished eating, Tug took the dishes to the creek to wash them. As he walked away, he mumbled something about a good supper. Logan laughed to himself. He decided he had lucked out having Tug for his first partner in the rangers.

They were up and on the trail just a little after dawn. They started spotting cattle once they started down the ridge toward the valley. It was cool and both Logan and Tug had jackets on. The jackets covered up the ranger badges. They were coming into a meadow when they spotted a small smoke coming from across the meadows. As they got closer, they could see two men branding a calf. When the men spotted Logan and Tug, they both ran for their horses and spurred off into the brush. When Tug rode up to the fire, the calf was still down with its legs tied together. Logan kept the mad cow off Tug while he untied the calf. Tug motioned to the brand partly done on the calf and then pointed to the cow. "These two brands don't match. I think we've caught someone trying to steal this calf. I think we have already started finding the problems around here."

Logan handed his reins to Tug and started looking for tracks up through the brush where the two riders had gone. Logan soon found a place where the ground was moist from a nearby spring. The tracks of both horses were plain to see. He motioned to Tug to come over for a better look. One horse's track showed it had one rear shoe built up on one side and the shoeing job had been done recently. The built-up cleat was still mostly square showing that it had not been on long enough to wear it smooth.

Tug looked over at Logan, "How come you read signs so well?"

Logan laughed, "I grew up living every chance I got with an old trapper. He could follow tracks that most people couldn't even see."

Tug grinned and shook his head as they headed down the trail toward Clover. They rode into the topical western town with the false front buildings. Clover was no different than any other town. You could tell the buildings that had been here for a winter or so and the new ones built that year. As they rode looking for the marshall's office, people along the wooden sidewalks were giving them the eye. You could tell they were looking mostly at the badges shining on their shirts. Tug motioned to follow him instead of stopping at the office. Tug rode up to a blacksmith shop. Both riders stepped down as a young man in dirty clothes walked out to meet them. He was looking at the horses. "Do you fellows have a shoe problem?"

Tug shook his head. "We're just after a little information right now."

Logan had gone over and picked up a newly made shoe from the anvil and walked back to where Tug was talking to the young smithy.

Logan held out the shoe. "Do you ever build up a shoe like this with metal added on one side?"

The young man looked at Logan. "I sometimes do make a special shoe to correct a horse's hoof."

"Have you built such a shoe in the last few days?"

The young man hesitated and Tug pointed to his badge. "We're Territorial Rangers, and if you tell us the truth, you won't get in trouble with us. We've found a track of a new shoe with the built-up side. All we want to know is if you made the shoe?"

The young man looked toward the shop and back at Tug. "I didn't make the shoe but my dad did."

Tug nodded, "Can we talk to your father then?"

In almost a whisper he answered, "He's down at the saloon."

As Logan and Tug turned to leave, they saw a fellow with a star on his vest walking toward them. The marshall smiled, "I'm Lenny Cook, Marshall of Clover."

"Tug Higgins and this is my partner Logan McTier."

"I saw you fellows ride in while I was visiting over at the barber shop."

Lenny introduced the young blacksmith as Bill. "He can fix any problem you have with a horse's hoof."

Tug nodded, "We didn't need any work done. We just had a question about a horseshoe track we found. We found this track while we were following two fellows we caught branding a calf."

Lenny nodded and walked away. He motioned for them to follow. As soon as they were out of hearing of young Bill, Lenny explained, "I didn't want to talk in front of young Bill. Bill's dad is the blacksmith, but he's usually drunk and young Bill does most of the work. He has to hide any money he makes or his father would drink it up. I know the horse that wears the built-up shoe, and Bill's dad is a drinking buddy of its owner."

"When they got to the marshall's office he invited them in for coffee.

As they were finishing the coffee Tug asked, "Would you point out this horse to us the first time you see it?"

"That's easy; it's tied to the hitch rail in front of the saloon now." He pointed out the window. "It's that bay on the far side. It belongs to Chip Brown. Anyway, that's the name he goes by now. He's a terror with a six gun and usually shoots first and talks second. So far he's always had witnesses that swear the other party drew first. He's killed two men in the last month."

Tug looked at Logan, "Let's go talk to this bad man."

When they neared the saloon, Logan looked over at his partner. "How about me going in the front door while you come in the back?"

Tug nodded, "I guess you need the practice of arresting a man legal like," and headed down between the buildings. Lenny had tagged along with Logan, and as they neared the front door, he turned to him. "You step aside as soon as we walk in the saloon."

As they walked through the door, Lenny whispered, "The fellow in the red shirt," and he stepped aside.

Logan stopped inside the door and looked over the room. About then somebody spotted his badge.

The fellow in the red shirt turned to face Logan. He smiled and announced in a loud voice, "We don't serve milk in here kid."

Everyone in the place laughed. "Which one of you fellows ride the bay outside?"

The fellow in the red shirt stepped away from the bar. "I do. What's it to you?"

Logan smiled, "I was just wondering why you didn't finish your branding job today when we rode up."

The fellow's hand flew toward the gun on his right hip. As he cleared leather, he was slammed back by a bullet to the chest. It had come from a smoking pistol in Logan's left hand."

The man standing to the right of the downed gunman started to pull a belly gun when Logan heard Tug's voice, "You just stand quiet."

Tug stepped up and disarmed the fellow and looked over at Logan. "I think this fellow looks like maybe he was helping brand that calf today with Red Shirt here."

Logan nodded and looked over at Lenny. He was as white as a sheet. When he looked at Logan he tried to smile. Lenny moved over to the body

172

and motioned to a fellow who had been playing cards at a back table to step forward.

"Jake, you take care of the body. Come over to the office later and I'll pay you." As he and another fellow packed out the body, Lenny motioned to Jake. "He's the local undertaker."

Tug walked the other calf brander ahead of him and headed for the jail. People were standing along the street on both sides as they walked to the jail. Once inside Lenny locked the man in a front cell. Tug walked over to the stove and poured a cup of coffee and offered it to Logan.

Tug poured himself a cup and turned to Logan. "Why the left gun? You seem to me to be mostly right handed."

Logan shrugged, "I try not to have a favorite gun side. I've heard it can get you killed sometimes."

Lenny looked over at them both. "I've never in my life seen a draw that fast."

"The main thing is it got the job done. In this business that's what counts," Tug said in his normal growl.

Logan figured Tug was just letting Lenny know he was also fast.

Logan was looking out the window of the jail and could see a stage-coach stopping in front of the general store.

"Lenny, how often does the stage come through here?"

"Every other day."

When he said that, Tug nodded to Logan. "Go over and hold the stage until I get a note written to Bennett. We're suppose to keep headquarters notified about where we are whenever possible. Maybe I can get someone appointed to this sheriff job before we leave." He turned to Lenny. "Marshall, would you be interested in being the sheriff of this area?"

Lenny grinned, "You bet. I'd really like that job."

"Good, I'll tell Bennett in this note we've found a sheriff already here and to get the paperwork done to appoint you."

Logan walked up to tell the driver of the stage to wait for a letter before leaving. The driver gave him a strange look, then looked at the badge. "Are you one of those new lawmen I hear we now have since we became a terri-tory?"

Logan nodded, "I'm Ranger McTier."

"You look mighty young to be carrying a badge. Wouldn't anybody else take the job?"

About then the store clerk who had been standing there listening to Logan and the driver's conversation asked Logan, "Was that Chip Brown the undertaker carried out of the saloon?"

"That's the name the marshall gave us."

The stage driver looked at Logan. "Brown was a terror with a six gun. How did you get him?"

As Logan started to answer, another person walked up. "I saw it all and Brown never even cleared leather."

The stage driver turned and looked at Logan. "What did you say your name was?"

"Logan Mc Tier."

The driver grinned, "The same McTier from Placer Butte?"

Logan nodded.

"Now I know why Brown never cleared leather."

About then Tug rushed across the street with his letter to ranger headquarters. The driver put the letter in his shirt pocket. "I'll deliver this myself."

As Logan and Tug started back across the street, they missed the conversation between the clerk and the others gathered in front of the store. The clerk asked, "Who's Logan McTier and what about Placer Butte?"

The next morning Logan and Tug decided they could cover more territory by splitting up to visit all the homesteads and small ranches. "Logan, I'll cover the north side of the valley and you cover the south side."

Lenny was standing in front of his office as they mounted. "There's a small religious settlement on the upper end of the valley."

Tug nodded, "Logan, I'll meet you this afternoon at that settlement."

Logan rode down the beautiful narrow valley and came to the first homestead perched along a good sized creek. As he rode up, a man with a long beard walked out from the barn carrying an old muzzle loading shotgun. Logan smiled, "I'm Ranger Logan McTier. I'm here to look into the rustling in these parts."

The fellow nodded and lowered the barrel. "The name's Sears. We've had no problem with them, but our neighbors have lost most of their small herd." About then a lady with three small girls walked out from behind the cabin.

Logan tipped his hat to the lady. "There's two of us around. We wanted to let everyone know that we're here in the valley." Logan decided this fellow was not as old as he first thought; the beard just made him look older.

He was still not sure of Logan and kept the shotgun in a two handed grip. "You look awful young to be a lawman."

"I was appointed by the governor and have my papers with me to prove it."

Sears nodded, "Like I said, I haven't had any trouble, but I mostly farm. We only have a few head of cattle. We've heard riders during the night but so far no trouble."

Logan nodded, "Where's the next place up this valley?"

"Up the valley along the creek. As soon as you get beyond the little ridge there, you'll see the place."

At the second place the lady was home alone. She would not come out of the cabin to talk to Logan. Logan could see a rifle barrel in the window from where she was talking to him. Logan rode closer to the cabin. "I'm Ranger McTier. I'm here to look into all the rustling going on. I'll be back by sometime when your husband is home." As he rode away, he was sure he saw a man's head looking out from behind the small barn.

All morning Logan found most people did not trust strangers. Most of them were not sure he was really a lawman. He decided he would head up the valley to meet Tug at the settlement. He rode over a small ridge and on top stopped to get an idea of the lay of the land. As he started to ride away, he heard a shot higher up the ridge. It was followed by more gunfire. It sounded like both pistol and rifle fire. Logan headed up the ridge using all the cover he could find to keep out of sight. The gunfire was getting louder when he spotted a smoke from a shot coming from behind some rocks across the draw. He dismounted and moved out where he could see better. He spotted a downed horse lying along the trail leading down into the valley. He recognized the horse as the one Tug had been riding. Logan had pulled the old Sharps when he dismounted so he moved out along the ridge to try to see where Tug was. He could hear pistol fire coming from trees just below him, then he spotted Tug. There was fire coming from three different gunmen with rifles shooting at Tug. Logan could see their horses being held by another man. Logan found a good rest and was glad he had the Sharps because these fellows were across the canyon. He pulled down, and when he fired, he saw the man knocked backwards. When he turned, he found another rifleman looking up his way. He fired at him before the man could move. He also went over backwards so Logan knew he had two hits. As he turned to find the third shooter, a bullet cut through the brush above him. The man holding the horses was now shooting up toward him. He figured the man had not spotted him; he was just shooting at the smoke from the old Sharps. Logan pulled down and fired. The man dropped. The horses the man had been holding broke away and headed down the trail toward the valley. The other gunman broke into view trying to head them off when Logan heard another shot and the man fell holding his leg. Logan looked down and could see Tug on a high run toward the downed man. Logan waited until Tug made it to the downed man before he headed back to get his horse. When he rode up, the downed man was yelling about his wounded leg. Tug was ignoring him.

Tug looked over at Logan. "Boy, was I glad to hear that old big bore."

Logan went to check on the other three men and found them all dead. Looking back at Tug, Logan motioned, "I'm going after the horses." He found them all eating grass along the creek

When Logan rode up to where Tug was, he tied a rag around the wounded leg of the fellow he had shot. Tug was mumbling, "I should just let the leg rot off for what they done to my horse. I hate people that shoot horses. That was a fine little horse to die from a bullet.

Logan helped Tug get his saddle off the dead horse. He unsaddled one of the shooter's horses and put his saddle on it. They were trying to figure out how to load the three bodies on the remaining horses when they heard a wagon coming down the road. A couple young kids were in the wagon along with a lady dressed in men's clothes. The woman was driving the wagon. She stopped short of where Logan and Tug stood. Logan walked over to the wagon, "We're rangers. I'm McTier and that other fellow is Tug Higgins. Would you consider helping us? We need to haul these three dead men to Clover?"

She looked over where Tug was helping the wounded man to stand up. "Where's the bodies?" Logan motioned over to the rocks.

"Four men tried to ambush Tug and now three of them are dead."

Tug pulled out a twenty dollar gold piece. "We'll pay you twenty dollars if you'll help us haul these men to town."

The woman looked back at the boys in the wagon. "You boys help these fellows load those bodies."

They rode into town with the wagon following them. Tug was leading the horse with the wounded man.

Logan figured they would let the wounded man ride the wagon but Tug had said, "No way. He shot my horse, so let him suffer."

The marshall was standing in front of his office when they turned down Main Street. Tug stopped, "We've got a prisoner for you and there's three bodies in the wagon."

By this time a crowd was forming and Lenny motioned to the lady driving the wagon to follow him. Logan took the prisoner into the jail and put him in a front cell. Tug had followed the wagon and helped unload the bodies at the undertaker's.

Tug walked over to the wagon. "Thanks for the use of the wagon. I owe you this," he handed her the twenty dollar gold piece.

She smiled, "I can really use this money."

As she drove away, Lenny looked at Tug. "That was big money to that lady. She's raising those two boys by herself on a small place up the valley."

When they got to the jail, Logan had a pot of coffee heating on the stove. Tug was explaining to Lenny, "I got ambushed by those four and they shot my horse out from under me. Then Logan showed up with his buffalo rifle and got three of them. I shot the prisoner. Do you know any of the dead men or the prisoner in the cell?"

Lenny nodded, "I know one of the dead men; he was a friend of Chip Brown."

About then the doctor walked in. "I heard down the street someone has a bullet wound."

Lenny motioned to the cell.

Tug mumbled, "Don't fix him up too good; he don't deserve it."

The undertaker, Jake, walked in. "Lenny, what do you want done with those bodies."

Tug spoke up, "Bury them and I'll see you get paid by headquarters."

As Jake turned to leave he stopped. "What kind of rifle do you fellows carry? Those bodies have some big holes in them."

Tug laughed, "My partner carries a buffalo gun. I'm glad he did today. He had to do some long shooting to get these fellows."

Lenny joined Tug and Logan for supper. They discussed what had happened since the rangers had arrived. Lenny grinned, "You two really seem to bring out the bad guys in a hurry. I think maybe Brown was the leader of the bunch. I also figure there's a money man involved too."

"I agree. I think Brown was the leader of the men doing the rustling, and like you said, somebody else is calling the shots. Lenny, this is your town. Do you have any ideas about who this person could be?"

Lenny shook his head, "No, I'm trying to think of anyone else Chip was friendly with. I'll keep thinking about this and maybe I'll think of someone I've seen Brown with."

As they started to leave the dining room, the door opened and a man with a badge stepped in.

Tug laughed. "Look what the cat just drug into town."

Logan and Lenny turned to see a man wearing a ranger's badge standing at the door. When he saw them, he started toward them with a grin on his face. He walked up to shake Tug's hand. "I should have known I would find you eating; you're always hungry."

"Logan, Lenny, this is Wes Miller. He's one of the original rangers selected by Bennett and Governor Davis. Wes, this is Logan McTier, my new partner and Lenny Cook. Lenny's the marshall here in Clover."

Wes shook hands and turned to Tug. "I've got new orders for you two. I also brought the appointment papers of Lenny Cook as sheriff of this area."

Tug looked over at Lenny. "Well, I guess that was quick. Congratulations on your appointment."

Wes stayed to eat while Tug and the other two returned to the marshall's office. Tug read the new orders for him and Logan. He handed Lenny his appointment to read. Logan was checking on the prisoner when Wes came back.

Wes looked over at Lenny. "I understand I'll be staying here for a short time to help you get your new operation in gear. Bennett told me to pass on to you the need to have the town council appoint a new marshall. I'm suppose to stay until you can find at least one deputy for now."

Tug brought Wes up to date on what had gone on in the two days since they had arrived. When Tug finished, Wes grinned. "You two have cut down on the population real fast."

Tug nodded, "My new partner seems to draw all the bad people to him."

Logan looked over at Tug. "I wasn't the one caught in a crossfire with my horse shot out from under me."

Wes looked over at Tug. "How come you left that part of the story out?"

Tug grinned, "Well, I've got to agree we've had some fast times since we rode in."

The new sheriff spoke up, "I think they are both guilty of drawing the bad people."

The orders Wes had brought Tug and Logan was that they were moving out back to the capital the next morning. Bennett wanted them back as soon as they could make it. As they rode along the next morning, Tug looked over at Logan. "I guess maybe there's more trouble somewhere else besides Clover."

They made good time and were in the capital two days later. They went to the ranger quarters first to clean up before they headed for George's office.

They were just changing clothes when in walked George. "You two better just put your traveling clothes back on."

He had brought a bottle with him and poured them a drink. He motioned for them to sit down. "We have troubles in more places than we have rangers, so I'm splitting you two up. We have more men signing up, but right now I'll need you two to work alone in different areas. "Tug, I need for you to head down into the breaks around Jewelsburg. We seem to have a nest of rustlers using that area as a base camp. There's a newly appointed sheriff down there but he needs some help getting set up."

He looked over at Tug. "Do you think Logan is ready to be on his own as a ranger?"

Tug nodded, "Logan has his own way of being a lawman. He'll get along alright. I do hate to lose him. He's a good cook. Besides that, he seems to be a good backup when trouble starts."

George looked over at Logan. "You must have really impressed him. He usually don't talk that much."

George went on, "Logan, I'm sending you up to a newly formed mining district in the Rapid River country. You will know some of that country; it's about fifty miles north of Kilgore. I know you spent a season on the winter range above Kilgore and know Jerry Crawford who runs the trading post there."

Logan nodded.

"Jerry's been having trouble with some men in Kilgore. I think they're the same ones who have been causing the trouble with mine shipments. It seems they've made Jerry's trading post their headquarters. This bunch have almost stopped the mines from shipping their gold. There's two big new mines up there and they are mining some real good ore. They both have stamp mills and are trying to ship the gold bars down to the railroad at Mill

City. It's a forty mile trip to Mill City. So far they've lost two shipments in the last month. I sent a man up there two weeks ago, and so far I haven't heard a word from him. His name is Rex Taylor. I think something has already happened to him. Check with Jerry when you ride through Kilgore to see if he's seen him."

George poured another drink. "Boys, I really need for you to get out of here at first light."

Tug looked over at Logan. "Let's charge supper to Bennett here. First we'll have a drink on him at the hotel dining room."

Logan nodded.

As the two of them started to walk out, Tug looked back at George. "You could join us."

George laughed, "Just tell the waiter I'll be over later to pay the bill. I'll see you two at dawn."

Tug ordered two big steaks and all the trimmings for them. When they both pushed back after finishing, Logan looked over at Tug. "I suppose it'll be awhile before we can do this again."

Tug nodded, "Logan, I've really enjoyed working with you. You'll do good as a lawman. I want you to remember when these men finally give up on beating you to the draw, then they'll get you anyway they can."

Logan looked at the gruff talking little law man. "You keep an eye peeled too. With your speed you will also be a target." As they walked back to the ranger headquarters, they both were pretty quiet.

The next morning as Tug and Logan were tying down their bedrolls, George walked up. He handed them both traveling pay vouchers and a hundred dollars in gold. Tug looked at the gold pieces. "Now this is something new, paying in advance."

Logan looked at Tug. "Maybe there is more to these jobs than we've been told."

George shook hands with them both. "All I can say is good luck and do your best. And please keep me posted." Tug, as he mounted, looked over at Logan, just tipped his hat and headed out the gate without looking back.

George, who had been watching all this, looked up at Logan. "I think Tug's really going to miss having you around."

Logan swung up, looking down at George, "I'm going to miss that little bantam rooster too," and headed out and up the trail for Kilgore.

It was getting along toward evening when Logan rode up where he could see the trading post and the town of Kilgore. He could see new additions to the town. Logan made sure his badge was under his vest when he rode up in front of the trading post. When he entered the trading post, Jerry was behind the counter. He looked around while Jerry was busy. He noticed the small bar was gone and most of the tables by the kitchen. When the last customer left the store, Logan walked over to the counter. Jerry started to say something then he recognized Logan.

"By God, Logan, I didn't recognize you when you walked in. You've filled out into a big man." He came around the counter to shake hands. He motioned for Logan to take a seat at the table. "We got two saloons in town so I closed my small bar," Jerry laughed, when he saw Logan looking around. "This way I don't have to put up with drunks and all the fights whiskey usually causes. How have you been and what brings you up here?"

Logan pulled his vest aside so the badge showed. "I'd just as soon not everyone see this badge yet."

Jerry smiled, "You can count on me not to say a word. I'm surprised that my letter has brought a ranger so quickly."

"Have you seen the other ranger they sent up; his name was Rex Taylor?"

"Yes, he passed through here a couple weeks ago."

A customer came in the door and Jerry got up to wait on her. When she left, Jerry came back to the table. "He stopped here one afternoon and told me who he was. When he left here he stopped at the hotel. I figured he stopped there to eat. I just happened to be watching as he rode out, and I noticed two riders come out from behind the saloon and head up the street behind him. I saw them both back in town that night."

Logan nodded and stood up. "I'm going to get a room at the hotel. I'll stop by in the morning before I leave."

Jerry shook his head, "No way are you staying in the hotel. You'll stay here with me and Bayou. You can stay in the same room you stayed in the last time you were here."

Logan grinned, "I was hoping you would say that. I need some of Old Bayou's cooking."

Jerry laughed, "Old Bayou is slowing down with age but he can still cook up a storm."

When Old Bayou saw Logan walk into the kitchen, he walked over to get a better look. Then he grinned, "I better put on another pot."

"I'm surprised you remember me Bayou," Logan responded as the old man shook his hand.

"Logan, he still talks about how much stew you ate that night when you were here with Dave."

Logan turned in early. Jerry looked over at him as he headed for his room. "Breakfast will be at dawn if you want to leave early, Logan."

"I'd like that."

While eating breakfast, Jerry told Logan all he knew about the bunch that was now called Kilgore home. "There's been a few gunfights among themselves. They always have lots of money to spend. There's somewhere around ten men in the group. The leader's name is Payne. I don't know his real first name but most of the men call him Blackie."

Jerry grinned. "Logan, you didn't hear this from me but there are two or three of the teamsters for the freight outfit that are real friendly with Blackie. It's the same freight company that hauls for the mines."

Logan just nodded, "I'd better hit the trail for the mines.'

As Logan started to leave he turned, "Jerry, do you remember the horse Rex was riding?"

"Sure it was a little bay and I noticed it had one white hoof, left front."

As Logan was mounting up, two men with tied down guns rode up and stepped down at the hitch rack. Logan looked over at Jerry. "Thanks for the help. I'll try for a job at the mine."

Jerry had caught on to what Logan was trying to do and went along. Logan hoped to keep the two men from asking Jerry too many questions about him after he left. With a wave Logan rode off up the street. The two men were from the saloon. They motioned to Logan. "What did he want?"

"He was out of supplies and traded me a pistol for some grub and a room last night. He's looking for work. I told him to try the mines."

It seemed to satisfy them and they went on into the store. If they would have looked back, Jerry had a grin on his face. Jerry was thinking, "I owe that young fellow a big favor for being so fast thinking."

As Logan rode along headed for the big mines in the Rapid River area, he kept thinking about Rex Taylor. If those two men Jerry had seen leaving from behind the saloon were following Rex, it was along this same trail. Jerry had seen them ride back in the same night so they did not follow him too many miles. He decided to spend a little time checking over what would be a half day ride from Kilgore. If those two had ambushed Rex, his body would have to be somewhere near here. Logan knew it was too long to find any special tracks but decided to follow any tracks that left the main trail. Logan found where someone had left the trail in some brush and could see broken limbs. As he rode around the brush on the hillside, he found the tracks of a running horse. As he followed the tracks, he could see where the horse had turned and plunged and slid down into a wash in the rocks. The bottom of the wash was too rocky for Logan to follow tracks, but he rode slow looking for any mark showing the horse had stayed in the wash. Ahead he could see where the horse had climbed out of the wash. When he got to the spot, he looked over where the horse had gone up. He decided the horse had lost his rider. Somewhere along this rocky wash the rider must have gotten off. Logan started back up the wash looking for sign. He had traveled about a hundred yards when he noticed a strange pile of rocks he'd missed before. Logan dismounted and then could see where rocks had been moved and piled up. As he got closer he could smell an odor coming from the pile. Logan removed a few rocks and uncovered a boot and leg of a man. As he uncovered the body, he spotted the badge on the vest of the man. He knew then he had found the missing ranger. Logan uncovered more and could see where the man had been shot twice, once in the chest and once in the head. The head shot had been from close range. Logan considered moving the body to higher ground for burial but decided to leave it owing to its condition. Logan took the badge and packet from the shirt pocket. Then he started covering the body back up. He spent most of the afternoon packing rocks and building a wall around the grave. It was in a wash and Logan was afraid high water might wash it out so he built the rock wall to turn the water away from the grave. When he finished, he went up on the bank above the wash and carved in a small tree a cross with Taylor below it and the year.

Logan rode away with a sad heart that this ranger had died without a chance to defend himself. He was ambushed. When he fell from his horse trying to get away down this wash, someone had finished killing him with a bullet to the head. Logan followed the horse tracks where it had left the wash. It was getting too dark for tracking so Logan found a good place to spend the night, with water and good grass. At daylight Logan was off following the tracks, and finally, the horse had found a game trail to follow. From there Logan could not find the tracks. Too many deer and other animals used this trail and hid the horse's tracks. He decided to follow this trail until he could find a good place to get back on the main trail to Rapid River.

Logan found a place he could get back down to the main trail. He had gone a half mile when he smelled wood smoke. Logan kept looking as he moved along and finally spotted smoke coming from the trees across a small meadow. He decided to find out who was camped there and started across the meadow. When he rode up, he found a small cabin with smoke coming from the chimney and a corral back in the trees.

Logan called out and soon heard a woman's voice, "Ride on in. Coffee's on."

As Logan swung down from his horse, a gray haired lady came around the side of the cabin. "Hello, I'm Logan McTier. I was just passing through when I smelled your fire."

"We're the Greys. We're homesteading this meadow. I got a pot of venison stew on the stove. You're sure welcome to a bowl."

"That's an offer I can't turn down." As he loosened the cinch on his saddle, he could hear a horse behind the cabin.

The grey haired lady called out, "Jess, we got company."

A little wiry gray haired man came from around the cabin with a big grin on his face.

"Ma and me don't get very many visitors around here. Come in and sit a spell."

The stew was really good, and Logan did not turn down a second bowl and a couple slices of warm bread.

When they walked back out of the cabin, Jess motioned to follow him. "Come, I'll show you where I've started a barn."

When they walked behind the cabin, Logan noticed a couple horses standing in the corral. As they were looking over the base logs on the barn, Logan noticed the one horse was a bay with a white hoof. When they left the barn, Logan walked over to the corral to look at the horses.

Jess spoke up, "That little bay showed up here one day with the saddle turned and was in bad shape. The reins or what was left of them were dragging and that saddle had been on for many days. When I unsaddled him, there were sores under the saddle. They've healed real good."

Logan walked up to the horse, and when he felt under the mane, he could feel the small ranger brand. He lifted the mane and showed the brand to Jess. "The owner of this horse was a Territorial Ranger." He opened his vest and showed Jess his badge. "I found his body and re-buried it. I've been trying to follow this horse's tracks since yesterday."

Jess nodded, "After the horse showed up, I back tracked him, and I also lost the tracks on the game trail."

"Jess, can I leave the horse for a spell? I'll pay you as long as he's here."

"You sure can. What you gonna do with the saddle and rifle?"

"Do you need a saddle and extra rifle?"

"I sure could use them."

"Okay, you can have them. We'll deduct them from the cost of pasturing the bay."

Old Jess grinned, "Son, you have a deal."

As Logan mounted to leave, he motioned toward the horse. "Use that horse and keep him in shape in case I need him in a hurry."

Logan arrived at the mine on the mountainside that evening. He could see the name Golden Rose Mine on the roof of one building. Logan stopped at the building with "Office" printed above the door. When he walked in, a man behind the desk said with a gruff voice, "Are you looking for work?"

Logan shook his head, "No, I'm not. But I would like to see the boss around here or the owner if he's around."

The fellow walked over to the counter. "The owners of this mine are the Griffith brothers. They're too busy to talk to each saddle bum that passes through here."

Logan pulled back his vest so his badge showed. "I was asked to come up here by your bosses."

The fellow stepped back, "You look awful young to be a lawman. Do you have proof to who you are?"

Logan started to pull his papers from his shirt when a voice from a back office said, "That won't be necessary." An older fellow walked out of the back office and held out his hand. "I'm John Griffith, one of the owners."

"Logan McTier." Logan handed John a letter from George Bennett introducing Logan.

Griffith, after reading the letter, nodded. "I will do it any way you want so long as we stop these robberies."

Logan nodded, "For now, no one needs to know that I'm a ranger. Only you and your man up front know who I am, so there shouldn't be any leaks about me being here." John walked over to where the clerk was standing. "Did you hear what the ranger said?"

The clerk nodded his head and John looked directly at him. "That means no one. Not even Frank."

185

John turned back to face Logan. "Frank's my brother and half owner of this mine."

Logan must have looked puzzled because John added, "I do trust my brother, but with this the less people that know the better."

Logan nodded, "Now I need for you to bring me up to date on the shipments and the robberies."

John motioned for Logan to follow him, and they went into his office. This room was filled with maps and drawing of tunnels of the mine. John went over to a map drawn to show the country from here to Mill City. He had clearly marked the sight of each robbery.

Logan studied the map. "When is your next shipment due to go?"

"We need to get a shipment out soon. Our storage areas are full. I'd figured on a shipment going out Friday morning, but no one knows that but me. I've always started the shipments on Monday, but this time I decided to change it. They'll accept the ore any time in Mill City. I thought maybe leaving Friday I could catch the crooks asleep. I have let everyone think that something is going to happen next Monday. Who knows, it might work."

Logan nodded, "Go on with the shipment on Friday, and I'll try to maybe shake up anyone with ideas of robbing it." Logan went over the route with John and checked on how many guards would be with the wagon.

As Logan started to leave, he turned to John. "Does Frank know about Friday's shipment?"

John shook his head. "No, my brother is back east right now."

Logan shook hands with John. "I'll be with your wagons all the way, not riding with them but close by."

John asked Logan as he started out the door. "How old are you, Logan?"

"Near twenty," and he walked out.

Logan rode out of camp traveling up higher toward the timbered country when he met some wagons with timbers headed down the grade. There was a man on horseback leading the wagons. When he got to where Logan waited in a wide place in the road, he stopped. "Would you mind waiting here until the wagons go by?"

Logan shook his head.

"Would you be looking for work? We need some muckers in the mine."

Logan just grinned. "I stopped by the office. They said they were looking for laborers. To me that's not really what I had in mind for a job."

The man tipped his hat. "We sure could use a big husky lad like you in the mine," as he headed down the trail.

Logan waited until the wagon hauling the timbers passed then he went on up the trail. That night found Logan a few miles back down the wagon road from the mine. Logan figured the outlaws would not try for the wagons this close to the mine. Logan knew he only had tomorrow to try to find a place where the robbers would try their holdup.

As Logan started out the next morning, he left the road and looked for a route where he could ride. He could still see the gold wagons on the road below. As he rode along he found most places where he could travel and continue to see the road. The gold wagons, according to John, always stayed at a big ranch along the route. The owner of the ranch made sure the wagon was safe while on his range with extra cowboys helping guard the wagons. Logan was sure he was on the ranch now because he had seen cattle and a couple riders off in the distance. By starting the wagon three days early, there was a good chance the outlaws would be late in finding out about the shipment. If their headquarters was Kilgore, that would mean they would have to hit the wagon the second day. John had said the wagons stayed the second night at a small army post ten miles from Mill City. From there on in, the army furnished a small patrol to ride along. Logan finally decided he better figure on the wagon being hit the second day, about midday if it did not leak out about the change.

Logan rode back toward the mine a few miles and camped for the night. He decided he would get up early and ride back to meet the wagon somewhere near where he camped last night. Logan was sound asleep when he heard a horse being ridden hard down the road by his camp. It was a clear moonlight night. Logan could see the rider was really making time down the road. Maybe this was the messenger riding to warn the outlaws in Kilgore. Logan figured it was a couple of hours before he could track the rider so he laid back down. He was wide awake, so he got up and stoked up the fire and put on some coffee. After a short breakfast, Logan headed down the road following the rider. Soon as dawn broke, Logan could see the tracks of the running horse real well. Logan knew a horse could not keep up this pace much longer so he figured the rider knew someplace he could trade horses. Logan had not seen any sign of camps or buildings while riding the day before. As Logan rode near a small rocky knoll, he could see where the rider had slowed and left the trail. Logan followed the tracks around the knoll.

187

On the back side he could see a small meadow with green grass, then a cabin came into view. Smoke was coming from the cabin so Logan rode into a dry draw out of sight from the cabin. He pulled his rifle and walked back out where he could observe the cabin. As he scanned the area, he could see a man walking a horse that looked pretty well worn out and could see lather on its neck. The fellow was sacked off the horse to dry him then walked him some more. Logan could see what looked like a trail leaving out the other side of the meadow heading back toward the main road. Logan watched the man water the horse, tie it in the corral and pour grain into a box mounted on a post. Logan decided if these men were part of the outlaws, they treated their stock pretty good. As he continued to watch, the fellow walked back into the cabin. Logan could see by the additional smoke, he had built up the fire. This must mean the fellow was alone and cooking breakfast for himself.

Logan moved back to his horse and mounted and went back out the way he had ridden in. Back on the main road he found where the rider had re-entered the road in a rocky place where tracks did not show unless you were really looking for them. The rider speeded up again and Logan could see he was making time in the direction of Kilgore. The rider would need at least one more change of horses before getting to Kilgore riding at the speed he was traveling. Logan passed the place where the gold wagon would turn off to spend the night at the ranch. Logan by now knew he was following a rider carrying a message to the outlaws. This meant the robbery would have to be tomorrow between the ranch and the army post. Logan kept watching as he traveled along to see where the rider broke off the road to hit the trail to Kilgore. He traveled only about a mile further when he saw where the rider turned off. The rider was not following the main trail so Logan figured this must be a short cut. Logan thought of turning around and going back to look at the main road when he spied a roof in the trees about a half mile ahead. He left the trail and stayed in the scrub trees and moved toward the building. Soon Logan could see three buildings. It looked to be a small horse ranch with corrals. In one corral a couple men were saddling a horse with sack over its head. This could only mean they were breaking a rough string. They were so busy they did not see Logan as he moved again into the trees out of sight. Another man was sacking down another horse. This meant the messenger had traded horses again.

Logan turned back toward the main road. As he crossed a small creek,

188

he rode up a short ways until he was out of sight. Along the creek was good feed. He pulled off his saddle and wiped down his horse with dry grass. He watered him and staked him out to feed while he fixed a little lunch for himself. He decided against building a small fire this close to the main road and settled for jerky with a water chaser. He dozed for a couple hours to let the horse rest before saddling back up. The rest did wonders for both him and the horse. Logan could see dust ahead of him along the road and decided it must be freight wagons headed for the mines. Ahead in the trees Logan could see what looked to be maybe a line camp for the freighters. There were horses in the corrals and a couple men moving around the camp. As Logan rode in he hailed the camp and back came an answer, "Come on in; the coffee's hot."

Two men soon appeared dressed like mule skinners, both with heavy whiskers. Logan pulled a cup from his pack and the one fellow poured it full.

Logan found a log to sit on. "How far is it to the army post and Mill City."

"You can make it on a horse in a half day's ride to the army post."

Logan nodded, "I've been up to the mines looking for work. I just can't see myself as an ore mucker, so I decided mining wasn't for me."

Both of the men laughed, "Neither of us like the idea of being underground, so we aren't interested in mining either."

Logan looked around. "Is this a stop over place for the freight wagons?"

"Yeah, we're paid by the company to maintain a camp here. Down the road below here is the worst part of the road to Mill City from the mine. It's hard on teams with the grade and the rocky road bed, so we keep extra animals here."

"I could see dust coming this way when I rode in."

As Logan looked over the camp, he could see a cabin with a large lean added on one end. "That's the kitchen. You're welcome to eat and spend the night. The cook charges fifty cents per meal."

"I think I'll do that," thinking to himself maybe he could hear something about the robberies.

When the five wagons were unhitched and the animals fed, the teamsters joined Logan around the fire. The meal was good. Logan was glad he decided to stay. "What time do you have breakfast?"

The cook growled, "These teamsters always wanted to be gone just at dawn so I feed early."

189

During the talk that night around the fire, Logan heard nothing much about the robberies. He decided he would scout out this bad part of the road the teamsters had referred to all evening. From their talk it was narrow and steep pulling up one side and was real rocky. One teamster had said the company was letting a contract to widen that part of the road. It was suppose to start in a week or two. The teamsters all turned in early so Logan joined them for a good night's sleep.

Logan rode out while the teamsters were still hooking up. It was just getting light when Logan found where the road started up a canyon; it was very narrow. The grade was only about a half mile long, but he could see why it was hard on teams, both up and down. Logan rode off the trail to where he could see for miles around. Logan decided this would be a good place to stop the gold wagon on either side. They could block the road real easy and the wagon would be going real slow over the rocky surface. If the wagons had left the ranch at dawn, it should reach here about noon or a little after. Logan knew this was a guess but decided to hold up near here and watch the trail coming from Kilgore. Logan tied his horse in a draw down from the top where he found some feed. He unsaddled and decided if he saw riders approaching he would put the saddle back on. Pulling the old Sharps, Logan took some jerky and a canteen from his saddle bag. He headed back to the top of the ridge. About noon he could see what looked like dust in the trail from Kilgore and soon spotted riders. As he watched they stopped below him on the road just below the top on the upgrade. Two men started rolling rocks off the bank into the road and soon had the road blocked. There were five riders. One of the riders took the horses and rode out of sight off the road. Logan could see all five from his perch on the ridge top. Looking across the valley, Logan could see wagons with three riders coming toward the canyon. Logan was grinning to himself and thinking what a surprise this will be to the men below when he starts shooting. The wagons were almost up to the rocks when the men below moved out of sight. The first wagon stopped and the driver stepped down to start moving the rocks. He was joined by the three other riders. The shotgun guard stayed in his seat on the wagon. He was looking around the rocks when four men stepped out with guns leveled. One had moved behind the lead wagon and had the guard covered. Logan could see they disarmed the group then herded them out behind the wagon. Two of the outlaws jumped into the wagon and started uncovering the gold bars. Logan's first shot hit the man holding the company men in the chest. He flew backward against the rocks beside the road. His second shot dropped one of the men in the wagon. Before the third one could move, he was also hit and knocked off the wagon. The fourth man threw up his hands. Logan then looked back towards the man holding the horses. He had his rifle and was trying to get a shot at Logan. Logan aimed dead center, and when he fired, he saw the man dropped. Logan hollered down, "You fellas cover that man; I'll be right down."

The five men with the wagon had retrieved their guns and were tying up the last remaining robber.

When Logan rode up, they all were just looking at him. "How many of you are up there?"

Logan smiled, "Just me. I'm Ranger Logan McTier," then pulled back his vest so they could see his badge. Four of the men started clearing the road while the shotgun guard watched the prisoner.

The guard looked at Logan. "I saw you at the mine the other day. They did not mention you were a ranger."

Logan grinned and walked over to talk to the prisoner. "You want to tell me who the messenger was that rode to tell you about this shipment?"

The man snarled. "You can go to hell, Ranger. I'm not saying anything."

Logan saw the man's eyes go to the men clearing the road. He did not like what he saw. Logan stepped sideways and drew as he moved. Two shots rang out. Bullets hit the rocks where Logan had just moved from. Two of the men clearing the road had guns drawn and were shooting at him. Logan fired two quick shots as he moved sideways. Both men were falling backwards. He glanced at the other men. They were just staring at him. Logan walked over to the two downed men, both were dead.

As he walked back to the prisoner he smiled. "Thanks for the warning." The man just glared at Logan.

The shotgun guard was staring down at Logan. "I've never seen anyone shoot that quick in my life. How did you know they were drawing their guns?"

Logan nodded toward the prisoner. "Their friend there let me know from the look in his eyes when he looked that way."

The driver and the other man had finished clearing the road. They had heard what Logan had told the guard. The old teamster walked up. "Son, you don't look old enough to be a ranger. That shooting wasn't normal either."

191

The other man spoke up. "I worked up in Butte City for a while before coming here. The name McTier rings a bell. A young fellow by that name worked for the Chinese moving gold up in the Placer Butte area. He wiped out the gang working that area. "Would you be that same fellow?"

"I did work up there for a spell."

"When that rifle opened up awhile ago it sounded like a big bore. If you are McTier, I always heard you carry an old Sharps rifle."

Logan smiled, "Would you boys take the prisoner and the bodies to Mill City? Tell the marshall there to notify George Bennett in Capital City. He'll take the prisoner." The driver of the first wagon nodded, "We'll do that for you."

Logan helped get the dead men loaded on their horses. They tied the prisoner in the wagon.

Before they headed out, the old teamster walked over to Logan. "You know we won't make Mill City until tomorrow. I think by then these bodies will be a little on the ripe side with weather this warm."

Logan nodded his head. "I guess you're right. Maybe I'll take them to Kilgore. I can use the same trail they used getting here and be there before dark."

As the wagon headed on down the road toward the army post, Logan, with the bodies in tow, headed for Kilgore. As Logan rode along, he decided to wait until dark to ride into Kilgore. He did not want whoever was the leader of this bunch to know they were dead. If Kilgore was the base for this gang, he needed time to find out who the leader was. Logan found a place close to the trading post but had hidden away in a draw. He left the horses with the bodies still loaded there.

The trading post was dark as he rode up. Logan could see a light coming from the sleeping quarters. He knocked and the door opened a crack, then Jerry opened the door. "You're up kinda late."

"I broke up a robbery over on the road to Mill City. I've got six bodies I need to take care of."

Jerry nodded, "I think maybe it's best if we just bury them and not tell the new town marshall anything about it. He was just appointed to the job, and I really don't trust him for some reason."

"Burying six bodies is going to take a while."

"You know, Logan, I think we can probably solve this by taking the bodies up to old Red Gilbert's place. There's a small grave yard up there where a bunch of settlers died of small pox. Others have been buried there since. Old Red is always needing money. So if the rangers could pay him, I'm sure we can solve this problem."

"I have no problem with the rangers paying for the service."

Bayou had come into the room. "I could lead Logan up to Red's place."

Jerry looked at his old friend. "Can you ride that far?"

Bayou grinned, "I've been wanting to visit Red. I can stay a few days up there and rest up before I ride back." Jerry just nodded at his old cook.

Bayou went back to his room and soon headed for the barn to get a horse.

It was only a two-hour ride up to Red's place. Even in the dark they had made good time. It was just getting light on the horizon when Bayou and Logan rode into the yard. Old Red came out with a rifle under his arm. When he recognized Bayou, he leaned it against the cabin wall.

Bayou laughed, "Red, I brought you some work. This young fella is Ranger Logan McTier and he needs these bodies buried."

"Well, if the money's right I can handle the burial alright."

Bayou spoke up, "I'll help you Red."

Red laughed, "Bayou, you just cook. I'll do the shoveling."

When Logan unloaded the bodies, both Red and Bayou knew them all except the two men that had been with the gold wagon.

Logan gave Red two gold pieces. "Will this cover taking care of the bodies?"

Red chuckled, "At that rate you can bring in all the bodies you want."

"Well, I'm going to find a place to sack out for a spell."

Red motioned toward his cabin. "You're welcome to use my cabin."

Logan shook his head. "I don't want anyone to know me just yet. If anyone asks questions, just say a group of rangers paid you to bury these men."

Logan headed back toward the Mill City road. He spotted a place off the trail where he could hide both himself and the horse. After staking out the horse, Logan rolled out his bedroll and was soon sound asleep.

When Logan woke up, he found it was early afternoon. He fixed a pot of hot coffee and ate some jerky from his saddle bag. Logan and his horse had really needed a little more rest, so he decided he would stay at the wagon camp again. As he rode along the trail back to the main road, he noticed tracks going the same way he was. The rider was moving right along.

Logan wondered if this was the messenger heading back to the mine. Logan rode up to the camp and the same two men were busy packing wood for the cookhouse.

The cook came out. "There's hot coffee and I just took some hot biscuits out of the oven. There won't be any wagons in tonight so we have the camp to ourselves."

"I never turn down hot biscuits. Besides that, if you don't mind, I'd like to stay for supper and spend the night."

After supper the crew told Logan, "A rider traveling to the mines from Mill City told us some ranger had stopped a holdup in the canyon yesterday. We thought we heard shooting once but it was too far off to be sure. According to the rider, he'd talked to the guard at the gate at the army post and he told him about it."

Logan grinned, "Looks like I missed all the fun. I was going to ride with that wagon. Was there another rider by here just before he rode in?"

The cook nodded, "Yeah, I saw a rider out on the road. He was riding pretty hard toward the mines just before you came in. I see riders like that every so often and they aren't very friendly. Most of the time people riding by just stop to get a drink of fresh water and give their horse a rest. These riders never stop and never even wave when they pass."

"How often does the mail stage to the mine go by?

The cook, thought for a minute, "Every other day. It's due early tomorrow morning, heading back to Mill City. We keep a team change here, so they make this an eating stop while we change teams."

"I need to send a letter on that coach."

He decided the less these people knew about him the better, for now. He found writing material in his saddle bag and wrote George Bennett a note about what was going on. He also reported the death of fellow ranger, Rex Taylor, and where he had re-buried him.

The next morning Logan waited for the stage to appear to send his letter, then headed back for the mines. He rode past the place where the rider first changed horses when coming from the mine. The horse ahead of him had a cracked shoe so it had been easy to follow the tracks. Then Logan saw where it had left the road. He rode real easy down toward the small cabin and corral. When it was in sight, Logan was surprised to see a saddled horse standing near the cabin door. There was a couple other horses in the small corral so Logan decided the wrangler had company. He tied up his horse and walked from tree to tree as he approached the cabin. When he noticed the cabin only had one window, he stayed on the other side away from the window as he moved closer. He could hear two men inside talking. It sounded like they were eating. He could hear the clink of dishes or cups. He worked his way near the window and stayed low hoping he could hear what they were saying. The window was open a crack so Logan could hear pretty good. Logan heard the one fellow say, "I'd better get back before I miss my shift and the boss gets mad."

Another voice asked, "Did you ever hear how come they moved the gold early?"

"I really don't know. Jess just told me to get a horse and get to Kilgore and warn Blackie. Jess picked me to ride because it's my shift change over and I had two days off."

Logan heard a chair move and heard the one say, "I wish I knew what our take was this time. The crew will be back in Kilgore sometime tomorrow from the cache, then we'll know what our share is. Blackie said he would send word with Charlie on the mail coach."

Logan moved back out of sight but stayed where he could see the fellow as he mounted his horse. Logan waited until the sound of the horse going up the trail was gone before he moved back toward his horse. He decided he would not arrest the fellow in the cabin right now. The less people that knew he was a ranger the better for right now.

Logan rode into the mine from a different way this time. He dismounted behind the office. John Griffith was alone in the office and the door was locked. When Logan knocked, John lifted the blind to see who was knocking. When he recognized Logan, he opened the door and let him in. He then locked the door behind them.

"Well, did the wagon make it? We haven't heard a word!"

Logan grinned at him. "They were headed toward the army post the last time I saw them." He then told John all about what had happened since he was there last.

John jumped up from his seat. "What do you mean two guards were involved?"

"John, do you have a fella named Jess that works here at the mine?"

John thought for a spell. "We have two men named Jess. But I think one of them has since quit and moved on." He walked over to the desk where the clerk worked and opened a file. "I was right, Jess Cross has moved on."

Logan told him about the conversation he had heard at the cabin.

John nodded, "The other Jess is Jess Owen; he's a shift foreman in the mine. It's true that when the crew changes shifts some have two and a half days off." John paused and then said, "I think we should keep this quiet for a day or two until we're sure who the second man is."

"I'll let you take care of this here; I want to visit the Milford mine."

John nodded, "The owners are Bill Milford and his son, Charley. It's about three miles from here to the Milford."

"I'll see you tomorrow." Logan turned and went out the back door to his horse.

When Logan looked at the Milford operation from across the canyon, it looked to be a big operation. As Logan approached the gate a guard stepped out.

"What do you want?" he growled.

"I'm here to see Bill Milford on business."

"What kind of business?"

"I think that's between Mr. Milford and me."

As the guard started to bring up his rifle barrel, he found himself looking into the big bore of a 44 Colt aimed right at his forehead.

Logan smiled down at the guard. "You and me are going to have an agreement here and now. First off I'm a Territorial Ranger." He pulled back his vest to show the guard the badge. "The second thing is you're the only man that knows that, and you're going to keep your mouth shut about who I am, understood?"

The man was still white as he nodded.

Logan holstered his pistol. "Where do I find the office?"

Logan walked into the office. There were two men working at the counter. One looked up. "What can I do for you?"

"I'd like to talk to Bill Milford if possible." The man turned and walked to a door in back of the room. He knocked and Logan heard a voice telling him to come in.

An older fellow walked back out with the clerk and looked at Logan. "How did you get past the guard at the gate?"

Logan grinned, "I just bribed him a little with a 44 Colt. If you're Bill Milford, I'd like to talk to you alone if possible."

Logan pulled back his vest enough to show his badge.

"I'm Bill Milford; follow me."

They entered the office and he closed the door behind them.

Logan offered his hand. "I'm Ranger Logan McTier."

"I'm glad to meet you, Logan."

Logan handed him the letter from George Bennett. After reading the letter, Bill grinned. "I'm sorry we got off on the wrong foot. To me you look too young to be a lawman."

Logan just grinned, "We all have our bad days."

Logan explained to Bill all about the shipment from the Golden Rose. "I came up here to see you because I figure there's a few spies working here too."

"Do you think you could get another shipment out to Mill City without any trouble?"

Logan thought for a while. "I guess the only way to find out is to try it. You name a date and I'll do the same as last time. I'll shadow the load. Let's try not letting anyone know about the shipment until the night before you head out. I have a way of checking if they have a spy here at your mine too. If a rider heads for Kilgore, we'll know you have a spy here."

Logan then smiled. "My way of knowing, I'll keep to myself for now."

Bill nodded, "That's okay with me. How about we leave the day after tomorrow with the shipment?"

"Sounds good. You won't see me again until after the shipment heads out." As Logan walked out, he noticed the two clerks were watching him. They both headed into Bill Milford's office when he closed the door.

Logan headed back down to the Golden Rose Mine to see if John had heard from his crew with the gold shipment. John had told Logan earlier that a rider usually heads back with word as soon as they reach the army post. Logan was sure the shipment had made it, but he still wanted to make sure. When he got to John's office, Logan noticed a horse tied at the hitch rail. He could tell it had traveled a good distance. As he entered the office, he heard his name called from the back office. Logan recognized the man John was talking to. It was the outrider that had been at the robbery attempt on the road to Mill City. "When the rider saw Logan, a big grin crossed his face. John, this is the fellow I was telling you about."

John introduced Logan to Mel Miller, a long time employee of the mine.

Mel shook Logan's hand. "I've never figured out how you knew those other two guards were drawing their pistols."

"I saw something in the eyes of the prisoner in the road I didn't like." John broke in, "Mel says the shipment made it in to Mill City alright with the army escort."

Mel added, "Those two riders you shot are good friends with a few fellows that worked in the mill. They've been seen with Jess, the shift foreman, and also with one of the muckers in the mine. I've seen all four at one of the cabins down on the line quite often."

After Mel left, Logan told John about Bill Milford shipping gold the day after tomorrow. "I'll ride up and see him tomorrow and offer riders if he needs more."

"Bill's not letting it out about shipping the load until tomorrow night after supper, so don't get up there before he lets out the word," Logan cautioned.

John nodded, "Bill and I get together quite often so me being up there won't be any different than any other visit to those that see us together."

When Logan got up to leave, John asked, "Why don't you come to supper? The wife would be glad to see someone besides me."

"Thanks anyway, but I need to get out of camp here before too many people get the idea of who I am. Where can I pick up some supplies without going to the company store?"

"You make a list. I'll get the supplies for you. Tell me where you'll be and I'll bring your supplies to you."

Logan camped along a trail not too far from the main road near a spring that evening. He had only been there about an hour when he heard a rider coming up the trail from the main road. He stepped back into the trees until he saw it was Mel Miller bringing the supplies.

Mel grinned as he stepped down. "The boss thought it better if I was seen leaving camp instead of him. Besides, he wanted to get up and see Bill at the Milford anyway."

"Coffee's hot if you'd like a cup," Logan motioned toward the fire.

"Sounds good. I'd just as soon get back after dark; maybe I won't be noticed."

Mel handed Logan a bag of supplies. "John said his wife added a few things to your list."

When Logan opened the bag, he grinned at Mel. "You might as well sit down and help me eat all the extra food; it's already cooked." John's wife had really sent out enough to feed an army plus the supplies Logan ordered.

Mel and Logan finished eating. After cleaning up, Mel headed over to his horse.

"I'd better head back to the mine. Thanks for sharing the grub."

"Mel, how well do you know this country? Do you know who owns the horse ranch on the trail to Kilgore?"

Mel shook his head. "I only know there's a ranch over there, but I don't know much about it."

"I played poker with a couple of the wranglers from there one night at the relay camp. I noticed another camp just off the main road between here and the relay camp. Do you know anything about it, or who owns it?" Logan asked.

"For a newcomer you sure must get around. You're finding all these places that are hard to find."

Logan grinned, "It's all part of the job."

Mel thought for a minute. "I think the cabin you are referring to belongs to Jess, the foreman at the mine. He built that place last year before he went to work at the mine. I believe his brother stays there and takes care of the place. Anyway, I heard the guy is a relative of Jess's."

Mel then looked at Logan, "I believe you know more about this gang than you let on. I've got many more questions about why you're interested in those two places. But I think it's best I don't know."

Logan grinned. "Have a safe ride back to the mine."

After Mel had rode off, Logan finished the coffee and decided to grab a little shut eye. If his plan worked, he should hear a rider sometime after dark headed for Kilgore. They may have a different meeting point each time but it would be somewhere close to Kilgore or the horse ranch. Logan figured they would try for this shipment and maybe move their contact point closer to the road. Last time they really had to hurry to get set up for the holdup. By moving the crew closer to the Mill City road, they could pick out a better place to stop the wagon. This was only a hunch. Logan figured he'd better be ready to follow the rider headed for Kilgore. If the rider turned off before the relay camp, then he would know the gang was close by. Logan figured he was about two miles from the cabin. He would let the rider change horses then try to follow him in the dark.

Logan had dozed off for about two hours. He woke and saddled his horse and packed up his supplies. If Bill had waited until supper time to notify the wagon crew, he should see a rider in about an hour. Logan figured he was about ten miles from the mine or maybe a little further. Logan had moved down the road toward the cabin, moving along really slow so he could hear a running horse. He pulled off the trail about a half mile from the cabin. He had just dismounted when he heard a horse coming down the road. The rider was making good time and acted like he knew the trail real well, even in the dark. Logan followed and could see where the rider had dropped off the road onto the trail to the cabin. He rode on down to where the trail from the cabin re-entered the road and waited.

Soon Logan was surprised when two riders came up onto the main road and headed down the road together. Logan began to wonder why there were two riders now. As he waited there, he started to wonder if maybe they were going to set up an ambush for him. Logan waited so they would get a little head start before he followed. As he started to mount, he heard another horse coming down the road from the mines. He pulled his horse back into the brush and watched as the rider hurried by. As the rider rode by, Logan recognized Mel Miller and wondered what he had to do with all this. Logan mounted and followed down the road. It was beginning to break dawn and he could see further down the road. As Logan rode into a rocky part of the road, he heard a shot coming from around the next bend. The area alongside the road was real rough country with big boulders and a few trees on the hillside. As Logan rounded the corner, he spotted a body laying in the road up ahead. A horse with reins dragging was standing close by. As Logan looked over the area before riding closer, he heard a horse coming down through the road above the road. He spotted a rider working his way down toward the man laying in the road. As the rider got closer to the body, Logan saw him lift his rifle to shoot the body again. Logan had his rifle in the boot with no time to pull it before the man would shoot. Logan drew and sent three quick shots at the man on the horse. It was a long shot for a pistol. The horse jumped and started bucking just as the man shot at the body. Logan heard the bullet hit the rocks on the hillside above the body. The shooter dropped his rifle as he fought to stay on the bucking horse. Logan kicked his horse into a run, and as he got closer, the horse quit bucking and the rider spurred it up the road. Logan slid to a halt pulling his rifle and swung down. He kneeled and shot the man from the running horse. He remounted and rode up where the man had fallen from the horse. The man was alive when Logan rolled him over. His first words were, "Who in the hell are you?"

Logan could see his shot had hit the man high in the shoulder. He would live. He took the man's pistol and searched for more guns. He walked over to the horse the fellow had been riding and grabbed the reins, mounted his horse and headed back down the road to the other man.

Logan swung down next to the man in the road. When he rolled him, he recognized Mel. Logan opened his shirt that was covered with blood and found a hole in his side. Logan felt on the back and found where the bullet had come out. Logan dug through his saddlebag and found the cloth his food had been wrapped in. He wrapped it around Mel's wound and tied it tight.

"Where did you come from? asked Mel. I was riding to find you when I got shot." "Bill Milford has his loaded wagon coming down from the mine right now." When Bill saw the rider heading out right after he announced the shipment, he decided to move out then with the gold wagon.

"Mel, can you ride if I help you mount up?

"I'm not hurting that bad from the bullet, but I'm still dizzy from this knot on my head."

Logan looked at his head. "You must have hit the road head first. You were knocked out for a good spell. You sit there for awhile. I'm going back to get the guy who shot you."

When Logan got back to the gunman, he was holding a rag in the wound to stop the bleeding. Logan dug through the saddlebag on the man's horse. He found a shirt and used it to finish plugging the hole in his shoulder. He pulled the man to his feet and led him over to his horse. As Logan pushed him up into the saddle, he noticed the notch in the cantle of the saddle. There was a fresh wound on the rump of the horse. Logan smiled. He figured that one of his bullets had hit the saddle then burned the horse across the rump causing it to buck.

The trip had been easy for the gold wagon, and, so far, no trouble. Logan had loaded his prisoner on the ore wagon. Then he left Mel at the relay station to catch a freight wagon going to the mine. Logan borrowed a horse from the camp and followed the wagon. When they got to the army post, Logan tied his prisoner on his horse and headed for Mill City. After leaving his prisoner at the jail in Mill City, Logan headed for the telegraph office to wire Bennett at headquarters. With orders from George to leave the prisoner at the jail, Logan went back to talk to the town marshall.

With this all taken care of, Logan headed for the freight yard to leave the horse for the night.  He introduced himself and told them he was riding one of their horses.  The manager told Logan he would take care of the horse. Logan asked for a good place to stay for the night and the old fellow motioned up the stairs.

"Grab yourself a room that's empty and make yourself at home."

As Logan started up the stairs the old fellow added, "The teamsters eat at the café just around the corner." Logan nodded.  After a good supper, Logan retired to his room for a good night's sleep.

The next morning Logan took the same horse and headed back up to the relay station to get his horse.  He was just a few miles out of Mill City when he met the ore wagon with the army escort.

Logan was just about to the Kilgore Trail when he noticed a cloud of dust on the ridge.  He rode off into the timber along the road.  He tied his horse and walked back where he could see the trail from Kilgore.  The cause of the dust was eight riders coming down the trail at a good clip.  They stopped when they got to the main road.  Logan could see them studying the tracks in the road.  One rider headed toward the relay station.  The rest moved off the trail.  As Logan watched, he could see them starting a fire. He knew then he was stuck there until they moved.

He walked back to his horse and loosened the cinch and dug out some jerky to chew on.  Logan waited about an hour then heard a horse coming from the direction of the relay station. It was the same rider that had ridden out earlier.  He stopped at the trail head and then saw the others ride up to their camp.  By all the cussing, Logan could figure from the group by the fire that they weren't too happy about missing the ore wagon.  They mounted and headed back up the trail toward Kilgore.  Logan waited until they were out of sight before he mounted and headed to the relay camp.

As Logan rode into the camp, he noticed a wagon just pulling in from the direction of the mines.  When he rode up, he saw John Griffith swing down from the seat next to the driver.  When John saw Logan, he walked over as Logan stepped down from his horse.  He held out his hand.  "I guess with you being here it means the ore wagon made it."

Logan told him about the events up to now.  "Mel's here and needs to get to a doctor.  He was shot from ambush back up the road this morning."

John nodded, "I'll take him back to the mine with me.  We have a doctor there. He takes care of both mines."

Logan and John walked into the kitchen.  They found Mel nursing a cup of coffee. He still didn't have much color. He grinned, "I'm feeling better. One of the cooks cleaned my wound and put on a new bandage."

"Mel, as soon as I discuss with Logan our next move in getting all the men connected to the robberies arrested, we'll head back to the mine."

Logan told John about the rider that had been on the road soon after getting notice of the shipment and rode to warn the gang. Logan told John about the cabin used by the gang as a relay station. "The man who lives there ambushed Mel."

"Mel thinks the man at the cabin is kin to Jess, the foreman for your mine. I discussed with Bill about Jess being involved after the shipment from your mine. Now we know both mines have men belonging to this same gang. When Bill Milford gets back from Mill City, the three of us should start weeding out the gang members."

Logan spent the night at the relay station. After breakfast, he headed back toward the mines. As he came to the trail leading to the cabin where the gang had changed horses, he stopped and looked for fresh tracks. Logan rode up the trail toward the cabin. He dismounted before the cabin came into view. He tied his horse off the trail where anyone riding in wouldn't see it. He pulled the old Sharps and started through the trees staying hidden from the cabin. As he got closer, he could smell smoke. When he could finally see the cabin, he saw smoke coming from the chimney. As he moved closer, he noticed two horses in the small corral. The saddles were on the top rail of the fence. Logan circled around the cabin checking for any other horses tied in the trees. Finding none, he moved over closer to the cabin. As Logan got next to the wall of the cabin, he heard the horses in the corral making noise like they were in trouble. The door to the cabin was around the corner from where Logan was leaning against the cabin wall. The door flew open and two men came out with guns drawn. They headed for the corrals. About then Logan heard a bear roar and heard two shots. All kinds of commotion could be heard. Logan moved around behind the cabin where he could see the corrals. About then the horses broke down the gate and took off.

A big bear was chasing both men as they climbed up onto the roof of a small lean-to next to the corral. Both men shot again into the bear. It was still trying to climb onto the roof where they were. Both men fired again and the bear fell over on its back. It was trying to get back up when they shot the beast again. The big bear quit moving and the two men climbed down from the building.

Neither man heard Logan as he walked up behind them. They had started reloading their pistols when Logan, in a quiet voice, said, "You two, real easy like just drop those pistols."

Both men spun around. With the loading gate open on their pistols, they could do nothing but drop their guns. Logan motioned for them to step back. He kicked their guns into the lean-to. The way they were dressed Logan figured they both were miners. Logan grabbed a rope off the corral fence and tossed it to the nearest man to him. "Tie up your friend."

The two started to argue. Logan cocked the old Sharps and pointed it at the man's mid section. The sight of the bore on that rifle ended the argument, and the man started tying up his friend. Logan watched as the man worked. "If he gets loose, I'll shoot you and let your friend go."

When the fellow finished tying up his partner, Logan tied him up. After checking both men, Logan headed back to get his horse.

When he got back, the two men were trying to get to a chopping block near the cabin.

Logan had tied their feet to the corral. Logan threw a rope on the bear and wrapped it around his saddle horn and mounted a very nervous horse. It was all his horse could do as he pulled the bear away from the corrals into the trees. He rode out into a small meadow to get the two horses feeding on the far side.

When he returned to the corral, both horses were pulling back. They could still smell the dead bear. He finally calmed them and saddled them. He loaded his two prisoners into their saddles. Logan checked over the cabin. He drank a fresh cup of coffee from the pot on the stove before closing it up.

When Logan, with his two prisoners, rode out on the main road, he could see fresh wagon tracks going toward the mine. As he rounded the first curve, Logan could see the wagon ahead of them. He recognized John sitting alongside the driver. As Logan caught up with them, John turned to see Logan leading two horses. Logan explained, "I found these two at the cabin."

"Do you want to load the prisoners in the wagon?" asked John.

Logan shook his head, "They're fine where they are."

Mel, who had been laying in the back of the wagon on some grain sacks, called to Logan. He asked, "How about I trade with one of the prisoners? This wagon's too slow and it's rough riding."

John laughed, "Until you see a doctor, Mel, you're not riding a horse."

John told Logan, "When you get to the mine, see the cook and tell him to use the new cellar to keep the prisoners. The building is still empty and it'll make a good jail for now."

Logan nodded, "I'll wait until you get to the mine before I start checking on any other gang members working there."

When Logan finished locking up the two prisoners, he headed for John's office to wait for him. The clerk who had tried to give Logan a bad time the first time he entered this office, now was real quiet. Logan had put his horse in the barn out back and had carried his saddlebags into the office with him. He went into a back room and dug out of his bags some gun oil and a rag and started cleaning his guns.

The clerk walked back and motioned to the stove, "The coffee in the pot is fresh if you want some."

Logan nodded and poured himself a cup and sat back down to finish cleaning his guns. As he was finishing his task, he heard a wagon pull up out front. John walked in, followed by Mel, who was still saying he didn't need to see the doctor. John told the clerk to get the doctor and bring him to the office. Soon an older fellow walked in carrying a bag, and John filled him in on what had happened to Mel. He started checking over Mel.

Logan and John moved into John's office. John asked, "How soon do you want to go round up Jess and his cronies?

"I've changed my mind about waiting for Bill Milford. I wanted to get Jess now before he gets word about the prisoners."

The doctor came in about then with Mel a step behind him.

The doctor told John, "I think Mel should rest for a few days. He's still a little dizzy when he moves too fast. The bullet wound, I redressed and it looks good."

John nodded, "Mel will check with you again tomorrow at your office." With that the doctor walked out.

John told Mel, "You go get some rest and check with me tomorrow."

"I'm alright but I do have a headache," Mel growled as he walked out.

After Mel left, Logan asked, "Where do I find this club or dive where Jess and his cronies hang out?"

John said, "Follow me and we'll go down there."

Logan noticed John was still wearing his pistol. As they neared the saloon, Logan could hear all the noise coming from inside. He figured there was a big crowd inside. Logan stopped at the window and looked in. To his surprise, all the noise was coming from a group sitting at the table in the back. There were six men sitting down and one standing at the bar. Logan asked John, "Which one is Jess?"

"The one standing at the bar." Logan told John to stay outside and John shook his head.

"He's my employee. If he's to blame for all these robberies, I want to face him with you."

Logan glanced over at him. "Okay, but step away from me when we get inside."

Logan moved his badge to the outside of his vest and walked in to the smoke filled room. No one noticed him until the bartender nudged Jess and nodded toward the door. Jess turned to the group at the table, "Boys, we've got company," and turned to face Logan and John.

Jess looked at John. "What can I do for you Boss Man? Why the lawman?"

Logan said, "I would like to talk to you about the gold shipments being robbed." Logan was watching both Jess and the men at the table. When he saw one man at the table reach under the table, he drew and fired. Jess also pulled his pistol. Logan shot him and turned back to the table. Two men were leveling their guns when Logan sent two fast shots their way. He heard the bullet from the one man hit John, who was just getting his gun out. The one who fired the shot was back against the wall with blood coming from his shoulder. He tried to level his pistol for another shot when Logan shot him. The other man was sprawled across the table, and the other three men just stood there. Logan's second gun appeared in his left hand.

"You three step out away from the table."

They raised their hands and Logan told them to drop the gun belts. As Logan started to look over at John, he spotted the bartender pulling a scatter gun from under the bar.

Logan yelled, "Drop it!"

The bartender kept swinging the gun for a shot when Logan shot him. The shotgun blast hit the ceiling as the bartender slumped to the floor behind the bar.

John was holding his leg when Logan looked over at him. He grinned, "I guess I wasn't much help."

The door swung open. Mel stepped inside with a rifle in his hands.

"Mel, watch these three while I tend to John's wound."

More people were crowding into the bar. Logan saw the doctor was one of them.

"Doc, will you look at John's leg?"

Logan walked over to look at the other men. Jess was dead with a bullet through the heart. Two of the men at the table were dead but the one sprawled on the table was still breathing. Logan walked behind the bar and found the bartender still alive. As Logan leaned down to see how bad he was hit, the fellow whispered, "I should have remembered your gun speed from when you were in Placer Butte." He went limp and Logan knew he was dead. Logan wondered where the man had seen him in Placer Butte.

The doctor had finished binding up John's leg. "The bullet didn't hit any bone but John will limp for a spell." A couple of mine workers offered to help him back to his quarters. Logan and Mel took the three men down to the cellar to lock them up with the rest.

"We'll need someone to watch this place now with five men locked up," said Logan.

Mel nodded. "I'll watch the door."

"We'll need more than one man. Why don't you go get two more men."

The cellar had two rooms. Logan decided he would fix a locking bar on the door of one room and the guards could stay in the outer room. When Mel returned, Logan put them to work installing a bar across the door. One man from the three just brought in kept saying he had nothing to do with any robberies and that he just worked the same shift as the rest. Logan told him, "I'll look into it, but until then you'll spend the night here."

When the door was finished, Logan posted one guard. "Mel, it's up to you to see he's relieved at midnight. Then the other guard will be relieved at sunup."

The one man Mel had brought spoke up, "I'll do the midnight shift."

Mel told Logan he would take the morning shift. As they turned to leave, Logan took a board laying on the floor. He turned to the guard, "Brace this board against the door after we leave and don't let anyone in except the three standing there now."

As they walked away, Logan asked Mel, "How's your head?"

Mel grinned, "With all that's been going on, I hadn't felt any sign of a headache."

Logan nodded, "You two get some rest and I'll see you come morning."

Logan walked over to John's house. The doctor was just leaving. "I just gave John something to make him sleep. I waited until it took effect; John is sound asleep."

Logan turned back and headed for the office and decided he would sleep on the bunk in the back room. As Logan started up the steps, he heard the doctor say, "Do you want to eat before going to bed?" The doctor motioned to follow him.

"The cookhouse is open twenty-four hours a day because the crews work two ten-hour shifts." As he and the doctor were finishing a good meal, the doctor asked, "Logan, how old are you?"

Logan grinned, "Twenty or close to it."

"I've heard stories about a Logan McTier up in the Placer Butte area. They say he's a mean gun fighter. Are you any kin?"

"I spent a short time up in the Butte country."

The doctor looked at Logan, then with a grin said, "I guess I heard wrong."

When Logan got back to the office, he looked at the clock on the wall. It was eleven p.m. As he sat on the bunk, he started thinking about the one fellow Mel had brought to help guard the place who wanted the midnight shift. Logan checked his guns and took his coat from the gear on the floor and slipped out the back door. He worked his way down through the buildings and found a place under a woodshed roof where he could see the door to the cellar. He didn't wait long before he heard footsteps coming toward the cellar. Soon he saw the fellow who had asked for the midnight shift knock on the door. When the door opened, he stepped in and the other guard came out and headed up the path toward the bunkhouse. Logan waited until he was out of sight and then he moved down closer to the cellar.

He could hear men talking. He heard the one say, "We'll meet at the cabin come morning." About then the door opened real slow and the guard stepped out to look around. Logan moved over where he could see in the cabin and drew both guns. Two more men stepped out. They both were holding pistols. "The guard must have come well armed," Logan thought to himself. When all three started to move out, Logan's voice broke the night, "Drop the guns." Two men with pistols in their hands spun to shoot as two shots rang out. Both men fired into the ground as they fell. The guard dashed for the corner of the building as he drew his pistol. Before he gained the corner of the building, Logan fired and the man fell against the building.

Logan ran up alongside the building to the door. He called into the building, "You fellas come out one at a time with your hands in the air." As they appeared, Logan moved over to where the downed guard was moaning and kicked his gun under the building. Logan stepped up to the fellow who earlier said he had nothing to do with the robberies.

"Are there any more guns around in there?"

The man started to motion to the fellow next to him when that fellow's hand dropped. Logan hit him with a gun barrel alongside the head. Men were pouring down the path from the bunkhouse with Mel in the lead. Logan rolled the man he had hit over and found a pistol in his belt.

"Mel, lock up those two standing against the wall."

Logan walked over to the guard who was rolling around holding his legs. Logan rolled him over to look at his wounds. He felt someone kneeling by him. The doctor said, "I'll take care of this."

The man Logan had clubbed was beginning to stir. Logan jerked him to his feet and drug him inside. Mel looked at Logan, "Do we lock him up too?"

"Tie him in that chair."

After Logan had checked over the two dead men, they were packed off to the doctor's office along with the guard who had been shot.

"He's been hit in both legs. One bullet broke the bone in his right leg and missed the bone in his left but left a big hole in the flesh," Doc told Logan.

"I'll spend the rest of the night with the prisoners," Mel added as he picked up his rifle. Logan headed back for the office.

Logan was up early and went down to see if Mel had survived the short night. Logan opened the interior door and told the two prisoners to step out. He told the man who kept claiming he had no part of the robberies to go back to work.

"If your story don't pan out, I''ll be looking for you."

As he turned to leave he said, "I think the other man is just a friend of Jess's crew and wasn't involved in the robberies." Logan looked over at the other fellow.

"That's true. I work on the shift where Jess is the foreman."

Logan told him to head out with the other man. Logan untied the fellow from the chair where he tied him last night , then put him in the room and closed the door. He turned to Mel, "See he gets fed sometime this morning."

When Logan got back to the office, John was sitting at his desk with his wounded leg resting on a chair. He grinned at Logan, "If you stay much longer, I won't have a crew left." He added, "But at least I'll have the gold we mine."

Logan was getting ready to head up to the Milford Mine when he heard a wagon pull up out front. When he looked out, Bill Milford was climbing down from the wagon seat. Dismounting behind the wagon were two men with badges shining in the morning sun. The two lawmen were George Bennett, his boss, and his old partner, Tug. After Logan filled them in on all that happened previous night, Tug laughed, "How come you get all the easy assignments?"

Logan suggested they get up to the Milford Mine and see if they could find any of the gang. When they got to the Milford Mine they were met by Bill's son, Charlie, who told them four men had ridden out real fast the night before leaving all their gear and pay checks. Bill wanted to know who they were. After Charlie told him, he just shook his head. Bill motioned for the three lawmen to find a seat after they entered the office.

"Those four men have worked here ever since I started the mine. One of them was lead man on the framing crew. One was a powder monkey. The other two were two of the best drillers in the mine. They all four drew top money. I don't understand this at all."

"This whole group has been people who were trusted by the mine owners. Bill, do you know the stagecoach driver named Charlie?"

"Everyone knows Charlie. Why are you asking?"

"I overheard a conversation at the horse ranch saying they would send word through Charlie on the stage."

Bill looked at his son, Charlie. "Isn't the stage due here at the mine about noon?"

"It usually rolls in a little before noon," Charlie answered.

George Bennett nodded, "Tug, you meet the stage when it comes in. Nobody knows you're here yet. Keep your badge under your vest when you meet the stage."

It was almost two o'clock before the stage arrived, and the first thing the Milfords noticed was Charlie wasn't driving the coach. Bill Milford walked out with Tug to meet the stage, "Where's Charlie?"

The driver stepped down to face Bill. "Charlie didn't show up for work yesterday. That's the first time he has missed work since the stage started making this run."

The three lawmen looked at one another and George said, "I guess they got word to him about Logan rounding up the men at the mine." George decided he and Tug would take the prisoners and head back to Mill City in the morning.

As they rode back down to the Golden Rose Mine, Logan told George he would like to ride with them as far as the cut off to Kilgore.

"I want to see if Blackie Payne is still around Kilgore. I figure the whole bunch has left by now, but I want to make sure."

When they arrived at the mine, John met them.

"Doc wants to see you, Logan, about the wounded prisoner." They all three walked down to the doctor's office.

"I don't think you'll have to worry about getting this one back to Mill City. He's lost a lot of blood and I don't give him much chance of making it till morning. That leg will have to come off for him to live and he wouldn't last through the operation," Doc told the three lawmen.

Logan nodded, "I'll check with you later."

John put the three lawmen in a cabin up behind the office for the night. They ate in the cookhouse. After eating they stopped by the doctor's office on their way back to the cabin. When they walked in, the doctor was putting on his coat.

"I was just getting ready to go find you fellas. The prisoner died about a half hour ago."

The next morning the three lawmen headed for Mill City with one prisoner. When they got to the relay station, they ate.

Logan told George, "I'm going to leave you two here and head for Kilgore."

George nodded, "Let me know what happens in Kilgore."

As Logan neared the horse ranch, he left the main trail and circled around behind the cabin. The corrals were empty and the cabin door was open with no sign of life around. When Logan looked in the cabin, it looked like they had just pulled out and left everything. The stove still had a coffee pot and some pots with spoiled food in them. Logan threw all the food out back, pots and all. He figured no sense ruining a good cabin with that mess. As he started to leave, he could hear what sounded like a wagon coming through the trees. He moved out of sight. Soon a wagon came in sight with a man and woman in the seat. Logan stayed out of sight, and when the wagon stopped, he heard the woman saying this must be the place. They walked up to the cabin and went in. When they went inside, Logan walked around to where he could see them in the cabin. The man saw him first and nudged the woman who stepped behind the man. The fellow then noticed the badge.

"Are you really a lawman? You look awful young?"

Logan held out his hand, "I'm Ranger Logan McTier. Do you folks own this place?"

"We just bought this place sight unseen from a man in Kilgore."

Logan asked, "What was this man's name?"

"Blackie Payne. "He told us we could get a wagon to the place. We've been four days clearing a road to get here."

Logan laughed, "I think there was a reason Blackie didn't tell you where the wagon road was. If you'll look out back, you'll find a road going down the ridge. There's an old wagon frame back there. Blackie Payne has been using this place as a front for a gang of men robbing gold shipments. You may have men stopping by for awhile who don't know it's changed ownership, so be a little careful." Logan shook hands and said he would stop by again.

Logan followed the tracks where the couple had cleared a path wide enough for the wagon. As he rode along, he couldn't believe the work those people had done to get the wagon through. Blackie must have wanted time to get his crew out before the new owner arrived.

Logan rode up in front of the trading post. The place was doing a good business. When he walked in, he could see Jerry Crawford working behind the counter. There were two other clerks working. Logan walked back toward the kitchen to get out of the way. Jerry noticed him and motioned to go on in the living quarters. When Logan stepped into the kitchen, he was met by his old friend, Bayou.

Bayou grinned, "I suppose you're hungry for Bayou's cooking?"

Logan, remembering Bayou's cooking, laughed, "Bayou, I can eat your cooking anytime, and I'm hungry." Logan was just finishing a second bowl of stew and more hot biscuits than any one man should ever eat at one time when Jerry walked in. They shook hands.

Jerry grinned, "You're getting to be a famous man that no one knows. That crowd out there knows all about you breaking up the gang. Yet not a one of them knows you by sight."

"Why the big crowd out front?"

Jerry laughed, "It seems Blackie was involved in a lot more than running a gang of thieves. He owned the big store uptown and the hotel, besides the saloon we knew he owned. He closed up everything one night and was gone by morning. I'm the only store in town right now and I can hardly keep up. The supply freighters found the store closed, so I was able to buy their loads. I heard a fellow showed up last night who said he had bought the store, but so far I haven't seen him."

"I need to get back out front. Are you going to spend the night with us?

Logan nodded, "I need to get some answers to a few questions from you later. I want to go uptown and look over things. I'll be back before dark." Jerry looked back from the door.

"Do you want people to know who you are when you walk around town?"

"I guess it's about time I let people know that the law is in town."

Logan put his horse in Jerry's barn then headed uptown to look things over. He noticed the stares when people saw his badge. He stopped in front of the closed up store when the door opened and the fellow stepped out.

Logan introduced himself and the man said, "I'm Jeff Milner, the new owner of this store."

"Did you buy the store from Blackie Payne?"

"Yes, I only met the man once and that was in Mill City. I stopped in Mill City to see if I could find some business to buy. I took a room in the hotel and later was sitting in on a small poker game in the bar when I met Blackie. I asked the group of card players if they knew of any businesses in the area for sale. Blackie was one of the players, and he said he had this store in Kilgore that he wanted to sell. Later that night Blackie came to my room with the deed and told me what he wanted for the store. When I started asking questions about why he was selling, Blackie said he needed the money quick and he needed to be gone by morning. When I left the card game earlier in the evening, I asked the hotel clerk where this town of Kilgore was and how big it was. When I asked about the store, the clerk told me it was almost new, and when he was there it was the only store in town. He added there was a small trading post that handled supplies but the store was the main supply house in town. So when Blackie came to my room, I had decided I would take a chance and buy it sight unseen."

Logan thanked him for the information and headed on down the street.

Logan noticed more people were watching every move he made. He walked past the hotel and the big saloon next door and the sign on both said "Closed." Further down the street he found another smaller saloon and decided he would have a beer. There was a table of card players and one man at the bar besides the bartender when Logan walked in. He walked to the bar and ordered a beer. When the bartender brought it, he asked, "Are you this McTier we've been hearing about?"

"My name is Logan McTier."

The bartender grinned, "This beer is on the house."

The bartender continue to grin at Logan. "I keep hearing the fast gun Territorial Ranger is just a kid, but I didn't believed it till now."

The group at the card table had quit playing cards and were listening to the conversation between Logan and the bartender. One of them asked if Blackie Payne was one of the gang members.

Logan nodded, "It seems he was the leader of the bunch."

The lone man at the bar turned toward Logan, "I think maybe you're wrong about Blackie."

Logan looked at the man closer and could see the tied down holster. "How do you figure that?" The fellow didn't answer he just turned back to his drink on the bar. Logan thanked the bartender for the beer and turned to leave.

The fellow at the bar snarled, "I don't think you're as fast as they say."

Logan turned and drew his left gun and fired as the other man's pistol cleared the holster. A bullet dug a groove in the floor in front of Logan. The gunman slowly slumped against the bar and then fell to the floor. Everyone in the room was standing by this time staring at Logan. The bartender walked around and rolled the fellow over and looked at Logan. "You hit him dead center."

Logan walked over to the fellow, "Do any of you know this fellow's name?"

One of the card players said, "I think he was hired by Blackie but everyone was gone before he got here. He's been asking questions about Blackie. He seemed mad when he found out Blackie had lit out a few days ago."

The bartender looked over at Logan, "I'll get a hold of the undertaker to come and get the body."

"Where can I find the local marshall?"

"Oh, he left when Blackie did," added one of the card players. "They haven't appointed another one yet."

Logan waited until the undertaker arrived. "The territory will pay you to bury him. I'll take the gun and holster." The bartender told Logan the man had a horse and rigging at the livery stable.

"Sell the horse and saddle and put the money in the town marshall's fund," Logan told the group.

As Logan turned to leave, the bartender asked, "How did you know he was drawing?"

Logan shrugged, "I guess I was lucky."

The bartender laughed, "That was the fastest draw I ever seen, and I don't think luck had anything to do with it."

Logan headed back to the trading post. When he got there, the crowd was mostly gone. Jerry was restocking some items. When he saw Logan he asked, "Were you involved in the shots I heard uptown?" Logan told him about the trouble and said what the other men had said about the gunman.

"I think I know the fellow you shot, and I agree with the fellows in the saloon. He came here to work for Blackie."

Logan spent the night and the next morning deciding there was nothing here to help him find Blackie and his gang.

"I'm going to ride up to the line shack where I spent the winter. From there I'll go over the pass and stop by the ranch on my way to headquarters in Capital City," he told his old friend, Jerry.

As Logan worked his way up the valley toward the Rafter T winter cabin, his thoughts went to what had happened in his life since that winter. It seemed like years since he spent his first time on his own and the last days of Claire Matthews life. As he looked back, he wondered to himself what changes Claire Matthew's influence had made on his life. As he topped the small ridge, he could see the cabin. There was smoke coming from the chimney. As he rode in, he noticed all the horses were carrying Rafter T brands. When he dismounted, a fellow with an apron on opened the door and stepped out with a pan of water he threw over the corral fence. Logan didn't know him. As he stepped back toward the cabin, he said to Logan, "There's hot coffee on the stove."

Logan followed him into the cabin and poured himself a cup of coffee. The fellow was eyeing his badge and asked, "What brings you up in this country?"

"I was headed over the pass to Benton and saw the smoke from the cabin."

The old fellow sat down next to the stove, "They call me Biscuit but I'll answer to most anything."

Logan offered his hand, "I'm Logan McTier."

The old fellow looked him all over, "So you're the fast gunny raised on the Rafter T. You're big like Ted but you look like your mom."

Logan smiled, "Who all is up here from the ranch?"

"There are six counting me up here to put up the hay from the meadow. We'll be done by week's end and head back toward the ranch. You should know Dave Olson and Jerry Miller from when you were home, and the others are just summer help."

Logan finished his coffee and told Biscuit he was going to spend the night, then grinned, "If that's okay with you."

The old fellow went back to cooking without an answer. Logan turned his horse into the corral. As he rounded the barn, he could see a loaded hay wagon coming toward the barn. As the wagon pulled up, Logan recognized Jerry Miller driving the team. When Jerry finally saw Logan, he let out a holler and baled off the wagon and ran over and grabbed him. Jerry stepped back and looked Logan over.

"I don't think I want to try to take you down like I use to. Boy, you must be eating good as big as you are now. Where did you ride in from?" About then the second wagon appeared and down jumped Dave Olson with a grin from ear to ear. As he shook Logan's hand, he looked over at Jerry.

"I do believe our boy has grown up." Logan and the crew had a good visit that night after supper. Dave looked over at Logan, "Did you know your old buddy, Dave Bowman the mountain man, died last month?"

Logan shook his head. "I'm really going to miss the old fellow; he was like a second dad to me."

The next morning Logan headed over the pass toward the Rafter T. He looked forward to seeing his folks. Riding down past the old cabin where old Dave had lived for so many years, Logan could see it was still being used. There was a fresh wood supply under the porch roof and new poles on the corral. There was no sign of smoke from the chimney so Logan didn't ride over closer. As he rode into the valley, he could see the only home he ever knew. The big hay stacks were all along the edge of Sheep Creek which wound its way across valley. There were trees along the creek which worked as a wind break during the winter and close to water for the cattle. As Logan was riding toward the buildings, he heard a horse running behind him. He turned to look. The horse was one of the two he had gotten from Matthews. The rider with hair flying was a girl. As she got closer, Logan knew it had to be his tomboy sister, Rebecca. She came sliding to a stop laughing.

"I knew that was you when I saw you coming down into the valley." She leaned over to kiss her big brother on the cheek, "I hope you don't mind me riding one of your prize horses." "Mom put me in charge of these two horses and told me to keep them in top shape like you would want them."

Logan nodded, "Well, keep up the good work. This one looks in prime shape."

"They don't like to work cattle but pull a rifle from the scabbard and they know what to do." Logan nodded. "That's the life they had with Claire Matthews. They probably saved his life a few times."

As they neared the buildings, Rebecca asked more questions than Logan had time to answer. One question that got Logan's attention was if he knew Laura Benton was getting married. Rebecca was off on other subjects before Logan could ask more about Laura. As they rode into the yard near the house, Lottie was already coming down the steps. Logan swung down, and before he could say anything, his mother was hugging him.

Lottie stepped back and looked at her oldest son. "You look older and I don't like that."

Lottie looked over at her oldest daughter. "Where were you when you found your brother?"

Rebecca grinned at her mother. "I'm on my way. See you tonight Big Brother."

Lottie just shook her head, "I'm glad she isn't a boy or I'd have two wild ones in this family."

Logan spent the afternoon around the ranch with his mother about two steps behind him. When he told her she asked more questions than Rebecca, she went stomping off toward the house. Logan could see she had a grin on her face. That evening they caught up on each other's lives since Logan had last been here. Ted and Logan spent some time going over the books and talking about the ranch. Logan was happy the way Ted was upgrading the cattle and thinning out the older cattle. Logan asked who was staying up at Dave's old cabin on the mountain.

"A trapper and his wife rented it for the winter. We were having some problems with cats and wolves last spring so I hired this fellow to thin them out. When he saw Dave's cabin he asked if he could rent it to trap the high country this winter."

Lottie walked in to join them and soon Rebecca also joined them in the office. Lottie told him John and Mary were both going to school in Benton.

When he looked over at Rebecca, "Don't you start on me too about going to school." Logan figured that was one subject he would skip from the look in Rebecca's eyes. When it started getting late Logan asked, "Is anyone using Dave's cabin behind the house. If not, I'll sleep up there."

Ted grinned, "That you can take up with your sister. She's taken it over."

Before Logan could say anything Lottie said, "You're staying upstairs tonight." With that Logan picked up his gear from beside the door and headed upstairs.

After a big breakfast, Logan went out with Ted while he got the crew lined out for the day. He knew most of the crew, and Ted introduced him to a couple of new hands. After the crew left, Logan told his dad he was heading on down to ranger headquarters in Capital City.

Ted nodded, "Could you wait until morning to head out?" then added, "It'd be nice to have you around more than one evening."

"Okay, they're not looking for me at headquarters at any set time. I can stay one more night." He enjoyed the day with his folks and even took a ride with Ted and Rebecca. They went out to look over some yearlings just brought down from the high country. He rode one of the Matthew horses.

That night Rebecca chased her mother from the kitchen and cooked supper for them. As she sat down at the table, she informed her big brother she could also be a lady. Lottie just grinned.

"We should keep your big brother around more often to keep you on the straight and narrow."

"I didn't know you could cook like this," Ted added. Logan couldn't keep from laughing at the look on his sister's face.

After supper Logan helped his sister do the dishes, then they all sat around the living room. Ted was curious about what had happened up at the gold mines above Mill City. Logan left out most the shootings that happened but told them about the gang stealing the gold shipments. When he said that the gang had their headquarters in Kilgore, this brought more questions about whether Jerry Crawford was alright. Logan told them the gang fled the area, and so far the rangers didn't know where they moved to.

218

Logan told his folks that area was his area to patrol so he would probably be back once more before it snows.

They retired early that night. Logan was up at first light and found his mother waiting for him in the kitchen with a pot of coffee.

"Did Rebecca tell you Laura is getting married about Christmas time?"

Logan nodded, "She just mentioned Laura was getting married. Is the new husband the same fellow she was seeing when I was last here?"

Lottie nodded, "I think so."

Logan knew his mother was waiting for him to tell her he had a woman friend. Finally, he told her he hadn't had time to look for a girl.

"You should move back here and start a family." Before Logan could say anything, she added, "I know you can't but I can still dream, can't I?"

After breakfast Logan saddled up, and Rebecca joined him in the barn. She was saddling her horse. As they went back to the house, Lottie came out and handed Rebecca a pile of letters. Logan started to ask what was going on when Ted spoke up, "Rebecca's going in to Benton for the mail." With a big hug from Lottie and a handshake with Ted, the two older kids of the McTier's headed for Benton.

As they rode, Logan found his sister had a serious side, and he was enjoying her company. She told him she had a boyfriend that lived on a horse ranch south of Benton. They had both gone to school in Benton one winter, and so far, they were just good friends. They only saw each other at social events in Benton a couple times a year. Rebecca asked him about the life of a ranger and if he likes it. She also knew a lot about the battle with the gang in Kilgore. She told him she knew he had killed a good bunch of that gang. Logan started to ask how she knew so much but decided if she wanted him to know she would tell him. "Dad knows it's been tough for you up there, but we don't think Mom knows anything more than you told her the other night."

Logan grinned. "Our mother has always known more than we ever suspected." Rebecca nodded. Finally, it come out Rebecca had heard most of the stories from Laura at the store in Benton. Laura always tried to listen in when the sheriff was in the store talking to her father. Then she would tell Rebecca.

They were riding into the outskirts of Benton. Rebecca noticed Logan pulled the loop off the hammer of his holstered pistol and unbuttoned his coat. She shuddered to think her brother had to be ready to protect himself everywhere he went. They rode up to the store, dismounted and entered the store. Ed Benton saw them walk in and rushed over to shake Logan's hand and give Rebecca a hug.

"Rebecca, Laura is at the dressmakers with her mother getting her wedding dress measured."

"Okay, I'll head down there as soon as I get the business done for Mom. If you have room, I'll spend the night with you folks."

Ed said, "You know where your room is. You don't have to ask."

"Well, Sister, I enjoyed the ride in. I'm going to head on down the trail a few more miles before night, and I'll see you the next time around."

As Logan untied his horse, he saw Sheriff Del Rogers motioning to him over to his office. The sheriff had some paper work he needed Logan to look over before he sent it on to ranger headquarters. Logan looked it over, "I'm headed for headquarters; I'll just take it with me."

Logan had just started to mount his horse when he heard Del holler, "Behind you Logan!" Logan dropped away from the horse and drew as he fell. He heard two bullets go by before he heard the shots. He fired as the two men in the street came into view. The first one he hit, fired his pistol into the ground as he fell. The second one was leveling his pistol for another shot when Logan fired the third time. The fellow had fired a split before Logan fired. Logan heard the bullet hit someone behind him. The fellow dropped his pistol and then toppled over. Logan looked back to see Sheriff Rogers crumpling onto the sidewalk. Logan heard another shot behind him and heard glass breaking. He spun around with his gun ready. He then saw a fellow lying on the sidewalk in front of the saloon.

People crowded out into the street. Logan spotted Rebecca standing by her horse with her rifle in her hands. There was a scared look on her face as she looked at the man lying on the sidewalk.

Logan walked back and rolled Del over. Then he saw the bloody pant leg and could see he had been hit in the thigh. It looked like it missed the bone. The doctor ran up and bent over Del. Logan walked over to the two gunmen lying the street. As he rolled them over, he recognized one of them from the Golden Rose Mine. When he rolled the second one over, he knew he had seen him before but couldn't remember where. Logan felt someone grab his arm. He looked up at his sister who was still carrying the rifle. Logan stood up and put his arm around her and grinned, "You're pretty fast getting that rifle out."

"He was going to shoot you in the back as you were turning to help Del. I was just getting ready to mount my horse to ride to the dressmakers when I heard Del holler, 'lookout Logan!' When you fell away from your horse, I thought they had shot you. Then when you fired at them, I knew you were alright. I just happened to look over to the alley beside the saloon and see this man holding three horses. He pulled a rifle from the scabbard and walked onto the sidewalk. When he started to lift the rifle to shoot you, I shot him. The bullet must have went through him and broke the window. Logan, I don't even remember pulling the rifle from the scabbard!"

Logan put his arm around Rebecca, "I guess the name McTier will really be bad around here now." About then Ed Benton walked up.

"Do you know these men?" He turned to look at Logan and added, "I think she just saved your life." Logan just nodded.

The doctor had some men carry Del over to his office and check over the three gunmen who were all dead. The undertaker showed up, and as they started to pack them off, one of the men standing there told Logan he thought he knew one of the men.

"That's Charlie, the stage driver, from Mill City. They always just called him Charlie. I never ever heard his last name."

Now Logan knew all three were part of the gang from Kilgore. Logan took the rifle from Rebecca and walked with her back to her horse in front of the store. He put the rifle back in the scabbard and looked at his sister, "Are you going to be alright?"

About then Laura came running up and took Rebecca in the store with her.

Logan walked over to the doctor's office. Del was lying in bed with his wife by his side.

He grinned at Logan, "It's pretty bad when a girl has to help you while the sheriff gets himself shot."

Logan looked down, "If you hadn't seen them and hollered we might both be dead now."

"I wish I knew what caused all this. Did you happen to know any of them?"

Logan filled him in on who they were. "I don't like the idea they're here around Benton. I hope this was a deal where they were just passing through and just happened to see me. I'm going to check around and see if any other people have seen them around before today. I'll let you know."

As Logan started to leave, the sheriff's wife asked, "Logan, is Rebecca going to be alright?"

Logan nodded, "I think so."

The bartender at the saloon told Logan, "Those three were in the saloon this afternoon when you and your sister rode in. That's the first time I've ever seen them. They said when they first came in they were just passing through and needed some supplies. When they saw you ride by, two of them wanted to get out the back way and ride out. The third one insisted they try to gun you down. The one the girl shot stayed in here so I couldn't get a word out to the sheriff. I've heard about you ever since I bought this place, and I heard you were fast. I always figured these people were just bragging up a local boy. Now I'm a believer."

As Logan walked out, he said over his shoulder, "I was just lucky today," and the bartender just grinned.

Logan went back and told the sheriff he thought it was just a fluke that they were in town when he rode in. Logan walked back to the store. Rebecca was in the back talking to Laura.

Logan sat down, "Sis, are you going to be able to explain this to Mom? If you want, I'll ride back out with you tomorrow."

Rebecca grinned, "I think I better do this myself. If you were there, she would get all over you for letting me get involved. You know Mom, she'll blow her top but she will come around after she thinks it over."

Logan nodded, "How about I take you two out for supper tonight?

The two girls looked at each other then said, "Okay!"

Logan was up early and stopped by to see how the sheriff was doing before stopping at the hotel dining room for breakfast. He had just ordered when he heard Rebecca's voice telling the waiter to bring her the same. After breakfast they both saddled up and with a hug they each headed their separate ways.

When Logan rode into ranger headquarters, he found the place almost deserted. He put his horse away and put his gear in his room then headed for the office. George was working at his desk and motioned for Logan to grab a chair. "Tug's away with a couple new recruits checking out a rustling complaint. The other men are out making rounds on their own areas," George told Logan.

Logan gave his report on the three men shot in Benton. "I think this gang is still together somewhere not too far from here."

George shook his head. "With winter coming on, the mines will be snowed in until spring. I think if this gang's going to do anything more this fall, it'll be before it snows. Maybe you should head back up that way while the weather is still good. Make sure you get out before those roads and trails snow in."

Logan spent the rest of the day resting up and getting cleaned up with some new clothes. He bought a new winter coat. His slicker needed to be replaced, so with that done, he headed back to the bunkhouse. As he walked into the area, he noticed three horses at the hitch rail in front of George's office. The front door of the office was open.

Logan heard a familiar voice, "Are you buying supper?" Logan recognized Tug's voice and saw his old partner hurrying across the yard with a big grin on his face.

As he walked up, he said, "I hear your sister had to save your butt this time."

"George talks too much."

Tug turned to the two men following him leading the horses and introduced them to Logan. Lee Taylor was a younger man a few years older than Logan and Fred Hitt looked to be Tug's age.

Both men looked at Logan and Lee said, "Tug has told us some stories about you."

Logan grinned, "I'll make you boys a deal. You forget what he's told you and I will buy supper."

That evening the four rangers ate at the hotel dining room. Logan kept his promise to buy, then after a drink in the saloon, they headed back to the bunkhouse. Logan filled Tug in about the fight in Benton.

"I think we'll see more of this Blackie Payne. This was a well-organized gang. I think they are just waiting for us to forget them before they strike again."

Logan told Tug about his trip back up to the mines before winter. Tug looked over at his old partner, "Logan, you need to watch your back on this trip. They know they don't stand a chance facing you so they will shoot you from behind if they get a chance."

George joined the four rangers for breakfast. "Logan, I want you to take one of the new men with you on this trip."

"Sounds good; I'd enjoy the company."

George looked over at Fred. "Pack your gear and go with Logan to the mines."

When Fred left to get his gear together, Logan grinned at George, "Are you sending Fred along to watch my back?"

"I've been considering moving you to another area. But right now you're the only one that knows that area and Fred needs some trail experience."

"I think I'll check out the area around Kilgore to see if any of Blackie's men have been around."

Logan and Fred headed up to Mill City, and from there they headed for the mines. The weather was clear but it was cold and the new coat felt good. Freight wagons were heavy along the road stocking the mines with supplies for the long winter. Logan and Fred stopped by the relay station and spent the night. The cook was the same fellow who had been there during the robberies. The other men working there rotated so they were new to Logan. After supper Logan and Fred stayed in the kitchen to talk to the cook. He told Logan there hadn't been many strangers coming by except men going to the mines looking for winter work. He hadn't seen anyone from the bunch from Kilgore, and from what he heard from the teamsters was that trail hadn't been used much lately.

Logan stopped to see John Griffith at the Golden Rose. "We're sending two gold wagons out tomorrow. The Milfords and me are shipping our gold together now since the gang has been broken up."

Logan smiled, "Fred and me will ride shotgun on this trip back as far as the army post." They were still in John's office when Bill Milford walked in. He shook hands with Logan and Logan introduced Fred.

Bill motioned outside, "I've got my wagon out front and I'm going along on this trip. This will be the last shipment until spring."

The next morning the two wagons headed out with four riders plus a guard on each wagon. This made ten riders with the wagons. Logan told them he and Fred would just be around if trouble started. Logan and Fred headed out ahead of the wagons, and Logan dropped down to the cabin the gang had used when they passed that trail. The cabin was closed up and looked like no one had been around for awhile. They rode back up on the trail and on toward the ranch where the wagons would spend the night.

A little after noon Logan spotted a grove of trees above the road and headed up there. He found a place where he could see the road and still keep the horses out of sight. Logan found some real dry wood and built a small fire for coffee. A light breeze was blowing away from the road toward them and on up the hill. Logan made sure the small fire didn't smoke.

"Fred, we'll stay here until the wagons pass."

Fred looked at him kind of funny and Logan grinned. "I find I have better luck stopping these robbers by not following what I've told these people I was going to do. They figure I'm out front, and if they're watching at different places and we don't appear, it ruins their plans for a spell."

Fred nodded, "That makes sense." It was an hour or more before they heard the wagons from the mine coming down the road. At the same time, Logan could hear more wagons coming up the road from Mill City with freight. Logan and Fred had a front row seat as the wagons met right below them on the road. Logan watched as the two groups were talking as they went by. Logan noticed one of the teamsters passed something to one of the men riding alongside the gold wagon. The guard put the whatever he was handed in his pocket and rode on up the road beside the wagon.

Logan motioned to Fred , "You saddle up and I'll put out the fire as soon as the wagons are out of sight."

Logan rode along behind the wagons for a spell before they finally caught up. Mel was riding in the rear when Logan rode up alongside.

"I thought you were out in front?" Mel told Logan as he rode up.

Logan grinned, "That's the idea." Logan motioned to the rider riding beside the rear wagon. "Who's the rider on the bay horse?"

"I don't know his name. He works for the Milford Mine and has for a long time."

Logan turned to Fred, "You stay here with Mel."

Logan rode up alongside the guard who had taken the note from the teamster.

"How's things going today?"

The fellow looked over at Logan. "Just like any other trip with the ore wagons."

"What was in the note you got back there from the teamster?" Logan asked in a very low tone.

Before the fellow could answer, Logan reached over and pulled the note from his coat pocket. The guard's right hand darted for his pistol. Before his hand hit the grip, he found Logan's pistol against his chest. Mel and Fred, who had been watching all of this, rode up alongside.

"Fred, watch him while I read this note."

225

The note had 'feather ridge' printed on it. Logan handed the note to Mel, "Is there a place along the road called Feather Ridge?"

Mel nodded, "It's about a mile south of the road going down to the ranch buildings where we'll stay tonight."

"Tie up the guard and put him in back of the front ore wagon," Logan told Mel. Logan rode up and told Bill what had happened. Bill shook his head.

"Jed's been with me almost from the start. I can't believe he would be involved in this." Logan handed Bill the note.

"Maybe this has nothing to do with a robbery, but until I find out, he stays tied up. How long will it take to get to the road to the ranch."

Bill thought for a moment, "About another two hours at the pace we're traveling now." Logan rode back to where Mel was bringing up the rear to talk to him. Logan found out there was another two freight wagons right behind the gold wagons coming from the mines.

Mel added, "Jim Stewart and his son are independent freighters and they only have the two wagons. The main freighting company don't give them too much trouble because they mainly haul mining machinery. They also haul most of the dynamite used at the mines, which is something most freight outfits hate to haul."

"Mel, do you think they can be trusted hauling the gold ore?"

"They're good men and they can be trusted. Why are you asking?"

"I just have an idea. Mel, ride back and see how far they're behind us."

It didn't seem long when Mel was back. "They're only about a mile behind us."

Logan nodded. "Ride up and tell Bill we need to fake a problem with one wagon until the Stewarts catch up."

Logan rode back to visit with the Stewarts. He introduced himself.

Jim grinned, "Hell, everybody knows about you. I'm glad to finally meet you."

"Would you consider hauling the ore in those two wagons to Mill City?" Logan asked. After explaining what he had in mind, both Jim and his son grinned, "You bet we'll do it."

When they caught up with the stopped ore wagons, Logan told Bill he wanted the ore transferred to Stewart's wagons. As they were transferring the loads, Logan finally saw why it took two wagons. The gold bars were in iron chests, but there was also many sacks of silver concentrates. When they talked of the gold shipments, Logan had always wondered why it took two wagons. He didn't know about the silver ore bags. When they finished, Logan took the Stewarts off to the side. "Will you take the prisoner with you and turn him over to the army at the post? Tell them I'll pick him up later."

"We'll take him, no problem."

The Stewarts headed on down the road. Logan rode over to where Bill was watching the Stewart's wagons. "I hope this idea of yours works."

"Me too. Now we need to find a place to load some rocks onto these wagons. We need these empty wagons to look loaded. Then you can go on to the ranch for the night and act as if they still had the gold aboard." As Bill started to walk away, Logan added, "Fred and I will meet you in the morning at the forks of the road." Logan moved off after the Stewart wagons and found out they didn't use the relay station as a stopover. It was company owned.

Jim said, "They charge too much for a night's stopover. I stop at the ranch on the west side of the road as you cross the first creek on the other side of the summit. The place belongs to my sister and her husband. He breaks and trains horses for the army post. It's about a mile off this main road. The gold will be safe there as long as nobody saw us loading it." Logan nodded. As they neared the Kilgore cutoff, Logan could see dust coming down the hill on the trail. Soon he made it out; it was a small Calvary patrol. Logan and Fred waited for the patrol to hit the road when Logan hailed them. The leader of the patrol was Captain Kock. When Logan introduced himself, the captain grinned.

"I have orders to watch for you and to be of any assistance you might need."

Logan grinned back. "You couldn't have showed up at a better time. Captain, would you escort the Stewart wagons and the prisoner onto the fort. If you can, do not let on the wagons that are loaded with gold."

When he told the captain about the Stewarts staying the night at the ranch, the captain nodded. "Staying at the Cline ranch is no problem. I'm to pick up two horses there, so I had figured on spending the night anyway." With all that taken care of, Logan and Fred headed back up the road.

Logan and Fred spent the night hidden in a grove of trees not far from the junction of the main road and the road to the ranch. Logan made a point to look over what was called Feather Ridge hoping that he was not being seen. At dawn they ate biscuits and jerky chased with hot coffee. Just before sunrise, Logan saw the wagons moving along the road below. He sent Fred down to tell Bill and Mel to travel along like normal. When Fred returned, they moved up the ridge above the road. Fred was the first to smell wood smoke. Then they could see it coming from a stand of trees along the creek below. Logan moved out on foot where he could look into the canyon better. As he moved out, he could see below into a deserted camp. Logan motioned for Fred to bring the horses, and they started on down the hill to the camp. The camp had held maybe six men but had been vacant for a couple of hours. They had left the camp in a hurry because the fire was still burning and part of their breakfast was still by the fire. As they looked over the tracks where the horses had been, Fred noticed where a rider had come in from the ridge at a fast pace. The tracks went out the same way they had come in.

Logan looked over at Fred, "I think they were warned about us being around and called off the robbery." Logan mounted up and worked along following the tracks as they headed out away from the road. He sent Fred to tell Bill and Mel what they had found. Logan followed the tracks until he was sure they weren't turning back toward the road, then he headed back down to the wagons. Bill and Mel had stopped along the road and had a fire built and a coffee pot on waiting for Logan to show up.

Bill took Logan aside, "I've got a list of supplies I need to bring back from Mill City. If you don't care, I'll unload the wagons and send them on in."

"Go ahead," said Logan. They all helped unload the rocks and the wagons headed out for Mill City. Bill sent the guards back to the mines with a note to let John know what had happened.

Everyone had left except Mel and Bill and the two rangers. "Bill, I think there's still at least one gang member working at the mine. How else did they send word from the ranch about the empty wagons? I think I'll wait here and pick up the teamster that passed the note when they stop at the relay station. They should be back down here sometime tonight and Fred and I can get a good meal while we're waiting."

Bill just shook his head, "During the winter, John and I will work on finding the leak at the mines. It won't be long before we're snowed in for the winter. We should be safe until spring."

Logan nodded, "The gang will probably leave this area and look for other places to rob until spring."

Bill and Mel left for Mill City, and the rangers rode with them as far as the relay station. That evening the freight wagons from the mines pulled into the station. Logan finally picked out the driver that had passed the note but decided to wait till morning to arrest him. After supper the rangers retired to the tent with the bunks they were assigned. With just the one freight train in camp, Logan and Fred had the tent to themselves.

When breakfast was over, Logan went out to where the teamsters were hooking up. Logan walked up behind the fellow as he was hitching up his teams. "I don't suppose you'll tell me who told you to pass the note to the guard of the gold wagon." The fellow spun around as his hand dropped toward the gun in his waistband. He was too late. He saw the gun in Logan's hand already pointing at his mid section.

"I don't know what you're talking about."

Logan pulled the gun from his waistband. The leader of the freight train walked over and asked what was going on. Logan showed his badge and told him about the driver passing the note to one of the guard.

The company man said, "This driver has driven for us almost all summer. He's a good hand."

"I'll take him to Mill City and try to find out his involvement with the gang. If it turns out he's only a messenger, I'll turn him loose when he tells me where or from who he got the note," Logan informed the boss.

Logan had borrowed a spare horse from the relay camp for his prisoner. He told them he'd leave it in the Mill City freight yard. He and Fred stopped by the army post and picked up the other prisoner and rode into Mill City. Logan wired ranger headquarters and George sent back word to bring the two prisoners to Capital City.

Logan found where the Stewart's corrals were in Mill City and paid them a visit. He had them fill out a pay voucher for hauling the load of gold to Mill City.

They both laughed, "Your prisoner offered us big money to let him go."

"Did he mention anything about where his friends were?"

"After he found out we weren't going to let him go, he didn't say another word."

Logan thanked them again for the help and headed back up town.

When Logan arrived at ranger headquarters, he had two quiet prisoners when they saw the size of the jail. George told the two rangers over a cup of coffee, "I think we're making a big dent in the size of Blackie Payne's gang."

Logan shook his head, "It's hard to tell with spies still working at the mines. This is maybe a larger gang than we think."

Fred headed back to the rangers' bunkhouse while Logan wrote his report. When he laid it down on George's desk, he added, "Fred is a good partner and will make a good ranger."

That night after supper, they were sitting around in a B- S-ing session when Tug asked Fred, "How many men did Logan shoot this trip?"

Fred shrugged, "It was a dry run, but I still can't believe how fast that gun can appear. A couple times when Logan drew his gun to arrest one of the prisoners, it just appeared in his hand."

Logan grinned, "Fred's just pulling your legs with these stories. He's been around Tug too much."

Logan spent the next three weeks around ranger headquarters before heading back up to Kilgore. The high country had been hit pretty hard by snow storms so Logan figured the mines were snowed in. Logan had thought about trying to get back to the ranch for Christmas, but with the snow in the high country, he would have to take the long way around. So he spent the holiday with Tug and a few other single rangers at headquarters. George had the group over to his house for dinner. This really made Logan think of home.

Logan rode into Kilgore and spent the next few days looking over the area. He made it back to Jerry's place every night but was hoping to find a base camp used by Blackie during his scouting trips. Jerry had told him about all the places he knew with buildings. Logan found most of them occupied by homesteaders. He rode out to spend the night with the couple that bought the horse ranch from Blackie and found them all settled in. They were still laughing about making a road to the ranch when there was already a perfectly good road over the ridge that Blackie hadn't told them about. Logan rode over to where he had buried Rex Taylor and fixed up the rock work on the grave. Later, he rode over to visit the Greys and to see if they still had Rex's horse. As he crossed the meadow, he couldn't help notice another barn and one other out building. He pulled up to the cabin, and Mrs. Grey stepped out with a rifle in her hands. Then she recognized Logan and lowered the barrel toward the ground. Logan stepped down, and about then Jess came walking around the house also carrying a rifle.

Logan asked, "Why all the guns?"

"We've been having some real bad men around this fall. It seems they've been hiding out from the law around the mines on Rapid River."

"What sort of problems?" Logan asked.

Jess shook his head, "No one has tried to harm us, but they're always snooping around. When they saw that ranger's horse, a couple of them got a little nasty. They wanted to know where I got the horse. I told them it belonged to the Territorial Rangers, and I was just holding it for them. The one fellow, I think was the leader, came over and made me tell the story again of how I got the horse. He asked if I knew you real well, and I told him I only seen you once. As he mounted to leave he told me, 'If I have my way, you won't never see that ranger again'."

Mrs. Grey spoke up, "We can talk while we eat."

As they ate, Jess went on with his story, "We haven't seen those fellows for about a month or more. We've had a couple fellows ride in and ask if we know of a camp nearby, and when we say no, they ride off. I might just know where the camp is, but I make sure not to go near the place."

Logan took Rex's horse with him and headed back to Kilgore. "Jess, I'll probably be back in a few days."

When he got back to Kilgore, he found Tug and Fred waiting for him. George had sent them over to see what Logan had found. With the high country snowed in, many of the rangers had their areas closed by snow. With extra help around headquarters, George was doubling up on areas that were open. Logan and Tug decided to go back up and see if they could find the old camp used by Blackie last summer. Tug told Fred to ride back and report to George and then come back if George didn't need him.

"Fred, why don't you take Rex Taylor's horse back to headquarters with you?"

After Fred left the next morning, Tug and Logan packed a few extra supplies and headed back up toward the Grey place. Logan took Tug over to where he'd buried Rex. It was better that more people knew about the grave and where it was located. Logan remembered seeing a miner's cabin not too far from the grave when he was following Rex's horse. With a little back tracking, they finally found the cabin. It was in good condition and vacant. There was some grass still along the creek bank for the horses so Logan and Tug decided to use this as their base camp.

The second day they finally found some buildings hidden in a grove of trees. There were some fresh tracks around but the camp was empty. Logan and Tug had left their horses in the trees and walked up behind the cabins.

Logan didn't want to leave any tracks around in case there were people still using the area. The biggest cabin had wood in the wood box and cupboards filled with supplies. Tug suggested they leave everything as it was and check back in a few days. As they rode away, Logan stayed off the main trail. That night back at the miner's cabin, they decided they would check every so often on the hideaway for a week or so. The weather turned for the worst so the two rangers headed back to Kilgore for more supplies.

It rained almost steady for the next two weeks while Logan and Tug stayed in Kilgore. Fred returned from headquarters and told them George's orders were to stick to this area. With the mountains snowed in, things were quiet in the territory. They weren't needed anywhere else. Finally, the weather broke, and the three rangers, with an extra pack horse of supplies, headed back to the miner's cabin. The second day they headed for the camp they had found earlier. They circled around and came in from the back side. From a small ridge, they could observe the buildings below. There were four horses in the corral and smoke coming from two of the cabins. As they watched, two men came out the bigger cabin and headed for the corral. They led the horses out into a small opening. The dead grass from last summer was still standing and looked to be good feed. They staked the horses out and headed back for the cabin. Logan noticed the one fellow was carrying a rifle. He was kinda looking over the camp as he walked back to the cabin.

Tug nudged Logan, "Do you think this was some of the Blackie Payne gang?" Logan nodded. They decided to work their way down and cover the cabin from three sides. They were about to move when Fred motioned up the trail. Three riders were moving toward the cabin. The three rangers stayed where they were. The riders pulled up in front of the cabin, and Logan noticed they had a pack horse with them.

"With that much supplies, they must figure on staying here for awhile," Logan whispered to the other two. The man Logan had seen earlier with the rifle came around from behind the second cabin. He stood behind the three which had just ridden in. Logan decided these fellows were ready for trouble and there must be a back door to the cabin.

Tug nudged Logan, "I don't remember a back door on that cabin." Logan nodded and motioned for the two to follow him back over the ridge. Once out of sight of the cabin, Logan stopped.

"Maybe we should just watch for a while before trying to take these men."

"I want to move around where I can see the back of that cabin." As Tug moved off, Logan and Fred moved back up where they could watch the cabins. They had unpacked the pack horse and moved the supplies into the main cabin.

As the morning passed, the door finally opened, and the three who had ridden in, came out and mounted their horses. Two men were standing in the doorway talking to the other three. With a wave, they rode back up the trail.

Logan caught Tug's attention and motioned him back over the ridge. Logan and Fred mounted their horses and led Tug's over to where he was waiting. When they were well away from the cabin, Logan pulled to a stop. "Let's go get the three who just rode away. Or at least find out where they come from. The four men at the cabin are going to be there for awhile so why not leave them for later."

Logan remembered the trail the three men had taken so he and the rangers took a short cut over the ridge. When they got to the trail again, they could see they were ahead of them. After waiting for a spell, Tug looked over at Logan.

"I think our three riders have taken a different trail."

The three rangers moved back up the trail. About a half mile up the trail, they found where the riders had turned off on another well-hidden trail. After all the rain, their tracks were easy to follow. As they moved along, Logan figured out they were heading back toward Kilgore. It was evening when they saw the three riders crossing a hay meadow leading up to some ranch buildings. They watched the riders pull up at the barn and lead their horses inside. Logan motioned to follow him, and they circled around the hay meadow staying out of sight of the buildings. As they moved up on the buildings, the three men came out of the barn and headed for the house. As they watched, another fellow came out of the barn carrying two pails.

Logan whispered to Tug, "This must be a working ranch and that guy's been in the barn milking."

They moved closer. Logan moved up where he could see in the window. All he could see was a woman cooking at the stove. She was setting the table. He counted six places. As he watched, the three men came in and sat at the table along with the man who had been in the barn. A girl of maybe ten or so also walked in and sat at the table. When the woman cooking took her place, that made the six places. Logan moved back and told the others what he had seen inside the house.

"Tug, you go in the back door. I'll go in the kitchen door. Fred, you wait until we're inside then come in the front door." Tug worked his way in the back door. Logan eased up to the kitchen door and tried the latch; it moved freely. He waited until he figured Tug was in place, and he opened the door and stepped in. He had both guns drawn, and when he stepped in, everyone at the table started to rise. A voice behind them said, "Just sit back down real easy like," as Tug walked into the room. About the same time, Fred walked in from the living room. Logan moved up behind the three men they had followed.

"You three stand up." Logan retrieved their guns. He motioned for them to move over away from the table. Tug moved up behind the other man and searched him but found no weapons.

The woman asked, "Who are you? Why are you in my house?"

Tug pulled back his coat to show his badge. "We're territorial rangers and we've been following these three."

Logan looked over at Fred, "Find something to tie these three up. After they were tied, hands and feet, Logan left them in the dining room.

"Fred, stay in here and watch them."

Tug was still in the kitchen talking to the people at the table. Tug looked over at Logan. "One of those men is this lady's brother. They're paying these people board to stay here for the winter. I don't think they are aware of what these men were doing."

Logan had holstered his guns and motioned for Tug to put his away. "Where's the bunkhouse? Do you have other hands working here?"

"The three in the other room have been helping me feed the stock, so I don't need any other hands," said the man at the table.

"Tug, what do you think of spending the night here and ride for Kilgore in the morning? I know it's only a two-hour ride, but I'd rather travel in the daylight with prisoners." Tug nodded.

The woman fixed them breakfast. Logan turned the prisoners loose to eat after everyone else was done. Logan was looking out the window when the lady set a plate of food on the table. He turned as the fellow sitting next to her pulled a gun from under her apron. Logan drew and fired in one motion as the fellow brought the gun level. The pistol went off and the bullet dug into the ceiling. The impact of Logan's bullet knocked the gunman over. When he fell, he knocked the woman down. The other two men at the table just stared at Logan. Tug dashed into the room with his gun drawn. Fred, standing by the stove, spun around drawing as he turned. The woman turned the man over that Logan had shot and screamed, "He's dead!" Then she started crying.

Logan told her to go stand by her husband as he checked over the downed gunman. He looked at the woman, "Is this your brother?" She nodded. "Why did you try to sneak him a gun?"

"He promised me he wouldn't kill anyone. He just wanted to get away."

Fred had the horses at the house by the time Logan and Tug had the prisoners and the body ready for travel. Logan turned to the couple, "For now we're not going to arrest you. If I find you helping more of this gang, we'll be back."

The woman looked up at Logan, "What are you going to do with my brother's body?" Logan looked over at Tug, "Do you have a problem if we leave him here for her to bury?"

The woman reached for the horse's reins of the one that carried her brother's body and turned to face Logan. She said, "Thank you," and led the horse away.

As they rode away, Tug said, "I really don't think they were involved other than helping her brother." Logan agreed.

As they rode along, one prisoner asked Logan if his name was McTier. Logan nodded. The man shook his head, "I've heard you were fast but nothing like what I saw back there."

Tug looked over at Fred, "You sure are quiet today."

Fred shook his head, "I'm a great lawman. I didn't even get my gun out until it was all over."

Tug laughed, "Fred, don't feel bad, most men that travel with Logan think the same thing."

Fred looked at Tug and smiled and shook his head.

When they got into Kilgore, they locked up their prisoners in the new jail. They went over to see Jerry at the trading post. "Jerry, if you get a chance, will you check out the prisoners to see if you recognize them?" Logan asked his old friend.

"I'll stop by after I close for the night."

The jail was empty except for the two prisoners so the rangers decided to bunk in the spare cells. Later, Jerry stopped by and, over a cup of coffee, looked the two prisoners over. When he left, Logan and Tug walked out with him. "I've seen them both at the hotel here when Blackie owned the place."

Tug decided he would take the prisoners back to headquarters and leave Fred to help Logan. Logan helped Tug get his prisoners ready to travel, then he and Fred headed back to the miner's cabin. The next morning they headed for the hidden camp. They hid their horses and made their way up on the ridge to watch the cabin. There was smoke coming from the cabin so the rangers figured they were just eating breakfast. The horses were still in the corral and Logan figure someone would be moving them out to the grass along the creek before long. Logan told Fred to stay on the ridge. He moved down closer to the creek where they had staked their horses. Logan moved into the willows along the creek when he heard the door open. One of the men stepped out pulling on a coat. He heard him say to someone in the cabin, "We should take turns doing this." Logan heard someone laugh in the cabin and the door closed.

As the man led the horses to the creek, he passed close to Logan. He was still grumbling to himself about being out with the horses. Logan moved over next to one of the horses and worked his way up behind the fellow without being seen or heard. He pulled his pistol, and with a sharp blow to the head, knocked the man down. Logan grabbed the halter ropes of the horses and led them up the creek and tied them up. He walked back to the downed gunman. He lifted him on to his shoulder and headed up the hill to where Fred was. After tying him up, Logan went back down and moved the horses up the ridge into a small draw with some grass showing. He spaced them out so they could feed then moved back to where Fred was watching the cabin. "You wait until I get behind the cabins before you move down closer," Logan told Fred.

Logan moved over behind the cabin and looked for a door or some other way the man used while they watched last time. Logan could see Fred moving closer to the cabin. Fred motioned to Logan he was in place at the same time the cabin door opened. One of the men stepped out and hollered out, "Kid, what's taking you so long? Did you fall in the creek?"

Logan heard Fred call out, "You, stand still and raise your hands." The man drove back into the door when Fred fired. From the sound Logan figured Fred had hit him. As Logan watched, a door pushed up in the leaves behind the cabin and out came the same rifleman. As the man started to move around the cabin, Logan called to him, "Just stand where you are, and drop the rifle."

In one fluid motion the man spun and leveled his rifle. Logan had already had the old Sharps trained on the man's chest. When he pulled the trigger, the man was slammed into the building and slowly slid down onto the ground. Logan could hear Fred firing out front as he worked his way to the cabin. Logan lifted the hidden door and could hear the two men inside talking to one another as they fired out the window and door. Logan, between the shots, called into the cabin from the cellar door.

"Your friend out back here is dead; drop your weapons and move out the door. If you don't, I'll set the cabin afire and burn you out."

Logan hollered to Fred to watch the door as the men came out. Logan walked around the cabin as the two men came out. He stayed at the corner.

"Keep your hands where I can see them." One had blood on his shirt and pants. The way he was walking Logan didn't think he was hurt too bad. Fred moved down and checked the men for more weapons. Logan moved them back into the cabin. Fred tied them to the pole bunks. Logan checked the wounded one while Fred tied up the other one. The bullet had gone through the fleshy part above the man's belt. Logan grabbed a shirt hanging on one bunk and made a bandage to cover the wound.

Logan went back around the cabin and opened the trap door and stepped into the cellar. It was a big room. When Logan lit a candle, he found a well-stocked supply room. There was food, plus ammunition, extra bedding, four extra rifles and a case of dynamite. Logan decided this was one of their main camps.

"I think we'd better head for the miner's shack to spend the night. We'll be better off there in case more of the gang shows up here." Fred nodded.

Fred got the two men onto their saddle horses. Logan helped him load the dead man. Fred retrieved their horses and the other prisoner while Logan checked through the other cabins. He found, to his surprise, there was sleeping area here for about twenty men.

"As soon as we get these men delivered to ranger headquarters I want to get back here and keep an eye on this place," Logan told Fred as they mounted up.

When they rode into Kilgore, they found George and Tug both waiting for them. Logan brought them up to date on what they had found.

"I would like to stay and keep watching the hidden camp," George nodded.

"Tug can stay with you. Fred and me will take these prisoners to headquarters.

They had Jerry stop by the jail again for a visit and coffee. "I've seen both of the prisoners before here in Kilgore, but the dead man, I don't know."

George and Fred left the next morning for headquarters with the body and the three prisoners. Logan and Tug waited around Kilgore until about noon then headed back to the miner's cabin for the night. The next morning they rode up behind the cabin again, but there was no sign of life. Logan and Tug decided not to ride into the yard and leave tracks. Logan led off over the trail away from the camp. He headed toward the Grey's place to see if they had seen any strangers around. When they rode in, Jess called to them from the barn where he was adding a tack shed. Mrs. Grey had been helping him. She excused herself and told them she wanted them to stay for supper. They helped Jess until supper was ready. After supper they rolled their bedrolls out in the barn for the night.

Logan and Tug spent the next two weeks riding the area looking for another camp. Their supplies were getting short so they decided to head back for Kilgore. That night as they packed up, Tug suggested they load the pack horse with some of the cache in the hideout cabin. The next morning they headed for the cabin. Before riding in, they checked from the ridge. The place still looked deserted. They loaded all the rifles and ammunition and the dynamite on the pack horse. They left all the other supplies and closed up the cabin.

They spent one day at Kilgore before heading back to headquarters. George asked, "Do you think the gang has left the country?"

"Wherever they are there's a good chance they won't do anything until spring; anyway, that's my guess."

Tug nodded, "I agree with Logan, but I think maybe this bunch may have moved to another area and won't be back."

The rangers spent the next month working around headquarters. It was the middle of May when George sent Tug, Fred and a couple of new rangers south to look into a rustler problem that had been reported. Logan made another quick trip up to Kilgore, but the hidden cabin was still vacant. Logan had heard the first freight wagons were getting ready to head for the mines when the road was open.

George told Logan, "You get ready to leave the first of the week and head up to the mines. I figure with the mines running all winter they'll have gold ready to haul out as soon as the first wagons show up."

238

Logan was awakened that night by the night watchman. "George wants you at the office as soon as you can."

Logan hurried over to the office. George was pacing the floor. As Logan walked in George said, "I think our Payne gang is back. Someone just robbed both mines. I got a telegram from the Marshall in Mill City. A rider had just come in from the mine with word of the robbery. There were some people shot during the robbery but they didn't say how many."

"I'll head that way before daylight. I'll take a spare horse so I can make better time." While Logan was getting his gear together, George walked in. "Logan, do you want to take one of the new rangers from headquarters with you?"

"If you don't mind, I'd rather go alone for now."

"Okay, Tug and his crew are on their way back but I don't expect them for a couple days. I'll send them to the mines as soon as they get in."

Logan mounted his horse with a spare horse on a lead rope. "George, I'm going by way of Kilgore. I think I can make better time that way, and time is what counts now," and with a wave headed out.

Logan stopped in Kilgore just long enough to see if Jerry had seen any of Blackie's gang around Kilgore. Jerry shook his head, "So far, I haven't seen any of that bunch."

Logan stopped by the relay camp for some grub and any news they had about the robbery. The cook was the only one at the camp.

"All I know is they made a big haul on the gold stored from the winter mining." He did know there were at least three dead men that were killed by the gang. Two were at the Golden Rose and the other one at the Milford. Logan changed horses again and headed on toward the mines.

When he rode up in front of the office, both bookkeepers rushed out to talk to him. They informed him, "John has been shot during the robbery. He's down at the doctor's office in bed. Doc said he would be alright in time."

The younger of the bookkeepers motioned to Logan's tired horses, "I'll take them to the barn for you." Logan thanked him, "I need to borrow one of your horses so I can ride up to the Milford after I talk to John."

The bookkeeper nodded, "I'll bring a fresh horse and your gear to the doctor's office for you."

The doctor had seen Logan ride in so he had already told John that Logan was in camp. John told Logan of how the gang had snuck in during the evening during shift change and almost got away without being seen.

"I was on my way home for supper when I noticed horses tied behind the assay office. The gold room and retort are in the same building. When I got closer, I saw a man standing at the corner of the building in the shadows. He stepped out and had a rifle leveled at me and told me to keep coming toward him. As I reached the building, the guard pulled my pistol and shoved it behind his belt. He told me to walk ahead of him back toward the horses." That was the last thing John remembered for awhile.

"The guard had clubbed me with either the rifle or something. As I started to come to, I could see six men loading a string of pack mules. I used the building for a brace and finally got to my feet and was leaning there as the six men mounted. When they rode by, they saw me standing there. One of them swung a rifle that was across his legs and shot me. That's the last thing I remember until the doctor was leaning over me in this bed."

"When Mel got to the assay office, he found both workers in the retort room dead. They had been tied up. They were both stabbed after they were tied up. They emptied the gold vault but left all the silver concentrates."

Where's Mel? I'd like to talk to him," asked Logan.

"He's down at the bunkhouse in bed with a broken leg. He was in that bed," pointing to the one next to him, "until this afternoon when Doc let him move back to his own bunk."

"Mel and a group of riders from here were joined by more men from the Milford. They rode after the robbers. They were ambushed not far up the trail. Mel's horse was shot from under him, and when it fell, it pinned Mel and broke his leg."

"I'm going to head up to the Milford and talk to Bill." Logan leaned over to shake John's hand.

Logan got the same story from Bill. "They made off with all the gold. We didn't know we'd been robbed until the night shift watchman went on shift. He found the day watchman dead. He had been knifed and the gold room was empty. This had to be during shift change same as at the Golden Rose. The two men working in the retort had gone off shift, and the night crew hadn't come on yet. We've been working two shifts on the retort so we'd be ready for the gold shipment next week. There were tracks of mules being used to pack the gold."

Logan decided he would head out at first light and try to follow the gang's trail.

Logan's horses were well rested the next morning. He borrowed a small pack saddle for the spare horse to carry extra supplies. While he gathering supplies at the Golden Rose store the night before, he spotted some 45-90 shells that would fit his Sharps. He bought all they had. He was getting a little low, and he hadn't loaded any for quite sometime. On his way back to the office he stopped by to see John.

"I'm going to head out at first light to see if I can find their trail."

"Don't you think you should wait for backup?"

Logan shook his head, "I need to hit the trail before any rain shows up. John, if the rangers show up, the leader will probably be Tug Higgins. You tell him I'll leave signs for him."

Logan stopped by the cook shack early, and they fixed him a hot breakfast and at first light Logan was on his way. As he passed the Milford, Bill was waiting along the trail.

"Logan, I could send along some men if you want the help."

"Thanks for the offer. Tracking will be slow, and a bigger body of men will be easier to spot so I'd rather go alone."

As Logan started climbing up the trail, he found the place where they had ambushed the men from the mine. Two men had waited in the rocks in a very narrow part of the trail. It was lucky none of the miners were killed. As Logan moved on up the mountain, he found more places where the two riders had stopped to check the trail behind them. This was well planned. When Logan neared the top of the mountain, the snow was still deep, and the trail had been shoveled before the raid. Logan could tell by how the snow melted it had been done on the way over to the mines. As Logan started down off the mountain, he rode into an area he had only heard about from Old Dave when he was growing up. As he got back down into the timber, it was big pine trees, beautiful country. Logan remembered Dave called this Raven Basin country and the small river was called White River. The trail came to a small meadow. As Logan got closer, he could see where the gang had camped for at least one night. The grass had been eaten from a large part of the meadow by the horses and mules. There was a carcass of a deer hanging from a tree near where the fire had been. The birds had been eating on it, and Logan thought he was maybe three days behind the gang. He decided he would ride on down river before he camped.

On the fifth day Logan got into more open ground, so he decided he would stick to the timber for better cover. From where he was riding, he could see the tracks of the pack string in the lush green grass. Logan could see ahead a ridge coming down on his right toward the meadow. There was an outcropping of rocks up ahead where the ridge met the trail he was on. The sun was high and warm, and a flash of something shining from the rocks caught Logan's attention. He dove from his horse pulling the Sharps as he fell. At the same time, he heard a bullet smack the tree alongside the horses. Logan crawled around behind some brush. Then another bullet hit the brush above him and off to the right. As he moved, he could see a rock outcropping. One man was waving his hat and looking down into the valley below. Logan steadied the old Sharps. When he squeezed the trigger, he could see his shot was true and the fellow was knocked over. As Logan reloaded, he saw a second person ride up to where the fellow had fallen. Just as he started to ride off, Logan's second shot knocked him from the saddle.

Logan took his time working his way toward the downed men. He made the rocks where they both went down. The first one Logan crawled up to was dead, but he could hear the second one moaning. Logan scooted over next to him and could see he was hit pretty hard. Logan looked down below and could see corrals and a couple of cabins. There were three men looking up at the rocks. One was waving his arms pointing to where Logan lay hidden. The outlaw moaning was looking at Logan when he glanced that way.

The fellow whispered, "Are you the ranger called McTier?" Logan nodded.

The wounded outlaw whispered, "We heard you was hell with a short gun, but nobody mentioned your rifle."

Logan looked at the fellow, "I just took up the pistol a few years ago, before that I only owned a rifle." The fellow started to speak and never got a word in before he died.

Logan moved over where he could see better and pulled down on the outlaw who had been waving toward the rocks. As the fellow was knocked over, the other two dove behind a small shed next to one cabin. Neither man had a rifle and their pistol shots were landing way below where Logan lay hidden. A bullet chipped the rocks above Logan. He spotted smoke from a rifle fired from the second cabin. Logan placed two shots into the door frame and heard no more from the rifle. He then saw a fellow run from behind the same cabin, so Logan decided he hadn't hit the fellow in the cabin. Logan went back to his horses and got a saddle bag with extra shells and jerky and a canteen and returned to his spot looking down at the cabins. He fired a few rounds to let them know he was still around. He could see one man move behind the corral. He figured this fellow was getting ready to make a mad dash for the nearest cabin. When the man broke from behind the corral, Logan was ready. When he fired, the fellow went sprawling. Before Logan could fire again, the man made it to the cover of the first cabin. Logan knew he had hit the man, but from the way he was crawling, it was a minor wound.

Logan watched for movement below as he bounced against the rock he was lying behind. Logan woke with a great pain in his back. He knew he'd been shot. He was very dizzy and soon passed out. When he woke, he could hear horse hooves getting closer. A horse stopped near him and Logan figured a bullet was next. Instead he heard a voice.

"McTier, I thought you were suppose to be tough," then Logan heard a short laugh as the horse moved off.

Logan knew he was hit bad, and there wasn't any help close by. He finally was able to roll over. He could feel the pool of blood under him. As he felt his side, he could feel a good sized hole. He could feel his saddle bag under his leg and finally pulled it free. He found a spare shirt and packed it against the hole. He tried to loosen his gun belt and pull it up over the shirt. He pulled the belt tight but could feel himself slowly passing out again. He was brought awake by gunshots coming from down by the cabins. Logan got to his canteen and took a small drink which seemed to help. He finally was able to see below. He could see two bodies laying in front of the first cabin. A rider was just moving away from the cabins leading six loaded mules. Logan thought maybe this was the man who had shot him. Logan passed out again. When he woke the next time, he could hear hooves on rocks. He slowly pulled himself around where he could see the trail above and could see the rider leading the pack string toward the top of the ridge. Logan reached for the Sharps which was leaning against the rock where he'd put it. With a lot of effort, Logan finally got the rifle over a rock in front of him and pointed toward the ridge top. He moved until he could finally see along the barrel and up the sights. He was getting dizzy again but knew if he didn't get a shot now he'd never see the man again. The rider came in line with the sights and Logan fired. The recoil knocked Logan back against the rocks, and he was out to the world. Unknown to Logan, the bullet had knocked the man from his horse. He lay, not moving, at his horse's feet.

The next evening four riders came over the ridge above the valley.

Shining badges could be seen on all four riders. They came in sight of the mules with heads down. The pack was turned on one mule. A body was lying on the trail by the lone horse.

Tug was the leader of this group of rangers. Fred was with him and two new men to the rangers. Tug told two of the men to get the animals down to water and unpack them. He and Fred walked back to the body. Tug rolled him over, "I think this fellow was shot by Logan because of the size hole in him."

They boosted the body onto the horse and moved down to the creek. When they got into the meadow, Tug then saw the cabins. Tug started that way when one of the other men asked if he should look in the packs. They opened all the packs and found nothing but gold bars. Fred had gone on over to the cabins. There he found the two bodies out front, and both had been shot in the back at close range. As he looked around, he found another body with a bullet in the back and a wounded leg. Tug looked over to where Fred was motioning to all the bullet marks in the door frame of the one cabin.

"Look at the size of these holes," Fred said as he put his finger in one of the holes.

Tug nodded, "I know this was some of Logan's work but where is he?"

The rangers decided to make camp. Tug mounted up. I'm going up to check out the ridge above these cabins."

Fred heard Tug hollering from above. He was motioning for them to come up. When they rode up, Tug was kneeling over two bodies. He looked up at Fred.

"Big bore and from a long way off."

They loaded the bodies on two of the saddle horses, and the two rangers walked back to the cabins leading the horses. As they ate supper that night, Tug kept saying. "I can't figure out where Logan could be. He left us a good trail this far, but now there's nothing."

Tug had made great time getting there following the good trail Logan had left for him. The next morning at first light Tug told the others, "After we eat, you three take all the papers off the bodies and then bury them. It's too far to try to take them back to the mines in this warm weather. Maybe we can figure out who they were from what's in their gear and what's on them."

Tug rode back up where they had found the two bodies and looked again for any sign Logan left for him. As he looked behind a rock overlooking the cabins below, he found two 45-90 brass cases. There was what looked to be blood covering a large area but no sign of a person. It almost looked like someone had brushed the ground to hide all tracks. To find the cases was unusual because Logan always picked up his cases so he could reload them the way he liked. Tug spent the entire day looking for some sort of sign of Logan.

The next morning he told Fred to take the gold back to the mines and then send word to George. "Tell him I'm going to keep looking for Logan and the rest of the gang."

They had buried six men, and according to the mine owners, had told them there were four who robbed the Golden Rose. Tug figured there was more than just two when they robbed the Milford.

Tug took Fred to one side. "I think it's better to keep the names we found on the bodies under wraps and give them to George."

Tug was thinking that the one name they found should be kept quiet until they could check more into it. The dead man found on the trail with the mules had papers with the name Frank Griffith on them. This was the same name as the part owner of the Golden Rose Mine. Tug wanted that kept quiet until they could investigate it more. As they all mounted to leave, Tug turned to Fred. "Fred, if I'm not back to the mines in three days after you get there, you head back to this camp."

For the next three days, Tug crisscrossed the whole area but could find no trace of Logan or his horses. As he rode into the mine a few days later, he found Fred and George getting ready to head up looking for him. George informed him mine owners had said there was still forty thousand in gold missing.

Logan, in a very dizzy state, could feel movement as he went in and out of consciousness. It was night and he knew he was being carried. When he woke the next time, he could hear talking but the words didn't make sense. He could feel the movement he had felt before. Logan felt like he was burning up. Then he could feel a cool feeling on his head and then he passed out again. Logan felt like he was in a floating world and couldn't make things stop. Unknown to Logan, he had been in this state for almost four weeks. It was mid-summer when he woke one morning. As he looked up, he peered into a smiling face that looked like someone he should know.

Finally, a voice said, "You look older, One Who Shoots Far." Logan was still in a foggy state. He whispered, "Little Feather," and she nodded.

He was again only half awake, but he could feel a warm liquid being held to his lips. It tasted good. Soon he was asleep again. One day when he woke, there was another woman looking at him. She was older. When he started to speak, she said something he couldn't understand. A curtain or something moved and the area became bright. Little Feather stepped alongside his bed.

Logan whispered, "Where am I?"

Little Feather smiled, "At our summer home in what some call Raven Basin."

As the days passed, Logan could finally sit up. He couldn't believe how weak he was. When he felt his face, he had a full beard and his hair was long. He asked Little Feather, "How long have I been here? Two moons?"

Logan still couldn't understand how he had gotten here and why it had been so long ago. Logan hadn't seen anyone except Little Feather and her mother since being awake.

"Where's Little Hawk and your father, Hawk?" he asked her one afternoon.

"They are higher up in the mountains hunting and fishing and picking berries."

"Why aren't you on the mountain with them?"

"Mother and I stayed here to take care of you." Little Feather added, "You were too weak to make the trip."

As time passed, Logan could finally walk outside. Each day he walked a little further. He noticed his guns were on a hide near his bed. One afternoon he decided he would clean them. The pistols felt heavy and he could hardly hold up the old Sharps. Logan knew he was still in poor shape and wondered if he would ever get totally well. He started strapping on the gun belt each day and trying to draw the pistol faster each day.

Tug had spent two months riding the area in search of his fellow ranger. He hadn't turned up anything. The man they had found dead with the gold turned out to be Frank Griffith, the brother and partner of John Griffith at the Golden Rose. They also discovered he was also known as Blackie Payne, the leader of the gang. John had figured he was still in the east. Now he knew his brother had never gone east. John Griffith was still trying to figure out why his brother had turned outlaw. They had all the money they would ever need coming from the mine.

Two weeks after Logan had been reported missing, George Bennett made a trip to see Governor Henry Davis. When he walked into the office,

246

Henry looked up. "I don't like the look on your face."

"We recovered most of the gold as you've already heard in some of our reports. What you haven't heard is, Henry, we can't find Logan. We know almost for sure it was Logan who was in a gun battle with the gang in a place called Raven Basin. A large bore rifle was used. From what we've found, Tug Higgins, his old partner, is sure it was Logan doing the shooting. There were five dead men found near the camp and one man dead on the trail leading out of the basin. The dead man on the trail was killed with a big bore rifle. He was leading the pack mules with all the gold we have recovered so far. These men had been dead maybe one day, two at the most when Tug and the other three rangers got there. The three men found near the cabins had been shot in the back from close range. The two found dead on the ridge above the cabins had been shot from long range by a large caliber rifle. It looks like the man on the trail may have been one of the gang. We think he killed the three at the cabins and took the gold for himself. We believe now the fellow on the trail was Frank Griffith, a brother and part owner of the Golden Rose Mine."

"Tug, from information he's dug up, thinks that this Frank Griffith was also know as Blackie Payne, the gang leader."

Henry just sat there for a moment. "George, what do you mean you can't find Logan?"

"That's the part I didn't want to have to tell you. We can't find any trace of Logan. Tug has spent the last two weeks trying to find any sign of him. He left Tug a good trail to follow from the mine to the camp and the dead men. Now there's nothing. Tug found two 45-90 cases on the ridge above the cabin where they found two of the dead men lying but that's it. Tug found what looked like blood near where he found the cases. There's no tracks or any sign of his horses or him. Tug says it almost looked like someone had swept the tracks away."

"Why did Logan go after the gang alone," Henry asked.

"All of the rangers at headquarters were out when the word came about the robbery, so he went alone. I offered to send one of the new men from here with him, but he said he'd make better time alone."

Henry just sat there for awhile then looked up at George, "We need to let the family at the ranch know about this."

George nodded, "I'll leave come morning and head for the Rafter T."

Henry nodded, "I'll ride with you on this trip."

That evening after supper, Henry told Becky and his daughter, Alice, about Logan's missing. He started to pack some clothes for the trip.

He turned to Becky, "I'm going with George to tell the family."

"I'm going too, Henry."

"We're going horseback so we can make better time."

Becky looked at her husband. Henry could see that look that meant she wasn't backing down.

"I will be ready come morning."

The three of them made good time, even on the second day when riding in on the old trail. That same trail Henry's dad, Hugh, Ted McTier and Lottie rode and had first seen the valley. The ranch looked so beautiful from the ridge. They all stopped and looked before riding on down. Henry wasn't looking forward to this trip into the valley. He was the one who had talked their son into being a ranger and now he was missing.

Ted saw the three riders coming in on the old trail and called to Lottie who was hanging up clothes. Lottie walked over, "Can you tell who it is?"

Ted finally said, "I think it's Henry and Becky but I can't tell who the other one is."

"I wonder why they are coming in on horseback and from that old trail?" she asked.

The three rode up and dismounted. Ted and Lottie both could tell something was wrong. Henry looked at Ted.

"We bring news that I don't know how to say in an easy way. We can't find Logan after he broke up a big gang that robbed the two big mines north of Kilgore."

Henry turned toward George, "Ted, you and Lottie remember George Bennett."

"Well, George just let me know a few days ago about this. I wanted to let you know as soon as I could. We've got rangers combing the White River and Raven Basin country but so far nothing."

Lottie motioned for the group to come into the house.

George spent the afternoon telling the story from the first. Becky who had been sitting next to Lottie admired the woman who hadn't changed expressions since George started talking. Ted looked over at his wife of many years as she stood. "Until you find a body, I'm not going to worry about Logan."

Lottie walked off into the kitchen. They could hear her starting supper.

248

Becky looked at Ted. He just grinned, and Becky walked into the kitchen to join Lottie. The men went out to put the horses away. Ted asked if they were going to keep looking.

George nodded. "Tug Higgins really liked Logan that he'll never stop looking. Logan was like a son or maybe a brother to Tug. He was the first partner Tug trusted when in a tough situation. I'll let Tug keep looking for as long as he wants."

When Rebecca rode in that evening, Becky went out to her cabin and told her the story. She was like her mother; she didn't shed a tear. "He'll appear one of these days."

The two women returned to the main house, and Becky admired the two women she had known for many years. They both were of a hearty stock like most pioneer women.

George and the Davis's headed back for the capital the next day. George and Henry both told Ted and Lottie any news and they would send word.

George smiled at Becky, "You're one heck of a lady. When Henry said you were going with us, I didn't know what to expect. You're one tough lady, and I'll travel with you anytime."

"Why thank you, George. I really enjoyed the trip, but I didn't like the message we had to deliver."

The McTier's sure took the word of Logan missing a lot different than I expected," George told Henry as they unsaddled.

Henry smiled, "Now you can understand why my father thought so much of those two. When Logan was able to buy that ranch for them, it was one of the greatest days I will ever know. "They are as much Rafter T as the Davis family, maybe even more," Henry said as he turned and headed for the house.

Logan was sitting in the sun one morning when he heard someone walk up behind him. He was still having a tough time moving, and to look back, was almost impossible. Then a voice he hadn't heard for a while said, "You look better than when I seen you last." Little Hawk stepped around where Logan could see him. He grabbed Logan's arm and Logan grasped his as they just looked at one another.

Logan smiled, "Do you still have the rifle I gave you?" Little Hawk nodded.

"I shoot real well now. We always have meat on the fire. You still shoot real well too. That was a long shot, when you shot the man leading the mules."

Logan looked at Little Hawk, "How did you know about that?"

"We saw you when you first rode into the Basin and we followed you." Little Hawk went on to tell Logan about what they had watched from a distance. As Little Hawk told the story about what they had seen, it was all news to Logan. Little Hawk told Logan the man who was leading the mules was the man who had shot him. He had come from the timber while Logan was watching and shooting down at the men at the cabins.

"I was too far away to try a shot to help you," Little Hawk added.

"We watched as the man rode into the camp after shooting you. The men there must have known him because they welcomed him. When the two men in the yard turned toward the second cabin, the man pulled his pistol and shot them. There was a wounded man by the other cabin. When he saw the other two get shot, he tried to get into the cabin. Before he could shut the door, he was shot. We watched as the man packed the mules and headed back up the trail."

Little Hawk stopped for a moment. "We thought you were dead. Then we heard the shot and saw the man fall from the saddle. When everything was quiet, we moved closer to see if there was anyone alive. Little Feather rode over to where you were. She told us you were still alive but hurt real bad. We made a sling between two horses and headed for this camp."

"I stayed there after the others left with you. I brushed out all tracks of you and your horses. I think maybe they'll find no sign of you ever being in the area," Little Hawk told Logan.

"When we got here, Father told Little Feather you would die from your wounds. She went to Morning Dawn, our mother, and asked if she knew any way to cure your wounds. She told Little Feather she would call a meeting of the women in camp and see what they could do. The older women in camp all agreed on the way to try to keep you alive. You have been taken care of by the best medicine known to the Shoshone.

"When the tribe moved to the high country for the summer, Little Feather and Morning Dawn stayed here with you. You didn't move for one moon, and Little Feather never left your side. The men have taken turns staying here to see that no one bothers the women. It was my turn off the mountain, and when I got here, I was happy when I saw you sitting outside. You look very weak. With the beard and long hair, it would be hard for anyone to recognize you."

"When did you learn to speak the white man's language so well," Logan asked his old friend. Little Feather had come out of the teepee and she answered for Little Hawk.

"It took many months to teach this one to speak English." Little Hawk smiled at his sister.

"I have many things to unpack after my trip off the mountain. Logan, I will see you later."

Logan was walking very slowly toward the small brush corral behind the teepee when he saw another rider coming up the trail. As the rider neared, he jumped from his horse and ran to Logan. Logan, then recognized Running Wolf from the winter at the horse camp.

"I'm glad to see my old friend walking," Running Wolf said as he shook Logan's hand.

"Do you still have the rifle I gave you on the mountain?" Logan asked.

Running Wolf pointed to the pony he had been riding. Logan could see the rifle butt sticking out of a well with decorated skin scabbard on the side of the horse. Logan waited while Running Wolf put his horse in the corral, then walked back to camp with him. Logan got weaker as they neared the camp. He knew he had pushed it a little too far today. He felt a strong arm grab him. With Running Wolf's help, he made the block where he usually sat. Little Feather had been watching all of this. The scolding she gave him would have made Lottie smile Logan thought to himself. He had spent much of his time lately thinking about the Rafter T and his folks. He had told Little Feather no when she asked if he wanted them to try and get word to his folks. In this condition he would only be bait for some gunslinger to kill him. If he got so he could travel and defend himself, then he would ride to the ranch.

One evening Logan sat outside near the fire talking to his two old friends. The nights were beginning to get cold and the fire felt good. Hawk had ridden in that day and joined them at the fire. He still spoke no English.

Little Feather had told Logan, "I think he understands more of the language than he lets on." Hawk had Little Feather tell Logan he was glad he was still with them and not in the spirit world. Logan grinned. Using sign language he told Hawk he was glad to see him too. Hawk signed to Logan.

"You still talk well with your hands."

"One man has ridden back into the basin many times since you were

251

shot. He spends much time looking for some trace of you. He always goes to where we pick you up and looks for something like he is trying to find a trail," Running Wolf said.

"What does this person look like?" Logan asked.

When Running Wolf described the man, Logan knew it was Tug. Hawk signed that this rider at one time had been on the ridge above the camp watching.

Little Feather nodded. "I saw him once as he watched this camp." With only Little Feather and her mother moving around the teepee, Logan figured Tug never thought to come down for a closer look.

Logan smiled, "That rider you saw is a fellow ranger and a very close friend."

Henry Davis was busy with the needs of the territory and the process of making the territory a state before long. He and Becky had made another trip over to the Rafter T to see Lottie and Ted. The family still believed that Logan was out there and one day would show up. Henry and Becky had talked many times about the McTier family still believing Logan was alive.

"I've always admired Lottie with her outlook on life and her beliefs," Henry said during one of these talks.

Becky agreed, "I still can't believe Logan wouldn't try to contact his folks if he were alive."

There was one other person who shared Lottie McTier's thoughts. That was Tug Higgins. George Bennett tried to convince Tug that Logan was probably buried somewhere and his horses driven out of the country.

Tug would always just tell George, "You've never ridden with Logan and know him the way I do. I know he was hit up on that bluff and I know someone helped him. I have crisscrossed that mountain many times. I know I'm missing some sign that will lead me to him. I used to watch Logan read sign. He'd been well taught. If I was the one lost, he would be able to follow the trail and find me. The only thing I have seen alive up there is a small Indian camp with two squaws and one brave. I know they have seen me but they never pay me any attention. There must be more of them close by because they have changed men a few times. The camp always has plenty of supplies and fresh meat."

Tug was wanting to go back once more before it snowed in. The rangers had been real busy with rustlers lately and George needed him. He knew once the fall rains and snow covered the ground he would never find the trail.

Tug and three other rangers were sent into the Benton area where both cattle and horse thieves were causing a big problem. Tug spent one night with the McTiers. He delivered some horse that had been stolen from the ranch a month before. So far the Rafter T had only lost horses. Ted told Tug he knew riders had been scouting the cattle herds. With winter coming on, the rustling would stop. With snow blocking all the passes, the rustlers wouldn't be able to move the cattle out to other markets. One evening after everyone headed for bed except Tug, Lottie asked him to stay. They were sitting in the kitchen. Lottie asked Tug about his many times up in Raven Basin looking for Logan. Tug told her about everything he had found.

"I still believe Logan survived the shooting," he told her.

"When he left the shell casing behind, it was one clue that he had been hit. Second, there were no tracks. Lottie, I know I missed something, and come spring, all signs will be gone." Lottie reached across the table and touched Tug's hand.

"We'll see him again come spring."

The next morning as the tough little ranger mounted his horse, Lottie thought to herself what a team her son and this man must have made. Lottie noticed the twin tied down holsters and the way this little man moved the first time she saw him. Logan spoke only good words about him. Lottie knew this man had given his best to find Logan.

Logan, one afternoon, was surprised when he looked up the trail to see dust. Many horses and people started moving into camp. Little Feather walked up beside him. "It's time to move to winter camp." Logan asked if they were going over to the same place they were when he knew them before. She said no.

"It's not safe for us to winter there anymore. Too many people have moved into the area. They complain to the army that there's Indians living off the reservation, and we steal from them. A small calvary patrol rode out two winters ago and met with Hawk. The captain of this patrol had talked with us before. He'd always told Hawk as long as we didn't start trouble he would look the other way when looking for Indians. This time he had said there were too many people reporting seeing Indians. Hawk had told the captain we'd find other winter quarters. Hawk thanked the captain for bringing the word. We wintered last year down the White River in the canyons of the steaming water. It was warm there, and we found plenty of feed for the animals," Little Feather added.

The next morning the people moved down the trail with Hawk. Little Hawk rode in the lead. Running Wolf and Little Feather started dismantling the two teepees at the camp. Little Feather's mother had moved on with the people so only Logan, Little Feather and Running Wolf remained in camp. When everything was loaded on pack animals, they headed for winter camp. Logan's horse was brought up, and with both Running Wolf and Little Feather's help, Logan finally made it onto the saddle. Running Wolf then tied Logan so he couldn't tumble out of the saddle. They started off with Little Feather walking and leading Logan's horse. Logan felt pretty good for the first few miles then he started getting tired and dizzy. When the sun was still high in the sky, Little Feather turned off the main trail and stopped in a small meadow out of sight from the main trail. They untied Logan and helped him off onto a robe Little Feather had placed under a tree. She got a fire started. Running Wolf unloaded the horses. Logan decided they were here for the night and soon he was asleep.

It was coming light when Logan heard people moving around camp. They had wakened him the night before after dark and fed him a hot meal. When he laid down after supper, he was asleep in minutes. Now awake, he was sore as he got to his feet and moved over closer to the fire. Running Wolf was again loading the horses while Logan ate breakfast. Little Feather smiled as he ate everything before him. Then she handed him what was left in the bowl. He had eaten more this morning than usual.

The soreness slowly went away as they moved down the trail. Logan felt better in the saddle. Logan could see the country around them was changing. The canyon walls were getting steeper. It was warmer and Logan knew they were getting into a lower elevation. Running Wolf rode up alongside Logan and handed him a water bag and a few sticks of jerky. Logan had noticed that Little Feather had mounted her horse after they had traveled a few miles. She had been watching Logan pretty close. She must have figured he was getting along alright so she mounted up. She was still leading the horse Logan was riding. Logan began to slump over a bit. The sun was almost going out of sight behind the steep canyon wall. Logan knew he had lasted better today. Little Feather again turned off the trail to make camp. After they helped him down, Logan walked slowly around camp before settling down on the robe. He ate a big supper that night and soon was asleep.

They made better time the next day. Just before sundown, Logan could see smoke ahead and the tops of teepees. They were entering the winter camp. Many people came to help set up the two teepees, and soon they were settled in. Logan, for the next few days, showed much improvement and walked more each day. As he walked away from camp, he started drawing his pistol and dry firing it. He was surprised that he was as fast as he was after being laid up for so long. The speed increased each day, and soon he wanted to shoot to see if he could hit anything. He really didn't want to be shooting around camp. He decided to wait until maybe he could ride out a mile or so.

One evening Little Feather was walking with him when a movement in the trail ahead caught Logan's eye. With speed that surprised him, the pistol appeared and fired in one fluid motion. In the trail ahead lay a dead rattlesnake. Men from camp came running up the trail. Little Feather motioned to the snake ahead in the trail. Running Wolf walked up and picked it up. Just the head was missing.

Little Hawk, who was now standing beside Logan, grinned, "You almost missed."

As they walked back toward camp, Little Feather was telling everyone the story about the snake. After everyone went back to their own camps, Logan and Little Feather sat alone by the fire.

"Why is it you can draw and shoot that fast?" Little Feather asked.

Logan shook his head. "It's a gift to have speed and also I had a good teacher. The man you helped me bury on the mountain by the cabin, taught me to shoot a pistol like that."

"Hawk told me when you were very young you traveled with an old man who once trapped these mountains. Hawk said this old man taught you the long rifle and how to track like an Indian. Is that true?" she asked.

Logan smiled, "I had no idea Hawk remembered me when Dave used to take me into the mountains. Dave used to talk of Hawk and the men of this tribe. I remember the times we stayed with warriors hunting for game, but I don't remember seeing Hawk. Dave taught me all I know about talking with hands."

The winter at headquarters was busy. Tug and the rangers stationed at headquarters were chasing rustlers. The stealing was small bunches of mostly horses. Tug figured the few cattle reported missing were being taken to feed the bunch. Tug was now in charge of ten rangers in the district. He found this new job kept him real busy. He made Fred Miller his second in command. Fred was becoming a tough fighting man. He had proven himself many times this last year. Tug could see that many of his habits he had learned from Logan. His gun speed was talked about among other rangers. He learned from Logan some tricks that had probably saved his life more than once. He and Lee Taylor had broken up a band of outlaws raising cane over in Clover. The rustlers had wounded Lenny Cook, the sheriff, and for a few days, taken over the town. Fred and Lee, in a gun battle, killed three of the gang and arrested three others. Tug had assigned a young ranger from headquarters to stay in Clover until Sheriff Cook was back on his feet and able to handle things.

George Bennett was almost never in the field anymore because of the paperwork involved in running a growing ranger department. The territory was growing each day as people moved west after the war between the states was over. Along with the growth, came the men who thought the law was something to break. In order to become a state, the territory needed to have law and order. Governor Davis pushed for a ranger outfit that could meet that challenge. Many a night George had lain awake wondering if Logan was still alive and would he show up come spring. Logan would be a big help trying to break up the rustlers that George knew would bring havoc this spring. Logan had a way of finding trouble before it started and that is what was needed now. George deep down figured Logan was really dead. Tug was so sure he was still alive he never let it show.

George and Henry talked in the governor's office one day about if Logan was alive and why hadn't he appeared. Henry was like George, deep down he figured him gone, but he, too, wanted to share Lottie's idea that he was alive.

The McTier ranch was a busy place in the spring with a big calf crop. The weather had been great for the surviving young calves. Ted knew the Rafter T would too have big trouble with rustlers come later when the mountain passes opened up. He had extra men hired.. He was going to keep the line cabins manned all summer to watch for missing cattle.

Lottie decided to have Ted build Rose a bigger cook shack to handle the extra men. So far they had been too busy. So, Lottie sent word to Ed Benton at the store to find someone to build the cook shack. Ted grinned to himself. He knew if he didn't build it she would take over the project. In fact, Rebecca had accused him of stalling on the new building for that reason. Logan was very seldom mentioned anymore and each day made it harder to believe Logan was alive.

Logan had gone riding with Running Wolf and Little Hawk. When they returned, Logan found Little Feather had moved to her parent's teepee. Logan motioned to Little Hawk he wanted to talk.

"Why did Little Feather move from the teepee she's been living in next to me?" he asked his old friend.

Little Hawk smiled, "Hawk told her family you no longer needed someone to care for you. You are well. She needs to find her own man and have her own family."

Logan nodded. He was going to miss having her with him to fix his meals. The next day while riding with Running Wolf, Logan asked, "What does it take to get married Indian style."

Running Wolf didn't understand the word married so Logan had to explain what he meant. When Running Wolf finally figured out what Logan was asking, he laughed. "First, you need to find out if the girl wants to have you for a partner. Then you need to ask her father. He will expect gifts from you for his daughter. Sometimes he wants many things."

Logan shrugged, "I have nothing except a couple of horses that don't belong to me and two rifles and two pistols and I need them."

Running Wolf looked over at his friend. "I will give you some ponies to give Hawk if you want Little Feather. You can pay me back later by teaching me to shoot a pistol like you do."

"I will ask Little Feather tonight."

After supper with the Hawk family, Logan asked Little Feather to walk with him. When they were away from camp, he asked if she would be his wife. Little Feather knew what wife meant. She walked along for awhile before asking him if he was going to leave come spring.

Logan nodded, "Yes, I'll leave as soon as I feel I'm strong enough to do my job.

"What will you do with me when you leave?"

Logan motioned her to sit beside him on a rock along the trail. Logan went on to tell Little Feather he had decided as soon as he could get back to Capital City, he was going to file on the land in Raven Basin. No settlers were here yet and he wanted this land for their home. He would fix it so Hawk and the small band would always have a home. Hawk would be a partner in the ranch. He went on to tell of his plans to build maybe near the cabins where he'd been shot. He would also file on ground near here for

257

winter range for cattle he figured on bringing into the area. As he talked, Little Feather snuggled up to him.

"I will be your wife."

The next day Logan went riding with Hawk while Hawk looked over the horse herd grazing away from camp. When he spoke of taking Little Feather as his wife, Hawk grinned. "Why did you take so long to ask?" Little Feather told me last night of your plans to settle in the basin. If you can make it so we don't have to worry about being moved to a reservation one day, it is well you marry."

Logan started to ask what he needed for gifts when Hawk motioned nothing. Logan had been using sign language when he started talking to Hawk. He was surprised when Hawk answered in English. Hawk still needed some sign language to talk to Logan. "It would be good if you don't tell my family I can speak some English." Logan grinned.

"If you could make this our home forever, that would be your present to me for Little Feather, " Hawk added.

The next week was taken up getting ready for the big ceremony of taking Little Feather for a wife. Logan sat one morning waiting for Running Wolf to stop by. When he showed up, he carried a Colt pistol. Logan took the gun when Running Wolf offered it to him. As he looked it over, he found it in good shape - almost new.

"I took two pistols from the two dead men when we were getting you ready to travel after you were shot. I didn't take the pistols in their holsters, these were in their waistband. I decided if I took the other pistols, people would have known somebody had been there. Little Feather insisted we leave no trace of being there."

"Where's the other pistol?"

"Little Feather has it," Running Wolf added.

"Will you teach me to shoot this gun?"asked Running Wolf.

"This pistol's the same caliber as mine. I don't have very many rounds with me," Logan told his friend.

"I have many bullets for this gun." Running Wolf hurried off toward his teepee.

When he returned he had six boxes of new 44-40 shells.

Logan grinned, "Where did you find these?"

"I found them in the cabins below where you were shot. Hawk and I later last fall after you were in camp returned to the place. The bodies had all been removed and the cabins closed up. We saw the little rider who kept looking for sign ride over the mountain. So we went into the cabins looking for anything we could use. There were blankets on the bunks. We took them, and when we moved one bunk, we could see a hole in the floor. There was a door to space under the floor. We found two rifles and one pistol and many boxes of shells. There was powder and other bullets and then we took, as you call, a bullet mold for making bullets."

Logan grinned, "How many boxes of these shells do you have?"

Running Wolf motioned many.

"Do you have a holster for this pistol?"

Running Wolf shook his head no. "I want to carry my pistol in belt like you do with your extra pistol."

After Logan was through with all Little Feather wanted him to do for the time being, he     motioned for Running Wolf and they walked away from camp.

"Running Wolf, have you ever shot a pistol before?"

"I shot Hawk's front loading pistol before."

Logan nodded, "Draw your pistol and slowly take aim and shoot that small rock by the   tree."

Running Wolf slowly drew down on the rock. He quickly learned the pistol had a hair trigger and the shot went high into the air. Logan chuckled. Running Wolf had almost dropped the pistol. Logan took the pistol. He found the former owner had filed down the action so this pistol had a very hair trigger. Logan fired and the rock went flying. Then he explained to Running Wolf about the easy trigger pull. After a dozen shots, Running Wolf finally hit the rock. "That's enough practice for one day. Let's head back to camp," Logan suggested.

The day of the wedding was a big day. Little Feather had sewn Logan a new shirt and pants from elk hides. Her mother had trimmed his hair and beard. Then he went to the hot springs for a bath. It was a big day for everyone. That night he and Little Feather shared the new teepee built for them.

The weather was getting warm and the grass was green in this part of the White River canyon. Logan was back to feeling good and had gained some of his weight back but was still skinny compared to when he was shot. Running Wolf practiced everyday and Logan was surprised at the speed and accuracy he had gained. He wanted to go with Logan when he left, and Logan decided to take him along. Logan and Little Feather decided he would help her move back up to the summer camp before he left.

It was, Logan guessed, May when Hawk's people started back to the mountains. When Little Feather was all settled in, Logan told her he would leave the next day. He had already told Running Wolf to be ready and what he wanted him to take. Logan looked more Indian than he did white. The clothes he wore when he was shot were destroyed. He had one change in his saddle bag which he had already worn out. He dressed in a buckskin shirt and pants and moccasins when he rode out the next morning. He had worn moccasins a lot traveling with old Dave in his younger days. His boots were totally gone so he had no choice but to wear moccasins now. It was hard to leave Little Feather, but Hawk said she would be fine with them and not to worry. Logan wanted to make it to Kilgore without anyone recognizing him. Jerry Crawford would know what was going on, and he could get some different clothes for him and Running Wolf.

They made the trip in six days. Logan waited till closing time to ride up to the trading post. They dismounted and walked into the store. It was empty except for Jerry behind the counter.

Jerry looked up, "Can I help you fellows? I'm about to close up."

Logan walked closer, "I sure could use some new duds," then walked toward the racks of shirts. Jerry stared at the guns Logan wore. He turned to look Logan over. Logan turned.

"What's the matter, Jerry, don't you even know your old friend?"

Jerry said in a low whisper, "Logan?"

Logan put out his hand, "How have you been, Jerry?"

Logan turned to Running Wolf and introduced him to Jerry. Jerry and Running Wolf both laughed.

Logan grinned, "I forgot you used to trade with Hawk and Little Bear, so you know Running Wolf from before. I want some white man's clothes for both me and Running Wolf."

They spent an hour picking out clothes. Logan bought a pair of boots, but Running Wolf decided he would keep his moccasins and leggings for the time being. Logan's old hat was in bad shape, but he decided it was good enough for awhile. Jerry told Logan he would cut his hair and beard off if he wanted, but Logan decided to wait. As they ate supper, Logan noticed a woman fixed their supper.

"Bayou died during the winter. I sure do miss him," said Jerry. "I hired a housekeeper and cook to take care of the place and also work out front when I'm busy."

After supper Jerry told Logan all he knew about the Rafter T and the ranger outfit.

"You know Tug has ridden all over the country looking for you."

Then he looked at Logan, "How bad were you hit? Tug figured out you had been hit by the blood he found with the rifle casing."

Logan told Jerry the whole story and that he was now part of the tribe since he married Little Feather.

Jerry told Logan, "From the stories I've heard, your mother still says her son will be back come spring."

Logan grinned, "I think that woman can look into the future somehow. She always seems to know about things like this."

"The rangers had trouble with rustlers last fall. The rustlers are back, and there's been many raids. I just heard today that Tug and some of his rangers were over around Benton this week chasing a big bunch that's been raiding there. A rider stopped by the other day. He said the Rafter T had been hit last week pretty hard," Jerry added.

Logan nodded, "Well, I guess come morning I'd better get back to work. I've been off too long."

Logan and Running Wolf rode up over the pass onto Rafter T land. They stayed in the timber as they rode down toward the valley. They skirted the buildings, and Logan could see where one hay barn had burned. Running Wolf touched Logan's arm and held his hand to his ear and pointed south. Logan then heard what Running Wolf had heard. It was gun fire coming from over the next ridge. It was real distant. They turned and headed up over the ridge. Staying in the thick timber, they soon could hear cattle bawling and the shots were getting louder. Logan worked them around where they could see into a small meadow. He could see a puff of smoke coming from the rocks across the meadow. As he searched out the timber across the meadow from the rocks, he could see a downed horse and a fellow shooting from behind it. Then he picked out a body laying in the grass near where the fellow was shooting from behind the horse. He soon could see a couple more men in the trees. Then he saw the reflection of a shiny badge on one of the men. These men were some of his fellow rangers, and it looked like they were being ambushed. He could see men moving in the rocks to get a better angle to shoot the men in the trees.

Logan dismounted and pulled his old Sharps. Running Wolf was right behind him with his Sharps. They both found a place where they could see into the rocks real well. This was going to be some long shooting.

Logan looked over at Running Wolf, "Shoot to kill."

The two big bores roared together. Two men in the rocks were knocked over backwards. Logan could see another fellow in the trees holding horses so he shot him. Then he put a shot into the dirt in front of the horses. They broke and ran into the meadow. He and Running Wolf poured a deadly fire into the rocks. Then he spotted a white flag being waved from behind a rock. He motioned for Running Wolf to stop firing. They both stayed hidden where they were. Finally, Logan saw two men walking into the meadow from the rocks holding another man between them. Two horses came from the trees below Logan and started across the meadow toward the three with the white flag. Logan recognized Fred, his old partner. When he looked back toward the downed horse, there stood Tug looking up the ridge.

Logan and Running Wolf moved back to their horses and mounted up and moved off through the trees toward Tug. Logan and Running Wolf were still dressed in the clothes they wore from the summer camp. Their new clothes were in rolls behind their saddles. Logan knew as he broke from the timber that Tug didn't recognize him. When Logan rode up, he said in a very low voice, "Why do you always get your horse shot from under you?"

Tug jumped into a run. He hollered Logan's name as he pulled him from the saddle. He grabbed Logan in a bear hug and almost caused Logan to fall.

Tug then stepped back. "Where in the hell have you been?" then added, "you look more Indian than white man."

Logan smiled, "It'll take many hours to bring you up to date so we'll do that later. What happened here?"

"This bunch hit the Rafter T last night. Me and my crew were staying the night there. We heard the shooting when they shot the night herder. We saddled up and took after the rustlers and the cattle. When it broke light this morning, we found the tracks of the herd going down this narrow valley. When we got here, they had this ambush set up, and we got caught in the middle. Then they pushed the cattle on past us. Part of the herd broke back here. But they still got a big bunch, and they're headed out over the pass unless we stop them." Logan motioned to the spare horse he had.

"Get your gear from your downed horse and use our spare horse." Running Wolf had jumped down to help Tug get his gear from the dead horse.

Fred rode over to where they were. He didn't recognize Logan at all.

262

"Fred, tell the other two rangers to take the three live rustlers and load the dead ones and head for Benton," Tug told Fred. Fred rode off to tell the other two what Tug wanted. Running Wolf and Logan helped Tug get his gear from the dead horse. When Tug was saddled, Fred rode back and Tug motioned to follow.

"Let's get after the cattle and the rest of the rustlers." Logan was already well ahead following the tracks of the herd. Fred looked over at Tug as they were headed down the trail, "Who's the help?"

Tug laughed, "You heard and saw that shooting, who do you think it is?"

Fred stared at Tug, "You mean that's Logan?" Tug nodded.

They broke into a trot to keep up with Logan and Running Wolf.

Logan motioned to stop and pointed down below them where the cattle were drinking from a creek, and the rustlers were building a fire off to one side. Tug moved up beside Logan.

"They think their friends finished us off and nobody is following them." Logan reached back and shook hands with Fred as he rode up.

"Tug, you and Fred move over to cover that bunch from behind the fire. When you're ready, wave and Running Wolf and I will greet our friends below."

When Tug got into position and waved, Logan and Running Wolf were lying on the hillside ready with their rifles. Logan's first shot took the fellow putting the coffee pot on the fire. The fellow was knocked over into another sitting on a rock. Running Wolf shot the fellow tending the horses and down he went. Tug and Fred poured two shots into the camp and the others threw up their hands. Logan and Running Wolf stayed on the hill while Tug and Fred rode down to get the prisoners. Logan watched the cattle. They were tired from the run and many of them had already laid down after drinking their fill.

"I think these cattle will still be here when someone from the ranch gets here," Logan told Tug. He nodded.

Tug looked over at Running Wolf. "You've been taking lessons from Logan the way you handle that big bore."

Running Wolf nodded, "He gave me this rifle many moons ago. Then taught me how to shoot well."

Tug looked at Logan. "This must be one story you forgot to tell me when we rode together."

They started back up the trail.

"I'm going to take these prisoners to the jail in Benton this afternoon," Tug told Logan. As they rode back up through a narrow part of the valley, they could see dust rising up the trail ahead. Tug and Fred glanced at each other when they noticed Logan and Running Wolf were no longer riding with them. They had slipped back into the trees and blended in so you could hardly see them. The group of riders came into view. Tug recognized Rebecca riding in the lead with Whitey Miller at her side. When they pulled up, Rebecca asked before Tug could say anything, "What Indians broke up the ambush with the big rifles?"

"How did you find out about the ambush," Tug inquired.

"We met the rangers taking the prisoners into Benton. While we were talking to the rangers, one prisoner spoke up. He said they had you rangers in a good trap and would have gotten away if the Indians with the big rifles hadn't shown up."

Tug grinned and motioned to the two riders coming out of the timber toward them. Rebecca dug her spurs and raced toward the two. She launched herself onto the big bearded rider before her horse had come to a stop. She almost unseated Logan as she landed in his lap. Logan's horse almost went down with the sudden extra weight. She yelled in his ear, "Logan, where in hell have you been?" When she had finally let go of him, Logan let her to the ground. He dismounted and hugged her.

Tug, who had ridden up, asked, "Rebecca, how did you know it was Logan with the beard and all.

Rebecca laughed "Tug, have you ever seen an Indian with a beard like that?"as she pointed at Logan. Rebecca then turned to look at Running Wolf, who was still wondering about who this wild woman was.

"Sis, I'd like you to meet Running Wolf. He's, I guess, what you call my brother-in-law." The others all turned to stare at Logan.

Rebecca started to laugh, "I really want to hear this story."

Logan turned to Tug and winked. "Don't we need to get these prisoners to Benton while Rebecca gathers the cattle." The riders from the ranch had moved up to join the group. Logan shook hands with Whitey Miller and his brother, Jerry, who had worked for Ted a good many years.

Rebecca turned to Whitey, "You find the cattle and head them back for the ranch. I'm not letting Logan out of my sight until I hear the story of where he's been."

Tug, who had been listening to all this, told Whitey where he would find the cattle, and the Rafter T riders moved off to get the herd.

"Tug, I can take the prisoners on into Benton if you want to get to the ranch with Logan," said Fred.

Tug nodded, "Good, I'll stay with Logan. Tomorrow bring the other rangers, and I'll meet you at the ranch."

As they rode up to the buildings, Ted stepped out from the barn to greet the four riders. Logan swung down and reached to shake hands with Ted before Ted recognized him.

He grabbed Logan, "It's about time you showed up. Lottie kept saying you would be back this spring. As time passed, I was thinking she might be wrong for once."

Logan looked over toward the house and could see his mother on the porch shading her eyes to see what was happening over by the barn. Logan stepped away and headed for the house. He was about half way there when he heard his mother call his name. She met him at the gate and held him, and Logan could feel her crying against his chest.

Finally she stepped back and looked him over, "Where have you been, and why the clothes?"

Logan grinned at her, "I'll tell the whole story tonight when everyone is here." The others had held back but now were walking up to the house. Running Wolf held back behind the rest. Logan motioned for him to step forward. As he walked up, Logan could see his sister grinning.

Logan turned to his mother, "I want you to meet my new traveling partner, Running Wolf." As Lottie walked up to greet Running Wolf, Logan added, "This fellow is also my brother-in-law."

Lottie told Running Wolf she was glad to meet him, acting like she hadn't heard what Logan had said. She told the group she expected them all for supper and walked back toward the house.

After supper that evening, Logan sat the family down and told the story about his life since the shooting. He told of how Little Feather and her mother had used everything they knew of Shoshone medicine to save his life. He told them for over one month he didn't move. Then he figured out where he was and who was nursing him back to health. He told Ted these were the same people he had helped while spending the winter with the horses.

Ted nodded, "I remember you talking of the Indians you met that winter."

As Logan went on about what he remembered of the shooting and what had happened before he was shot, he looked over at Tug.

"When you were on the ridge looking down at the two teepees and the two women, I was in one of the teepees."

Tug grinned, "How come they didn't let me know you were there."

Running Wolf, who had been listening, added, "They didn't know you were a friend, so they only watched you. I also watched you one day looking to find sign at the place where we found Logan. Until Logan was able to talk, we weren't letting anyone know he was with us. Little Feather didn't let any of us in the teepee except to move him when she changed the medicine on his wounds."

Everyone just sat there after Logan finished his story. No one said a word. Finally, Lottie looked at Logan, "When do I get to meet my new daughter?"

"Soon I hope."

Logan went on to tell about Raven Basin and that he was going to file on the land and make Little Feather's family equal partners. He needed to have Henry help him get the Indian bureau to let the family stay in the basin and not move them to a reservation. Logan told them once he had buildings and was ready, he wanted to buy cattle to stock the basin.

"I'll keep on working for the rangers as long as they want me, but my home will be in the basin.

He looked over at Lottie. "I'll bring Little Feather to see you one day when things calm down. She speaks real good English and has taught her brothers the language." He hugged his mother, "You'll like Little Feather. She is a lot like you. You're both strong-minded."

The next morning the rangers showed up ready to head back toward headquarters. As Tug mounted up, Logan told him.

"I want a couple days before I ride into headquarters to see George."

"Do I tell George and Henry you're back?" asked Tug.

Logan nodded, "I think you should."

After the rangers left, Logan told Running Wolf, "It's time for us to try out the new clothes we bought. I need a haircut and get this beard trimmed."

Lottie had heard this. "You get ready. I'll be glad to do that for you."

After Logan was all cleaned up, Lottie stepped back and looked at her oldest son.

"Logan, you're no longer my young-looking son; you look so much older. You need to put some weight back on; you're too thin."

"When I started to come around after I was shot, I didn't even recognize my own arms and legs."

Running Wolf was still wearing his buckskin pants but had put on the shirt they had bought at Kilgore. Logan went out to the tack room and dug through boxes of his stuff he had gotten from Dave. He found some holsters he had found in Claire Matthews' belongings. He finally found a cross draw holster and the belt to go with it. He showed it to Running Wolf and showed him how to wear it around his waist. Running Wolf kept changing it until he found the position he liked and could draw with good speed.

Logan grinned at his speed. "I was worried that your pistol would hang up on your clothes the way you've been carrying it. This way it would always come free. You need to keep the holster well-oiled and soft."

Rebecca had walked up and watched the two as Running Wolf tried out the holster. They looked over at her, "I see you have taught him well, Logan."

Logan and Running Wolf left the next morning for ranger headquarters. Lottie walked out as they were ready to leave. Logan knew she was having a hard time trying not to shed a few tears.

He looked down at her. "I will keep in touch and hope to see you soon."

As they started to leave, Rebecca motioned toward the road from Benton. Two riders were making good time toward the ranch buildings.

Lottie laughed, "I was hoping they would hear Logan was here and show up."

As they rode into the yard, Logan figured out it was the rest of his family, John and Mary. Logan dismounted to greet the youngest of the McTier family. Logan couldn't believe how much both of them had grown since he last saw them. Logan and Running Wolf stayed for about an hour. Logan put his arms around John and Mary, "I hate to leave, but I need to get back to work."

When they rode into headquarters, it was evening. George had seen them, and he hurried from his office to greet Logan. Logan introduced Running Wolf.

"George, I think you should think about making Running Wolf the first Indian ranger."

Tug spoke up, "George, from what I've seen, Running Wolf will fit right in."

George nodded. "I'll think about it and talk it over with Henry."

The ranger headquarters now had a kitchen and dining hall, so after getting settled in Logan's quarters, they joined the crew for supper.

After supper Tug, Fred and Logan went over to George's office to meet with him. Logan told them what had happened the day he was shot. As he told the story, Tug sat back and listened with a very sober look on his face. When Logan finished the story up to the part where he shot the man leading the pack string, Tug spoke up, "I guess you don't know who that fellow was, do you?"

Logan shook his head.

"It was Frank Griffith."

"Do you mean John Griffith's brother? He was part owner of the Golden Rose Mine."

"Frank Griffith was also known as Blackie Payne."

"When we got there, we found the dead man and the pack string. On him was papers saying he was Frank Griffith."

This was hard for Logan to figure out. He decided in the near future he would ride up to see John Griffith at the Golden Rose. Logan was curious why someone with a good mine and plenty of money would rob himself.

"Logan, we've been curious about how you shot Frank and then totally disappeared; now we know," George added.

Later Logan told George, "I better stop by to see Henry and Becky or I'll be in a lot of trouble."

Running Wolf told Logan he would stay and talk to Tug and Fred. So Logan went alone to the governor's house. Logan knocked on the door. It opened and there stood Alice, their daughter. Logan could tell she didn't recognize him.

With a straight face he said, "May I see the governor?"

With a yell, "Logan!" she grabbed him into a big hug.

Henry and Becky heard her and they rushed into the room. Henry grabbed his hand and shook it while Becky grabbed him around the middle and planted a big kiss on his bearded cheek. Alice, as everyone stepped back, added, "I didn't recognize you with that beard."

They went into the living room and Becky brought coffee, "Start from the beginning, Logan, and don't leave anything out."

When Logan got to the part about Little Feather, both women really watched him with interest. When he said they were married, all three looked at each other and then back at Logan. Becky grinned, "What did Lottie say when you told her?"

"She only asked when she was going to meet her new daughter."

Henry laughed, "I think it's great."

Logan then told them his plans for filing on the land in Raven Basin. "Henry, I'm going to need some help with the legal part."

Henry nodded. "Logan, I'll get the paperwork started. You'll need to meet with the colonel out at the army post about keeping Hawk's people off the reservation."

It was late when Logan returned to his quarters. He found Tug and his crew packing to head out. George was with them.

"Logan, I want you to stay here at headquarters in case more trouble starts elsewhere. I just got a telegram that rustlers have hit a big ranch down near the territorial boundary and three ranch hands have been killed. Tug's taking four rangers with him. They're leaving on a special train as soon as they can get loaded."

The next morning after breakfast, Logan and Running Wolf stopped by George's office. Henry was there, and they talked about making Running Wolf a ranger. Logan introduced Henry to Running Wolf.

Henry told the three, "I have no problem making a lawman out of Running Wolf if Logan thinks he can handle it."

George reached into his desk and pulled out a badge and handed it to Henry, "You pin it on."

Running Wolf didn't understand that part of the obligation and looked at Logan.

"Just say, 'I do'."

With a big grin Logan told his partner, "You are now a ranger, and, as far as I know, the only Indian lawman in the area."

That afternoon Logan and Running Wolf rode out to the army post to see the colonel in charge. They were ushered into the office and introduced to Colonel Muller. He offered his hand to Logan, "I've heard many things about you as a lawman."

He turned to Running Wolf, "What tribe are you from?"

"I'm the son of Hawk, of the Little Bear clan of the Shoshone."

The colonel nodded, "I know Hawk, and I guessed you were one of his sons."

"The governor just made Running Wolf a full fledged ranger this morning," said Logan. Colonel Muller shook Running Wolf's hand. "I wish the best on being a lawman."

Logan then told the colonel what he wanted to do up in Raven Basin on White River. The colonel thought for a moment. "I have no problems with Hawk and his family staying in the basin, but I don't have final say on this. I'll contact the Bureau of Indian Affairs, to see if they have any problems with your proposal. When I find out, Logan, I'll get word to you."

As Logan and Running Wolf rode back into ranger headquarters, people hurried everywhere. Logan heard his name being called. He looked toward the office to see George waving for him to ride over. "One of the banks uptown just got robbed. Two clerks were shot. The town marshall got a couple of shots at the robbers as they rode down the alley but didn't stop them. Get up there and see the marshall. Find out what he knows, then get after the robbers if you can find a trail to follow."

As they rode up near the bank, a man with a badge came hurrying up to them. "There were five riders leaving down the alley when I shot. I don't think I hit anyone. From what I can find out, four men were in the bank, and the fifth must have been holding the horses in the alley."

Logan and Running Wolf rode around to the alley and found where the horses had been held. The back door of the bank was still open. Many people had walked around out there so they moved down the alley to check the horses tracks. Logan motioned to Running Wolf the horse track with one new shoe. Running Wolf pointed to another track where the horse had a side cast track on one rear hoof. They followed the tracks out on to the main street where the tracks were more confusing with all the traffic since the word of the bank robbery got out. About a half mile out of town the tracks got plainer as the traffic thinned. They started making better time. Another mile and they found where the riders had separated. Three riders headed up a little used trail that headed up toward a rocky ridge and from there up into the timber country.

Logan told Running Wolf, "You follow the three, and I'll stay on the main trail."

Logan went another couple miles when the two he had been following headed up another trail heading into the mountains. Logan could see where they had stopped and checked their back trail. Logan looked for a place to leave the trail and still be able to see the trail as he rode along. Logan got into thick timber when he heard a magpie chatter in the trees ahead. He stopped. Then he heard a bird call over to his right and knew Running Wolf was letting him know he was close by. Logan dismounted and moved ahead real quiet-like. The next thing he knew, Running Wolf stood next to him. He motioned for Logan to follow him. Leaving his horse, Logan followed Running Wolf through the timber to a clearing. There was a small fire smoking in an opening and one man drinking a cup of coffee. They watched and could count six horses in a makeshift corral behind the man. They looked lathered, and Logan started thinking the robber had spare horses stashed here. This fellow was probably just a man hired to shuffle the horses. Running Wolf motioned he would circle in behind the fellow to make sure he was alone. When Logan saw Running Wolf was in place, he moved up and had his pistol covering the fellow as he walked into camp. The fellow heard Logan. He dropped his cup and started to draw when he saw Logan already had him covered. The fellow noticed the badge.

"What the hell do you want, lawman?"

Logan moved over and pulled the man's pistol and then tossed a nearby rifle into the brush. The man's hand started under his coat when he felt a cold sharp object touching his neck. He dropped his hand. He slowly turned to find an Indian standing there with a long bladed knife touching his neck. He turned white as Running Wolf reached under his coat to get the pistol stuck in his belt.

Logan motioned to a log, "Sit down on that log. How long ago did your friends ride off."

"I'm here alone, what are you talking about?"

Then he noticed Logan was holding a rope and Running Wolf was talking in his native tongue. Logan nodded and turned back toward the man sitting on the log.

"We know those horses in the corral are the horses used in the bank robbery in Capital City. If you don't tell me the truth, I'll let Running Wolf tie you between two horses and turn them loose on the trail."

Logan looked at the fellow, "You're not worth the trouble and turned away."

The fellow hollered at Logan, "Why is that damn Indian wearing a badge?"

Logan grinned, "Running Wolf is a full fledge territorial ranger."

"Now you're wasting our time. When did your friends leave?"

271

Logan turned to Running Wolf. "Go get ropes on all the horses and get ready to travel."

Logan retrieved the rifle from the brush. He gathered up all the saddle bags from around the fire. When Running Wolf came back, Logan put the fellow's gear on the horse that was already saddled. Running Wolf had also brought up their horses.

"Now take off your boots." Logan tied them to the saddle of the spare horse then mounted his horse. Running Wolf had the lead ropes of the other horses. Logan motioned for him to head out. The fellow sitting on the log jumped up, "What about me?"

Logan looked back, "There'll be a posse along after awhile; you can join them or walk to town."

Logan rode along behind Running Wolf who was already on the tracks of the bank robbers. When it got dark that night, they stopped near a creek and made camp.

They were in the saddle moving out at first light. The gang they were following got a little sloppy and didn't even try to cover their tracks. They came into a long valley and Logan could see buildings ahead. The men they were following had stopped and dismounted here out of sight of the buildings. The tracks looked like they were made either early that morning or late last night. Running Wolf rode on up the road. He pointed in two different directions. Logan rode over and could see where two of the riders had rode off from the rest of the group. They followed the other three for a ways and then another rider left the bunch. The last two riders rode another mile then they separated, each traveling into the valley. They rode back to where the first lone rider had left to travel into the valley. Following his tracks led them down into the valley and toward the buildings they had seen from above. As they got closer, Logan could see tall false fronts on a couple of the buildings. It looked like a small town started up in the valley. Looking around, Logan could see cattle along the small creek running through the valley. On one hillside there looked to be a mine because of the tailings pile along the ridge. Moving closer Logan could read a handwritten sign, saying, "Welcome to Mercyville." In small print below the name it said 'no guns allowed.' As they rode up in front of a building with "General Store" in big print on the false front, two men came out to greet them. One fellow motioned to a sign on the post on the front porch of the store.

"We don't allow guns in town."

Logan pulled back his coat and showed them the badge. The same fellow said, "That doesn't mean you can wear guns in our town, even if you are with the law."

Logan swung down and walked up to the fellow and in a very cold tone said, "It does now, and besides, we're here on business." The tracks they followed led around behind the building. Logan followed them into a barn behind the store. The two men were trotting to keep up with Logan's long strides. Logan walked up to a horse. It had been ridden in the last few hours. He walked over to a saddle blanket hanging over the saddle rack; it was still wet. He turned to the two men.

"Who belongs to this horse?"

"It belongs to the store owner's son."

"Does he have a name?"

They both answered at the same time, "Larry Kimbell. His dad, Ralph, owns the store."

Logan motioned to a small cabin behind the store. There was smoke coming from the chimney.

"Who lives there?"

"It belongs to Kimbells. Larry and his brother stay in it.

Logan motioned to Running Wolf, "You watch these two." He stepped over to the cabin door. Logan pulled his pistol and opened the door and walked in. A sleepy head appeared from the bunk.

"What's going on? Who are you?"

Logan jerked the fellow from the bed and sat him down in a chair in the middle of the room. The sleepy man was awake now. Logan could see he was about his age. Logan spotted a saddle bag lying on the upper bunk above where the fellow had been sleeping. As Logan moved toward the bunk, the fellow dove for his gun belt laying under the bed. Logan rapped him with his pistol barrel behind the ear before he got half way there. The fellow hit the floor and didn't move. Logan opened the saddle bag and found it almost full of green bills, and in the bottom, he could feel coins. He heard Running Wolf tell someone to stand still. He stepped to the door to find a small group of people had gathered. Running Wolf had his rifle trained on the man trying to get through the crowd. Logan motioned for Running Wolf to let him by. The man stopped in front of Logan.

"I demand to know what is going on."

"Who are you?" Logan asked.

"I'm Ralph Kimbell. I'm the owner of this store."

Logan motioned him to step into the cabin. He pointed to the fellow laying on the floor, "Is that your son?"

Ralph kneeled beside his son who was starting to wake up. He turned to Logan, "Why has my son been knocked out?"

Logan tossed the saddle bag over to him, "What do you know about this money?" Ralph knocked the bag away. When it hit the floor the cash and gold coins spilled all over the floor. He stopped and looked at the money on the floor.

"The bank in Capital City was robbed, and the tracks led us here," said Logan.

Ralph turned to Logan, "We are of the belief that's against any type of violence."

Logan told both Ralph and his son, who was now standing, to step outside. Logan turned to the crowd. "The bank in Capital City was robbed, and two clerks in the bank were shot during the robbery. We've been following the tracks of the robbers and it led here."

As Logan spoke, a big tall man dressed in a black flock coat came pushing his way through the crowd. As he pushed his way up to Logan, he said in a loud voice, "You'll leave my town now and take your heathen friend with you. I'm Reverend Ballard and these are my people. We don't recognize your law here."

As he started to push his way up next to Logan, a pistol appeared in Logan's left hand. His right grabbed the front of the man's shirt. The crowd started to push forward, but when the gun appeared, they stopped. In a very cold voice, Logan spoke in the reverend's ear, "You tell these people to back off or they're going loose their leader."

The big man glared at Logan. He must have seen something in Logan's eyes that made him turn to the crowd, and he told them to stay back.

After the crowd moved back, Logan pointed to the man he had clubbed in the cabin. "Reverend, the bank in Capital City was robbed. In that cabin lying on the table, you will find a gun belt and pistol belonging to him. On the floor, you'll find money that spilled from this fellow's saddlebag."

Running Wolf, who had moved over closer to the horses the men were holding in the crowd, nodded at Logan. Running Wolf then moved up behind a younger fellow holding a horse in the back of the crowd. Logan walked through the crowd and motioned the Reverend to follow him. As

Logan walked toward the fellow, he started to step back. Then he felt Running Wolf's gun barrel against his back. Logan noticed the saddle bags behind the saddle on the man's horse were the same as the ones they had found the money in. As he stepped over to get them, another young man in the crowd started backing away from the group. Logan told the fellow to stand where he was.

"Reverend, look in the saddle bags on the horse."

Logan heard the crowd gasp, and he knew what had come out of the bag. As Logan looked back, he saw the preacher take a rolled up gun belt from the other saddle bag. He threw them to the ground. Running Wolf had moved over and moved the other young fellow to the front of the crowd. Logan noticed this fellow's saddle didn't have any saddle bags. There was a bedroll tied behind the saddle.

"Running Wolf, see what's in that roll behind the saddle." When Running Wolf unrolled it, he found a gun belt and two pistols.

Logan turned back to the reverend. "Are these three part of your clan?"

The reverend scowled, "They are sons of elders of our church."

"I think, Reverend, if someone would ride out, they'll probably find this fellow's share of the bank robbery. It can't be far away," Logan added.

Logan tied the men up. "I'm taking these fellows back to the capital. Then I'm coming back to look for the other two and the balance of the bank money."

The reverend turned to Logan, "If you'd like, we have a new jail that is still unused, and you're welcome to use it tonight. That way you could get an early start tomorrow."

Logan and Running Wolf were just about to the jail with the reverend and four other men when Logan saw movement out of the corner of his eye. He hollered to Running Wolf, and he dove sideways drawing as he did. He heard one shot come from between the buildings. Then another shot from a building to his right. Both bullets had hit flesh behind him. Logan fired at the man leveling his pistol for another shot from between the buildings. Logan fired and the man was knocked back into the alley. Logan heard two shots coming from Running Wolf's direction. He glanced that way and saw a fellow slumped against the wall of the new jail. Logan walked over toward the alley. When he got closer, he could see a boot, then he could see a body; it wasn't moving. As he walked up, he could see he had hit him dead center in the chest. The man was dead. Turning back to the street, Logan saw people huddled over two men lying in the street. As he walked closer, he could see the black coat of Reverend Ballard. He struggled to sit up. Logan could see blood coming from his shoulder. There was another man lying close by. They covered him with a coat. Logan recognized the man they had covered up as the store owner, Ralph Kimbell.

Running Wolf stood by the jail and motioned for Logan to join him. Logan could see the man up against the building was still alive. Logan bent down to look and could see the fellow had been hit twice in the chest.

In a low whisper he asked, "How bad is the reverend hit?"

"I think the reverend will be okay." The man's head dropped, and he was dead. One of the town's people walked over to see who had been shot. "Oh, my God, it's Danny."

"Who's Danny," Logan inquired.

"That is Danny Ballard, the reverend's son."

Logan walked back toward the people helping the reverend into a wagon bed. Logan turned when he heard horses galloping up the street. As he turned, he saw about eight men moving toward them, most were wearing badges. The posse from Capital City had followed Logan and Running Wolf's tracks. Logan brought Marshall Cromwell up to date. He motioned to the three prisoners now sitting on the steps to the new jail.

"Those three are part of your robbers, and we've recovered part of the money."

Later that night Logan and the marshall made a call on the reverend to see how he was. He sat up in bed and shook hands with both Logan and the marshall. "I've been told about my son, Danny, being dead. I'll help you find the rest of the money."

As they left, Logan thought the preacher was taking his son's death a lot different than most fathers would.

"I want to go to the jail and talk to the prisoners," Logan told the marshall.

"I'll walk along to see how my deputies were getting along."

As they rounded the corner, Logan could see the jail door open. In the lantern light, he could see a deputy with his hands in the air. Logan touched the marshall's arm and motioned him back into the shadows.

"Marshall, you stay here, and if whoever's in there tries to come out the door, shoot to keep them inside." Logan went back around and crossed the street in the shadows. He moved up to the jail real slow. He suddenly heard a low sound of a night hawk coming from the shadows behind the jail. As he moved that way, Running Wolf appeared from the shadows.

Running Wolf whispered, "I cut the cinches on the horses behind the jail."

As they moved up closer to the jail, the back door opened and the three prisoners were peering out into the dark area behind the jail. Two more men appeared behind them. They were joined by two more as they slowly walked out toward their horses. Logan and Running Wolf stood in the shadows behind the horses. As the men mounted up, all hell broke loose. Men fell under the horses when their saddles turn on them. The horses stomped on the men on the ground. A couple of them broke loose and ran out onto the street in front of the jail. Logan could see the marshall appear in the door of the jail. He then moved into the shadows next to the door. Logan, in a voice that all could hear over the confusion, told everyone to stand still. One man ran a shot that broke the night air. The man folded to the ground. The shot had come from Running Wolf. About then the marshall shot as one man broke for the open jail door.

The remaining men hollered that they were giving up and their hands went into the air. About this time more deputies came out of the jail. The jail breakers had locked the deputies in the cells. The marshall had seen, from where he was, the men moving out the back door of the jail. He crossed the street and went in the front door. He unlocked the cells before he had moved over to the back door where Logan had seen him. They herded the men back into the jail. By now there was a crowd in front of the jail. The four men who tried to break into the jail were older men that Logan had seen in the crowd earlier at the store. There were four cells in the new jail, so they divided up the prisoners as they put them in cells. The two wounded men were put into a cell by themselves. One of the deputies tended to their wounds.

Logan walked to the door and told the crowd to go home. A woman from the crowd moved forward. "What's going to happen to the men involved in the jail break tonight?"

"All of the prisoners will be taken to Capital City to stand trial," Logan told her. As she walked closer, Logan could see she had a child, and she was crying. "My husband didn't want to do this. The reverend ordered him and the others to break the prisoners out of jail."

Someone in the crowd yelled for her to shut up. The marshall had been watching and told one deputy to go into the crowd and get the man that yelled at her. The man started to move back and a voice behind him said, "Just stay where you're at."

Logan smiled. He recognized the voice of Running Wolf.

Logan was really getting to like this Indian as a partner and the way he moved when involved with a crowd.

He heard another man in the crowd say, "It's that damn Indian behind us."

About this time two other women stepped up alongside the first woman. "We're with her."

Logan ushered them inside and pulled some chairs from the office for them. The man from the crowd who had yelled at them was put into a cell. The marshall and Logan listened as the women told how the operation was run by the reverend and some of the other elders. The lady that first spoke up told Logan to look at her husband's back to see where the reverend had beat him for not going on any of the raids. She told him that when they came for her husband tonight to help break out the prisoners, he refused at first.

"They told him they would not only beat him but also me if he didn't help. So he went with them."

Logan nodded, "I'll talk it over with the marshall, and we'll let you know come morning if your husband will be charged."

Logan and the marshall got the names of the other elders involved and decided that they would arrest them in the morning, then take them back to Capital City along with the reverend and the prisoners. Logan was awakened by someone beating on the door of the back room of the jail. One of the deputies poked his head in, "You're needed out front." When Logan walked into the jail office, two young boys were crying and talking to the marshall. They were telling him they went to the barn to milk and found their dad hanging from a rafter. Logan and the marshall followed the boys to a farm about a mile from town. They cut down the body. They learned from the mother of the boys that her husband was an elder in the church. They loaded the body into a wagon. A deputy rode up with word two more men had been found hung. As the morning wore on, Logan and the marshall found that all of the elders not in jail had hung themselves, except one. When they rode out to that farm, they found no one. Breakfast dishes were still on the table and nothing was out of place. Running Wolf went to the

278

barn. He found tracks of a wagon leaving up the road out of the valley. One of the men that led the lawmen, told them the man had a wife and two kids.

As the marshall got ready to head back to Capital City with the prisoners, he and Logan decided to let two of the men from the jail go home. They both had scars on their backs from recent beatings and were not part of the reverend's trusted thieves. With everyone loaded, the marshall left for Capital City.

"I'll be heading back to headquarters when I'm sure we haven't missed anyone," said Logan.

Logan held a meeting with the townspeople and told them the law wasn't going to bother them as long as they stayed straight. Logan kept the two men who had been released from jail as the crowd broke up from the meeting. He told them he was putting them in charge of keeping this place free of any of the reverend's men that might still be around.

After returning to headquarters, Logan told George he would like to ride over his area to see how things were. George went to a rough drawn map on the wall of his office and drew a line around the area he wanted Logan to patrol. As they discussed the boundaries, Logan noticed his area included the White River drainage which would include Raven Basin.

When Logan saddled up to leave, George told him a messenger from the army post had just brought word that Colonel Muller wanted to see him.

Logan nodded, "I'll stop by on my way out."

George shook hands with Logan, "This new larger area will keep you busy, and you're going to be on your own. This area is too big for you to keep me informed of everything, so use your best judgement and I'll back you up. This large area has few people now but I look for it to grow once people hear about it. If something comes up, I'll send word to Kilgore and also up to the mines. If you need to contact headquarters, you can send word back the same way."

"I figure on covering the whole area before winter sets in. Then I'll winter down along White River with Little Feather." George again shook hands with Logan and then walked over to Running Wolf and shook his hand.

"I'm glad we made you a ranger."

When Logan was escorted into Colonel Muller's office, the Indian agent was also present. Running Wolf had walked in with Logan. The agent looked at the colonel, "You didn't tell me he was a ranger."

Colonel Muller grinned, "From the reports I've heard, these two make a good team."

The colonel turned to Logan. "We've talked it over. If you hire the people of Hawk's band to work for you, the army or Indian Affairs won't interfere. If trouble starts between this group and settlers moving into the area, then the army will step in."

With their agreement worked out, Logan and Running Wolf headed for Kilgore. Logan needed to see Jerry at the trading post.

Logan and Running Wolf were traveling along a month later into the upper reaches of Logan's territory. They had been traveling along an open ridge when Running Wolf pointed to wagon tracks in the tall grass. They looked to be a week or so old, and they were traveling deeper into mountains. Logan thought to himself why was a wagon so far from any main road or even a good horse trail. It would have been a feat to get a wagon into this part of this range of mountains. Logan decided they would follow and see where the people were headed. The next day about noon they could smell wood smoke and finally could see a camp through the trees. As they rode closer, Logan hailed the camp and heard a woman's voice call back, "Come on in."

As they rode in, Logan could see a grey haired lady cooking over a fire. To Logan's surprise, there were two wagons parked just behind her. She smiled, "Climb down and have some coffee, and if you're hungry, I'd be glad to feed you."

"I'm Logan McTier, and this is Running Wolf. We are territorial rangers. We'll be glad to pay for a meal if you have the extra grub."

While they ate, she told them that they were moving through the area. "All this rough going had taken its toll on the wagons." My husband and two boys are out looking over the area trying to find place where we can winter. We know this is too high a country to spend the winter so they're out looking for way down off the mountain."

Running Wolf, who had been listening, said, "I think I know a place where they maybe can get the wagons down to White River."

Logan could see the surprised look on the lady's face when Running Wolf spoke English so well. "We'll ride over and look it over to see if the wagon can make it down to the river."

Logan and Running Wolf camped that night near a long bare ridge leading down off the mountain. The next morning they rode on down below the timberline and could see the headwaters of White River below them. They rode on down a ways further, and Logan could see where the ridge leading to the bottom was a good grade to get the wagons down. As they headed back up toward the camp, Logan found one place where they probably would have to rope the wagon down one real steep stretch. He figured he and Running Wolf could help these people before heading down to find Hawk's camp.

When they rode back into the camp, a big grey haired man and two big boys were standing by the fire. As Logan dismounted, the older man walked over and introduced himself.

"I'm Acel Helmick." The lady that had fed them stepped over next to him, "This is my wife, Caddie, and my sons, Boyd and Cliff."

They shook hands all around. "I think Running Wolf and I have found a way down to the river."

"Why don't you two spend the night, and we'll discuss this road you've found for us?" Logan agreed.

After supper Logan asked Acel what his profession was and learned he was a craftsman. "Back in the east before we headed west my favorite thing was to build big barns. I've built many houses, too, but my favorite is barns. My boys were also skilled, and as a team we built good buildings."

Logan grinned, "Would you be interested in building all the buildings for a large ranch?" The whole family was staring at him after he asked them that question. Logan laughed, "I'll pay in gold or anyway you would like to be paid."

Old Acel chuckled, "Where's this place at? Can we get our wagons there before winter?"

"If we get the wagons down to White River, the hardest part is over," Logan assured them.

On into the night Logan explained what he was doing. Before they all turned in for the night, they had a deal worked out.

It took them three days to get the wagons down to the valley floor, then another three days into Raven Basin. Logan took the family to the cabins used by the outlaws. Caddie was thrilled to have a roof over her head for winter. As they made camp, Logan saw the Helmicks all looking down the valley they had just traveled. Then he saw the Indians riding their way. Running Wolf stepped out to wave.

"It's my brother, Little Hawk."

When they rode up and dismounted, Logan introduced them to the Helmicks. Two of the braves with Little Hawk spoke very little English. Logan greeted them in their own tongue.

Little Hawk said, "Our camp is a half day's ride away."

Logan turned to Acel, "I'm going to leave you here to get settled and ride back to camp to see my wife, Little Feather. I'll be back in the morning to show you the whole basin and what I want built."

As they rode into the Indian camp, there was yelling and greetings from everyone. Logan then saw Little Feather running his way, and he jumped down to meet her. When she finally stepped back, Logan must have had a strange look on his face because she broke out laughing. She grabbed his hand and placed it on her bulging mid section.

"You will be a father come winter." Logan just stood there and then pulled her to him.

"Are you alright?"

She smiled, "I've never felt better."

They all ate together. Later, he and Little Feather went to their teepee to be alone. Logan told her of all that had happened and about building a ranch at Raven Basin.

Logan went back over to Helmick's the next morning to show Acel what he had planned for the ranch buildings. They spent the morning going over the location of the house and main buildings. Later, Logan and Acel rode up into the timberland to look for logs to build the house. It was decided with winter season getting close, Acel should go out with a pack string to Kilgore for supplies for his family.

"It's a long trip," Logan told Acel. "Kilgore and Jerry's trading post will be the best place to buy what you need. You tell Jerry that I'll be in later to pay for all the supplies. "Can I find this place on my own?"

"If you want a guide and a helper for the trip, I'm sure Little Hawk would enjoy the trip. He can probably get you there quicker because he was raised in that area. While you're gone, the boys could start falling trees. After it snows, they could skid them to the location of the buildings," Acel nodded.

With all this done, Logan headed back to spend the night with Little Feather. That evening Little Hawk came riding in and stopped by to talk. "Shot a big buck and took it down to the Helmicks' camp. Acel asked me to go to Kilgore with him. I'll be looking forward to seeing my old friend,

Jerry."

Logan spent one more day with Little Feather. The following day he and Running Wolf headed out to cover the area he was suppose to patrol. They went over into the east fork of White River. This was new country to Logan. Running Wolf knew this area from hunting trips with Hawk, so he led the way. They rode along a ridge looking down into a small valley when Running Wolf pointed to some buildings on the ridge across the valley from them. As they rode further on, they could see a tailings pile next to one building. They decided it was a mine they were looking at. Logan decided they would stop by to let people know they were in the country. As they rode up a rutted road toward the mine, they were stopped by a man with a rifle. "This is private property. Are you fellows looking for work?"

Logan shook his head, "We're not looking for work. I'm Logan McTier and this is Running Wolf. We're the territorial rangers for this area. We just stopped by to say hello.

The guard still had the rifle pointed at them. He told them, "You two just turn around and leave. We don't need any lawmen around."

Logan grinned, "Running Wolf, I think they must be hiding something if they don't want us around."

The guard growled, "What is your name again? I'll let the boss know you were around."

Logan noticed the look on the man's face when he said his name again. He dropped the rifle barrel. "Were you ever near Placer Butte?"

Logan laughed, "Yes, I spent over a year there working for the Chinese miners."

The guard smiled, "Then you're the kid that put an end to Tiny Lang's gang."

"I was only packing gold for the Chinese miners and Tiny's men kept trying to rob me. Tiny killed himself when the girls working for him spiked his shotgun."

"Well, you sure made a name for yourself with those two girls. They have a great business up there," the guard said with a smile. The guard motioned for them to follow, and he untied his horse and headed for the mine. The guard introduced them to his boss and mine owner, Cliff Stroup. When the guard told Cliff they were territorial rangers, a grin came to his face. "Sit right down here. I'll tell you of the trouble I'm having with four men living at a small store in the valley. They're robbing everyone who tries to pack gold out to Mill City or any other place to sell it. I hadn't made a shipment since my men were robbed and killed two months ago."

Cliff went on, "I loaded a small pack string with gold and sent them out the back way in the middle of the night. Two days later a trapper found their bodies shot to hell about ten miles from here. The horses and the gold were gone. We looked but couldn't find any trail to follow. It had rained the day before the bodies were found. I really need to get some gold into Mill City so I can pay my men and buy supplies."

Logan nodded, "When do you need to get a shipment out?"

"I owe many people for supplies and back wages. I've got the gold to pay them if we can get out of here."

"Okay, we'll look around. Why don't you plan on getting a shipment out in a couple of days. You get the shipment ready but don't tell any more people than you have to about what you're doing."

Logan and Running Wolf headed down the trail. Cliff had told them where they found the dead packers and what their horses looked like. As they rode up to where the guard had been they found, he was now back on duty. "Where's this store in the valley that Cliff spoke of?" Logan inquired, "How do we get there?"

As they started to ride away, the guard laughed, "If only those fellows knew what was in store for them."

They spent the night where the bodies had been found. Between the two of them they found enough sign to follow. At noon the next day, they were in the trees behind the store. There were two horses tied up out front  Four more were in the corral in back of the main building.

Logan and Running Wolf tied their horses out of sight and eased their way toward the buildings. As they neared the corral, they heard the front door open and men talking. Logan worked his way around where he could see the men. Then he heard someone say, "Now remember, keep us posted on the next shipment."

As the riders left, they rode by very close to Running Wolf and Logan. They were on the trail heading back toward the mine. Logan found a back window and eased himself up to look into the bar part of the store. There were four men in the room, three playing cards and one pouring himself a drink.

Logan moved back to where Running Wolf was waiting. "Get ready to sneak in the back door when I walk in the front door."

Logan eased around front and over to the front door. He waited a second then pushed open the door and walked in. The man watching the card game spun around.

"Where in the hell did you come from?"

The other three men in the card game stood. Logan motioned, "You three sit back down."

All three started to draw when two shots from the back of the room dropped two of them. The third turned to see Running Wolf with his pistol aimed at his mid section. The other fellow at the bar, with good speed, drew when a bullet caught him dead center. Logan turned to the only one still standing. "Drop the pistol, and do it easy."

"Who the hell are you fellows?"

Logan pointed to the badge that was partly hidden by his coat. The man just groaned. "Where is the gold you robbed from the pack string,"

Before the man could answer, Running Wolf motioned to Logan. "A rider is coming in from the trees. I can see him through the front window."

Logan turned to the fellow with his hands up. "Sit in the chair behind the table and keep your mouth shut."

Logan pulled the three bodies behind the bar as the rider pulled up out front. Logan stood by the bar. Running Wolf stepped out of sight in the back room. As the man walked in, Logan noticed the two tied down holsters. He stopped at the door and looked around then saw the man at the table.

"Where is everybody, Curly?"

He looked back at Logan, "Who are you?" Then he noticed the badge. Both hands dropped for his guns, but as he cleared leather, he was knocked backward by a bullet from Logan's pistol. As he slid down the bar, the man at the table jumped up.

"How in the hell did you beat him?" The man just stood there. "He never even cleared leather. Who are you?"

Logan shrugged, "Someone just a little faster than he was."

The man finally told Logan where the gold was hidden and where the horses were.

Running Wolf retrieved the pack horses. With the bodies and the gold loaded, they headed for the mine with their one prisoner.

It was sundown as they rode up to where the guard sat on a stump. He looked over at the prisoner. "Curly, how come you didn't try McTier. You're always telling everyone how fast you are?"

Curly scowled and glanced at Logan. "You're Logan McTier? I thought they said you were dead." Logan just grinned.

When Logan rode up to the mine office, Cliff ran out. "Is that my gold on those horses?" Logan told him what happened.

"I'm not through with this yet. There were two men at the store when we got there. I think they are the lookouts for this bunch. If I see them again, I'll know them."

Logan walked with Cliff to the cook shack that evening when everyone was eating. As they walked in, Logan filled his plate and walked over to sit across from the men from the store. He had spotted them as they walked in. Running Wolf started to sit down next to Logan when one of them said, "You sit somewhere else. I don't eat with Indians."

Running Wolf sat down anyway, and as the fellow started to rise, Logan told him to sit down. Cliff, who by now had joined them at the table, told the fellow to shut up and eat. As the fellow jumped up, he found himself looking at two gun barrels pointed right at his chest. He slowly sat back down glaring at Running Wolf and Logan. "Now both of you put your hands on the table," Logan said in a low voice.

The guard from the road, who Cliff called Jeff, had been sitting at a table in back of the room. He walked up behind the two.

Cliff nodded to Jeff, "Take them to the office and hold them until Logan here decides what he's going to do with them."

As Jeff started to leave, Logan held up his hand. "Ease those pistols out and lay them on the table."

Running Wolf had finished eating. "I'll walk along with Jeff and the prisoners."

Logan and Cliff just finished eating when they heard two fast shots outside followed by a third shot.

Logan said, "That last shot was a rifle."

Logan busted out through the door on a dead run. Across from the cook shack next to the office, Logan saw Running Wolf with his pistol drawn. He was looking down at a body lying at his feet. Jeff held his pistol on the two prisoners. As Logan walked up, one prisoner said, "My God, is that Indian fast on the draw."

Running Wolf looked over at Logan. "When Jeff and me and the prisoners got close to the office, this fellow with a rifle stepped out from behind the outhouse. He started to swing the rifle toward us. I drew and shot twice. The rifleman went down to his knees then fired the rifle into the ground as he fell over."

Jeff told them, "When the two shots rang out, I looked over at Running Wolf as he walked toward the man with a smoking pistol in his hand."

Logan rolled the man over. You could cover the two bullet holes with a gold piece. Cliff, who had just walked up, looked at the man, "I fired that fellow a few months ago."

"Do you have a graveyard where we can bury these people?"

"We had a couple miners die since I started the mine. They're buried in a small graveyard on the ridge."

"Is there someone I can hire to bury the four men from the store and the one Running Wolf just shot?"

Jeff, the guard, spoke up, "I'd do it if the price is right."

Logan grinned, "You tell me what you think is a fair price."

They agreed on a price and Logan tossed him the gold coins to cover it. Running Wolf helped another fellow load the bodies on a wagon. When he walked into the office, he handed Logan a vest he had taken off the fellow Logan had shot at the bar. Logan heard the thump as the vest hit the table. When he turned it over, there was a holster sewn into the inside of the vest. Logan pulled a small caliber six shooter out.

"I've never seen a gun like this. It's the smallest caliber I've ever seen in a pistol," said Logan as he examined it. It looked like a toy in Logan's big hands. As he looked it over, he noticed it had only a five shot cylinder. It could cock and fire without cocking the hammer. Logan cut the holster loose from the vest and put the pistol and holster in his coat pocket.

Logan and Running Wolf rode back the next day to the trading post to look around.

Logan looked through a saddle bag in the back of the building. He found four boxes of small caliber shells. They were the same as the little pistol he had in his pocket. As they looked through the store supplies, they found another six boxes of these same shells. Behind the bar they found another pistol of the same caliber in a holster under the bar. Logan took the pistol and ammunition and put them in his saddle bag.

Logan picked up his prisoners the next day and headed back over the mountain toward the Milford Mine road. He hoped to catch the stagecoach or a freight wagon and pay them to deliver his prisoners to Mill City. As they rode into the Milford Mine, Logan noticed three horses in front of the office. As they dismounted and Logan started for the office, out stepped his old partner, Fred.

He shook hands with Logan. "We've been sent up here to look into a gang robbing a mine over near Spirit Lake. We traveled this way hoping to find some sign of you and Running Wolf."

Fred turned to look at the prisoners Logan had brought in. "Who are these fellows?"

Logan turned to Bill Milford. "Do you have a place where we could lock these fellows up for the night? Bill nodded and motioned for Logan to follow.

They locked up the men and put a guard on the door. Logan then answered Fred's question. As they compared notes about the robberies, they decided maybe Logan and Running Wolf had shot the fellows involved in both places. The only problem was they hadn't found any gold other than what had been stolen from Cliff Stroup's mine. Logan decided to pay a visit to Curly, the only survivor from the shooting in the bar. Logan took Curly into another building to question him about the robberies. At first he wouldn't say anything, but when Logan mentioned Spirit Lake, he had a strange look.

"Curly, I'm going to take you over to Spirit Lake to see if the people from there recognize you." Curly shook his head and admitted they were the ones who also robbed Spirit Lake. When questioned about where the gold was, he told them they had sold the gold in Mill City and deposited the money in the bank in Capital City. Logan turned the prisoners over to Fred to take back to headquarters. He sent along all they knew about the ones they had buried and all papers found on the bodies.

Logan and Running Wolf headed over the mountain toward Spirit Lake to let them know about the men who had robbed them. With this done, they headed back toward Raven Basin and the White River area. The winter weather was setting in, and Logan knew his area to patrol was going to shrink to the low lands along the rivers. When they rode into the basin, the Helmicks were all set for winter. Acel was able to pick up all the supplies he needed in Kilgore from Jerry. Logan thought with the trouble at the mines, he had forgotten to get over to Kilgore to pay for the supplies Acel and Little Hawk got. He decided he would make a quick trip back over the mountain. He figured if it snowed too much to get back over the mountain he could take the long river route back. Acel said Little Feather, with her family, had moved to winter quarters down river about two weeks ago. Logan nodded, "Acel, I filed on a section down along the river too. If it gets too bad up here, you could move down to build winter quarters along the river."

Logan and Running Wolf made good time getting to Kilgore. It had started snowing hard when they crossed over the mountain. Logan figured he would have to take the long trip home if it didn't let up soon. Jerry was glad to see them but gave Logan hell for making the trip just to pay the bill.

He told Logan, "You can charge anytime and don't worry about the bill. That's what good friends do for each other."

The route they took on leaving Kilgore took them back past the cabins where they had found the gang living. They stopped by the grave of the fallen ranger, Rex. They added a few rocks to keep it in good condition. As they neared the small valley where the buildings were, they left the trail and came in behind them. They topped the little ridge where they spied on the cabin before. They could see smoke coming from the biggest cabin chimney. Logan noticed the small meadow was fenced, and about a dozen horses could be seen across the meadow. Logan looked down closer at the buildings and could see smoke also coming from another cabin. There was smoke coming from a shed by the corrals. About then they heard a hammer striking metal. Logan decided that smoke from the shed was coming from a forge. Logan looked over at Running Wolf, "You stay out of sight while I ride down to see who's there."

Logan rode back the way they had come, and when he hit the main trail again, he headed for the cabins. As he rode closer, he could see an older, big man making horseshoes. The man hadn't heard Logan as he rode up to the shed. When he turned and saw Logan, he jumped and reached for a rifle leaning against the wall.

Logan smiled, "You don't need that friend," and the big man leaned it back against the wall.

Logan started to tell the old man who he was when he heard a voice behind him say to just stand still. He turned his head. Two younger men stood there, both had rifles aimed at him. Logan looked at the old man. "Tell those two to lower their rifles now."

The old fellow laughed, "You're mighty brave with two rifles aimed at you to demand anything."

Logan slowly pulled back his coat to reveal the ranger badge.

The old man nodded. "That don't mean much out here."

"Well, I can say this for sure, if those boys don't lower those rifles now, they will be dead soon." My partner has never missed at this range in his life.

As both men looked behind them, Logan drew both pistols and stepped behind the old man. The two men spun around. Logan told them to drop the rifles. They both were eyeing their chances when a click of a pistol being cocked was heard behind them. They dropped their rifles. Running Wolf stepped out from behind the nearest cabin.

Logan disarmed all three, "Now who's in the cabins?"

They found two women in the main cabin. When the three decided to calm down, Logan holstered his pistols. He found out they had just moved into the area this spring and found the cabin deserted and moved in. Two riders had showed up during the summer and tried to run them off. They took the two into Kilgore and found out the cabin had been used by the gang robbing mines in the area.

"The marshall in Kilgore told us he didn't have any authority outside of Kilgore," the old man added. "He told us that to him the cabin didn't belong to anybody. If we wanted, we could homestead it."

Logan assured them he thought the same as the marshall and he did have the authority here. As he turned to leave, the older man wanted to shake hands. "I'm sorry about the greeting you got."

Logan laughed. "Well, at least it was settled without anybody getting shot." One of the boys spoke up, "What's your name, Ranger? Is the Indian really a ranger?"

Logan introduced Running Wolf. He about laughed out loud when he saw their expressions when Running Wolf spoke to them in good English. As they mounted he told them, "My name is Logan McTier," and he could tell they knew the name.

It was a two week trip around the long way home, but Logan also made some side trips when he found trails that showed fresh sign. They found some remote small mining operations. Some of these would probably grow into big operations later. Some of the places they were welcomed. Others were not so friendly. Logan figured probably some of these men had a 'wanted' poster on them from somewhere. They didn't like having the law move into the area.

Logan stayed pretty close to the Indian winter camp and Little Feather who was about to have their first child. When he and Running Wolf had returned from their trip to Kilgore, Logan was surprised to see Acel's two boys building a cabin at the Indian camp. He asked them why they were down there. Dad decided he could handle the logging and kept two horses up in the basin. If it snowed much in the basin, he worried about having enough feed for all the horses. So he sent us with the rest of the horses to the Indian camp. He rode down with us to show us where you wanted the buildings."

"I'm glad to see this cabin going up. You can use it when it's finished while you're building another one for Little Feather and me."

A daughter was born in the early spring. Little Feather named her Fawn. Little Feather told Logan, "She should also have a white man's name. Can we name her after your mother?"

Logan laughed, "I'm all for that."

That spring he and Little Feather started riding on short rides. Logan made her a present of one of the small pistols. "I still have the pistol Running Wolf took off the men on the bluff where you were shot."

"I know, but that pistol is too big to hide. I want you to start carrying this pistol with you all the time."

Logan spent time teaching her to shoot it. He was surprised how well she picked it up. He told her with all the new people coming into the mountains, he wanted her to know how to shoot.

"Some of these people hate Indians. They won't hesitate to shoot any they see, man or woman."

Little Feather nodded. "I know this is true."

Running Wolf was riding with them one day when Logan had her shoot at a pine cone hanging from a tree limb. The first shot she knocked it off, and before they could say anything, she shot off the second one. Logan grinned as he looked at Running Wolf who was just staring at his sister. Then he looked at Logan. "I wondered why you wanted those small pistols."

As winter snows closed down most of the area under Logan's care, he made a few trips out to check over lower areas where men were still mining. During one trip, he found another valley being homesteaded by two families. When they rode in to introduce themselves, they were surprised the law was in the area. Running Wolf always drew stares wherever they went, and usually the same question was asked. "How come an Indian is wearing a badge?"

By spring Acel's boys had completed two cabins on the winter area. As the snow melted, they headed back to the Basin to help Acel with the buildings at the main ranch. Acel had finished cutting all the logs for the barn and main house. When the boys arrived with more horses, they started construction of the barn. Logan wanted it up first. That way come summer they could fill it with hay for the coming winter. Hawk and Little Hawk and any of the other men that wanted to make the ranch their home worked with Acel. Logan helped move Little Feather and Fawn up to one of the cabins at the ranch before he and Running Wolf went back to work as rangers.

The first trip took them back to Kilgore. Logan found the pass over to the Rafter T was open so they headed for there. Benton now had a resident ranger, and Logan was looking forward to seeing if the rustling had slowed down with him present. As they rode into the ranch yard, Logan was surprised to see a new house going up.

Lottie was first to spot them as they rode up. She greeted them as they dismounted at the yard fence. Logan grinned at her. "You're now a grandmother. The girl is named after you."

"When do I get to see both daughter and my granddaughter?"

Logan gave her a big hug, "I'll bring them the first time I get a chance."

After supper that night and Running Wolf had retired to their sleeping quarters, Logan sat down to talk to his folks. He told Ted about the ranch being built. "Now I'll need some young stock to raise. I want this to be a cash sale for these cattle. I'd like to start with two hundred head this summer."

Ted looked up to study his son. "You're the main owner of the Rafter T. You can have them for free."

"I want these two ranches operated as totally separate places. I'll pay cash to buy the cattle. You add that money from the sale into the operating fund for the Rafter T. It could be used to do more upgrading of the herd."

Rebecca, who had joined them, asked, "When you're ready, can I bring the cattle to the new ranch."

"That would be fine with me, but you'll have to ask Dad about that."

Ted thought for a spell. "If you pick a good crew, I don't see any problem with you going." With that all taken care of, Logan retired for the night.

The next morning Logan drew a map for Rebecca on the best route to the new ranch. "You hire five riders besides yourself. Take the money from my account in the Benton bank to cover all of your expenses."

"I think five riders are too many," Rebecca protested.

Logan shook his head. "That's what you will need." She didn't argue. As Logan was getting ready to leave, he asked Rebecca how her love life was going.

"That's none of your business." Then with a grin she said, "I may bring him along on the drive and see what you think of him."

When Logan and Running Wolf rode into Benton, Logan couldn't believe all the new buildings going up. They pulled up in front of the sheriff's office. Logan noticed a new sign saying 'Territorial Ranger' hanging by the door. Sheriff Del Rogers was at his desk when they walked in.

He looked up with surprise, "How did you find out so quick?"

Logan must have had a blank look because the sheriff then added, "Aren't you here because the ranger here was shot?" Logan shook his head. "Running Wolf and I spent the night at the ranch and were just passing through."

"The resident ranger here was shot while trying to arrest a drunken cowboy yesterday. The man was wanted for questioning on some missing horses. When the ranger walked into the saloon to arrest him' he was shot by a friend of the wanted man." Del added, "Some people brought the wounded ranger to Doc's last night. The doctor had told me it would be a few days before he knew if the ranger would live. He lost a lot of blood. If infection doesn't set in' he's got a chance to live."

"Did you follow the shooter's tracks?" asked Logan.

"The shooting was out of my jurisdiction, so I couldn't do anything. The shooting happened at a small trading post and saloon down along the river. It was built to supply all the rustlers and thieves in the area a year ago. The rangers raided it last winter and arrested some men and told a few to leave the area."

Del told Logan, "It had been real quiet down there since the raids until this shooting. I figured with spring here a few of the outlaws from last year would start showing up again."

Logan nodded. "Do you know who the shooter was?

"I've heard it was a fellow they called Jake. I've tried too find Jake's last name with no luck."

Logan and Running Wolf rode out toward the trading post. As they approached the small settlement, Logan noticed a few tents and a couple of new buildings going up. They rode up in front of the saloon and dismounted. Logan, as he walked up to the door, saw a man running out the back toward one of the tents. He kept looking back at the two rangers as he ran. Logan and Running Wolf walked in. There were five men playing cards and four standing at the bar plus the bartender. Logan moved off to one side. Running Wolf moved off the other way.

The bartender walked up behind the bar. "What can I do for you?" Before Logan could say anything, another man at the bar said, "We don't allow stinking Indians in here."

Logan watched as the five playing cards all stood up.

"I'm Ranger Logan McTier, and this is Ranger Running Wolf."

Logan noticed a couple of men at the table were getting real nervous. About then two more men walked in from the back door. Logan recognized one of them as the man he had seen running to the tent. Logan knew this could explode any minute into a deadly shoot out. The man who had come in the back door asked, "What do you want, Ranger?"

"I'm looking for a fellow named Jake."

The fellow looked at everyone around him, "I don't know anyone by that name."

The others all spoke up and agreed they hadn't heard of anyone named Jake around there. Logan motioned to the bartender. "You walk around in front of the bar. The rest of you drop your gun belts, real slow like."

The bartender started down the bar. As he did, Logan saw him slowly pulling a greener from under the bar. Logan drew and shot the bartender just as the barrels of the greener were clearing the top of the bar. One of the men at the table drew a pistol from a shoulder holster. He fell backward as he was hit from a bullet fired by Running Wolf.

Gun belts started falling, and Logan moved over by the bar so he could see the back door in case they had more people outside.

With everyone lined up against the bar, Logan again asked for the man named Jake. About this time the back door opened and two girls walked in. From their dress Logan figured they worked in the bar. Logan motioned for them to move on into the room. "You two find a place to sit down at the table. Do either of you know a fellow named Jake?"

One girl started to speak when the fellow from the tent yelled for them to keep their mouths shut. Logan, over his shoulder, told Running Wolf, "Shoot that guy if he says another word. Now ladies point out the man called Jake if he's in the room."

The girls both shook their heads, they weren't going to talk.

Logan, by this time, could see a small crowd forming out on the walk in front of the saloon. He backed to the door, "Do any of you know a fellow named Jake? He shot the ranger here the other day."

An older man wearing a leather apron stepped forward. He looked into the saloon. "Jake's the man on the end of the bar." Logan grinned. It was the fellow that had come in from the tent.

One of the other men yelled at the old man, "You are a dead man for that."

"You loud mouth, step forward. You are joining your partner in jail in Benton," Logan snarled.

Logan turned to the old man. "How about you stepping in here and collect all the gun belts."

Running Wolf kept a close watch while Logan checked over the bunch for hidden guns. Running Wolf saw movement as the back door was slowly opening. A gun barrel appeared. Running Wolf fired a shot through the door. The door flew open and a man was laying sprawled in the doorway. One of the girls started to rise when Logan told her to sit back down. Logan started for the back door when running horses could be heard coming up the street. He stepped over behind the bar where he could watch the back and front door.

Running Wolf smiled, "We have more rangers now."

George Bennett walked through the door with his gun drawn. Crowding behind him were two more men with ranger badges. George looked over the room. "I guess you have this under control here," as he looked over at Logan.

Logan told George, "We were just riding through Benton from the ranch when Del Rogers told us about the ranger getting shot." Logan pointed out which one the blacksmith had told them was Jake.

"He's supposed to be the shooter of the ranger."

George asked the two rangers with him if they knew any of these men from their raid last winter. They had been here when they cleaned out the place during winter. They both nodded. "All but one of these men were here during the winter raid."

"We'll take them all back to headquarters and separate them there," George said.

George looked over at Logan. "Where were you headed from here?"

"I was coming into headquarters to report to you when this all happened."

"We've got a report of some trouble over near Spirit Lake again. Why don't you head that way?"

"Okay, I'll head that way now."

Logan and Running Wolf decided go back to Benton and spend the night. Tomorrow they would head back toward the Rafter T and out over the trail to Spirit Lake. Logan and Running Wolf slept that night in back of the jail. With an early breakfast, they headed back up the trail through the Rafter T. Logan stopped by long enough to see his mother then headed on up the trail past Old Dave's cabin. They camped that night near where Logan had shot the two men years before that were watching the ranch looking for him.

They rode into Spirit Lake the next day. It looked about the same and didn't seem to be growing any. They found the local town marshall. They told him they were there to see about the trouble reported to ranger headquarters. He nodded, "I figured that's why you were here. The trouble is a feud concerning the ownership of a mine. Last fall two men rode in and told everyone they were true owners of the Blue Bird Mine. The mine owner had been killed in an explosion at the mine during the summer. He had a wife and son living on the claim when these two men showed up. They told her to move; they owned the mine."

"You know I don't have any jurisdiction that far out of town. I tried to talk to the men and they run me off at gunpoint. The former mine owner's wife and son are staying in a cabin on the edge of town. She's been washing clothes for miners to make enough money to buy food. Her name is Martha Tidwell, and her son's name is Willy."

"Why do the two men think they own the mine?" asked Logan.

"Nobody has ever got close enough to ask that question without being shot at."

Logan rode out to where Mrs. Tidwell was living. He found her living in a cabin with part of the roof caved in. When he introduced himself, a smile came to her face. "Is there any chance I will get paid for the mine or get it back? I've never seen those men before, and they told me that my husband owed them money."

Logan and Running Wolf decided they would ride around and come in on the mine from the back side.

They found a place with good grass and tied their horses so they could feed while they moved over the ridge to spy on the mining operation. They watched for most of the afternoon and saw only six men working. They waited until almost dark and watched as the crew left the mine and walked down to the bunkhouse and cook shack below. They were about to leave when Running Wolf motioned to a rider coming in from the main road. He had a rifle across his knees. Logan figured he must be a guard stationed on the road to keep people out. Logan and Running Wolf went back to their horses and headed back for town. They rode past the road leading to the mine and up a ways to look for where they had been stationed. It was easy to find because they had built a small shelter next to a tree. After that Logan and Running Wolf headed for town.

The next morning Logan stopped again at Mrs. Tidwell's cabin. Logan wanted to find out how many men her husband had employed at the mine.

"We only hired one man. He was outside the tunnel during the explosion. His name is Rodney Davis. He is just a young man who stopped by one day and told my husband he needed work."

From what Logan could find out he had only worked for them a month before her husband had been killed. When she explained what he looked like, Logan thought to himself that sounded like one of the men at the mine.

When they were getting close to the road leading to the mine, Logan told Running Wolf to circle around and come in behind the shelter they had found the day before. Running Wolf tied his horse off the trail and disappeared into the timber. Logan waited giving Running Wolf time to get in place before he headed up the trail. Logan rode along, and as he rounded the trail close to the shelter, a man stepped out with a rifle pointed at him.

Logan pulled up, "Just turn around and ride back down the trail. This is private property.

Logan slowly moved one hand up and pulled back his jacket to show the badge. The man started to cock the hammer of the rifle when a voice behind him said, "Drop it."

The guard next felt a knife at his throat, and the rifle fell to the ground. They tied him on his horse and gagged him. Then Logan headed up the trail leading his prisoner while Running Wolf retrieved his horse. As they neared the mine, Logan kept an eye out for anyone else watching the trail. When he dismounted near the cook shack, Logan could hear somebody working inside. He left the prisoner on his horse, worked his way to the door of the kitchen and slowly opened it. At the stove was a man with his back to him. Logan eased up, and with his pistol pressing against the man's back and his hand over his mouth, he backed him out of the kitchen into the bunkhouse. He found some rope and tied the fellow in a bunk then gagged him. He went out and pulled the other man from the saddle and took him into the bunkhouse. He tied him to another bunk.

Logan figured it was nearing noon, and the miners would be showing up to eat, so he stayed out of sight near the cook shack. It wasn't long before the miners walked out of the mine and headed for where Logan was waiting. Logan noticed only two of the men wore visible guns. He figured the others probably also had a pistol stuck in their belt or boots. When they were about half way to the cook shack, Logan stepped out. The six stopped when they saw him. One of the men, with a pistol in a tied down holster, started moving his hand when Logan drew. "Just stand easy," he told them. "You two with the pistols, drop your gun belts and move back." The man who had started to draw seemed to be the boss. He yelled at Logan, "Who in the hell do you think you are?"

Logan pulled back his jacket. "I'm Ranger Logan McTier. Might I ask who you are?"

One of the men in back of the boss pulled a pistol from under his coat. As he stepped out to fire at Logan, a bullet from the trees hit him. As the man fell, two of the other men clawed for guns stuck in their belts. Logan fired twice. The three still standing all held their hands up. The boss had been one of the men who tried to draw a hideout pistol. He was now lying dead along with the other two. Logan searched the men but found no guns, just two knifes. Running Wolf came walking toward the men with a rifle still in his hands leading his horse.

Logan took the men into the cook shack dining room and set them against the wall. He untied the guard and the cook. "Now go sit down at the table in front of the other men," Logan ordered.

Running Wolf walked over and stood by one of the miners. "I think this is the one the lady was talking about." Logan nodded.

He walked over to the fellow, "Is your name Davis?"

The fellow started to say, "Go to hell," when Logan hit him with the barrel of his pistol before he finished. Logan reached down and pulled him up. "Now again, are you Davis?"

The man nodded. Logan turned him loose.

Logan turned to the other man who had been wearing a pistol. "Are you one of the partners in this mine?"

"Yes, me and the man you shot are the owners."

As the afternoon wore on, the cook kept saying he was just the cook. He wanted to get out before there were any more shootings. Logan told Running Wolf to go saddle up the horses. "We'll take this bunch into the Spirit Lake jail for the night then take them on to Capital City tomorrow. We'll let the courts handle the ownership of the mine and who was involved with who."

Logan looked over at Davis. "I know what the court will do with you if you had anything to do with killing the miner."

When Running Wolf walked back leading the extra horses, he and Logan tied each prisoner to his horse. Running Wolf smiled at Logan. "I've got a way to keep them from trying to get away."

Logan watched as Running Wolf put a rope around each prisoner's neck and tied it with very little slack to the horse behind. Each prisoner was hollering they would get hung if one of the horses jumped or moved quick.

Logan grinned, "I agree, so you better hope those horses don't get nervous."

As he started to mount, the cook hollered, "I'll tell you what you want to know if you'll take this rope off my neck."

The owner of the mine spurred his horse, and as the horse jumped forward, it jerked the rope around the cook's neck. Running Wolf was near the horse the cook sat on. When the horse jumped forward, the rope on the cook's neck jerked then fell to the ground. Logan had stopped the owner's horse and held his pistol on him. The cook was white as a sheet when he turned to look at Running Wolf, who was grinning at him. Running Wolf picked up the rope that had been tied to the cook's neck and the horse behind him. There was a light piece of broken rawhide on the end of the rope.

Logan told the cook, "Now speak up on what you know."

The owner started to yell when Logan hit him with his pistol. Logan grabbed him and slipped the noose from his neck and let him fall to the ground. He was out cold.

The cook told Logan he had heard them talking about how they had got the mine. They had been robbing miners all over the country the same way. They would find out about a miner working alone who had a good claim. One of them would get the miner to hire them to help with the mining in exchange for a grub stake. They would find a way to kill the miner and make it look like an accident then move in and high grade the mine. Whenever the law started getting too curious, they would move on looking for another victim.

Logan nodded. "Okay, if this is true, I'll see about letting you go when we get into Spirit Lake."

Logan and Running Wolf picked up the man Logan had hit and tied him over his saddle. He was coming to. He started yelling his head off about how he was tied over his saddle. He was still raising hell when they rode up in front of the jail. They put them in different cells in the jail. This included the cook.

Logan took the marshall into his office, "Do you know the cook?"

The marshall nodded. "He's been working around the area for a couple of years. I don't think he'd be involved in stealing the mine."

Logan walked back to where the cook was and let him out and led him up front. He told them all he knew about the operation. "They've had a big amount of gold ready to be moved out and sold. The owner you shot made a deal to sell the gold this coming week." From what the cook had picked up listening to them, they always sold to the same guy, and he usually picked up the gold himself.

Logan thought for a minute. "I've got one more job for you before you're a free man. Have you ever seen the man who buys the gold?

The cook shrugged, "I think so. When I was first hired, there was a stranger at the mine the first night I cooked for them. This fellow left the next morning with a couple loaded pack horses."

Logan looked over at the marshall. "Let's keep quiet about the prisoners being in jail. If anyone does ask questions, say that the prisoners we brought in were from somewhere else."

Logan, the cook and Running Wolf left town out the back way and headed back to the mine. The next morning Logan told the cook that Running Wolf would be up at the mine. "I'm going to take the guard's place on the road up here."

As they started out the door, the cook said, "When that fellow left that morning, he didn't use the road. He used the trail out behind the mine shaft."

Logan nodded. "Running Wolf, go on up to the mine and keep out of sight. I'm still going to watch the main road."

Logan had just got back to the cook shack that evening when he noticed Running Wolf motioning from the mine. He pointed down the trail behind him. Then Running Wolf ducked back into the tunnel, and Logan moved back into the timber behind the cook shack. A rider soon appeared leading two horses. Behind them was another rider. They rode on down and put the horses in the corral and unsaddled them. While they were doing this, Logan moved under cover closer to the buildings. He watched as Running Wolf also moved toward the kitchen and bunkhouse. The two men headed for the cook shack. Logan moved over close to the window of the kitchen. Logan heard one of them ask the cook where the crew was. The cook told them that they were still working in the mine.

Someone laughed, "Those boys are getting greedy."

"We're going up to see what they're doing. We'll be back for supper." As the two men walked out and headed up the hill, Logan stepped out from behind the kitchen. They noticed him and both turned toward him. Logan noticed they both wore two tied down holsters. One fellow looked Logan over.

"Who the hell are you? You're not part of the crew that I remember."

As Logan turned more their way, they also saw Running Wolf moving into view. This was when they noticed the badge on Logan's chest. Both men's hands flew toward their pistols. Neither man even came close to getting a shot off when bullets from both Logan and Running Wolf cut them down.

Running Wolf, as he walked up, grinned. "I think maybe you are getting slower or I'm getting faster."

Logan heard a door slam. The cook peeked around the corner of the cook shack. As he walked up, he shook his head and looked down at the two dead men. He mumbled something about, "I didn't know Indians could draw that fast." He looked at Logan. "I know who you are. I saw you draw on a man up near Butte one time." Then he looked at Running Wolf, "Are you a real ranger?" Running Wolf just nodded.

The next morning Logan loaded the two dead men and the gold. They headed for Spirit Lake. As they rode close to the cabin where Mrs. Tidwell lived, Logan rode on over. As he started to step down, Mrs. Tidwell and Willy walked out. Logan smiled at her, "Do you have a way to get to town?"

"Oh yes, I have a wagon and a team."

"Why don't you come into the marshall's office as soon as you can."

As he turned to leave, Mrs. Tidwell noticed the horses up on the trail and the two bodies. She turned toward Logan. He grinned, "You've got your mine back."

That evening with everything done, Logan and Running Wolf headed for the saloon for beer. The cook joined them. The bartender told Logan he wouldn't serve beer to an Indian and Logan grinned. "Would you sell one to a territorial ranger?"

Running Wolf pulled back his coat, and the bartender looked at Logan. "Is that badge real?" Logan assured him it was. As they finished the beer, they decided to go eat and invited the cook to come along.

While waiting for their meal, the cook turned to Running Wolf. "You knew that rope would break didn't you?"

Running Wolf grinned, "It was only tied by that thin piece of rawhide, and I just wanted it to scare you."

Logan grinned. "I was going to ask you about that trick you pulled up at the mine."

"Old Indian trick," said Running Wolf as he looked at Logan.

George Bennett had told Logan and Tug once before they had the power to appoint a sheriff in any of the new areas to handle local problems. This appointment would be good until the local government could be formed and an election held. Logan decided this would be a good place here to do this. That way he could let the new sheriff handle the prisoners. They had appointed a judge here in Spirit Lake and had a town council. Logan told the marshall, "I'm now appointing you as the sheriff."

The marshall's only question was, "Is this legal?"

Logan assured him he had the power to do this. The marshall said the local barber was the mayor and chairman of the town council. When Logan told the mayor of his appointing the new sheriff, the mayor said he was all in favor. Logan told them he would send word to ranger headquarters to let them know about the new sheriff in this area.

The next morning the two rangers were in the saddle at first light. Logan was a day's ride from Sweetwater, and this was the northern part of the area he was suppose to cover. He figured he would probably be in another ranger's area when he got to Sweetwater. He wanted to visit Jeff Rogers, the sheriff in Sweetwater, maybe even ride up into Butte as long as he was that close. The area they rode through now was where he had found

302

Mollie's folks and buried them. He found the place. Someone had erected a stone with their names carved into it. As they rode away, he told Running Wolf the story about finding the bodies and later shooting the men who killed them. As he rode past the pond where he shot the crazy family, his thought went to Mollie. He wondered if she was still working on that same ranch. It was mid afternoon when they rode up in front of the house belonging to the sheriff. As Logan started to step down, a voice behind them said, "Just stay in the saddle."

As Logan eased back into the saddle, he looked back and could see a young man standing in the barn door holding a double barrel shotgun on them. Logan started to say who they were when he heard a woman's voice," Logan, is that you?"

He looked toward the house. Mrs. Rogers was on the porch smiling at him. The fellow holding the shotgun was their son who had grown since Logan had last seen him. Logan dismounted and was given a big hug by Mrs. Rogers.

Logan introduced Running Wolf. Then he found out why they had been met with a shotgun pointed at them. The sheriff was in bed in the house recovering from a bullet wound. He had been shot during a bank holdup two weeks before and his deputy had been killed. The local ranger was gone following the trail of the robbers. So until they found someone to replace the dead deputy, Sweetwater was without a lawman in town until Jeff was back on his feet. When Logan walked into the bedroom, he found a very sick man trying to recover from the wound.

Mrs. Rogers told Logan, "The doctor says Jeff is on his way to recovery, but it'll take some time."

Logan assured Jeff, "I'll stay around until the local ranger is back before I move on." Sweetwater now had a telegraph so Logan sent word to George where he was. He also told him of the appointment of the new sheriff in Spirit Lake. Logan was in the sheriff's office when a telegram from George arrived and was delivered to him. George had sent two rangers out on the train the night before. They would be in Sweetwater sometime the next day. Logan's orders were to stay in Sweetwater until they arrived.

That evening Logan heard horses out in front of the jail. When the door opened, an older man with a ranger star stood there. When he saw the badges on Logan and Running Wolf he smiled, "I know you two."

He held out his hand, "I'm Stan Clark, and you've got to be McTier, and you must be Running Wolf," and shook hands with them.

"I lost the trail of the bank robbers three days after the robbery. I've been out there ever since trying to find any trace of those four riders." As he talked, Logan figured out where the ranger had lost the trail. It had been in the mountains along the South Fork. That wasn't too far from where he and Frank and Skinny had moved the gold out for the Chinese. Logan nodded. "I'm familiar with that area, Stan. We'll head up there in the morning."

The next day Logan and Running Wolf started finding miners working along the river, and Logan started to recognize places. They didn't find too many miners very friendly when they stopped to talk. It was close to dark when they rode up to a small mining operation, and the old miner had just started supper.

He looked up, "Step down fellas. I'll add a few more spuds and we'll have supper."

Logan untied a sack from behind his saddle, "We'll add this to the meal."

When Logan dug through the sack, the old fellow's eyes lit up when he saw the canned peaches.

"You fellows can stay as long as you want if you pack grub like this."

Running Wolf had unsaddled the horses and staked them out on grass along the river. As he walked up, the old miner leaned over to see Running Wolf in the fire light, "Are you part Indian?"

Logan started laughing, "I'm afraid he's all Indian."

The old miner saw the badge when Running Wolf took off his jacket. "I never heard of an Indian lawman before."

He looked back at Logan who also had taken off his jacket and saw his badge. The old fellow grinned then turned toward the brush behind the fire. "You can come in now ,Carl, these fellows are lawmen."

An old fellow carrying a rifle stepped into the fire light. Running Wolf looked over at Logan. "I was hoping he belonged to this camp."

Logan laughed, "I was thinking the same thing when I heard him out there."

The two old miners looked from one lawman to the other. "You both knew he was out there?"

Running Wolf nodded. Both miners started laughing. They chatted about a little of everything while eating their supper. Logan said the dishes were his to do. Logan asked if they had seen four riders riding around the last couple weeks that weren't miners. The one called Carl thought for a spell.

"We've had these same four fellows riding around for maybe the last month. They ride real good looking horses and all wear their guns tied down and aren't very friendly. They were through here about maybe a week or so ago. Their horses were tired like they had been rode hard. Only three fellows rode by, then later just before dark the fourth man rode by."

"Do you have any idea where they're holding up?" Logan asked. Both miners shook their heads

The next morning Logan fixed breakfast for the miners. Later, he and Running Wolf headed up the trail. Logan decided he was going to look at the places he and Frank had used. Del Rogers had told Logan the only thing he could remember was one of the robbers rode a sorrel horse. He said the sorrel was tall and well put together. He was the man who shot Del. As they rode off, Del saw something shining on the saddle horn.

Logan and Running Wolf wore jackets that morning, and their badges were covered up. While crossing a small meadow, two riders came riding up the trail from the direction of Butte.

As they met Logan asked, "How far is it to the nearest town?"

The lead rider rode a beautiful sorrel horse. Logan glanced at the saddle. He saw a silver plate on the horn. The man on the sorrel growled, "Just keep riding, and you will find out for yourself."

As the back rider rode by he said in a low voice, "Ten miles," and moved on following the sorrel. Logan and Running Wolf rode up the trail another mile then pulled off into the trees.

"Let's wait a short while, then follow those riders," Logan told his partner.

Running Wolf liked nothing better than tracking something, man or beast. He was out ahead of Logan with his head to the ground when he pulled up and held up his hand. Logan rode up alongside Running Wolf who pointed to the tracks leaving the main trail. The tracks started following another trail leading up along a creek.

Logan smiled, "There's some cabins up this trail about a mile."

Logan remembered this trail led to the cabin where he and Frank and Skinny buried two men Logan had shot. Logan motioned for Running Wolf to follow him away from the trail. Logan headed over the ridge to get in back of the cabin. Once in place they could see the cabin and the corrals and the trail up along the creek for another quarter of a mile. Smoke was coming from the cabin and the front door was open. There were just three horses in the corral. They watched as one of the men in the cabin stepped out and drew his pistol and fired one shot in the air. He stepped back in out of sight. As they watched, Logan and Running Wolf spotted another rider coming up the trail with a rifle across his knees. When they had ridden in the back way, they had missed the guard posted out along the trail. The rider tied his horse in front of the cabin and loosened the cinch and went into the cabin.

Logan motioned for Running Wolf to take the ridge and move up on the back side of the cabin. Logan waited until he saw Running Wolf behind the cabin when he started to move down the hill. As he moved down, he looked over at Running Wolf. He motioned for Logan to stop and motioned toward the trail. Logan got behind a willow bush and soon saw a rider moving in toward the cabin. Two men appeared at the door with guns drawn. Another had come out the back door and moved in behind the rider coming in. Logan watched as the men in the doorway re-holstered their guns. They moved out to meet the man on the horse. The man stepped down from the horse and all shook hands. They all turned and went back into the cabin. Logan started moving on down the hill and had just reached the bottom and stopped behind the wood shed when the guard walked out to his horse. Logan moved around and stood within ten feet of the man as he cinched up his saddle. As the man turned his back to mount, Logan stepped out. He jerked the man back and at the same time hit him over the head with his pistol. The horse jumped sideways and bumped into the another horse. Logan drug the uncon-scious guard behind the woodshed. He heard someone from the cabin call a name and ask what the hell he was doing out there. With no answer, two men could be seen standing in the door. Then a shot echoed from behind the cabin and brought a yell from the cabin. The two men in the door both drew their guns and dove out of the cabin. They started sneaking to the corners of the cabin.

Logan's voice brought them both around, "Drop your guns." Both men spun with guns level looking for the voice when Logan fired with both of his guns. The two men went down. Two more shots came from behind the cabin. When the firing stopped, Logan checked the guard to see if he was still out, then called to the cabin for anyone in there to step out.

"This is Ranger Logan McTier. You're covered from behind so just step out with your hands up."

All was quiet for a minute then the noise of someone moving in the cabin could be heard. The fellow who had just ridden up appeared in the door with his hands up. "Just keep walking into the yard."

Running Wolf was now standing in the doorway behind him.

"He's the only one left in the cabin except for a dead one," said Running Wolf.

Logan revived the guard. He tied both men to the hitch rail while he and Running Wolf searched the cabin. In the cellar under the house, Logan found three money sacks and a saddle bag full of cash. When Logan looked out the window, he could see the two prisoners talking. The guard motioned with his head toward the woodshed. The other man smiled at what the man was saying  Logan then figured either someone was hiding in the shed or there was more loot hid there. He walked out and tied the saddle bags to Running Wolf's saddle and put the money sacks in his saddle bags. The guard grumbled about his sore head and how they had gotten past him on the trail.

"I've arrested men living here before and getting here was no problem."

"Why are you here? We haven't done anything."

"Well, first off, we'll see if the sheriff and bank clerks in Sweetwater recognize you."

The other man spoke up, "I didn't have anything to do with any bank."

Logan nodded. "We'll see later how you are involved."

Logan winked at Running Wolf where the others couldn't see him. "I guess we might as well burn this wood shed."

The guard looked over at the other man. Logan could see the fear in his eyes. As Running Wolf started gathering chips to start the fire, both men yelled, "Don't burn it!"

Logan walked over to the shed. He could see where the wood pile had been moved in one section. As he moved a layer of wood, he uncovered a large metal box with Wells Fargo written on it. It took both him and Running Wolf to slide it out into the open. The lock had been shot off. When Logan opened the lid, he found it full of money sacks filled with gold coins.

Logan decided he needed a pack string to move all this into Butte. He could leave the bodies and use the saddle horses. Running Wolf took Logan aside. "I'll stay here and guard the gold while you take the bodies and prisoners into Butte tonight. Tomorrow you can bring horses to pack the gold out."

Running Wolf helped Logan load the dead bodies and the two prisoners and then Logan headed for Butte. As he rode into Butte, he headed for the livery stable to see Wade if he still worked there. He saw a boy on the street looking at the dead men draped over the saddles as he rode by. "I'll pay you a buck to go get the sheriff," Logan told the boy. "Tell the sheriff to come to the livery stable."

As Logan rode up, a black streak came from within the barn and started barking when he saw Logan. Wade appeared in the door and started laughing. "That dog hasn't moved that fast in a long time."

Logan reached down to rub his old traveling partner's head.

The sheriff came hurrying down the street with a deputy. The boy Logan had sent to get him was tagging along behind them. As he walked up, he saw the badge on Logan's shirt.

"It's been a long time, Logan," and stuck out his hand.

Logan filled him in on what he had found. The sheriff knew both prisoners. "The better dressed fellow is the Wells Fargo agent here in Butte. Now I know how the gang always knew what banks and stages to rob."

"The two dead ones and the other prisoner are known to be a outlaws. Until now they hadn't been caught doing anything wrong around Butte."

"I need a pack string tomorrow to bring in the rest of the loot, and maybe we'll find more," said Logan.

The next morning the sheriff joined Logan as he headed out leading a pack string. As they passed Ling's store, Ling stepped out to wave at Logan. Logan waved, "I'll see you tonight for supper." Ling waved he understood.

Traveler, who joined Logan for this day, was out front leading the group out of town just like he had a few years ago.

When they got close to the cabins, Traveler let Logan know someone was there. As they dismounted, Running Wolf appeared from the timber above the cabins. Logan could see the old dog was really watching him as he walked toward the group. Running Wolf nodded toward Traveler.

"That must be your old traveling partner you talk about."

Before they loaded the gold, they found more cash in other buildings as they searched each one. Logan told the sheriff he figured there was probably more hidden loot. As they were getting ready to leave, Running Wolf pointed toward Traveler. He was all bristled up and looking up into the timber. Logan moved over his horse and pulled the old Sharps. He used the cabin for a shield and walked over near where Traveler was. He motioned to the sheriff to mount up and start moving like he was leaving. He looked over to find Running Wolf had disappeared. Logan grinned. He figured Running Wolf was already in the timber. Logan worked his way around the cabin where he could look up the hill without exposing himself. The sheriff gathered up the lead ropes on the pack horses and started down the trail. Logan then saw a flash as someone darted to another tree. He was ready for a shot the next time the person moved. Then he saw Running Wolf move up to the tree where the person had just left. Logan waited until Running Wolf looked down his way and then pulled up and shot the tree where the person was hiding. In a flash Running Wolf crossed the opening. He heard a scream. Running Wolf stepped out holding a woman. When they were closer, Logan could see the woman was young, probably in her teens.

The sheriff, who had turned back when he heard the commotion, said, "I know her." Running Wolf let her go. The girl turned on Logan.

"How did you know I was up there?"

The sheriff grinned, "This is Jane Sims. Her father was the stage driver who was killed in the stage holdup."

Logan looked over at her. "Why are you up here? How did you know about these cabins?"

"I worked in a café in town. I heard last night that the men who killed my father had been caught. This morning when I saw you leaving town with pack horses I decided to follow."

Logan looked at the sheriff. "I think she's telling the truth."

Running Wolf handed her back her rifle. "My horse is over the ridge."

After Logan mounted up, he looked over at her. "We found the outlaw's stolen loot, or at least most of it. We're through looking. If you find more, it's yours to keep."

When they got back to town, Logan turned the stolen loot and prisoners over to the sheriff.

"I'll see Sweetwater gets their money back and turn the prisoners over to the judge when he comes through." Logan nodded and headed for the livery stable.

Back at the livery Logan and Running Wolf put their gear in the same cabin Logan had used before. Then they went back down to the barn to talk to Wade. Frank had shown up to see Logan. Wade had sent a kid out to the ranch to let him know Logan was in town. Both Wade and Frank grinned at Logan.

"We've heard stories about a fast gun ranger and his Indian partner."

As usual Logan shrugged, "You know you can't always believe what you hear."

Frank laughed, "That's a good job you left me. I'm still packing up to the girls in the basin and the Chinese miner. The girls have really fixed up the place, and the store is twice a big as when you were up there. Rachel done what you suggested. She runs gambling games and her biggest customers are the Chinese miners."

They decided to all go up to Ling's for supper. When they started to leave, Traveler just stayed in the corner on an old saddle blanket.

Wade laughed. "I believe you fellows wore him out today."

Ling welcomed them. "I'm buying supper for all and I will join you."

They spent the whole evening talking about old times and how the area was changing. Logan told them about Little Feather and his daughter and the ranch he was building.

The next morning Logan stopped by to tell the sheriff they were leaving. The sheriff asked, "Are you going back through Sweetwater?"

"I hadn't figured on it. I could if you need something."

"I just wanted to get the money back to the bank there. If you were going that way, I was going to send it with you rather than send it with the stage."

Logan nodded, "I'll take it, and that way I can wire headquarters and let them know how things went."

When they rode into Sweetwater, Logan stopped by the rangers' office to leave off the money. Stan Clark was at his desk. Two other men with badges were packing their gear into saddle bags. When Stan saw Logan and Running Wolf, he smiled. He turned to the two packing their gear. "Maybe you two won't be riding to Butte after all."

Logan filled them in on the trip to Butte and turned the money over to Stan to deliver to the bank.

"I'm going to send George a wire to let him know what happened in Butte. Then I'm going over to visit the sheriff."

Jeff was sitting up in bed when Logan walked in. "I'll be getting back to the office soon and ready to get back to work."

This brought a swift response from Mrs. Rogers like, "over my dead body," or something that sounded like that. Logan told Jeff about their trip. Jeff nodded. "You going to stay around awhile?"

310

Logan shook his head, "I'll be leaving tomorrow."

Mrs. Rogers looked over at Logan. "I think you better stay for supper. I know a young woman who'll be mad if she doesn't get to see you."

Running Wolf and Logan were in the barn putting their horses away for the night. Logan heard what sounded like a buggy pulling up out front. When they walked out of the barn, Logan noticed a young couple at the gate walking toward the house. A buggy and horse was tied to the hitch rail. The young couple knocked on the door. When Mrs. Rogers answered the door, she pointed at Logan. The girl turned and started toward him with a big smile on her face.

When she got up to him, "Logan, don't you recognize me?"

He kept a straight face, "You kinda look familiar; should I know you?"

By then Mollie had her arms around his neck and gave him a big kiss. She grabbed his arm. "I want you to meet my husband, Dave."

The young man shook Logan's hand. "From what I've always heard, you were at least ten feet tall."

Logan laughed, "I think she sometimes gets me mixed up with someone else."

Logan introduced them to Running Wolf. When Mollie moved over to shake his hand, Logan could tell Running Wolf wasn't use to this treatment. Mollie looked at Running Wolf then back to Logan.

"We've heard many things about you two. You're becoming famous at running down outlaws." Before she could say anymore, Mrs. Rogers invited them in to eat.

Logan and Running Wolf were near the divide overlooking Raven Basin three days later. As they descended to the river, they were met by two young boys from the Indian camp who asked if they could ride with the rangers to camp. When they rode into the camp, the boys were telling all their friends they rode with Running Wolf, the big lawman. Logan headed for the new ranch building a mile up the valley. He heard a horse behind him and turned to see Little Feather. He stopped and picked Fawn off from in front of her mother's saddle when she stopped. Logan put Fawn in his saddle with him. With his wife riding close, he headed for the ranch. Logan couldn't believe all the work Acel and his boys had done since he was there last. The main house was done, and the barn was nearing completion. Little Feather told him that some of the young Indian boys were becoming good builders with Acel as their teacher.

Logan spent the next few days working with the Helmicks. His new home was one to be proud of. Running Wolf stayed over at the Indian village. Little Feather told Logan she thought he was busy courting one of the young girls. He was about to marry when he headed off with Logan. The girl had other men asking for her hand, and Running Wolf was trying to make up for lost time.

One morning just as Logan got up, he heard a horse running fast coming into the yard. When he stepped out onto the porch, one of the young Indian boys from the village came sliding to a halt. He was talking so fast Logan couldn't understand him. Little Feather, who had stepped out on the porch, told Logan the boy was saying a wounded rider had ridden into the village looking for him.

"He's one of the riders that's bringing the cattle in from the Rafter T. They were ambushed by rustlers, and he was sent for help."

Then the boy added, "Running Wolf and Little Hawk and two other men from the village have already left to help with the rustlers."

"Did he say where they were ambushed?" Logan asked.

The boy nodded, "Near the pass."

Logan was on a high run for his horse. Little Feather hurried to gather his gear for him. In twenty minutes Logan was spurring his horse out across Raven Basin. Logan was climbing near the top when he first started hearing gun shots. As Logan neared the pass, he could hear cattle bawling and could see dust coming his way. Logan pulled his rifle and moved off the trail, and a rider appeared pushing cattle ahead of him. Then Logan spotted the second rider. He didn't recognize either rider, and their horses had brands he had never seen before. As the rider drew close to where Logan stood behind a big pine tree, he stepped out with rifle leveled on the startled man. The man's hand flew to his pistol when Logan shot him out of the saddle. The second man dodged behind a tree and fired at Logan. Bark flew from the tree beside Logan. When the gunman stepped out for another shot, Logan was ready. Logan saw the fellow fall over backward. Logan jumped across the trail, and as he did, he heard more cattle coming and shouts from riders pushing them. As the lead rider got closer to Logan, he spotted the body in the trail. The second rider rode up, and Logan could see he was wounded and having a hard time staying in the saddle.

The wounded man pointed, "Who shot Red?"

Logan stepped out, "I did."

312

Both men turned and looked into the muzzles of two 44-40 colts. Logan told them to drop their pistols real slow like. Logan moved forward and pulled the rifles from their scabbards. He told them to step down. The wounded rider looked at Logan.

"I can't do that. I'm tied to the saddle."

Logan motioned to the other man. "You untie him and help him down."

Logan was watching the wounded man being helped down when he heard another horse racing up the trail. As the rider came into view, a shot rang out, and he was knocked from his saddle. The man helping the wounded man down spun. He dropped to the ground and leveled a pistol when Logan fired. Logan had seen the first quick movement and was ready as the outlaw spun to get a shot. The wounded man fell from the saddle and was laying face down on the trail as Logan walked up. As Logan rolled him over, he saw the empty shoulder holster and knew where the other rider had found a pistol.

The wounded man opened his eyes and looked up to Logan. "Who are you? Where did all the Indians come from?

Logan pulled the man's head up. "Where's the people with the drive?"

The wounded man must have figured his time on earth was going to be short if he didn't answer this big fellow real quick. He motioned back up the trail. "They're holed up in some rocks back about two miles."

As Logan laid the wounded man back on the ground, he saw another rider in the trees looking at them. He recognized Little Hawk. He motioned for him to ride on down. As Little Hawk started down toward the trail, another rider could be seen coming off the other side of the trail. Logan grinned when he recognized one of the Indians from the village. He noticed the rifle across his saddle.

"Little Hawk, keep an eye on this fellow so I can ride back to where the Rafter T riders are."

Little Hawk nodded. "Rebecca is okay, but two of her riders are wounded pretty bad." Logan headed back up the trail, and as he rode along, cattle were scattered all along the trail. Most were moving down toward the creek where there was good feed. He found two dead rustlers in one place and three more laying in some rocks along the trail. When he found the last three rustlers, Logan stopped to look because he could tell by their wounds they had been caught in a crossfire. Most of the wounds looked like they were from big bore rifles. This must have been where Running Wolf and his crew had joined the battle. Logan heard his named called. He looked up above the trail to see Rebecca waving at him. As he rode up to dismount, he could see two wounded men being looked after by Running Wolf. As he stepped down, Rebecca grabbed him in a hug.

"Boy, I'm glad to see you." Then she added, "When we heard the big rifles turn loose I thought it was you."

Before Logan could add anything Rebecca said, "Logan, those Indians can really shoot." Logan about then spotted movement down close to where the three dead men were. He worked his way down the ridge to where he had seen the movement. He found another wounded rustler. The fellow was hit pretty bad. Logan opened his shirt to look at the wound and the fellow asked in a whisper, "Who are you people? We figured this would be an easy take. That girl and those five riders fought like crazy. We thought we'd killed the first rider. They headed for the rocks up there and then all hell broke loose. Then the rider we thought was dead got to a horse and spooked our horses and headed out over the ridge. During the night, we found our horses, and come daylight, we decided to take what cattle we could get easy and leave. They poured lead down on us every time we tried to move toward the cattle. Then all of a sudden some big rifles opened up from behind us and we were cut to pieces. The boss and two other riders finally broke free but I heard shots from over there so they must have found more riders." Logan checked over the rustler's wound and figured this one might live if they could get him down to the ranch.

Logan could see Rebecca kneeling near two bodies. He walked over. She was covering the head of one of them. Logan looked at his sister, "Were any of these riders part of the home ranch crew?" Rebecca shook her head no.

"I hired five riders like you said and didn't take anyone from the ranch."

"Is one of these riders the good friend you talked about?"

"Jerry was the rider I sent for help. When the Indians showed up, I knew he made it."

While they were talking, Running Wolf rode up.

"I think we have them all; two wounded and seven dead."

"The wounded man from my crew will need help getting to the ranch. We can't put him on a horse," said Rebecca.

Running Wolf spoke to an Indian from the village in their language. The man nodded and rode off. "I told Walking Bear to build a travois for the wounded."

Rebecca bandaged up the wounded rustler that was lying in the rocks. When she finished that, Little Hawk rode up with the other wounded rustler tied to his saddle. Little Hawk nodded toward the wounded outlaw, "I bound his wounds good enough to get him down to the ranch."

Walking Bear showed up with two travois for the two wounded men. They soon were ready to travel. As they started to leave, Little Hawk told Running Wolf, "We'll stay and help the wranglers start rounding up the cattle." Running Wolf motioned for Logan to look over on the ridge top. There were ten riders skylined on the ridge; most were Indians. Logan recognized Acel and his two boys with them. Logan waved and the riders came down off the ridge toward them. As they got close, Logan could see Little Feather was riding in the lead. Logan turned to Rebecca. "You're about to meet your sister-in-law." When they rode up, Logan introduced Rebecca to Little Feather. Little Feather smiled at Rebecca.

"It is good to meet someone from Logan's family."

As the girls talked, Logan asked Acel if he and the boys would bury the dead rustlers here on the mountain, then bring the dead rider down to the ranch with them.

It was a slow trip down the mountain with the wounded. By evening all were resting at the Indian village. Little Feather's mother helped care for the wounded rustlers. They moved the two riders from the cattle drive up to the ranch. Mrs. Helmick was a rather bossy nurse, and she seemed to know how to care for bullet wounds. Both riders were pretty badly wounded. They brought Jerry back to the ranch with them from the Indian camp. Little Feather's mother had bound up Jerry's wounds at the Indian camp soon after he rode in to give the warning. Rebecca checked on him then started to help when Mrs Helmick told her she could handle this by herself. When Rebecca started to argue, Little Feather grabbed her hand and took her outside. "Caddie has already decided how to treat your wounded and we best leave her alone," Little Feather told Rebecca when they got outside.

Logan and Running Wolf rode in toward the buildings. A small head could be seen behind Logan. As they got closer, Rebecca could see that Logan had a child standing behind him with her arms around his neck. Little Feather scolded Logan for letting Fawn ride behind him standing up. Logan just grinned and reached around and grabbed her by her belt and handed her to Rebecca.

"That's your niece, Fawn, or little Lottie. She answers to both."

Logan told Fawn, "This lady is your aunt, and she'll probably spoil you if we don't watch her."

"You're a cutie. If Grandma Lottie ever gets to see you, you'll really get spoiled," Rebecca told her as she hugged her.

Logan told the women he was going back up the trail and help bring down the herd. When Logan neared the pass, he could see cattle coming down off the ridge. He pulled off the trail and waited for the cattle to come by. Little Hawk was out front, "The wranglers say we've got them all.

Logan nodded. "Take them up into that small meadow above the barn and just turn them loose. The green grass and water will keep them close by until they're rested up from the drive." After the cattle passed, Logan headed on up to see how Acel and his crew were getting along. When Logan topped the ridge, he saw them coming toward him. When Acel rode up, he motioned to a bundle behind his saddle.

"We brought all the possessions we could find on the bodies." The pistols and rifles were in a bundle behind his saddle. "While they were burying the outlaws, a couple of young Indian kids from the village rode up. They told me they had found the pack horses from the cattle drive. One horse's pack had turned and they couldn't lift it back on. They said they had cut the cinch so the horse could get up but needed help packing the horse. Boyd went with the boys to get the gear. He took one of the dead rustler's horse in case the downed horse was hurt."

Over on the next ridge, three riders leading pack horses were moving along the trail toward them. It was Boyd and the boys from the village.

As they rode into the ranch Acel asked, "Where should we bury the men from the cattle drive?" Logan looked over at Acel.

"A person always hates to start a burial ground on a new ranch. Other people are going to die, so we should have a place nearby for those who belong to this ranch."

Logan thought for a minute. "For this ranch the grave site will be up on the ridge where I was shot." He pointed to the ridge above the cabins where Acel and Caddie lived.

Cliff nodded. "I'll head up there now to dig a grave. Logan nodded, "I'll go up with you and help."

Once up on the ridge, it brought back many memories to Logan as he looked down on the ranch he was building. Tug had buried the three men from the cabins and Frank Griffith on the same ridge only further down toward the valley. Logan motioned to Cliff, "We'll dig this grave on the open ridge overlooking the valley. There'll be room here for more along this ridge. We know more will die before this country is settled."

That evening as the sun was setting, they laid to rest the young cowboy, Benny Melton. Rebecca had hired him to help move the first herd into Raven Basin. Acel told them he would carve a wooden cross with his name on it for the grave. He was twenty years old. He'd just come west two years ago to get away from city life. He had been a handy man in the livery stables for a year and finally got to herd cattle for local ranchers during roundup. When he heard Rebecca was looking for riders, he rode all the way to the Rafter T one Sunday to ask for a job. Now she was standing with the two remaining riders at the head of his grave, with a Bible in her hand, saying the last words over him. Logan had offered to say the prayer. Rebecca shook her head, "I hired him and brought him along. I'll do it." Logan found another side of his sister he had never known.

The next day Logan and Rebecca rode out over the ranch so she could see what he was trying to build. When they were down along White River, they decided to eat the lunch Little Feather had fixed. Logan built a fire. When the coffee boiled, they enjoyed their lunch. Rebecca looked at her big brother. "I love this country. Even though the Rafter T is a great place, I'd like to move here."

Logan looked over at her. "You're welcome anytime. I'll make you half owner. I do worry about our folks being alone on the Rafter T."

Rebecca nodded. "John's really starting to help run the ranch. Soon Mary will be moving out to the ranch full time too. I'll go back, and if they say they can't get along without me, I'll stay. If they say they can handle it, I'll be back to take you up on the deal."

Logan smiled, "I hope you come back. I need help here, too."

When they finished lunch and started back toward the Indian village, Logan told her, "I figure on quitting the rangers before long and spending all my time here developing this place."

Rebecca looked over at her big brother. "Why leave the rangers now? You seem to have everything working alright."

"I can't be gone so much and expect this ranch to grow. If you do come back to live here, then I would probably stay with the rangers a few more years."

When they got back to the village, Little Feather was there. She had ridden over to see how her mother was doing with the two wounded rustlers. Logan walked into the teepee where the two wounded men were being held. They both were propped up on some robes and were still pretty sick men. "I'm Territorial Ranger Logan McTier." they both just stared at him. Finally, one of them asked, "Where are we?"

"You're in an Indian village." Running Wolf had walked into the teepee and Logan also introduced him as a ranger.

"Those cattle you tried to rustle were from the Rafter T down near Benton. I own this ranch here and these Indians are my partners. The cattle were being brought here to start a herd."

"What's going to happen to us?"

"As soon as you can travel, I'll take you back to ranger headquarters for trial."

The one said, "It looked so easy to steal that herd. Then all hell had broke loose." The other one nodded.

As Logan turned to leave, the one that had been tied to his horse asked, "Did any of the others get away?"

Logan shook his head. "We just buried seven rustlers and one cowboy. We buried them near the ranch building."

"I'd like to know the spot. One of them was my brother."

"Okay, before we head out for headquarters, I'll take you by the graves."

The month passed quickly, and the two outlaws were well enough to travel. Logan and Running Wolf were packing getting ready to leave when Rebecca walked up.

"Jerry wants to travel out with you. He decided he's well enough for the trip. He says he wants time to see if he wants a life here in the basin."

The three ranch hands that Rebecca brought in with the herd had asked if they could hire on to help build the new ranch. The wounded one was recovering. Logan told them they were welcome and he'd pay them top wages.

"When we hired on with Rebecca, we were looking for steady work."

Rebecca was going to head back to the Rafter T later that month. She wanted Little Feather and Fawn to go with her to visit Ted and Lottie. Logan smiled when she told him. "I'll let them go if you'll take Little Hawk and one other rider from the village with you." She nodded.

Logan asked Acel if he would take over as ramrod, and he declined. "Boyd doesn't like being a builder like Cliff and I do. I think you should make him ramrod," Acel added. Logan talked to Boyd. "I'd really like the job, but I've got a lot to learn about running a ranch."

Logan spent one day riding with Boyd and two of the new hands to show them what he wanted done. With Little Hawk gone, Logan needed someone the Indians trusted. Boyd had always got along good with the young braves in the village. With this settled, Logan felt better about leaving.

The trip over the mountain and to the mines took longer than Logan had figured. The wounded fellows he found weren't in good enough condition to stay in the saddle all day. When they got to the Milford Mine, Jerry, Rebecca's friend, decided to wait until the stage came through and ride it on to the capital. He was still showing the effects of his wounds more than the two outlaws. He was riding a Rafter T horse. Logan told him he would see it got back to the ranch.

Logan decided to spend the night at the Milford, and that evening Charlie rode up from the Golden Rose Mine. He'd been down helping install a new mill at the Golden Rose for John Griffith. When he rode in, he spotted Logan and stopped to talk. Then he asked, "Why are there so many rangers around?" Logan shrugged his shoulders.

Charlie laughed. "From your looks, I guess you didn't know there are two rangers staying at the Golden Rose tonight."

Logan decided he would ride down to see who they were and if they would take his prisoners back to headquarters for him.

When he got to the Golden Rose Mine, he stopped at the office. When he walked through the door, he was greeted by John Griffith who had seen him ride up. "I hear you have a couple of rangers staying the night," commented Logan.

"They're down at the cook shack. They should be back before long. They're bunking in the back room. These two rangers are new to me. They said this was their first trip out alone." John asked, "Have you eaten?"

"I ate at the Milford before I heard there were rangers down here."

They passed the time, and soon two young men with badges walked into the office. Logan stood up and stuck out his hand. Before he could say anything, one of the rangers said, "You must be Mc Tier." Logan grinned and nodded.

"I'm Jess Smith and this is Daryl Morgan." They shook hands.

"We took our training time under the eye of your old friend, Tug. We've heard many stories about you from Tug and George Bennett."

Logan laughed. "You know you shouldn't believe all you heard from those two. I've got two prisoners. I need them taken back to headquarters."

"We're headed back that way tomorrow anyway. We'd be glad to take your prisoners."

Logan nodded. "Thank you. I'll bring them down from the Milford in the morning."

Running Wolf and Logan went down to the Golden Rose at first light. The two young rangers had just finished breakfast and were saddling up when Logan found them. He introduced Running Wolf. They both look surprised when Running Wolf spoke. Logan gave the rangers all the effects from the dead rustlers and a map showing where they were buried. He also sent a letter to George telling about the shootings. He included in the letter they were going to start another trip around the area.

The stage pulled into the Milford Mine as Logan and Running Wolf were packing their gear to head for Kilgore. Jerry walked over to say good-bye. Logan told him he always had a job anytime he wanted to come back. The two rangers headed out with the extra horse that belonged to the Rafter T.

When they rode into Kilgore that evening, Logan was surprised to hear Rebecca and Little Feather had spent last night with Jerry at the trading post. Logan figured Rebecca must have decided she wanted to get over and tell the folks her new plans. When Logan had last talked to her, she was going to wait to see how Boyd got along as ramrod before she left. Jerry told them supper would to be in about a hour, so they had time to get their horses put away. They were about through eating when shots were heard coming from main street about a block and a half away. Logan looked at Running Wolf. "We'd better head up that way." They were just walking out when a clerk from the store up town came running up the street toward the trading post. When he saw the badges, he rushed over to them. "Two men up at the saloon shot a man during a card game. The sheriff is out looking into a rustler complaint in the valley. The town marshall is in Benton."

Logan walked along at a fast pace with the clerk trotting along side trying to keep up. The clerk kept saying the guys were dangerous and he'd need help. As they neared the saloon, Logan stopped.

"You go back to the store. We'll handle this."

As the clerk started to leave, he turned back to Logan. "Those men in the saloon stopped at the store when they first rode into town. There was a third guy with them then, but when the shooting was reported, they only mentioned two men doing the shooting." Logan nodded.

Logan moved over where he could look in the window. Two men were standing with their backs to the bar. The bartender was in the crowd in front of the two at the bar. Logan noticed a third older fellow standing on the stairs. He seemed to be coming from one of the girls' rooms up above the bar. The two at the bar weren't paying him any attention so Logan figured that was the third man. They had their guns holstered. They were laughing at someone in the crowd. Logan and Running Wolf stepped into the bar, and each stepped to the side so their backs were covered from the street.

The two men at the bar spun around when Logan said, "What's the problem here?"

Logan noticed the man on the staircase was pulling a shotgun. He'd been holding it out of sight behind his leg. The two men at the bar went for their guns. Logan drew and fired just before the man on the staircase could level the shotgun. As Logan turned toward the bar, he heard two fast shots coming from the other side of the doorway. Both men were crumbling against the bar. They both fired into the floor, and their guns fell from their hands to the floor.

As Logan turned to the crowd, they were all raising their hands and yelling, "Don't shoot." The man on the staircase was still breathing when Logan kneeled down beside him.

He looked at Logan. "Are my boys dead?" Logan nodded.

You must be McTier. His last words were, "I figured so when I saw the Indian."

Logan could see where his bullet had hit the man, but the blood was coming from the other side of his body. When he looked under his coat, he found a money belt which had deflected the bullet.

The bartender Logan knew from before was there. The man grinned, "If they only knew who you were before they tried to out draw you."

The crowd was beginning to mill around, and Logan told someone to find the undertaker. When the bartender got behind the bar he shouted, "Free drinks on the house." Logan heard someone in the crowd say, "Did you see the speed of those two rangers. I've heard McTier's Indian partner

321

was also fast, but I didn't believe it till now."

"They both fired at the same time," came from another bystander.

The undertaker removed the bodies. "Did the two men in the card game have families close by?"

The bartender nodded. "I already sent a person over to tell the one fellow's wife."

Logan shook his head over the situation. He told the undertaker to charge the territory for all five bodies. The lady had lost enough without paying to have her husband buried. As Logan turned to leave, he looked back at the bartender.

"You make sure the wife doesn't get charged too," The bartender nodded.

As the two rangers walked back into the trading post, Jerry looked up. "From the sounds I heard, I guess they didn't surrender."

Logan gave Jerry a brief story on what happened and told him the one card player had a wife. They were having a cup of coffee when the store clerk who had brought the warning walked in. He looked over at Logan. "You could have told me you were Logan McTier. I ran into the store telling my boss we needed to get some men to help you. He laughed at me and told me who you were."

"Who was the card player that had a wife?" Jerry asked. When the clerk answered, Jerry just shook his head. He turned to Logan, "They've been customers of mine for a long time."

The next morning as they got ready to leave, Logan told Jerry to fill the sheriff in on what happened. As they topped the pass looking down on the Rafter T buildings, Logan wondered how Little Feather was making out with Lottie. When they rode up to the hitch rail in front of the new house, out walked Lottie holding her granddaughter's hand. Little Feather was walking behind. She had a grin on her face. Logan reached down and picked up Fawn, and she gave him a big kiss. Logan held her back away from him. "You sure are mushy for being an Indian," and he got a giggle from his daughter.

Lottie was all smiles, "I'm keeping this kid here with me."

Rebecca walked up from the corrals, and Logan could tell by the look on her face she was happy. She gave him a hug. "Well partner, I guess you're going to have to get used to me in Raven Basin."

With all the family around during supper, a lot was discussed, and

Logan could tell his folks were proud of their new daughter-in-law. When they were alone that night, Little Feather told him how well she had been greeted when they arrived.

While Logan and Running Wolf got ready to leave, Fawn was talking to her uncle in Shoshone language. Lottie laughed at Fawn, "She changes from one language to another sometimes in the same sentence."

Rebecca and Little Feather walked out with Logan, "We'll start back to Raven Basin in another week. We'll take a couple of pack horses or whatever it takes to pack my belonging to my new home." Logan nodded, "Rebecca, why don't you buy the extra horses from my account in the Benton bank. We can always use more horses up there."

Ted, who had been listening, told them, "I just bought a bunch of horses off a horse trader the other day. I'll sell you whatever you need." With that all taken care of, the two rangers headed for Benton.

When they stopped by the sheriff's office, Del Rogers was doing paperwork. He motioned them to sit, "Why don't you two sit a while and bring me up to date on what's happening in the territory." He handed Logan a paper. "That's a list of items missing from the hardware store here in Benton. Ed has turned the hardware store over to his nephew. When the nephew came to work last Monday, he found the store had been robbed. The robbers hadn't even tried to open the safe or taken any change from the cash register. What was missing mostly was fire arms and ammunition. They cleaned out the rifles and pistols and all the loaded shells on hand. Ed later found they had also taken some kegs of powder from the store room. He also found bullet molds and lead missing."

"Why don't you keep that list of items missing. There's one thing that might help catch these crooks. There was a new model 73 Winchester and 45 Colt that will be easy to trace. Winchester gave Ed this new series 73 for selling so many Winchester rifles over the years. It had a gold trigger and a plate on the stock with Ed's name on it. The Colt was also a gift to Ed for promoting the Colt pistols. It's 45 caliber and has oak leaves engraved on the cylinder. The grips were made from a stag horn with E carved on one side and B on the other side."

"When I was notified of the robbery, it was too late to find tracks. I did find wagon tracks in the alley behind the store. I don't know if they were made by the robbers or someone else using the alley over the weekend. Ed and I both figure the robbery had taken place Saturday night after the store closed."

Logan nodded. "We'll keep our eyes open for the missing guns. I don't like hearing they only took guns and ammunition."

Logan telegraphed a report to George at headquarters and then waited around for a reply. It was evening before George wired him back. The rangers slept that night in extra bunks in back of the jail. They had breakfast with Del before heading back up the trail toward Sweetwater and Butte and the rest of their area.

They made a short stop in Sweetwater to see how Jeff was mending. Jeff was back on the job but mostly confined to office work. He'd hired a new deputy and the ranger was still in town. With everything good in Sweetwater, they headed for Butte. When they rode into Butte, they put their horse in the livery. Logan was again with his old friend, Traveler. Wade had kept him in good health and said he had made one trip with Frank over to the Chinese diggings. They had supper with Ling, and just like before, he wouldn't let Logan pay for anything. Ling told Logan the mines along the basin were doing good. The girls were now handling almost all the supply business. "They're now my biggest customer. I just heard they're going to build another gambling hall."

With everything quiet, they headed for Spirit Lake to see how it was making out with the new sheriff Logan had appointed.

Logan thought about how the area had changed since he first rode in a few years ago. He thought more about how he had gone from a young ranch hand to a gunfighter and now a territorial ranger. Logan was startled by the quick movement of Running Wolf, who rode ahead of him down the trail. Running Wolf pulled his rifle as he jumped from his horse into the brush along the trail. Logan followed his lead and pulled his horse off the trail and dismounted also pulling his rifle. He moved real slow up next to Running Wolf who was watching something in the trail ahead. Running Wolf pointed. "There's a body lying in the trail up near those two big trees." Then he pointed to an opening below the trail to a horse with its head down eating grass. As they moved forward toward the body, Logan moved off across the trail toward the horse. Logan noticed the horse didn't have a bridle but instead a hackamore. It was unusual in mountain country to see someone riding using a hackamore. Logan moved on past the horse. As he neared the trail, he heard a low whistle from Running Wolf. Logan moved up slowly into the trail. The body was only ten feet away. He rolled the fellow over. He was a small man. He'd been really worked over. Logan felt under his shirt. He could feel the slow movement of his chest. Running Wolf moved up near Logan. "I can't find any sign of the attackers. They must have rode off." Logan motioned to all the marks on the little man's face. "This man has taken one hell of a beating. There's a small spring near where the little man's horse is grazing so let's move him down there."

Later Running Wolf moved back up the trail to retrieve their horses. Logan built a fire and heated some water and bathed the man's face. As he removed all the dried blood, he recognized the little man. It was Henry, the store clerk from Placer Butte.

Logan had boiled a pot of coffee, and they were chewing on some jerky when Logan saw a small movement from the little man under the blanket next to the fire. He moved over. Slowly the eyelids moved and then he opened his eyes. He started to pull his arms up over his head when Logan told him they weren't going to hit him. The little man's eyes were riveted to Logan's face. Then he whispered, "McTier?"

Logan nodded. "You lay quiet. I'll get you some water."

While the coffee boiled, Running Wolf cut up some jerky and poured some meal like flour into a small cup of hot water. As they sat the little man up to drink, Running Wolf told him, "Drink from this cup, and then I'll give you some water."

He drank all the liquid from the cup. Then Running Wolf gave him a cup of water. Logan went back to his gear and returned with some salve Lottie always used on cuts. He put this salve on all the wounds on the little man's face. The fellow then laid back on the blanket and fell asleep.

Logan fixed a bigger fire ring, and as he started making camp for the night, Running Wolf moved off into the trees. He later came back with three big blue grouse.

Logan grinned, "Where did you find them?"

Running Wolf looked over at Logan and with his same slow talk, "I found them asleep."

Logan decided the Indian wasn't going to tell him how he caught them without firing a shot. When the grouses were about to be eaten, Logan woke up their beat up guest. He was really favoring his chest. Logan figured he'd also been beaten on the body, and maybe he had some broken ribs.

After eating Logan asked Henry, "What were you doing out here? Who worked you over like this?"

"This man and his two big sons rode into the trading post. He told us he was Tiny Lang's brother. Then he said he was taking back what belonged to him. When I objected, he told his sons to get rid of me. The next thing I remember was waking up tied over a saddle and the horse moving along through the woods. They'd tied my hands but there was some slack, and I got my hands untied. I guess when I tried to move, I fell off the horse. I remember waking up a few times but then I would pass out again."

"What happened to the girls?" asked Logan. Henry just shook his head.

By morning the little man stood up and could move around slowly. After breakfast he told Henry, "I'm now a territorial ranger and so is Running Wolf. We'll get you on the horse and head you back toward Sweetwater. Running Wolf and I will ride over to see what's happening at the trading post." Henry grabbed Logan's arm, "I want to go back with you. That's my only home."

As they neared the buildings, they hid the horses in the thick timber and moved out on foot. Logan found a place where he could observe both the store and the saloon. He saw a big, young man come out of the saloon and head over toward the store. He told Running Wolf to circle around and come in from behind the saloon. Logan moved off to get behind the store, and the little store clerk was right on his heals. Logan knew this little man was hurting but admired his courage. As Logan got around back, he was surprised to see a pack string tied up. It was then he recognized a black dog laying in the brush not far from the horses. The dog's ears went up. He moved off into the brush and soon was at Logan's side. With Traveler here, that would mean that Frank was close by. Logan told the little man to stay put until he got to the back door of the warehouse. With Traveler right on his heels, Logan moved toward the building. As he neared the back door, he could feel Traveler moving up and could hear a low growl. He stepped back behind the door just as it opened. Frank was pushed out ahead by a big fellow holding a bung starter. The big man told Frank to get busy unloading the pack string. Logan hit the big, young man over the head with his pistol as he moved away from the building. Logan grabbed him and eased him to the ground. He looked up grinning at a startled Frank. He motioned into the building.

"Is there anybody else in there?" Frank shook his head.

Frank helped Logan tie up the young fellow. They gagged him and put him in the wood shed. When the little clerk came up Frank said, "I heard they killed you, Henry."

Frank stuck out his hand. "Logan, where in the hell did you come from?"

"We found Henry up along the trail more dead than alive. When he could finally talk, he told us what happened. So we headed out to see what was going on."

Henry went into the store, and when he came back out, he was carrying a double barrel sawed off shotgun. He had two pistols in his belt. He handed them to Frank.

"This old man with these two boys played rough," Frank informed Logan. "I think they also worked the girls over, too. They broke a Chinese miner's arm yesterday. They sent him back down the trail with orders to tell the other miners they would be down to collect their share of the gold."

"Frank, you and Henry stay in the store while I work my way over to the saloon."

As Logan started to leave, Frank grabbed his arm. "Two riders came in last night and I think they are with these men. They put their horses away and spent the night in the saloon. They both wear a tied down six shooter." Logan nodded.

Logan moved up alongside the saloon where he could see in the window. There were four men sitting at a table near the stove. One of the girls was bringing food from the kitchen, and Logan could see her face was swollen. As he watched, he caught a glimpse of a shadow in the hallway. A smile came to Logan's face. Running Wolf was already inside. How that Indian could move around and never be heard still amazed Logan.

Logan loosened both pistols and opened the front door and walked into the bar. The big, older man faced the door, and when he saw Logan, he grabbed for a pistol laying on the table. Logan's first shot hit the big man as he turned to fire, and he fell into the stove. The other two men froze when a shot from the back room knocked over the big man's son as he stood up with a pistol in his hand. Logan moved over towards the two men with their tied down holsters.

"You two get up real slow."

Logan pulled their guns. When he checked them over, he found two hideouts, both Derringers. The kitchen door opened, and Logan could see two heads peeking out into the bar. Logan grinned, "It's all clear. You can come on out."

Rachel and Gail both rushed into the room. From their looks, it had been a rough couple of days. Running Wolf called to Logan, "This man wants to talk to you." He motioned to the big man laying by the stove.

Logan walked over and kneeled down next to the old man. He was hit bad and probably wouldn't live much longer. As Logan leaned down, the old man asked, "Who are you?" Then he added, "I own this store. You had no right coming here."

"Are you Tiny Lang's brother?"

The wounded man shook his head. "No, we're cousins. I heard about him owning this place so I was headed out to see him. I didn't know he was dead until we stopped in Sweetwater. When I heard that two girls that worked for him were now the owners, I decided I would take over."

He looked up at Logan, "Are both my boys dead?"

"No, the one over at the store is tied up in the wood shed."

Logan stood up. "I will bring him over to see you."

When Logan started for the door, gun shots were heard coming from the store. He dashed to the door and could see two riders lying in the street. Two horses were tied in front of the store. Logan thought he heard a shotgun blast during the shooting. Henry, the store clerk, stood over the two men. Logan walked over to Frank. "These two fellows rode up and said they had been hired by the old man. They decided to fight rather than surrender. Are the girls there alright?"

Logan nodded. "Go in and see for yourself."

Logan untied the son in the wood shed and headed him toward the saloon. As they passed Henry in the street, Henry growled, "Why don't you try to beat on me now?"

The big lad looked over at the beat up little man, "I should have killed you like Dad wanted."

Henry just grinned, "Logan, if you'll step aside, I'll save the expense of a trial."

"Henry, you calm down. We'll take care of this," and they headed on up the steps into the saloon.

When the son saw his father laying by the stove with blood coming from his chest, he kneeled down close to him.

The old man looked at Logan. "You never did say who you are and why you're here?"

"I'm Logan McTier, territorial ranger for this district."

"How did you know we were here," asked the son.

"We found Henry, the store clerk, lying in the trail, and he told us."

As Logan talked to the father and son, Henry, the little store clerk, walked up. He grinned down at the two men who had almost killed him. The old man started coughing up blood, and when it stopped, he told Henry, "I should have just gut shot you."

Before Logan could move, Henry pulled both triggers on the shot gun. Logan grabbed the shotgun, but the damage was already done. Both father and son were ripped apart by the blast. Henry turned and walked out the door and headed for his store.

Logan looked at the little store clerk's back as he walked out. He just shook his head. Running Wolf was standing off to the side watching the two gunmen the old man had hired. He looked over at Logan. "I guess he thought they were still a threat to him."

Frank and the girls were still looking at the bodies of the father and son who had caused them so much pain. Logan turned to Frank, "We'll ride with you back to Butte to let the sheriff know what's happened here."

Rachel grabbed Logan's arm. "When I heard that voice, I knew it was you."

Gail, who was still looking at the bodies, mumbled, "I wish I had been the one holding that scatter gun."

Both girls looked at Logan. "What will happen to Henry."

Logan shook his head. "That'll be up to the sheriff. As far as I'm concerned, I'm not doing a thing."

Traveler, who had warned Logan at the door of the warehouse, was at his heels all the rest of the day. Frank smiled as they unloaded the pack string load into the warehouse.

"That damn dog and you will always be a team."

Logan smiled and reached down to pet his old trail partner. "I wish I could make him young again."

The next morning with the prisoners mounted and the bodies loaded, Logan wished the girls good luck. With Frank and Running Wolf, Logan headed out toward the trail to Butte. Logan noticed Traveler bristled up as they neared the main trail. He eased his rifle out, and Running Wolf moved off the trail. About then Logan saw his old friend, Lo Lin, step out onto the trail. Behind him were more of the Chinese miners Logan had moved the gold for. Lo Lin and the miners were armed.

"We're going to fight the new owners at the store."

Logan smiled at Lo Lin. "Those bodies on those horses are the men who tried to take over the store."

With much Chinese chatter, Lo Lin explained to his fellow miners they could go back to their mines. With all of them grinning and laughing, Lo Lin smiled at Logan. "We're going to the trading post to celebrate."

Logan stopped in front of the sheriff's office. He turned over his prisoners to the sheriff. Logan told him the story about Henry killing the two men with a shotgun. The sheriff told Logan he would talk to the traveling judge on his next trip through. Then he would do whatever the judge wanted. That night Frank and Wade and Running Wolf had supper at the livery stable kitchen with Wade doing the cooking. Traveler spent the whole night at Logan's feet.

After supper the four of them were sitting out front of the livery stable when the stage from Sweetwater came to halt across the street. The passengers stepped out on the sidewalk. The coach blocked the passengers from the view of the four men across the street. As the passengers got their luggage, Traveler rose to his feet. He was making a low, whining sound.

Logan stood up. "I think Traveler knows one of those passengers," and he followed Traveler across the street. When Logan and Traveler were in the middle of the street, a young couple with luggage walked out from behind the stage. The woman was carrying a child as they walked toward the hotel. Traveler was off like a bullet heading for the young couple. When he got close, he started barking. The girl dropped to her knees. She threw one arm around the dog. Logan heard her say, "Traveler," then he recognized Mollie. The young man was her husband, Dave. The old dog was sniffing the blanket. Mollie opened it and showed him their young son. When Mollie looked up and saw Logan walking toward her, she started crying. As he walked up to Mollie, she grabbed him and buried her head in his chest. When she stepped back, she opened the blanket.

"Logan, this is David Logan MacIntire. Where did you find Traveler?"

Logan pointed to the livery, "That's his home now."

By then the other three had walked across the street. Logan introduced Frank and Wade to Mollie and Dave. They already knew Running Wolf. Logan told her Wade kept Traveler and had been since Logan started traveling so much.

"He makes trips with Frank and his pack string into Placer Butte sometimes. He's well taken great care of. In fact, he helped me on a recent problem over there. He's still a great partner."

Mollie and Dave headed on to the hotel. As they walked away, Mollie told Logan she would stop by the livery to see him later.

It was a nice evening so Logan just waited on the bench in front of the livery stable. Soon Mollie came walking down the street and crossed over to join Logan. They were joined by Traveler who was happy to lay at their feet.

Mollie shook her head, "I can't believe that Traveler remembers me. That was so long ago." Logan assured her animals always remember those who treat them well.

Mollie told Logan they were in Butte because Dave had been offered a job by an aunt that lived in Spirit Lake. "I'm going to stay here while Dave travels to see this aunt about this job offer. He's never met her."

"Running Wolf and me are going over to Spirit Lake tomorrow. Dave's sure welcome to ride with us."

Mollie went on, "Dave received this letter from a Mrs. Tidwell who said she is Dave's father's sister. Dave's dad died some years before, and his mother remarried so Dave was raised by his stepfather. Mrs. Tidwell had said in her letter she had found out where he was from a relative still living in Missouri. Dave's mother told him when he showed her the letter that his dad still had a sister back there when her and Dave's dad were married. This aunt said in her letter that her husband was dead and she needed someone to manage her mine."

Logan started laughing, and Mollie just looked at him.

"What did I say that was funny?"

Logan then told her the story about Mrs. Tidwell and her mine. When he finished, Mollie had this almost blank look on her face.

"Do you mean you know this lady and she does have a mine?"

"From what I have seen, a very rich mine."

Mollie stood up. "I've got to tell Dave about this."

As she turned to leave Logan said, "Tell Dave we'll be leaving at sun up."

Logan was just getting into bed when someone knocked on the door of the cabin they were staying in. A voice from outside said, "This is Dave McIntire. Mr. McTier, can I talk to you for a minute?"

Logan told him to come on in. Dave had all kinds of questions. Logan grinned at him. "Why don't you ride over with us tomorrow and ask your aunt all these questions?"

Dave told Logan, "I couldn't believe what Mollie said when she got back to the hotel. "I'll be here at sun up to go with you." He hurried out the door.

They made good time getting to Spirit Lake. When they stopped at the sheriff's office, Logan looked over at Dave. "Wait while I check in with the sheriff, then I'll take you up to the mine."

The sheriff reported all was quiet. Mrs. Tidwell had told him she had a nephew coming to run the mine. Logan introduced Dave to the sheriff.

Dave looked at the three men looking at him, "I've been a cowboy all my life, and I know nothing of mining."

The sheriff grinned. "I think Mrs. Tidwell knows that. She's hired one of the old local miners to work for her. She made the old prospector a deal. If he would help you get started, she would grub stake him for a year. I never knew that old miner could move so fast. He was packed and moved up to the mine the same day."

When they rode up to the main buildings, Mrs. Tidwell and Willy stepped out to meet them. "What brings you back here so soon Logan?" Before he could answer, she turned to Dave.

"Are you Dave McIntire?"

When he nodded his head yes, she smiled, "You look just like your father."

With the family all together now, Logan and Running Wolf headed for Raven Basin.

Two weeks later Logan was helping Acel on the barn when an Indian boy from the village came riding in fast. He told Logan a calvary patrol was coming off the pass toward the valley.

Logan saddled up and rode back to the village with the young Indian boy. When they arrived, Running Wolf was already saddled and ready to ride. They headed out to meet the calvary patrol. As they rode up, the captain with the patrol asked, "Are you McTier, the territorial ranger?" Logan nodded and introduced Running Wolf.

The captain smiled, "My name is Sines, and we've been sent up here to find Ranger Running Wolf. They looked over at Running Wolf. "It'll take a while to explain to you why I'm here."

"Captain, why don't you and your patrol stay at the ranch?"

The captain grinned, "Lead the way."

When they got to the ranch, Logan asked Mrs. Helmick if she would mind feeding these men. The captain spoke up, "I will gladly pay with army script if that's okay. I'll also furnish kitchen help to take care of all dish washing."

With a big grin Mrs. Helmick said, "I like cooking for men that like to eat." This brought a cheer from the soldiers. The soldiers set up camp out by the creek. While they were doing this, Captain Sines told Logan, "I almost forgot to give you a message from your sister and wife. While I was in Kilgore trying to locate you two, I met Jerry at the trading post. Jerry introduced me to Little Feather, Fawn and Rebecca McTier. They have a big pack string with five riders and two Indians. Rebecca's message is they'll be at the ranch in two days."

"I guess my partner must be moving everything she owns."

He explained to the captain his sister was coming to operate the ranch while he was away on ranger duties.

After supper that evening, the captain opened a case filled with papers. "This is why I'm here. Governor Davis has suggested to the army that Ranger Running Wolf could solve a big problem with the Shoshone tribe. It seems the tribe has been a victim of a crooked Indian agent, and they've left the reservation. It's a small part of a tribe, and Little Bear is their leader. He's the oldest member of the Shoshone tribal council. His wisdom is much needed in keeping the rest of the Shoshone tribe from following his group off the reservation. The other chiefs were willing to work with the army, but only if Little Bear was present at all the meetings."

"Governor Davis has told everyone that Running Wolf is a good lawman. He wants him to work with the army to settle this. My orders were to find Running Wolf and ask him if he would return to headquarters. Once there, he's suppose to meet with the army, Bureau of Indian Affairs and the Territorial Governor. The governor hopes maybe they can settle this trouble with Little Bear before it's a big problem."

Logan looked over at his partner. "I think you have been promoted to a higher rank."

Running Wolf nodded. "I need time to think this over. I'll let the captain know by morning." Running Wolf saddled up and headed back toward the Indian village.

Captain Sines asked Logan about his years as a lawman of the area. "When I was ordered to find you, I didn't realize how big this area was. I've

333

heard many stories about the fast gun carrying a badge and later about his Indian partner."

The captain laughed. "When my patrol passed by the Blue Bird Mine, the owner said you two were pure hell with six guns. It seems you solved a problem with robbers real quick for him."

Logan told the captain, "Most generally, I'd just as soon bring them in alive. But instead, when cornered, they always seem to want to fight it out."

Running Wolf rode into the ranch way before sun up and headed for Logan's place. Logan was up, just getting ready to head for the cook shack to see if Caddie had any hot coffee. As they sat down to drink the coffee, Running Wolf told Logan, "I didn't sleep much last night. I've decided if it's alright with you, I'll ride back with the captain to talk to Governor Davis."

Logan nodded. "Running Wolf, I think you've made a good decision." He also added, "If you can help your people to adjust to this different life without blood shed you should, by all means do it."

Then Logan continued to add, "I think Little Bear will listen to you. Then, if a good agent could be assigned to the reservation, it'll work out." Running Wolf nodded.

"I'm really going to miss you. I wish you luck on this new job."

After breakfast the army patrol got ready to mount up. The captain tried to pay for his troop's meals. Both Caddie and Logan shook their heads. "No, we've been glad to have the company."

They both told the captain, "Any time you're in the area stop by. The coffee pot is always on."

As the men mounted, Caddie told the captain so all troops could hear, "If any of these soldiers ever want work , they can help in her kitchen."

This brought grins from the soldiers who had helped Caddie in the kitchen. Logan shook hands with the captain. He walked over to his partner of many years and offered his hand. Running Wolf looked down from his horse at Logan. "I'll try to remember all you have taught me."

As they rode away, Caddie walked over and stood by Logan. "I'll miss him. I hope he does well." Logan nodded as he walked toward the barn to help Acel.

The next evening Logan saddled up and headed out toward the place where Little Feather and Rebecca would be coming into the valley. The ranch buildings were still in sight when Logan could see the long string of horses crossing the open ground before him. As he rode up, Fawn was riding a horse by herself. She came galloping up to greet her father. Logan noticed she rode very well. He knew Aunt Rebecca and Little Hawk had something to do with this. Logan turned to ride along with Little Feather and Rebecca. Rebecca laughed at the look her brother had given the long pack string.

"I bought supplies that I know we'll need to handle more men. Two of the riders are from the Rafter T. They'll head back later. These other three I hired to help get this ranch built and into full operation."

"All the extra horses I bought from Dad and some from a horse dealer in Benton." She laughed, "I told the horse dealer these better be legal horses and not stolen from other parts of the country. Their new owner is a territorial ranger."

She added, "He almost backed out on the deal because he wasn't real sure where some of this stock had come from."

As Little Feather stepped down from her horse, Logan noticed she was carrying a baby in her. About then Rebecca smiled at her brother. "You could have told me I was going to be an aunt again before we left. I didn't know for a while if we were going to make it home before it was born."

Before Logan could say this was all news to him, Rebecca added, "Wait till Lottie sees you next time. She was mad as hell that you sent Little Feather on this long trip while she was carrying a child."

Little Feather came to his rescue. "He doesn't ever know when I'm with child. Last time I had to explain it to him," Little Feather laughed at her husband. "This one will be healthy and already knows how to ride horse."

Little Hawk and his partner rode up to Logan, "If you don't need us, we're going back to the village."

Logan shook Little Hawk's hand, "Thanks for looking after my family." Little Hawk nodded and rode off.

They unpacked all the horses, and Logan took them down to the big pasture below the barn for the night. "Caddie and I will start putting away the supplies tomorrow." said Rebecca.

When Logan and Little Feather got ready for bed, she told Logan, "I really enjoyed my time with your mother. She would have kept Fawn if I would have let her; they got along great. Your father is so quiet but he is so strong willed, and now I see where you are like him. He'd also have spoiled our daughter given a chance," she laughed.

Logan smiled, "I'm glad you enjoyed the Rafter T. We'll make another trip maybe next summer."

With Rebecca back, she kept Boyd as foreman. She was in control of what needed to be done to make this ranch go.

Logan decided to wait until their new child was born before heading out over his area. Little Feather told him it would be in the next few weeks. Logan had been out with Boyd locating where Logan wanted a line cabin built when a rider from the ranch came with word the baby was near. As Logan rode back into the ranch, Rebecca met him with a big smile. "You're now the father of a fine young son. Both mother and child are doing great."

Logan went in to see Little Feather. She showed him their new son. "Can we name him Ted?"

This was a surprise to Logan. " I'm thrilled with the idea Little Feather, but how's Theodore Hawk McTier sound?"

She grinned and nodded. Rebecca, who had walked into the room, added, "You won't be able to touch Dad with a ten foot pole when he hears this."

Two weeks later Logan started his first trip alone since he was shot on the ridge above the ranch. He would miss having someone to back his every move. Running Wolf was one of the best at doing that. As he rode into the Milford Mine, he saw it looked kind of deserted, but he could still hear the mill running. Charlie Milford saw him ride into camp and walked out of the office to greet him. Logan shook hands, "Why do things look so empty?"

"We're having some labor trouble. The miners want better wages and living conditions."

"There's a union man from down in the Colorado mines who has been here stirring up trouble. This rep wanted the men to join the miners' union which is causing problems in the bigger mining districts. The Golden Rose had the same problem and is totally closed down."

"Has ranger headquarters been notified?" asked Logan.

Charlie nodded, "George Bennett himself just left yesterday. Dad's still at the capital getting paper work done. He has a meeting set up with George when he gets back to the capital."

Charlie went on, "Both mines need to do some more work under ground to relocate the main ore vein. We're still in good ore on one level but we need to explore more to find the main vein again. We've kept some miners who want to work to re-timber many of the old tunnels, and the rest are exploring for better ore. The Golden Rose was doing the same thing. We've both decided not to get back into full production until next spring."

Charlie motioned toward the mill. "It'll shut down in about two weeks. By then they'll have all the stock piled ore milled."

Logan shook hands with Charlie, "I'll see you later. I'm going to ride down and spend the night at the Golden Rose with John."

When Logan rode up to the office at the Golden Rose Mine, his old friend, Mel, was the first to meet him. He never did lose the limp from the broken leg he got when he chased the gold robbers. While talking to Mel, John Griffith, the mine owner, walked out of the office to join them. "Do you have room for me to spend the night?" Logan asked.

"They both laughed. "Room we've lots of."

Logan told them he knew about the miner's demands and the mine being closed down. Logan joined them at supper and discussed the mine problems. John filled him in on what George Bennett had told him and what the rangers were going to do.

"George is sending two men into the area. They're going to work under cover. That way nobody will know the law is close by."

"We're hoping with both mines running skeleton crews during the winter, we'll miss having any big troubles. My main worry is if we find good ore this winter, trouble will start when we try to go into full production next spring."

Logan nodded. "As soon as the mines are snowed in for the winter season, things should remain calm."

As the evening rolled on, Logan told them about his new ranch and that Running Wolf was working for the governor now. John said his wife had gone back east to see relatives and should be back before the roads close. It was getting late. John headed for home. Logan spent the night in back of the office with Mel.

Logan had an early breakfast with Mel and was well on his way toward Mill City before the sun was up. When he rode by the relay station, the cook invited him in for a meal. While they ate, the cook filled him in on what he knew about the labor problems at the mines. He agreed with what Logan had heard at the mines. These people had shown up just to cause trouble. The workers had good working conditions compared to some other mines Logan had seen. With lunch over, Logan headed on toward Mill City.

As Logan rode along a few miles from the army post, he heard gun shots coming from just around the ridge from him. He spurred his horse into a lope, and as he rounded the end of the ridge, two freight wagons were stopped in the road. One horse was down thrashing and there were shots coming from the rocks above the road. Logan pulled the old Sharps and slid his horse to a halt. He jumped from the saddle as the sound of a bullet passed over his head. He dropped to one knee and fired into the rocks where he had seen a puff of smoke. He then fired again and heard a man scream. Then two men broke from the rocks. They ran for their horses, but they made a mistake in leaving their horses too far across open ground. This was too easy for Logan. With his old Sharps, he dropped both men. Three men appeared from the wagons looking back toward Logan. From their dress, Logan figured they were teamsters with the wagons. As Logan walked up, one of the men pulled his rifle up and shot the thrashing horse.

He turned to Logan, "I hate people that shoot helpless stock."

Logan watched the hill side. The men he had shot in the open hadn't moved. "I'll be right back as soon as I check the rocks where they were hiding," Logan told the teamsters.

When Logan got near the rocks, he could hear someone moving around. He stepped down from his horse and drew a pistol and moved forward. He soon could see a boot moving behind a big rock, so he stepped around the other side of the rock. As he eased forward, he spotted a bloody-faced man trying to move over to a rifle laying close by. Logan stepped over the man and grabbed the rifle. He rolled the man over and searched for another gun but found nothing. Logan could see a wound on the man's face and one shoulder was bloody.

The fellow looked at the badge on Logan's vest. "Where did you come from? We waited until those two rangers that were here yesterday left before we followed the wagons," the man whispered.

Logan knew from the sound of the man's voice the wound was in his chest and not the shoulder. Logan leaned down closer to the man. "Why were you after the freight wagons?"

"We were paid to destroy the new mill parts on those wagons," the man whispered.

"Who hired you for this job?"

The wounded man slowly shook his head, "I don't know his name, but he is staying in room six at the hotel in Mill City. He paid us half and the rest was to be paid when we got the job done. We're suppose to leave a note in his box at the hotel, signed Jessup. He'll leave our money at the stage stop under the name Jessup."

Logan knew the fellow wasn't going to last much longer. Logan picked up a coat that was laying near him and put it under the man's head. He opened his eyes again, "What kind of rifle do you use? There was lead flying all over when you hit the rocks behind us."

Logan nodded, "I shoot a 45 - 90 Sharps."

"Then you must be Mc Tier," the wounded man whispered. He closed his eyes and died.

One of the teamsters walked up and heard the man's last statement. "We were wondering when you rode up here if maybe you were McTier, but the Indian wasn't with you."

Logan nodded. "How about you checking the other two men on the hill side."

The old teamster nodded and walked over toward the downed men. He called back,.

"They're both dead."

Logan helped get the dead horse away from the wagon, and the teamsters helped him load the bodies on their horses. The teamsters told Logan they could make it to the relay camp with one horse missing but it would just take longer. Logan rode on toward the army post leading the horses with three dead men. Logan stopped by the post just long enough to tell them of the ambush. "Are you going to have any patrols out between here and the relay station later in the day?" Logan asked.

"Not this afternoon, but I have a patrol scheduled for first thing in the morning," the captain answered.

Logan rode the back way into Mill City so people wouldn't see the bodies. When he stopped behind the jail, a deputy stepped out the back door. "I glanced out and saw you when I heard horses in the alley."

Logan filled the sheriff in on what had happened and told him about the fellow in room six at the hotel. Logan told him about the message they were suppose to leave in his box at the hotel. The sheriff smiled. "You know, I've seen a well-dressed man gambling lately in one of the saloons, and he stays in the hotel."

"Being as I'm in your town, maybe it would be better if you checked on this for me."

The sheriff nodded. "The deputy that just left is a good friend of the hotel clerk. When he gets back, I'll have him go over and visit his friend and see who's in room six."

When the deputy got back from the hotel, he told them the man's name was Granger. "He's from Denver, and he is suppose to be checking out in the morning. He's leaving on the stage at nine."

The deputy grinned. "When I walked back from the hotel, I went by way of the saloon, and the fellow is playing poker."

The sheriff looked over at Logan, "I'll wait until he goes back to his room to question him. By doing it that way, it won't cause any fuss among the poker players."

Logan wrote out a note "Job Done," signed Jessup.

The same deputy said, "I'll deliver it over to the hotel now before he returns to his room."

"You got a place in back where I can sleep?" Logan asked.

The sheriff motioned to the door, "Sure it's empty back there."

Logan picked up his gear and headed that way.

Logan felt a hand on his shoulder and looked up to see the sheriff standing there. It was breaking dawn.

"The man in room six played poker all night. He just went back to his room about a half hour ago. I'll arrest him when he walks out of the hotel on his way to the stage stop."

Logan thought a minute. "How about we let the man drop off the package before arresting him. This will be proof we've got the right man."

Logan stationed himself across the street from the stage stop in front of the hardware store. There was a bench there so Logan sat down with a stick to whittle on. Logan saw the well-dressed man leave the hotel carrying a bag and a package. As he neared the stage stop, he glanced around. Logan could see him make eye contact with another fellow standing on the street corner. The man on the street corner turned and walked over to another man holding three saddled horses. Logan quit whittling and moved down the street toward the two men with the three horses. Logan walked across the street so he was on the corner where he could see both the two men and the stage stop. Logan heard a shot coming from the stage stop building. The well-dressed man came running out of the stage stop with a gun in his hand. About that time the two men started to mount when Logan told them to step back down. They both dove sideways away from their horses, drawing as they fell. Logan had drawn both pistols when he told them to step back. He

340

fired twice before either of them got a shot off, hitting both men. As Logan turned, the well-dressed man ran towards him. Two shots rang out and the man stumbled and hit the sidewalk with his pistol sliding toward Logan. Logan looked back toward the stage stop and saw the deputy with a rifle and another with a pistol standing in the street. Logan walked up to the man lying in the street. He tried to pull a derringer from his vest pocket. Logan reached down and pulled it away from him. Logan stood and heard one of the deputies holler, "Lookout behind you." Logan drew as he dove sideways and rolled as a bullet hit the sidewalk where he had just been. He saw a fellow with a rifle trying to get another shot. He fired two quick shots then rolled off into the street. When he jumped to his feet, he was ready to fire again. The man was lying face down in the street. The two deputies came running by him. They rolled the man over, then they both turned to look at Logan.

"He's hit twice in the chest."

Logan walked over to the deputies. "Thanks for the warning."

The one deputy with the rifle said, "I couldn't see him good enough to shoot. You were between us."

"What was the shot in the stage depot?"

"When the sheriff started to arrest the fellow, he pulled his gun and hit the sheriff alongside the head. When the sheriff fell, the gunman shot the deputy standing by the back door. Then he ran out the front door."

The deputy, standing over by the well-dressed gunman, hollered, "This one is still alive."

Logan kneeled down next to the gunman, "Why were you paying to have the freight wagon stopped."

The man looked at Logan, "We'll still shut those mines down."

"Who's paying you to do this?"

The fellow just said, "Go to hell," and slumped against the deputy holding him up.

The sheriff walked up holding a towel to his bleeding head. Logan looked over at him, "We've got four dead men, and we still don't know who was paying them."

Logan and the sheriff headed back towards the sheriff's office while the deputies helped the undertaker clean up the street. Logan asked one deputy to bring all the belongings and papers found on the dead men to the jail.

Later that afternoon when they had gone through the papers and gear of the dead men, the sheriff said, "I think we know who they were now. The three with the horses are on 'Wanted' posters for killing a mine owner in Colorado. They blew up his house, killing the man and his family. The fancy dressed fellow was Granger, according to this stuff found on his body and from papers in his bag."

Logan looked over at the sheriff and said, "I think this trouble at the mines is just starting." The sheriff nodded, then Logan picked up his gear. "I've got a good many hours of daylight left so I'm going to head for headquarters at the Capital City. I'll camp along the way and get a good night's sleep."

Logan started to walk out when one of the deputies from the shooting in the street that morning offered his hand. "I've always heard of you from the sheriff and other people, but now I know for myself about your gun speed. You were moving and yet both bullets were almost side by side in that man's chest."

Logan grinned as he shook the young deputy's hand. "We all get lucky sometimes."

As Logan mounted his horse, he heard the young deputy tell the sheriff, "I don't think that was luck."

Logan spent a good night camped along a small creek. It was afternoon and he was looking at the buildings of Capital City up ahead. As he swung down at the barn at headquarters, he heard his name called. When he turned, he found George walking toward him. They shook hands.

"I hear we had a little trouble over in Mill City."

Logan grinned. "I'm not use to people having telegraph service where I work."

George laughed. "The sheriff sent word about the three wanted men killed in Mill City. I guess you know those three were on reward posters for planting the bomb that killed the mine owner in Colorado. Your name was just mentioned at the end."

Logan put his horse away and walked with George to the office.

After filling George in on the attack on the freight wagon and the shootings in Mill City, they decided to go eat. George had some bad news for Logan. His old partner, Tug, had been shot up on a raid on some rustlers down in the lower part of the territory. He was going to make it but his days as a ranger were probably over.

Logan shook his head, "I hate to hear that. George, you tell Tug he's welcome to come up into Raven Basin anytime. Tell him we'll cure him of his gun shot wounds."

Before Logan left, he told George he was thinking of quitting the rangers in the near future.

"With the ranch and my family getting bigger, I want to start spending more time near the ranch. I know with the mine problems it's going to be a busy time for the rangers come spring. I'll stay until this mess is settled, but then I need to change."

"Logan, would you consider staying with the rangers if you had a smaller area to cover?"

"What do you have in mind before I answer that question?"

If you'd be available to cover the two mines this coming summer and the Spirit Lake area, I'll find someone else to cover the rest of your old territory. You get me past next year's problems with the mines, and I'll make you a better deal. If we get this mining problem settled next summer, I will let you keep the badge and only work if needed in your area around White River."

Logan grinned. "George, I can't turn that deal down, but this arrangement is just between us."

"I'll put this in writing and seal it in the safe to be opened only in case of my death." They shook hands on the deal.

"I'm going to visit Henry and Becky this evening, if you need me," George just nodded.

Logan stopped by Henry's office in the capital and found him in a meeting. He left a note saying he'd stop by the governor residence that evening. When he got back to the bunkhouse to clean up for his visit, a messenger knocked on his door with a note from Becky. She wrote, "Supper is at 6:30 pm. See you then."

Logan laughed to himself. That woman would never change.

He was met at the door by a maid and shortly Henry appeared. "Logan, how about joining me in the sitting room for a drink?"

They discussed how the Rafter T was getting along these days.

Henry said, "I heard Rebecca is moving up to Raven Basin to join you."

"She's already moved up and running the ranch for me."

Becky joined them shortly and greeted Logan with a kiss on the cheek. As she stepped back to sit, she smiled. "Logan you look tired and you're skinny."

343

"It's been a busy year, and I've been looking forward to spending the winter in the basin."

Becky smiled, "I got a letter from Lottie. All she wrote about was her granddaughter. She also said your wife was about to have another child."

Logan nodded. "I now have a son. His name is Theodore Hawk McTier."

Becky smiled, "From what Lottie wrote, Little Feather must be quite a woman."

Logan smiled, "She's a great partner, and I'm looking forward to spending more time at home." This comment brought a quick look from Henry.

"Are you thinking of leaving the rangers?"

Logan told them he would have to leave some time but didn't tell them of the deal with George.

During supper Logan finally asked Henry how Running Wolf was getting along with his new job. So far, neither George or Henry had mentioned him.

Henry laughed, "We made a good choice when we brought him here to help with the reservation problems. He's doing great. He's got Little Bear and his people back on the reservation."

Becky spoke up and said he also proved his authority. "Two men tried to grab two young girls one night. He rode into their camp and told them they were under arrest. They tried to draw on him, and he shot them both. He returned the girls and made it known this practice of stealing girls was going to stop."

Henry added, "He's chased many of the worthless white men lying around the reservation off. Any white that doesn't have a job there is told to leave. So far the new agent and Running Wolf are getting along. I don't think there'll be any more stealing Indian rations."

After an after dinner drink, Logan thanked the Davis's for a great evening and headed back for his bed.

Logan left early the next morning and headed for the Rafter T. He decided to head over the old trail by passing Benton. He made good time. His horse was well rested, and they rode into the ranch a little after dark. Ted met him at the door, and John, who was now living at the ranch with his new wife, came walking out of the dark. He carried a rifle, "When I heard someone ride in this late, it made me curious."

He took the reins of Logan's horse. "I'll put your horse away," and walked off toward the barn.

Ted opened the door and called to Lottie, who was in another room, "Do you have an extra bed for the night?"

When Lottie walked in, she smiled and gave her oldest son a long look and then a hug. "Logan, you look like hell," she sputtered at him.

"You're the second woman in two days to tell me that. Becky told me that last night when I had supper with her and Henry."

Lottie poured him a cup of coffee. "Do you want something to eat?"

He grinned, and she headed for the pantry. While she fixed him something to eat, she asked, "Did Little Feather have her baby yet?"

Logan, with a grin, said, "Yes, Theodore Hawk McTier is doing well."

Both Lottie and Ted turned, "Who?"

Logan grinned, "We named him after his two grandfathers."

Then Lottie gave him hell for sending Little Feather on a long trip while carrying a child.

Logan told her, "You kept telling me you wanted to see your daughter-in-law and granddaughter, so I let them go with Rebecca." Then he added before she could say anything, "I didn't know about the baby until they got back to the basin."

Ted was beaming when John walked in and he told him he had a grandson. Lottie then smiled. "Naming him Theodore was nice. When do we get to see him?"

Logan looked over at John, "I hear you have a new wife. Do I get to meet her?"

"It's kinda late tonight, but come morning I will bring her down before you leave," John said as the kitchen door opened.

In walked a tall, red-headed girl. She looked over at Logan. "You must be Logan."

As she walked up to Logan, he was surprised how tall she was. "I'm Beth. Don't I get a kiss from big brother?" She then kissed him on the cheek. "I just about stole that daughter of yours while she was here."

They all talked for a spell, and soon Lottie told everybody to get to bed since it was late. The next morning Logan joined Lottie in the kitchen as she fixed breakfast. Lottie looked back at her oldest and shook her head, "Logan, you need to quit chasing bad men and settle down on that ranch of yours."

He grabbed her as she set bowls on the table. "That'll be happening real soon."

Before she could say more he added, "This is only between you and me but it's in the works."

The door opened and in walked John, Beth and Ted. Ted had been out to the barn to feed the stock. After they finished breakfast, Logan reached back and got his saddle bags lying against the wall. He pulled out some papers he had Henry fix up for him a year ago. He unfolded them. "As of today, you now own the Rafter T free and clear."

Lottie looked over at Logan. "I thought you said it was already free and clear." Logan held up his hand to silence her. This deed names Ted, Lottie, John and Mary McTier as sole owners. Logan looked over at Beth, "We'll add you on now. I had this made out before you were part of the family. I have the ranch in Raven Basin and Rebecca owns part of it, so now we're separate ranches."

Ted looked over at this oldest son. "Logan, this is a big deal. Are you sure you want to do this?"

Logan nodded, "I've always known I'd never get to stay here, but I wanted something with my name on it. So when I bought this for us, it was a place I could call home. Now I have my own home and you have yours. I only ask that this place stays in the McTier family." Logan moved his chair back, and as he stood up, said, "Business is done; now it's time I get back to work."

John, holding Beth's hand, walked over to his brother. "Brother, I can never repay you for this."

Logan grinned. "Oh yes you can. Have a big family with many boys and keep this place in the McTier name."

Beth grabbed Logan, and with her head buried in his chest, said, "You're like they say, a tough act to follow. You're maybe that terrible fast gun fighter but you're also pretty soft when it comes to family."

Logan gave her a smile, "Welcome to the family, Beth."

"I'd better make an appearance at the cookhouse or I'll probably get shot leaving the ranch."

The crew had already left for work when Logan walked in and saw Rose washing dishes. She turned to look at him. "It's about time you got your butt up here young man."

Rose dried her hands, poured two cups of coffee and walked over to the table. She set the cups down then gave Logan a big hug and just kept hanging onto him. When she stepped away, a tear could be seen running down her cheek. Logan reached out and pulled her to him and asked, "Why the tears?"

Rose drew back. "What tears," as she wiped her eyes. "Logan, every time you're here, I keep thinking about when you were shot. We didn't know whether you were dead or alive. When you were traveling with Running Wolf, you had backup, but now you're riding alone again. When your family was here, I kept thinking you should be with them and not be a target for every outlaw in the territory."

This lady was like a mother to Logan, and he knew she was afraid for him. As they finished their coffee, Logan told her his days being a ranger were getting shorter. When he told her this, he asked her not to pass this on because he didn't want it out yet. Logan reached out and pulled this tough old, grey-haired lady to him. "I'll be careful just for you."

As he walked out, she motioned to a package laying next to the door. "Take that to Fawn, and don't you open it."

Logan headed for Kilgore with snowflakes starting to fall as he rode over the summit. When he rode up in front of the trading post, the rain came down hard. Jerry looked up from the counter with a grin, "Now look what the cat drug in."

Logan shook hands. "Do you have room for this wet, tired old fellow?"

After rubbing down his horse and giving him grain and hay, Logan went back into the living quarters behind the store. After supper Jerry laughed, "That's quite a sister you have. When she stopped here on her way back with Little Feather, she almost bought me out of everything. I asked her why she hadn't bought it all in Benton, and she informed me. "Logan always buys here. So will I."

Logan laughed. "She's her own boss and I leave her alone."

Logan asked Jerry if he had heard anything about the problems at the two mines. Jerry told him a few of the laid-off miners had passed through but he hadn't heard much grumbling from them. They seemed to think come spring they would have jobs if the owners could find more good ore during the winter. Logan told him of the shootings and the men hired to wreck the mining machinery. Logan then added, "I figure come spring the men from the mines in Colorado would be back. I just hope we can keep it from becoming a shooting war."

"Well, old friend, I think I'll find me a bed. I want to get an early start to get over the mountain into the White River country before the snow gets too deep."

It was snowing hard as Logan topped over to look down on the White River canyon. The snow was up to his horse's knees. In places where it had drifted, it was up to the horse's belly, and Logan had to get off and help the horse break trail. The snow turned to rain real fast as Logan headed down toward the river.

Logan stopped by some of the friendlier placer miners to pass the time of day on his way up to the ranch. It was getting late by the time Logan made it to the Indian winter camp. Many of the cattle he could see had already been moved down to winter range. Logan was greeted by Little Hawk and invited to spend the night. Little Hawk said Rebecca had told him to move his family down here so he could look after the stock already here. Logan asked him how he liked being a rancher. "I figured this is better than reservation life."

"Did you see Running Wolf during your latest travels?"

Logan filled him in on all he had heard about Running Wolf and his new job. Little Hawk nodded. "Running Wolf has sent word to his wife-to-be's parents that he had many horses to offer for their daughter. The messenger is a grandson of Little Bear, and he's still in camp. He'll be going out over south pass in the morning."

Logan left the next morning to ride up to the ranch. Rebecca and Boyd Helmick seemed to make a good pair. As Logan rode by the big barn, he could see the mow was full of hay. There were stacks of hay fenced in down in the meadows toward the river. This new crew plus the Indians had been busy since Logan had ridden out. Logan stopped at the barn to unsaddle when he heard running feet. He looked up to see Fawn coming full speed from the house. He picked up his daughter. "I have a package for you from Rose."

Logan opened his saddle bag and handed Fawn the package. She was into it before Logan could tell her he would cut the string for her. With a big grin, she held up a knitted cap and mittens, and with a wave, was running toward the house.

Little Feather waited for him on the porch and was laughing. "You must have stopped at the Rafter T." Fawn was fascinated watching Rose knit. Rose told her she would make her something. Logan watched as Fawn came out wearing the new presents.

Ranch life was quiet for the next month, and Logan gained back some weight. Rebecca told him to stay around the ranch and enjoy his kids and that she could handle running the ranch. Logan made a couple trips down to the Indian winter camp to see how the cattle were surviving the winter. The whole family went on these trips, including Rebecca. Logan thought Ted might be kinda young for a winter trip, but Little Feather informed him he would be fine. After looking over the winter range, Logan and Rebecca decided it could handle more cattle with no problems. In the steep canyon, there were creeks coming down from the high country that had good winter feed for stock. Little Hawk had shown Rebecca the sheltered valleys that were up the different canyons. It seemed that all of the area had many valleys hidden in the isolated mountains. The different valleys were generally still at lower elevations and made good winter pasture for stock. The Indians had used these valleys for years for their horse herds. In the summer up these same canyons, you could find high mountain valleys where the different creeks started. Logan had ridden many of the high mountain valleys during his travels but never realized what was here for a cattleman, high country during the summer and good winter range below the snow line in the winter.

As they rode back up toward the main ranch, Rebecca mentioned to Logan they should register a brand. "These cattle and horses are all branded with the Rafter T, but now they are two different ranches."

Logan agreed. "Let's think on this and draw out some different choices before we make our decision." Logan had thought of the teepee brand but it would be easy to change by rustlers.

Logan was busy one day in the blacksmith shop when Boyd rode up with a horse that needed shoes. As they put the new shoes on the horse, Boyd mentioned that Rebecca told him they were trying to figure out a brand. Logan looked up from his work with a smile. "I know you have an idea so let's hear it."

Boyd told Logan that when he and Running Wolf first helped his family down into the valley, he got an idea for a brand. "I'll always remember looking back up the river seeing the three snow covered peaks. When we got to the cabins, which is now my folks' home, I could still see the three big peaks. Now each morning when the sun comes up it shines through those three peaks."

Boyd went on to say there are three different forks of the White River that head up in those peaks. "I think a good brand would be three forks." As he drew out the brand in the dirt with a stick, he added. "Some people will probably call it the pitchfork instead of three forks."

Logan put down his working tools and walked out to look up at the three big mountain peaks and nodded. "I think you have a great idea there, Boyd," Logan said, as he walked back to look down where Boyd had drawn out the brand.

That evening at supper, Logan told the family that Boyd was coming over to have a drink with them. When Boyd arrived, Logan told the group, "Boyd's got an idea for the brand for this ranch. I'll let him explain it to you the same way he told me."

Nobody said anything for a minute after Boyd drew it out. Then Rebecca said, "I like it."

From that night on, the pitchfork brand was now the official brand of the ranch in Raven Basin  Logan agreed with Boyd, "If we call it three forks, all strangers to see it will probably call it the pitchfork. On my next trip out to headquarters, I'll get it registered. Until then we'll stay with the Rafter T brand."

Spring was in the air one afternoon when a stranger came riding into the ranch with a young Indian boy from the winter camp. The stranger introduced himself as Jeff Taylor. He was a miner down at the mouth of White River. "I've been sent to find a lawman. Everyone I've talked to told me I could find a ranger at the ranch up on White River. I met an Indian named Little Hawk down along the river and he said you were up here. He sent one of the older boys in camp to show me the way up here."

"Well, you've found the right place. I'm Logan McTier, the ranger for this area. What's the problem?"

"There's been a shooting at a claim along the river, and one man's dead. The shooting was over a claim, and the dead miner's partner has been run off their claim. The man doing the shooting said they were crowding his claim. He rode over with a shotgun and killed the miner as he walked out of his cabin. When the partner told the gunman to leave the claim, he pointed the shotgun at the him and told him he had five minutes to get his belongings and be gone.

When the partner packed up to leave, the gunman took the miner's gold. He told the miner it was his gold because he owned the claim."

When Jeff finished his story, Logan nodded. "I'll get my gear, and we'll head out now."

It was the next afternoon when Logan and Jeff got down to the mining area. They stopped at the claim Jeff shared with his father and two brothers.

There were five other miners at the cabin when they rode up. The miners told Logan that the gunman had just hired two other men to help him.

"Since Jeff left to find you, they've gone to other claims and threatened the owners. They were told to pack up and be gone when they came back."

"Where are these claims?" Logan asked.

They pointed up the creek.

When Logan started to leave, some of the miners started to follow him. Logan stopped, "I'm just going up to talk right now, and I'll do that alone."

When Logan got close to the claim, he loosened his Colt and unbuttoned his coat. As he rode up, a shotgun barrel was sticking out of the door of the cabin. A voice told him to just keep riding.

"I'm Territorial Ranger Logan McTier and I've come to talk." A bearded little man stepped out of the cabin still holding the shotgun pointed at Logan. Logan, about this time, saw a movement in the trees behind the cabin. Logan looked at the little man.

"I was asked to come here to settle something about ownership of these claims." Logan continued on by asking, "Do you have this claim recorded?"

About then a younger man walked out from the cabin. "We own this claim and those other men jumped our other claims."

Logan, still sitting on his horse, asked again, "Do you have this claim recorded at Spirit Lake?" Logan knew it was the nearest claims office.

Both men looked at each other. "We didn't know there was a claims office in Spirit Lake."

Logan shifted in the saddle, and the little man brought the shotgun up to cover Logan again. "Well, the best way to handle this is to stop all mining here until the ownership of these claims is settled."

The older man growled, "We own these claims. You better ride on before someone gets hurt."

Logan looked down at the two men. "If you shoot me, you'll get ten rangers up here within a week. I'll be back tomorrow. When I get back, you let me know how you want to handle this."

The little man yelled at Logan as he turned to ride away, "You come back tomorrow we'll shoot you on sight."

Logan rode away not looking back. He watched out of the corner of his eye and saw movement on the ridge. Then he saw a rifle barrel sticking out from behind a tree.

Logan rode down the trail about a mile then headed up the ridge. As he doubled back toward the claim, he moved real slow making sure he stayed out of sight of the claim. Once he was sure he was above the claim, he tied his horse and took his rifle and headed down toward the cabin. First thing he needed to do was find out where the fellow in the trees was. As he worked his way down, he saw a man slowly working his way towards the cabin. Logan worked his way down making sure there wasn't another person on the hill besides the one he saw. As he neared the cabin, he could hear loud voices coming from the cabin. The cabin door opened and the same fellow Logan had seen on the hill walked out still talking back to someone in the cabin.

Logan heard him say, "What do you want me to do if I see him coming back?"

A voice in the cabin said, "Shoot and kill him."

The fellow told whoever was in the cabin, "I want to be relieved before dark so I can eat," and then slammed the door. He grumbled with his head down to himself and never noticed Logan standing next to the wood shed. As he passed, Logan moved over and hit him with his pistol barrel over the head. Logan drug him into the wood shed. Once inside he could see it was also a storage area. He found a coil of rope and tied up his prisoner, and with a rag, he gagged him. Once he had this done, Logan walked up behind the main cabin real quiet like. He could hear the two men talking inside.

"We should've just shot that ranger and buried his body." Then another voice added, "I think we should just ride down to the cabin where all the other miners are and have it out. Those miners aren't going to fight. We'll shoot the ranger as we ride up."

Logan could hear them moving around so he moved back by the shed where he left the other man. The door opened, and the two men stepped out both carrying shotguns. They walked to the corral and got three horses saddled. Then one of them hollered up the hill, "Jug, get your butt down here. We're going to visit the other miners."

Logan stepped out behind the two men, and in a low voice said, "Why don't you two just drop those shotguns?" The two spun bringing up the shotguns. Logan heard the hammers cock as he fired both pistols. Both men, as they fell, pulled the triggers, and the blast from one shotgun almost blew the legs off one of the men. The other blast hit the corral gate next to where their horses we tied. Both men were dead.

Logan started toward the shed when he heard horses coming through the trees. He stepped back out of sight. When he looked down toward the sound, he saw Jeff and two other miners looking toward the cabin. He stepped out and motioned them to ride on in. As they rode up, they saw the bodies lying by the corral. Jeff walked over and looked at the bodies. "You tangled with two shotguns?" as he looked at Logan.

Logan pulled the tied up prisoner from the shed. He looked over at Jeff. "I had the edge when I told them to put down the guns." He motioned to the dead man with his legs almost blown off, then pointed to the other shotgun blast that hit the corral post, "Those were the only shots they got off."

He pulled the gag from Jug's mouth and he started yelling, "Untie me and I'll see how tough you really are."

About then he saw his two friends. He looked back at Logan with a puzzled look. "Who shot them," he yelled.

Jeff motioned toward Logan, "The ranger did."

Logan asked Jeff if the trail to Spirit Lake was open.

Jeff nodded. "We've been using it all winter to get supplies."

"Help me load these bodies, and I'll take them and the prisoner over to your camp tonight. Tomorrow I'll take them over to Spirit Lake."

While getting ready the next morning, Jeff walked over to Logan. "Me and a couple of the other miners would like to ride over to Spirit Lake with you."

Logan turned to Jeff. "Why?"

"The miner, whose claim they stole, wants to get word to his partner's wife. They both were married and were going to bring their wives out from the east come summer."

Jeff grinned at Logan. "I'm just going along to keep from shoveling all day." He laughed and said, "I don't mind hard work but I'd just as soon find another job." As Logan mounted his horse, he looked at Jeff and said, "If you want to be a ranch hand, let me know."

Logan turned his prisoner and bodies over to the sheriff and turned in his report. As a deputy led the prisoner to his cell, he told everyone what he would do to Logan if he ever got free. The deputy locked the cell and stopped before leaving and said, "I doubt if you could even touch your gun before McTier would have three bullets in you."

Jug looked at the deputy with surprise. "That's Logan McTier?" and the deputy nodded yes. Jug sat down on his bunk and said, "Boy, did we ever pick the wrong place to stop."

He wrote a brief note to George at headquarters and dropped it off at the post office. The miners told Logan they were staying in Spirit Lake. Logan stopped by the sheriff's office before leaving town. "If you don't need me for anything I'll head back up the trail for home."

Jeff rode up just as Logan mounted up, "I guess I'd better get back to work before my family disowns me." As they rode up to the forks in the trail leading to Jeff's family's mine, they stopped. Jeff leaned over to shake Logan's hand, "Will that job offer still be good come spring?"

Logan nodded. "If you ride up looking for work I might be gone. If I am, just ask for either Rebecca or Boyd and tell them who you are. I'll let them know when I get back you might show up looking for work," and with a wave Logan headed on down the trail.

It was late spring before Logan could finally get over the pass. He headed for the mines knowing their road would also be open before long or maybe was open now. As he rode into the Milford Mine, he could see freight wagons unloading. Bill Milford stepped out of the office. "We figured you'd be showing up. These are the first freight wagons to get through." Logan walked down to where they were unloading the freight. He found one of the teamsters he knew from last year and asked him how the road had been coming up.

"We had to unhook one place and break a trail through some snow, but other than that it was a good trip. As Logan walked around, he heard his name called. It was the old teamsters he'd helped last fall. The old fellow walked over and shook Logan's hand.

"I got a letter for you in my gear." As they walked back toward a wagon being unloaded at the kitchen, the old teamster asked, "Do you figure on trouble with the union fellows this spring?"

Logan shrugged. "I hope not, but I'm going to be ready just in case. I hope if there is trouble, whoever's involved leaves you freighters alone. To lose freight is one thing, but to kill men that are only doing their jobs hauling freight, that I won't stand for."

The old freighter climbed up in his wagon and handed Logan a letter. As he climbed down he said in a low tone, "Nobody knows I brought you a letter from ranger headquarters. I would just as soon you not let on about it to the other drivers."

Logan nodded and put the letter in his pocket and headed back toward the office.

Bill Milford had gone down to check over the supplies being unloaded. Logan walked back into his office and closed the door. He opened the letter and found it was from George. It was a long letter. Logan was surprised when he read that the two men he'd shot at the mining claims last winter were wanted. It seems they were wanted in about every territory in the west. The shotgun murders had happened almost everywhere they'd been and usually were over mining claims. George said he had sent rangers to Spirit Lake to bring the prisoner back to headquarters. George wrote he was proud of Logan for stopping the three before any more men were killed.

George wrote that he had assigned two undercover agents to the mines. One would be working at each mine as miners. He passed word to them to let Logan know who they were only if they could do it without anyone else knowing. He also stated there were four rangers now stationed in Mill City. They would also be traveling with the freighter at times. Logan smiled and thought to himself maybe they could stop this labor problem without too much blood shed now.

Logan grinned to himself when he read the last of the letter about Tug. George wrote Tug was now back at headquarters healing up from his wounds. "Tug told me to tell you he would take you up on your offer. He's headed for the basin as soon as he can stay on a horse. He'll travel by way of Kilgore. That way he can rest for a spell with Jerry at the trading post."

As Logan put the letter away, Charley, Bill's son, walked in, "Dad said you were here," and shook Logan's hand.

Charley told Logan they had found some good ore during the winter and were ready to get back to full production. "Many of our old crew are drifting back to see if they still have a job."

"How many new men have been here looking for work?" asked Logan.

"Well, so far we've only had two."

Logan nodded. "These new people I think you should really watch. Mainly to see how much they know about mining before you hire them."

Charley nodded. "Dad and I have discussed this. Mel Miller is our new foreman, and he says the same thing about hiring new men."

Bill walked in while they were talking and joined in on the conversation. Bill told Charley, "I think we should hire that kid that rode in yesterday looking for a job. He's down helping the freighters unload just for something to do."

"His name is Ben Tate. He told me he didn't know much about mining but he needed a job, and he'd learn if we hired him."

It was decided by the two owners they would hire the young fellow. Logan told the two Milfords he was going to ride down to the Golden Rose Mine.

"I need to see John Griffith and let him know I'm around."

When he arrived at the Golden Rose, Logan could see John talking to some men in the office so he rode on down to the horse barn. He knew the old man they called Slim who took care of the horses for John from his other trips to the mine. As Logan unsaddled, the old fellow told Logan, "I'm glad you're here. When you're around, things are a little safer for the boss," he said with a small grin on his face.

When the old fellow finished putting Logan's horse away, he nodded toward his living quarters, "I've got fresh coffee in there."

They had built a living quarters in back of the barn for the old fellow to live in. As they talked, Logan asked, "Have you-seen anybody around here who's just looking the place over and not looking for work?"

Slim thought a moment. "No, most of the men in here right now looking for work are men who worked here before."

He then went on. "I went down the trail this morning to see how the grass is growing in a pasture we have a couple miles out. John took over that claim where those guys lived who were robbing the gold shipments and we now use it for pasture. John just left the old cabin, but I saw smoke coming from the chimney this morning."

Slim went on to tell Logan, "We just fenced the meadow and left the ground where the cabin was untouched. A trapper used it last winter. He moved out over a month ago so I don't know who's there now."

Logan smiled to himself. "I'll check it out tomorrow."

They were about through with their coffee when John walked in and poured himself a cup. "I saw you ride up when I was talking to those men looking for work. Then when you rode on by, I figured I could catch you here."

They shook hands. "Those men in the office were men who's worked here before. So far I've only had one fellow looking for work that's new to the area. I hired him when he told me he had done some work as a blacksmith and had sharpened tools before."

Logan nodded. "What name does he go by?"

"Skip Bolen is the name he gave."

That evening Logan joined John and his wife for supper. Logan found out they also had found more good ore during their winter project. John's wife was curious about Logan's ranch and the fact he was married.

Logan smiled. "My wife is Shoshone, and her name is Little Feather. We have two children, a boy and a girl. My sister has moved up from the Rafter T to be my partner. She runs the ranch when I'm gone."

John smiled. "Then you are related to the McTier's that own the Rafter T?"

"Yes, my family owns the Rafter T."

Logan didn't tell them he had been a part owner until he homesteaded Raven Basin. He did tell of his folks and Hugh Davis building the ranch. He told them Territorial Governor Henry Davis was Hugh Davis's son.

John shook his head. "I always just figured you were a drifter with a fast gun hired by the rangers."

"The story of my gun speed is a long one, and we don't have enough time now to tell it."

He thanked Mrs. Griffith for the supper and headed up to spend the night with Mel in his cabin.

While Mel and Logan walked to the cook house the next morning, Logan asked, "Do you know who's living at the cabin by the pasture?"

Mel shook his head. "I didn't know anyone was out there but I'll check into it."

"I need something to do for a few days so I'll check it out, if you don't care."

Mel nodded.

Later that morning Logan rode out but stayed well off the road as he headed south. He soon was high on a ridge looking back toward the mine and could see the cabin below. Logan staked out his horse and moved over where he could see the cabin and corrals. There were three horses in the corral and smoke coming from the chimney. As he watched, a fellow walked out carrying a pail and headed for the small creek behind the cabin. When he walked back to the cabin, he handed it to someone just inside the door. The fellow then walked out to the corral and haltered the horses. He opened the gate and staked them out to feed on grass at the edge of the meadow. Logan could see the fellow wore a tied down pistol on his left side. The fellow headed back to the cabin. He sat down on a bench along-side the cabin and rolled a smoke. Another man walked out and leaned up against the cabin while he rolled a smoke. As Logan watched, a third person walked out of the cabin and joined the other two. From what Logan could see, two of the men were armed. The last fellow out was dressed more like a miner. He had suspenders on and his pants looked like the heavy canvas pants the miners wore underground. Logan was about ready to move on when he spotted movement in the trees coming off the ridge away from the road. As he watched, a rider leading three pack horses came into view. Logan then caught sight of a second rider bringing up the rear.

Logan moved back to his horse, and from the saddle bag, he took a small telescope. He had never used it before but decided to try it now. He had picked it up at the store where he found the small bore pistols. Logan moved back where he could see the cabin and with the telescope watched as they unloaded the pack string. Then as they were unpacking two of the horses, he recognized the boxes. They were marked, "Dynamite." They packed the boxes to a small shed over by the corrals. The pack from the other horse was food supplies, and they packed that into the cabin. Logan figured these fellows were here to stay for awhile. Logan decided he needed to talk to John about them using a cabin on his claim. Thinking back Logan wondered if maybe some of these men had been part of Blackie Payne's crew. If John didn't have enough trouble now, maybe part of his brother's old gang was back thinking this cabin still belonged to someone else.

Logan mounted up and rode back to the mine. He found John in his office and told him about the people living in the cabin.

John frowned, "You know I told Slim once right after I took over the claim that we should burn that cabin. Then I decided if I needed someone to take care of the pasture and the horses, they'd have a place to live, so I didn't burn it."

"Slim's going to take some horses from the mine down there this afternoon." John looked over at Logan. "If you want, I can tell Slim to wait a few days?"

Logan nodded. "Let's do like you figured and see what they do when Slim shows up. I don't think they will harm him. They wouldn't be using that cabin if they weren't worried about drawing attention to themselves."

Logan spent time talking to Mel about any trails that were used near the mine besides the main road. Mel went over to a map on the office wall. "We've got a steep road that's used when we take some mining machinery up to the main mine shaft. It's grown in with brush and young trees but a horse wouldn't have any trouble going up there."

He told Logan how to find the old road and Logan headed up to look it over. When he got up the old road a ways, he found fresh horse tracks heading up the mountain. The tracks had come in from a game trail along the mountain slope. As he looked, he saw the tracks of two horses, and they'd come back down the same way. He rode up to where the tracks stopped and could see where two men had dismounted. From where they stopped, he could look through the trees and see the main shaft house. Logan followed the tracks back down to the game trail. He rode down the game trail for a ways then the horse tracks turned off down a ridge toward the main road below. As Logan sat there, he could see the small valley where the cabin stood. He figured he could follow these tracks all the way to that cabin but right now didn't want his tracks showing and leading into the main road. He headed back up the ridge where he found another way back down to the mine. If someone saw his tracks up along the mountain, they would think he was just hunting.

Later Logan was back at the mine and was in Mel's cabin when Mel dashed in. "We just got word somebody had blasted the road shut. It's down near the relay station and at least one freight wagon was hit."

Logan saddled up his horse and headed that way. It was dark when he got to the station but the cooks were still up. They fixed him a meal. While he ate, he found out the blast had killed one teamster and his team. The other two wagons were okay but they had to put a couple horses down because of wounds.

"Do you know the dead teamster's name?"

The cook shook his head. "I didn't know his name." But when he described him, Logan knew it was the one who had delivered his letter.

Then the cook added, "Two rangers were in for supper, and they'd told me about who got killed."

Logan thought, "Why blow up empty wagons headed back unless it was to scare the freight company."

Logan slept a few hours and before dawn was back on the road to the mine. As he neared the cabin turnoff, he left the road and rode through the timber coming in behind the cabin. He tied his horse. It was still early and no smoke was coming from the cabin. He worked his way down near the cabin. In the shed he saw one dynamite case had been opened and left with the lid off. A small sack was lying there so Logan put ten sticks into the sack and tied it shut. He slowly moved over next to the cabin. He found a notch in the logs up near the roof and put the sack with the dynamite in it. It couldn't be seen unless you were standing close or back beyond the shed. Logan heard movement, and it sounded like they were just getting up. The window in the back had one pane missing and Logan could hear more as he eased closer. He heard one voice saying, "They'll be a few days cleaning up that road and dragging off those horses."

Another voice said, "We need to get up to that shaft tonight before it's total dark."

The first voice answered, "Don't worry, I'll take care of that tonight, and we will be up at the Milford tomorrow night."

Logan eased his way back into the timber, and before he had gone very far, he heard the door open and two men stepped out. Logan froze behind a tree as one walked to the outhouse and the other one rolled a cigarette. Then both men went back in the cabin. Logan worked his way back to his horse. As he looked down at the cabin, he grinned when he noticed he could still see the sack under the eaves of the cabin.

That evening Logan told Mel, "I'll be gone tonight, but I'll see you in the morning."

Logan rode up the road toward the Milford until he was out of sight. He then turned off and headed up the mountain. He found a place across the canyon from the old road where he had been yesterday while following the fresh tracks. He could see real well where the two riders had dismounted across from the mine shaft. He unsaddled his horse and left it in a draw with some grass not far from where he was now lying on his back looking at the sky. Logan thought about the ranch in the basin and his family. He knew this could be his last job as a ranger, and in some ways was sad, yet glad to be able to be with his family. It was an hour before dark when he heard horses across the canyon. He watched as two men unloaded a box of dynamite and then led the horses back out of sight. They returned, and as it got darker, Logan watched as they started to move toward the mine tunnel. Logan grinned as he laid the old Sharps against a tree for a steady rest. As he pulled the trigger, he said to himself, "This is for my friend, the teamster you blew up." The roar broke the night air. When the sound died down, Logan could hear men hollering down at the mine. He watched as lights from torches could be seen coming up the hill toward the mine tunnel. Logan saddled his horse and headed down across the canyon. He found their horses and untied them and tied up the reins and slapped them both on the rump, and they went running down the old road. Logan moved off at a slow pace following the horses. Logan crossed the main road and again rode through the trees to get behind the cabin. Logan tied his horse and moved closer to the cabin. A light could be seen through the window. As Logan laid there, the door opened and a man walked out and turned toward the corrals. He heard the man at the corral shout and two other men came running out of the cabin. One was carrying a lantern, and as they got to the corral, he heard one of them say those are Red and Jesse's horses. Logan could see when the man held up the lantern that it was the two horses he had turned loose earlier. "I wonder what happened. We heard the explosion," Logan heard one voice say. Logan could hear them talking about saddling up to go see what had happened. Then he heard one fellow say, "We'll stay here until daylight. By then the boss is suppose to be here."

"It's still dark up there, and Jesse said they were using a brushy trail to get to the tunnel. If we go out in the dark, we'd probably run right into some angry miners."

Logan watched as the men unsaddle the horses then went back into the cabin.

Logan moved his horse back up the ridge and found a place well off the ridge trail and made a cold camp. It was still moonlight enough for him to find his way around, but the moon was about ready to hide behind the ridge. It was just getting light on the horizon when Logan was awakened by the sound of running horses. It sounded like it was coming from the main road. Logan saddled up and was about to start down the ridge when he heard horses on the ridge above him. He was in the draw with thick brush, and the riders couldn't see him. Logan held his horse's nose so it wouldn't make any noise. As the riders moved on down the ridge, Logan rode out where he could see down toward the cabin. There were three horses and a couple pack horses ahead of him that were using the same trail the riders had used to bring in the dynamite. Logan decided he had better follow that trail later on and see where it was coming from. When Logan reached the place where he had been watching the cabin, he saw the three riders dismounting. He could see three other horses by the corral and they appeared to be in bad shape. A man was rubbing them down and all three were standing with their heads down. These must have been the running horses that woke Logan up. Two men walked out of the cabin and shook hands with the three who had just ridden up. Another man walked out of the cabin. Logan was surprised to see a man dressed in a suit. As the men talked, another rider came racing in from the main road. Logan heard him say there were four rangers coming down the road. The men grabbed rifles and moved out to get cover behind all the sheds. Logan heard one man holler to move the pack horses back out of sight. They had been unloading the horses when the rider came in from the road. One fellow grabbed the horses and headed back into the trees while the other two moved the packs to the shed. Logan grinned to himself when a tarp came off the one pack and he could see a dynamite box. Another man headed for the corral and led the remaining horses back into the trees leaving the saddles still on the corral poles.

Logan watched as the rider who had ridden in with the warning move back out the trail toward the main road. All was quiet until Logan heard a shot coming from the road, and a horse ran into the area with a rider slumped over the saddle horn. The man fell from the saddle, and the horse ran off into the timber. Logan looked back toward the main road. He could see movement and soon picked out four men working their way toward the cabin. Logan saw a shiny badge on two of them and figured they were the rangers from Mill City. One of the rangers called to the men at the cabin to surrender. He got three or four bullets over his head for an answer. The shooting got pretty heavy when Logan decided he would join in. He laid the old Sharps over a small downed tree and searched the eave line of the cabin for the sack he had put there. When it came into view, he pulled the trigger, and the cabin roof flew up and the walls collapsed. Men were laying and crawling everywhere when Logan's next shot hit the shed. Trees flew and Logan had debris falling all around him. The explosion almost deafened him. When the dust settled, Logan could see two men standing over on the next ridge looking his way. Logan walked down toward the cabin. He saw two or three men with bad wounds but most were dead. A man walked from the trees with blood streaming down his face with his hands over his head. The four rangers were now moving up toward what was left of the cabin. Logan had his badge where they could see it. When they got closer, one of them said, "You must be McTier?"

Logan grinned. "I hope you didn't mind me joining your party."

"Tug told us when you were in a fight you were fast but we didn't know he meant the party didn't last long," a tall young ranger answered with a laugh.

They had more alive than Logan first thought. He asked one of the rangers to ride up to the mine and get a wagon. Logan moved over to where the man wearing a suit was lying, and when he kneeled down, he could tell he was in bad shape, but alive. The man's hand move up to grasp Logan's shirt and in a whisper asked, "What happened?"

Logan said, "I guess that dynamite you brought to blow up the mines and innocent people blew up on you."

The fellow laid back down. Logan moved over to check out another moaning near by. Logan looked up to see Mel and other men from the mine coming through the trees. Mel walked up and looked around. Then he looked at Logan. "What the hell happened here."

One of the rangers spoke up. "We were having a little gun battle until McTier joined in. He only fired two shots and it was over."

Mel grinned. "He's always showing off," as he patted his old friend on the shoulder. "We've got a wagon coming down from the mine. I figure John will send the doctor down with it."

Logan let the others tend the wounded, and he headed up the ridge to get his horse. Mel walked along with him. When they were out of ear shot from the others, he looked over at Logan, "Were you involved with the blast at the mine last night?"

Logan nodded.

Mel laughed, "Boy, they did piss you off when they killed that old teamster ."

"I figure the only way these men were going to be stopped from killing other innocent people was to use their own tactics. To blow people up is a coward's way as far as I'm concerned."

Mel nodded.

When they got back to the cabin site, the wagon from the mine was there. The doctor was loading the men who were still alive. He looked over at Logan. "Most of these men won't make it, and if they do, they'll be cripples."

Logan shook his head. "They started this dynamite deal so let them suffer when someone returns the favor." The doctor started to turn away when Logan added, "The old teamster was just hauling freight when they killed him. I heard them talking yesterday and they had more blasts planned for both mines. Doc, you could have been one of their victims."

As the old doctor turned away he muttered, "I'll never understand you frontier people code for survival."

Mel waited until the doctor walked away. "Doc's from the east, and our ways befuddle him. He came out here with John when he started the mine and still thinks we're crude people."

Logan nodded. "Who can we get to bury the dead men?"

Mel said, "I'll take care of that."

The wagon with the wounded had left when John Griffith and Bill Milford came riding in. John looked at Logan and grinned. "I guess I don't have to worry about that cabin anymore."

Logan filled them in on what had happened.

John looked at Logan "Do you think this will stop the union problems?"

Logan looked down for a minute then looked over at the two mine owners. "My idea is if this was a local project, it's over. From what I've heard and seen, the fellow wearing the suit was the big push to shut these mines down. When I was behind the cabin listening yesterday, they kept talking about the big boss showing up. When I got back last night, there were more horses here then others showed up with more dynamite."

Logan pointed up the hill. "Twice men with pack horses have come in from over that ridge. I think when we leave today I'm going to follow those tracks and see where they're coming from."

The rangers had finished looking over the area. The leader had introduced himself as Ray Johnson. Ray looked at Logan. "Your first shot blew the roof plumb off the cabin."

Logan nodded. "I planted that charge yesterday while I was listening behind the cabin. I figured before long this would end up a gun battle and I thought I might need an edge."

Everybody laughed. Then Mel added, "Since when do you need an edge?"

They were still talking about the battle when horses could be heard turning off the road and coming through the trees. There were five riders, and George Bennett was in the lead. George looked over where the cabin had been and the big hole where the shed had been. He shook his head and looked over at Logan. Logan just shrugged as George shook his head.

Logan told George what had happened so far and his idea about the wounded man with the suit. George nodded, "I brought along a fellow who can identify a fellow named Wilmarth, who is the master mind behind this trouble. We think this fellow was trying to force both mines out of business and was using tactics taken from the Colorado union problems. If we're right, this trouble here is a local issue and nothing to do with the Colorado killings."

"The fellow you're talking about is at the mine with the other wounded people."

George nodded. "I want to get up there and see if it's Wilmarth."

"I'm going to backtrack those men with the pack strings." As he turned to walk toward his horse, George added, "I want to talk to you before we head back with the prisoners." Logan nodded.

George turned to Ray Johnson. "You go with him to see he doesn't blow anything else up."

Logan followed the trail up over the mountain to a valley just north of Kilgore where it hit another trail. This trail had been used by more riders. Logan lost the tracks he was following. Logan figured this trail would lead him to the main trail coming over from the Mill City road. After another hour, they hit the trail Logan usually used when traveling from the Mill City road to Kilgore. Logan told Ray, "We'll spend the night in Kilgore with my friend, Jerry, at the trading post."

It was evening by the time they pulled up in front of the trading post. Jerry had seen them ride up. He walked out on the porch in front of the store. "You got room for two men for the night?"

Jerry laughed. "I'll find room. While you get the horses in the stable behind the store, I'll tell the cook we've got a couple more to feed."

While they ate supper, Logan filled Jerry in on the trouble at the mines and that they were looking for who was selling the dynamite.

"The big store uptown sells dynamite to many of the local miners and ranchers."

Logan grinned. "When we finish eating, I think I'll visit the store uptown."

Jerry looked up at the clock on the wall. "It'll be open for another couple of hours."

When Logan walked on the porch, he looked over at Ray. "You want to walk along and see more of Kilgore?"

Ray nodded. "This is the first time I've been here."

When they got near the business district, Logan adjusted his pistol and holster and flipped the throng off the hammer. Ray looked over at him and checked his side arm. "Do you expect trouble?"

Logan told him, "In this business, I always expect trouble."

The big store was still busy. Logan walked in looking for Jeff Milner. Logan had met him when he first bought the store from Blackie Payne. Jerry had told Logan he was still the owner. Logan asked one of the clerks if Milner was around, and he was told he was home for supper but would be back anytime. Logan nodded. "I'll wait around, and when he comes in, tell him that Logan McTier wants to see him."

Logan and Ray walked over by the guns and ammunition to look while they waited. Logan was tall enough he could see over most of the crowd and saw Milner walk in. He watched as the clerk talked to him, and he then hurried toward the back door. Logan nudged Ray and motioned to follow him. Logan stopped on the porch and looked between the building and saw Milner hurry down the alley. Logan walked on down the sidewalk and in front of the saloon looked in the window just in time to see Milner come in the back door. Logan moved over where he couldn't be seen looking into the saloon and watched as Milner stopped at a table where two men were sitting. He pulled out a chair and sat down and was talking real fast to the two men. Then he got up and hurried out the back door. "Ray, you watch those two men at the table, and if they try to leave, arrest them. Be careful. They both look to be on the rough side. If you arrest them, take them over to the jail, and tell the sheriff to lock them up."

Logan then headed back toward the store.

Logan walked into the store and went back over to where the guns were and acted like he was real interested in buying a gun. A clerk walked up to see if Logan needed anything when Milner walked up. "I'll wait on Mr. McTier. He stuck out his hand. "It's been a few years since I saw you."

Logan shook his hand. "Is there a place we can talk?"

Milner led Logan to an office in the back. He closed the door and turned to Logan. "Do you keep records of the dynamite you sell?"

"Well, I really don't sell that much, and I generally do know who buys it. It's mostly to miners but sometimes to local ranchers and farmers."

Logan nodded. "I've been having a little trouble over near the big mines on Cary Creek with men who had dynamite they bought here."

Logan used the name Cary Creek for a reason. That creek, as far as Logan knew, hadn't ever been named. It ran between the Golden Rose and the cabin.

"I heard there was trouble at the Milford and Golden Rose mines."

Logan grinned at Milner. From the look on his face, he knew he had fallen into a trap.

"How about we walk down to the sheriff's office real peaceable like," as Logan motioned toward the door. When they walked out by the clerk behind the counter, Milner told him he would be out for awhile. As they neared the jail, Logan saw Ray coming down the street with the two men from the saloon and a deputy sheriff with him. When Logan got to the door, the sheriff was standing just inside the office.

"What's the trouble Jeff?" the deputy said looking at the store owner. Logan replied, "I've got some questions for Jeff and his two partners Ray's bringing in."

Ray and the deputy brought the two men into the office. Logan saw Milner's face turn white when he saw the two men. Logan then recognized the two men as the ones who'd brought in the first dynamite while Logan watched the cabin. The two had tried to get away from Ray but the deputy had stepped in to help.

The sheriff and his deputy had seen Logan and Ray look into the saloon. Then Logan walked off with Ray still looking in the window. The deputy had made the comment to the sheriff, "Those men are wearing ranger badges."

The sheriff nodded. "I just recognized the one walking away. That's McTier. Why don't you walk over that way and see what's going on."

Logan filled the sheriff in on what had happened at the mines. "These two men packed the dynamite in for the people causing trouble at the mine. Their trail led to Kilgore. I knew only one store handled dynamite."

Logan went on to tell the sheriff what had happened when he went to see Milner. Logan looked over at Milner. "I was just there to find out who was buying dynamite and you fell into a trap."

The sheriff looked at Logan. "What trap?"

"I made up a name for the creek in the area between Golden Rose and the cabin they were using. There's no Cary Creek. Milner here then named the mines where the trouble's been."

The sheriff grinned. "I wouldn't have thought of something like that."

Logan laughed. "I hadn't either. It just popped out and Milner fell for it."

Milner just glared at Logan.

Logan turned to the three. "Your partners at the cabin are all dead or

367

badly wounded. It seems the dynamite you sold and packed in for them blew up before they could blast any of the mines." The two men from the saloon glared at Logan. "You can go to hell. We haven't done anything wrong.

Logan turned to Milner. "What was Wilmarth paying you?"

Milner just stared at Logan when he mentioned Wilmarth. "Wilmarth is in bad shape from the blast, but the last I heard, he'll live. The rangers will take him back to the capital for trial as soon as he can travel."

Logan turned to the sheriff. "I need you to hold these three until rangers arrive to take them to the capital."

The sheriff nodded. "That'll be no problem."

Logan walked out; the sheriff followed. "Sheriff, you better be on your toes because there could be more people involved in this."

The sheriff nodded. "I'll post extra guards and step up patrols around town."

Logan and Ray walked back toward the trading post. When they rounded the corner, Logan gave Ray a push sideways just as a bullet whined past their heads. Logan, as he hit the ground, fired twice at a shadow across the street. The shadow Logan had seen slumped to the ground. Logan dashed for cover of the building behind him when another bullet hit the boards near his shoulder. Logan heard two fast shots from the street behind him. He turned to look, a man staggered into the street and fell. Logan looked across the street at Ray who had his pistol in his hand as he moved over toward the downed man. Logan could hear running feet coming from the direction of Main Street.

The sheriff and two deputies dashed around the corner with guns drawn. Logan moved over toward the man he had shot as Ray checked out the other one. The sheriff looked over Logan's shoulder as he rolled the man over.

"That's the chief clerk at the store," about the same time Logan recognized him.

One of the deputies that was over with Ray called to the sheriff.

"This is Carl, the day bartender from the saloon."

More people showed up. The sheriff saw the old fellow who was the part-time undertaker and told him to take care of the bodies.

Ray walked over to Logan. "I guess Tug was right, trouble just follows you. What gave them away? I didn't see a thing until you shoved me aside and I heard the bullet go by. When you fired, I saw the man go down, and then I saw a flash from a shot by the other building. I fired at it and got lucky."

"The fellow must of had his rifle down at his side when he looked around and saw us. I saw the movement of him bringing it up to shoot when I pushed you."

The sheriff smiled, "I guess you were right. We better be on our toes until these prisoners are moved."

Logan nodded. "We'll head back to the mines in the morning. I'll get word to George about the prisoners. He'll probably be after them on their way back from the mines to headquarters."

When Logan and Ray walked into the trading post, Jerry was there to greet them. His first words were, "You were involved in the shooting?" as he looked at Logan.

Logan poured them a drink from a bottle Jerry had placed on the table. He told Jerry what happened. When Logan finished, Jerry just shook his head. "I would have never believed Milner was involved in this."

"If he hadn't panicked, I probably never would have figured it out unless one of the wounded from the cabin talked."

Jerry looked at Ray and grinned. "I've known this guy since he strapped on the first gun, and he still amazes me on the trouble he gets himself out of."

Ray shook his head. "I guess George wanted me to get some action so he sent me with him."

Logan looked at them both. "It's been a long day. I'm going to bed."

It was evening when Logan and Ray rode into the Golden Rose Mine. Slim saw them ride in and walked up to take care of the horses. Slim motioned to the cook house, "Your ranger buddies are over there eating." When they walked in, George grinned at Logan. "We were about ready to send another rescue party."

Logan filled his plate and sat down next to George. Logan filled George in on what happened in Kilgore. "You've got some more prisoners to pick up there."

George nodded. "We found two more men, one at each mine, that were connected to the group."

Logan saw two men sitting at another table with ranger badges. As they got up to leave, George called them over and introduced them to Logan. Logan figured they were probably the undercover rangers hired on at the mines. He smiled when he shook their hands. "I kinda figured you two were the undercover men."

George smiled. "They had figured out the two spies the same way you caught the store owner in Kilgore they spooked. When we brought wounded men into camp, the spy here had saddled up and rode up to the Milford. Skip followed him, and when he got to the Milford, Skip watched who the fellow contacted. In the meantime, Ben had seen Skip ride in, and he worked his way over to where Skip was watching the bunkhouse. The two men came out, one carrying his bedroll, and hurried to the barn. Skip followed them as they rode back to the Golden Rose, while Ben saddled up and headed down toward the other mine. The two men rode off the road, and the fellow from the Milford stayed in the brush while the other one rode into the mine. Skip had seen them turn off the trail so he stayed back out of sight. When Ben showed up, they waited until the one from the Golden Rose rode back with his bedroll tied behind him. As the two men rode back up to the road, they found two rangers waiting for them."

Logan grinned, "I guess these fellows were new at this business."

"We didn't get too much out of Wilmarth, but the other wounded were talking plenty. We can convict him without any problems."

"I hired a freighter to haul the wounded back to Mill City. They're all leaving in the morning."

When Logan and George got back up to the office, everyone else had either gone to bed or were out somewhere. The office was empty. George looked over at one of his older rangers in service. "How about you taking some time off? I think it's time to semi-retire you to Raven Basin. You were one of the first rangers we put to work, and you were just a kid. I hired you to keep you from becoming another fast gun trying to stay alive. Logan, it's been eight years now, and you have aged way too much for your years. I know the shooting at Raven Basin took a bigger toll on you than most people think. I would like you to keep the badge for two reasons. First off, if you took that badge off, every young kid that thinks he's fast would be here looking for you. By being a ranger, they know every ranger in the country would be after them even if they got lucky and out drew you. The second reason I want you to keep the badge is, I'll need help once in awhile in the White River area as people move in. You know that is a hard area to cover in the winter with snow on all the mountain passes."

Logan looked over at his old boss. "I would like to spend some time at the ranch. I'll gladly take you up on your offer, " Logan said with a smile on his face.

"Your comment about my wound aging me is more true than you know. What I'm going to tell you now is between only you and me. I have trouble from that wound. Some days my side really hurts. Other days I have real trouble eating. I'm getting so I have to favor my right side at times, and in a gun fight, this isn't good," Logan went on. "I'm lucky that when Claire Matthews taught me to shoot, he wanted me fast with both hands and now I know why."

George nodded. "I won't repeat any of this to anyone." They shook hands and both headed for bed.

Logan decided he would ride with George back to headquarters and get some business taken care of before heading for the Basin. First off he wanted to get the brand registered. He needed to check with the Chinese banker on how much money he still had. He also wanted to ride by the Rafter T and let his folks know about the change in his life.

Logan rode along with George and Skip and Ben who were picking up the prisoners from Kilgore. Ray and the other rangers stayed with the wagon hauling the wounded to Mill City. It was decided the rangers would stay in Kilgore for the night and get an early start in the morning with the prisoners. George got rooms in the hotel for himself and two of the rangers. Logan told George he'd spend the night at the trading post.

When Logan got to the trading post, Jerry was just closing up. Logan and Jerry spent the evening hashing over old times. Jerry told Logan he was glad he was slowing down as a law officer and devoting more time to his family. Logan told Jerry he was headed for bed and would see him in the morning. As Logan walked away, Jerry looked at his old friend who was really just a young man yet, but only in years. Jerry thought about all the gun battles this fellow had gone through in the first years after leaving the ranch at seventeen years old. Jerry had only heard stories about those years while he was packing gold for the Chinese. He knew many men had died trying to kill this man. The Chinese had paid him well. It still changed this young man into a gunfighter real quick. Jerry had agreed with what George Bennet did when he asked Logan to join the rangers. There was no doubt someone would have put a reward poster on his head if he hadn't joined the rangers. Probably not because he had done anything wrong but just to get him out of the way. Now he was among the last of the early rangers still on duty. The others were either dead or forced to retire because of wounds or age.

Tug had stopped by to see Jerry on his way to Logan's ranch. He had talked about how much longer his old partner, Logan, would last as a ranger. He was really looking forward to living near Logan and see if he could just be a ranch hand. He had lost some use of one leg and was still having trouble with one shoulder. The doctors had told him the shoulder would heal, but the leg would always bother him. Tug was like Logan and all the early rangers. They were the first to bring law into a lawless land. Their whole life depended on their gun speed and toughness. They were going to be a dying breed as this western country became civilized. Jerry, as he headed for bed, smiled and said to himself, "I've had the privilege to know some of the best."

The trip to headquarters was an easy trip, and the prisoners had offered no problems. Milner hadn't said a word the whole trip. When he found out Wilmarth was alive, he just shook his head and had been quiet ever since. Logan put his gear in his room at headquarters. Then he headed uptown to buy some clothes. After supper that night, Logan saddled another horse from the barn and rode over to the new governor's mansion. He was greeted at the door by the maid and escorted to, as she called it, the sitting room. Henry walked into the room. When he saw Logan, he almost dropped his pipe. He rushed over and grabbed Logan's hand, and at the same time called, "Becky, we have a visitor."

Becky walked in. She grinned and put her arms around Logan, "It's great to see you, Logan." Logan spent the evening talking to his oldest friends about what was going on. He found out from Henry statehood was less than a year away. It sounded like Henry was in line to go to Washington as a senator from the new state.

Becky shook her head. "I hate leaving our old friends but this is something Henry has always dreamed of."

Logan had told them of his talk with George. Henry told Logan that George had come to him earlier with the idea. They both wished him well. As Logan got ready to leave Henry said, "I have some legal papers for Ted and Lottie. Being as you're going that way, you can take them with you."

While Henry went to his study to get the papers, Becky walked up to Logan and hugged him again. "I'm so glad you're going home." As she stood there still holding onto him, Logan felt her trembling against him. "I have died a thousand deaths every time I hear a ranger has been killed thinking it could be you. Logan, you went from a child to a man without ever knowing the middle years of life. This job has aged you so much, and this territory can never repay you and the other rangers for what you have done." There were tears in her eyes as Henry walked back into the room. She pulled Logan's head down and kissed him. "Please, take care of yourself," and she walked out of the room.

Henry watched as his wife left and looked at Logan. "That woman will never get used to your way of life."

Henry gave Logan the papers. "These are the legal papers to transfer the ownership of the Rafter T. Lottie and Ted also have their wills in those papers." Henry looked up at his oldest friend and grabbed his hand. "Good luck and thank you for all you have done for this territory."

Logan rode up to the bank in Chinatown. As he walked into the bank, he hoped Lu Chung was still the manager. Lu Chung sat at his desk in a back room. He saw Logan walk in through his open door. He got up from his chair and rushed out to meet Logan.

Lu Chung had all the records of Logan's account brought to his office. He looked over his desk at Logan, "You are still a very rich man." Logan was surprised at the balance. Lu Chung told Logan he had been using the money and paying him a high interest rate. They talked and Logan told him about the ranch and his plans. Lu Chung convinced Logan to leave most of his money with him and transfer a smaller amount to the new bank in Kilgore. "If you need more transferred, we can do that anytime. By leaving it here, I will pay a lot higher interest rate than the smaller bank."

Logan agreed to leave the money in Lu Chung's bank. "I want my sister, Rebecca, added to the account. I still have the will naming my folks as my sole heirs. I want that changed to Rebecca, Little Feather, Fawn and Theodore."

Before he left, he told Lu Chung he wanted ten thousand dollars in cash to take with him. Lu Chung smiled. "With most people I'd talk them out of carrying that much, but with you I won't even try. I will get it now."

With all that taken care of, Logan headed for the capital building to get his brand recorded.

Logan rode that afternoon down to the army post and Indian agency to see if Running Wolf was around. The Indian agent told Logan Running Wolf had left for a few days to visit the reservation. Logan left him a note and headed back to headquarters. After having supper with George, Logan headed off to his room. Ray Johnson was sitting out front when Logan walked up. So Logan joined him for a spell before going to bed.

Logan rode into Benton. He decided he would check at the store to see if they had any mail for the ranch. Ed Benton was at the front desk when Logan walked up. Ed jumped up and grabbed Logan's hand and shook it. "We're being invaded by McTiers today," Ed laughed and pointed to Mary who was in the back of the store. Mary turned around when she heard the name McTier mentioned. She smiled and came over and gave her big brother a big hug. "What are you doing in Benton?"

"I was just checking on mail for the ranch before I headed out there."

"If you'll wait until morning, I'll join you on the trip home."

"Good, I'll wait. Where can we meet later for supper?"

Mary blushed. "I've got a date tonight."

Logan laughed. "Where do we meet come morning and what time?" Mary shrugged her shoulder, "You name it."

"I'll meet you at the café across the street at seven sharp."

Logan walked over to visit his old friend, Del Rogers, the sheriff. When he walked in, Del reached for a shotgun on the back counter. "Who we after this time?"

Logan just laughed. "You're safe, I'm just passing through."

Logan spent a couple hours with Del. Logan asked Del, "Have you heard from your brother, Jeff, in Sweetwater since he was wounded?"

"He's over his wounds and back on the job."

Logan stood up and stretched. "I'm going over to the hotel dining room to eat then I'm heading for bed at the hotel."

Del started laughing when Logan started for the door. "If you spend the night here and there's no gun fire, it'll be the first time."

Logan looked back and grinned. "I'm getting too old for such things," and walked out.

Logan enjoyed his meal as he thought to himself he was glad he hadn't told Del about his change in life. The less people that knew, the better. Logan had decided he would tell his family to keep it to themselves.

Mary met him the next morning for breakfast, then they headed for the Rafter T. Logan thought this was the first time he had ever been alone with his kid sister. She had grown up while he was running all over the country. Logan found Mary was a lot like her older sister, Rebecca, in knowing all

374

about ranch life. Mary talked about the cattle and the ranch in general. She was different than Rebecca in the fact she seemed happy just living the life of a woman on a ranch. Rebecca was always the tomboy who wanted to be the best at everything she tried. Logan grinned. "How was the date last night?"

Mary grinned back at Logan. "I haven't told the folks yet but I've got wedding plans to make. My husband-to-be asked me last night to marry him. I said I would."

Mary went on to tell Logan. "I went to school in Benton with Charley Rote and we've dated ever since we finished school. He works for the stage line breaking horses, and is learning the blacksmith trade from the local blacksmith."

As they rode along, she did most of the talking. "I've discussed with Charley about him moving to the ranch after wer'e married. He has a problem with me owning a share of the Rafter T and him working there. I told him once we're married he'd become a partner in the ranch." Mary went on, "Charley and John are good friends, and I hope John will help me convince Charley to move to the ranch."

"What if he won't change his mind?"

"I will do whatever I have to, and if it's not living on the ranch, so be it."

Logan was glad he made this ride with her just to get to know her. When the buildings came into view, Mary added, "Now don't say anything about what we've been talking about." Logan held up his hand. "I'll not say a word."

She looked at him and smiled. "I'm glad you're my brother."

Logan looked over at her. "I'm glad we had this trip together," then winked at her and added, "You'll do as a sister, too."

As they rode up to the house, Lottie and Rose walked out to meet them. Mary, with a laugh, said, "Look what I found along the trail."

The crews were just coming in, and Logan could see John out by the barn. He helped Mary get the stuff off her horse and then grabbed the reins. "I'll take care of the horses."

As Logan walked up to the barn, his dad walked out to greet him. "I thought that was you riding in with Mary." When they had the horses put away, John joined them as they headed for the house. That evening Lottie had the whole family over to her house for supper. Rose joined them.

Logan looked at her, "Who's feeding the crew."

Rose looked at Logan. "I'm now in management. I have a helper, and she is cooking tonight." Logan just grinned at her, and she walked over and punched him. "I can still handle you young man."

Logan noticed when Beth and John walked in that he was going to be an uncle before long. Beth came over and gave Logan a hug and sat down next to him.

After supper they were all sitting in the living room when Logan surprised them with his news. Logan could tell by the expression on his mother's face she was glad her son was finally settling down to family life. Everyone was talking at once when Logan held up his hand. "Now I have one favor to ask."

He went on to say he would like them not to pass it around that he wasn't a full-time ranger. He explained the badge caused many a young gunny trying to gain a reputation by shooting Logan McTier to leave him alone. They all agreed not to pass the information on to anyone.

Mary took the floor with her news about getting married. Logan kinda grinned when his dad asked her, "What other news do you have. We all knew you were to going to marry Charlie. We just didn't know when."

Mary acted like this broke her heart, then finally grinned and gave her dad a big hug. The rest of the evening the women planned a wedding and the men discussed cattle and ranching in general.

Logan left the next morning heading for Kilgore. That evening while in Kilgore, Logan purchased four pack horses with gear. He figured out a load of supplies for the ranch and gave it to Jerry to fill. Jerry, with Logan's help, packed everything and placed it by the door to be loaded in the morning. When they retired to the living quarters, Logan took five thousand from his saddle bag and gave it to Jerry. Jerry looked at his old friend. "What am I suppose to do with this?"

I want an account opened for the ranch, and when this is used up, let me know and I'll give you another five." Before Jerry could say more, Logan told him about his change in life.

Jerry reached over, "Old friend, that's the best news I could ever get, and it's about time," as he shook his hand.

He then continued, "Logan, it's not necessary to pay cash for your supplies for the ranch."

There's a reason I want it done this way. This way anyone from the ranch can stop by and pick up supplies and you won't have to wait for your money."

Jerry grinned, "I like your way of thinking, but you do know your credit with me is good."

The next morning Logan skipped going by way of the mines and headed over the trail leading over the mountain to White River country. He camped one night near a small creek with lots of feed for his animals. After supper he laid back and thought of all the things he wanted to do with this ranch. Logan loaded up the next morning, and by sunrise, was well down the trail. When the ranch buildings came into view, Logan stopped. He just wanted to look over what now would be his full-time home. As he rode into the yard, Little Feather came running. Logan could tell something was wrong. He swung down as his wife grabbed him. "Rebecca and Tug didn't come home last night."

Logan got her slowed down. "Tell me the whole story."

"Some men have built a cabin up on one of the high meadows on third fork. One of our riders told them this was deeded ground and they would have to move on. They beat him and tied him over his horse and sent him home with a message that it's their land and the next rider would be shot." Little Feather added, "Tug and Rebecca rode up yesterday to talk to these people and they haven't come back."

"Where's Boyd and the main crew?"

"They're over on the south fork branding calves."

"I'll change horses and ride up there to see what was going on."

He headed for the barn to get a fresh horse. Acel and Cliff Helmick walked up. Acel asked Logan, "Do you want us to ride along?"

Logan shook his head, "I'd rather go alone."

Then he asked, "Acel, will you unload the pack horses I just brought in?"

Acel nodded.

Logan rode up to the house. Little Feather grabbed his hand. "You be careful. I already sent Fawn to the Indian camp to get Little Hawk."

Logan headed across the meadow toward the creek that would lead him up to the third fork area. When he neared the timberline, he glanced back. He could see two riders coming toward him at a good pace. Logan stopped in the trees. As they got closer, he recognized Little Hawk. The other rider was dressed in white man's clothes. Then Logan grinned when he saw the other rider was Running Wolf. As they rode up, Logan asked Running Wolf, "Are you lost?"

He reached to shake Logan's hand. "No, I'm visiting my new wife's family."

Logan filled them in on what Little Feather had told him. They decided it was a two to three hour's ride up to the lower meadows.

"I figure anyone building a place up there will build in the lower meadows."

They rode for about an hour when Logan stopped them. "Let's all take different trails in case they have someone watching the main trail."

When the lower meadow came into view, it was almost dark but Logan figured they had at least an hour of shooting light yet. As he moved down through the trees, he could see a corral and a half cabin built along the creek. When he got closer, he could see a man tied to a tree not far from the cabin. He hung there slumped over like he was either dead or unconscious. From the size and build, Logan figured it was Tug. Then Logan spotted Rebecca near the fire; she looked like she had been beaten up. Her clothes were torn and her hair was matted. There were three men sitting near the fire drinking from a bottle. They were passing it around. Logan could see at least one more over by the corral. Then he spotted a movement in the cabin. That made five for sure. He figured Little Hawk and Running Wolf were also watching. As Rebecca walked by the men with a pail in her hand, one of the men tripped her and she fell flat. The man stood up and kicked her and told her to get supper on.

Logan laid his rifle alongside a tree and pulled down on the man that had kicked Rebecca. Rebecca had gone back down to the creek to get more water when Logan fired the first shot. The echo from the old big bore hadn't died down when two more large bores echoed across the meadow. Three men were knocked backward. The other two drew their weapons as the rifles sounded again. One of the men at the corral had started to move over to grab Rebecca when he was knocked backward by a shot from across the meadow from Logan. Two men had come from the cabin to be met by bullets from the rifles. There was a stillness as the echos died across the valley.

Rebecca stood like a statue looking into the trees that surrounded the camp. The man tied to the tree lifted his head. "Rebecca, I think your brother and a couple of his friends have arrived." Little Hawk walked up behind the tree where Tug was tied. His knife cut the rope before Tug knew he was there. He caught Tug before he could fall. Rebecca was at Tug's side helping to lay him down. Logan walked into the firelight checking over the bodies. One of the men by the cabin groaned as Running Wolf walked out of the trees. He leaned down as the man looked up at him. "Where in the hell did you come from, and who are you?"

"Territorial rangers."

The man just stared at him.

Logan walked up with Rebecca at his side. She reached down, grabbed the man's hair and jerked his head up. "Meet another McTier you lousy bastard."

Logan couldn't believe his sister's language but smiled anyway. She let go and his head hit the ground. The wounded man just stared at her. Then he slowly went limp.

They had beat on Tug pretty bad. "I'm well enough to ride back to the ranch," he growled. Logan decided to send Little Hawk back in the dark to let Little Feather and the people at the ranch know they'd ride in tomorrow. Logan figured a night's rest would help both Tug and Rebecca after their rough couple of days as prisoners.

Rebecca pulled Logan aside. "There's another one that belongs with these men. He left yesterday to get supplies. When he left, they told him to be back by tonight. This one is crazy and told me when he got back I was his."

Logan nodded. "If he heard the rifle fire, he probably turned back."

Near dawn Logan heard horses coming down toward camp. Logan then heard someone trying to sing and a woman sounded crying. The singer hollered, "Wake up! I got girls and booze," as he rode into camp. Logan started to get up when a hand grabbed his arm. There was a whisper, "This one is mine," as Rebecca moved away from him. Logan moved so he could see the horses coming through the trees. He noticed Running Wolf wasn't in his blankets. Logan grinned, remembering his many months with this guy as a partner. The fire had died down, but all of a sudden it flared up. Rebecca had thrown some dry wood on it. The rider rode up and started to swing down when he noticed Rebecca standing with a rifle pointed his way. He clawed for his gun when the first bullet hit him. Two more followed before he fell as the horse jumped away. There was screaming from the pack horses behind in the trees. When they looked, two almost naked women were tied onto the backs of two horses. Running Wolf, who had been in the trees watching Rebecca, walked up to cut them loose just as Rebecca got to them. They covered them with blankets and led them to the fire. Both looked to be in their teens. Rebecca told them they were safe now. Running Wolf, who had gone over to move the body, motioned for Logan to join him. As Logan walked up, Running Wolf pointed to the bullet holes in the man's chest. Logan saw that you could cover all three holes with a gold piece. Running Wolf looked at Logan, "I don't think your sister liked these people."

A voice came from behind them. "One thing about this family, there's always something going on." Logan turned to find Tug grinning at him.

"These girls were taken from a small farm near a trading post east of here," Rebecca told them.

"I heard there was a small settlement over on the other side of Three Peaks but haven't had a chance to check it out. It's in an area that isn't really part of my territory patrol so I haven't checked it out."

Rebecca cooked breakfast from the supplies that were on the pack horses. She found some new clothes in the supplies in the same packs and had the girls put them on. After breakfast they loaded the bodies, and Logan set fire to the cabin. This way no one else would try to use it. It wouldn't have lasted one winter but Logan wanted it gone. As they neared the ranch, they were met by Acel and Cliff, who rode out to see if they could help. Acel looked back at the seven bodies.

"Where do you want those fellows buried?"

"Bury them up there with the men that were killed when I was shot."

Tug had been listening. "That's going to be the largest boot hill for outlaws in the country if these people don't quit trying the McTiers."

Rebecca looked back. She started to say something then turned back with a grin on her face.

Little Feather and Rebecca took the two very scared, shy girls into the house. They cleaned them up and found clothes they could wear.

Tug was going to be alright. He had taken quite a beating but the tough little ex-ranger cleaned up and was back out helping Acel bury the bodies. Logan put the horses away. He decided the first time anybody rode out to Kilgore he'd send the outlaw's horses and gear with them.

Acel had built Rebecca her own cabin. It was up the creek from the main buildings. After building and spending a winter, Acel found a small hot springs along the creek. He noticed steam on the first real cold morning coming from along the creek about a quarter of a mile from the cabins. After Rebecca moved in, she had Boyd and some of the crew dug out a pool in the bank above the creek. They found a good stream of hot water. Acel then built a bath house over the spring. It became a popular place with everyone at the ranch.

Rebecca walked out of the house. When she got close, Logan could see the bruises on her face. Her hair was still a mess. As she walked by Logan, she mumbled, "I'm going up to my cabin. Later, I'm going to the bathhouse and soak for a spell. Little Feather has the girls calmed down, and they're both asleep." She reached out and touched her brother's arm. "When the fellow tripped me, then kicked me just before you fired, I was praying you were near. It was like a dream when I heard the rifle and saw that no account knocked over backward. Then the other two rifles fired from a different direction and the other two went down. I knew from the sound they were buffalo rifles and that had to be you. Then when Little Hawk and Running Wolf walked out of the trees, I knew we were safe. Those fellows were animals, and the last one was crazy. I'm glad I killed him."

Logan smiled, "Sis, I think you should maybe control your temper a little. One shot would have killed him."

As she walked away, she said over her shoulder, "I did control my temper. I wanted to gut shoot him!"

Logan grinned and decided his sister was maybe a little on the tough side.

The two girls helped Little Feather with breakfast the next morning. Logan asked them where they were from and how the little crazy man had grabbed them. They told Logan they lived with their folks on a small homestead near the new settlement called Penny Springs. "We were working in the garden when this little man rode up. He asked to water his horses. When our mother walked out of the cabin and up to him, he pulled his pistol and hit her. He tied our hands behind our backs then gagged us. Then we were loaded on top of the packs on the horses. As he tied us on the horses, he tore off our clothes laughing all the time."

Rebecca, who had come down for breakfast from her cabin, touched Logan's arm. "I'll tell you the rest later."

Logan nodded and looked back at the girls. "Where did you move from before homesteading near Penny Springs?"

Both girls answered, "Mercyville! It's a small new town that most people haven't even heard of."

Logan never let on that he had been the ranger that caught the bank robbers there. As they talked, Logan thought maybe this was the family that had left in a big hurry leaving everything behind. Their father could be the last of Reverend Ballard's gang. Logan decided he'd leave this alone for now and maybe someday pass the information on to George.

That evening as Logan worked in the barn with Tug, Fawn came running in, "Riders are coming across the meadow."

Logan stepped out where he could see. As they got closer Tug said, "That one rider is wearing a badge." When they rode into the yard, Logan recognized Ray Johnson. There were seven riders with Ray. Logan noticed one of the other men was wearing a badge too. There was a big grin on Ray's face.

"So this is where you hide out to keep from working," Ray said as he stepped down from his horse. As they shook hands Logan asked, "Why the posse?"

"These fellows are from a new settlement over the mountain. They're looking for two girls that's been kidnaped. We followed the tracks to a meadow up above here and found a burned-out camp. There were signs of maybe a gun battle. Then we found more tracks and we followed them here."

Logan nodded. "You fellows might as well step down." He noticed most of them were wearing bib overalls. He figured that meant they were all farmers from Penny Springs. "We have the girls here, and they are fine. They had a rough time before we got them back but they will be fine. The crazy little gunman that stole the girls is dead. He had six more friends up in that meadow. He was bringing the girls to them."

Logan went on to tell the whole story. When he finished, he told Ray he had the papers found on the bodies to send back with him. The door of the house opened, and the two girls came running toward the men. One of the older men with the group stepped out to greet the two girls. Logan heard them ask how their mother was. The man, he figured was their father, said she was going to be alright.

Logan told the men they had room for them to spend the night. With a good night's rest, they could get an early start in the morning. That evening after supper, the men and the two girls talked on the front porch. Logan and the two rangers walked over to Tug's quarters. The two rangers were going to spend the night with Tug. Ray introduced the new ranger as Roger Stills,

"He's been on the force about a month." Roger had told everyone at the supper table, "To sit with two ranger legends is something I'll always remember."

Tug laughed, then looked over at Logan, "Do you know these two fellows Roger is talking about?" This brought grins from everyone at the table.

Logan gave Ray all the papers Acel had found on the bodies before he buried them. "If you don't mind, I'll send their horses back with you."

"Why don't you just keep them and pay the going price for horses to George?"

"I figure from the looks of that bunch of horses they were probably stolen. George can post them at headquarters, and maybe their owners can be found."

As they sat there that night talking, Logan told them the story about Reverend Ballard and his gang. "I figure the father of those two girls could be the last member of that gang. Ray, I want you to tell George about this before we say anything to the girl's father."

Ray nodded.

The next morning as the group got ready to leave, Running Wolf rode in from the Indian camp. "I'm heading back to headquarters. My wife is staying here for a spell before coming to the reservation. I decided to ride along with Ray and the group back to headquarters."

Logan grinned when he saw the look on Roger's face when Ray introduced Running Wolf. This big Indian dressed in white man's clothes was becoming well-known by many people in high places.

The girls were in tears when they thanked Rebecca and Little Feather for taking them in. They both had a big hug for Fawn, who had been their shadow since they had been there. As they walked up to Logan and Running Wolf, they both were very shy with these two men that saved them from hell. Their father spoke up. "You thank those men properly, and they both blushed and held out their hands."

Logan held their hands, "You both want to forget that night."

There father had frowned when he had seen them dressed in pants. He changed his mind after Rebecca scolded him to use a little common sense.

Logan, for the next few months, found out what it was like to be a full-time rancher. Boyd and the crew were busy getting in hay. Logan told Rebecca the next trip she made to Kilgore to see if Jerry could get them a mower like they had at the Rafter T. This would make haying a lot faster.

383

Tug had become Rebecca's full-time partner. Logan thought sometimes her bodyguard. Tug was a few years older than Rebecca, but Logan figured he would be a good brother-in-law. When he mentioned this to Little Feather, she told him he should mind his own business. So Logan decided maybe she was right before his sister or Tug found out and gave him hell. Fawn was now with her father more each day, and she was one heck of a good rider. Little Ted was still pretty small for long rides, but his mother took him whenever she went riding. He was going to be a big man if he kept growing the way he had been. Between Little Feather and Aunt Rebecca, both kids were getting well schooled. They had studies to do each day, and both were good with English and the Shoshone language.

One evening while Logan and the family sat on the porch just before dark, a rider was seen coming across the hay meadow. When he rode up, it was Ray Johnson.

"We got some problems down at the mouth of White River. I was just passing through and figured I'd better stop by and say hello."

"Why don't you spend the night? Come morning I'll ride down there with you. I was planning a trip down there anyway to see if I could sell some beef cattle to the miners."

They rode out early the next morning for the mining camps at the mouth of White River. As they rode along, Ray told Logan, "When we left with the girls and rode back to Penny Springs, the girl's father gave himself up. He knew who you were, and with Running Wolf with us he was sure we were going to arrest him when we got to Penny Springs."

"I told the old man I'd bring it up to my boss and we'd go from there. The old man told me where his share of the money was buried. He confessed he had nothing to do with the raid but he was one of the planners of the robbery. When he got his share, he buried it in the barn at the homestead. When we dug there, we found it right where he told us to dig. George has dropped the charges against him."

When they neared the mining area, it was getting late, and Ray said he wanted to ride in the morning. They made camp by a small creek. "I'm here to settle a problem with some mining claim boundaries." Ray laughed, "George gave me a crash course on mining law and then said, 'Go settle this problem'."

As they sat around the camp fire that evening, Logan told Ray about the claim problem he had settled here once before. Ray smiled. "Logan, I'd just as soon settle this without any gun play."

It was just after sunrise when the two rangers rode into the first mining claim. The two men working the claim saw the badges and stopped working to talk. They told the two rangers they knew about the problem, but so far, they hadn't had any trouble. They explained what was happening was these two men had come in and filed claims between two existing claims. They were saying the existing claims were filed too far apart and they had the right to claim ground between them. The older miners say when they filed their claims they were adjoining. Logan asked the miners if these older claims were on rich ground. They said it was some of the best ground around. Ray thanked the miner, and he and Logan headed on down along the river. They stopped at another claim, and the miner told them the conflicting claims were on the next creek.

When Ray and Logan rode up to the two tents on the next creek, they couldn't see any mining equipment. Two men stepped out. Logan noticed both wore tied down holsters and the pistols were the newer Colts. When they saw the badges, Logan could tell they weren't happy the law was here. Ray asked, "Are you the fellows that are cross claiming these other claims?" The older of the two spoke up. "We are, and we don't need the law butting their noses in here."

While Ray talked to the miners, Logan noticed two men walking down from a cabin up the creek. Soon other riders and miners on foot started showing up. The two men who walked down from the cabin told the rangers, "We're the owners of the original claims here."

Ray nodded, "I'd like to see your claim notices, and do you have them recorded?" The two miners replied, "We do."

Ray motioned to Logan. "Let's check these location markers on the original two claims."

The two with the guns started to follow. Ray turned, "You two stay put while we check out the recorded description."

They paced off the width of the claims and then the length of both claims. They were according to the written description for the location markers. As they walked back to the group of men, they could tell things were heating up and tempers were getting out of hand. Logan walked off to one side. Ray called the four men involved to meet him off to one side. As they started toward Ray, someone in the crowd hollered, "How come you're not running this meeting Mc Tier?"

Both men who were contesting the claims spun around to face Logan but kept their hands away from their guns.

"This is Ranger Johnson's problem. He's the one sent here to settle it."

Ray told the two, "From what I can find, you two are cross filing on valid claims. You're just trying to bluff yourselves into some good ground and it won't work. I suggest you load up and find yourselves claims in other places, and this time do it legal. I will send a copy of this case to all the mining areas around and include your names."

One of them looked at Ray and snarled, "You're lucky you brought him back up or you'd leave here draped over a saddle."

This brought a laugh from Logan. "You two couldn't handle Ray if he was sick in bed." This brought a laugh from the crowd, and the two gunmen just glared at Logan.

The two moved over and started gathering their gear and saddling their horses. As they mounted, they looked over the group of miners, "This isn't over yet," and they rode off.

One of the miners standing there hollered, "What about your tents?" The two never looked back.

Ray told the miners, "I'll ride into Spirit Lake and let the claims office know what has happened here." While Ray worked with the miner committee, Logan asked around if any of them were interested in buying some beef for winter. Logan told them he had beef for sale, and he would be glad to deliver before winter set in. They all said they were interested and would get together and send word on how many they wanted. With Ray done, they headed for Spirit Lake. Logan decided to ride along to see if he could sell any beef over there.

When they were out of sight of the miners, Logan motioned for Ray to pull off the trail. "I figure we're riding into an ambush somewhere between here and Spirit Lake. We can do it two ways. We can ride up above the main trail and find our way through to Spirit Lake. Or I will ride along above you and a little ahead to try to spot the two we just chased out. If we do it this way, you'll be a sitting duck if I don't spot them first," Logan grinned at Ray.

Ray nodded, "I think it will be better if we flush them out now, if you're right about them trying to kill us. I'll give you a head start before I move out. I hope you're as good as they say at tracking people."

Logan moved up above the trail and worked his way through the trees as he moved toward the summit. The trail got steep just below the summit, and Logan knew his cover was beginning to thin out. This worked two ways; it was more open and hard for the gunmen to find cover. Logan almost walked right into a trap but his horse stopped. It started to whinny when Logan grabbed his nose. In the trees just ahead stood two saddled horses. Logan dismounted and led his horse down closer to the horses. Once the horses could see each other, the chance of them whinnying was almost gone. He tied his horse, pulled the old Sharps and moved down through the rocks toward the trail below. As he looked up the trail, Ray was just coming into view. Logan slowly moved forward, and all of a sudden could smell cigarette smoke. He moved closer and then could hear one of them say, "Here they come."

"There's only one rider. McTier isn't with him," he heard the other one say.

Logan moved around behind a tree, and when he looked below a few yards, he could see the two men behind a windfall watching the trail. They both had rifles laid over the windfall and were watching Ray below on the trail. Logan leaned the Sharps against a tree and pulled both pistols.

"McTier must have gone back up river. We'll get him later." The two below Logan picked up their rifles and started drawing a bead on Ray.

Logan stepped out above them. "Just let them hammers back down and drop the rifles real easy." Both men dove sideways trying to bring their rifles around to get a shot at Logan. Logan was ready. He fired both pistols almost at the same time as the men moved. Neither man had come close to getting a shot at Logan when they were hit. Logan moved over to look down at the two; neither were moving. Logan looked below and could see Ray's horse but Ray was nowhere in sight. Logan hollered down, and Ray appeared from behind a rock with his rifle ready.

Ray worked his way up and helped Logan get the bodies loaded on the horses. When they hit the trail and headed down the summit toward Spirit Lake, Ray turned to face Logan. "What made you think they'd ambush us?"

"They were the type that don't like being shown up in front of a crowd. When they said it isn't over to the miners, I figured they would try to get us then go after the miners."

"I kinda had the same idea but I didn't think they would try it so quick."

When they rode into Spirit Lake leading the two horses with the bodies draped over them, people stopped to stare. They pulled up in front of the marshall's office, and he stepped out to greet them. When he saw Logan, he laughed. "With the bodies, I should have known you were near." The marshall walked out to look at the bodies and turned back. "Were these the two causing the problem over on White River?"

Logan motioned toward Ray. "This is Ray's case. He'll fill you in on what happened at the mine."

While Ray talked to the marshall, Logan crossed the street to a new store. This was a new business in town. What drew his attention was the meat market sign. He walked in and made himself acquainted with the owner. The meat man was surprised that there was a ranch just over the mountain with beef cattle to sell. Logan told the butcher, "We'll deliver any amount of cattle you can handle at twenty dollars a head, fifteen dollars at the ranch."

As they talked, Logan told him the miners over on White River were also interested in buying beef for the winter. The butcher wanted to know when Logan was going back home. He told Logan, "I'd like to ride along and talk to the miners about me furnishing their meat."

"I'm figuring on heading back first thing in the morning."

With that done, Logan headed back to the marshall's office. Ray and the marshall were at the saloon having a beer when Logan found them. They all decided to meet in a couple hours for supper at the hotel dining room.

Later that night after Logan and Ray went to their room, they decided to part company in the morning. "I'm going back to headquarters by way of Sweetwater and Kilgore then through Benton," Ray told Logan. They were eating breakfast when the butcher showed up dressed like a cowhand. Later Logan found out the butcher had grown up on a ranch and knew his way around a horse and knew good beef.

When they parted company, Ray told Logan. "I suppose with winter coming on I probably won't be seeing you until spring."

The butcher told Logan his name was Harvey Lewis. He was married and had two kids. Logan gathered the miners that evening to let them know what had happened on the trail over to Spirit Lake. As the evening went on, Harvey and the miners came to an agreement that Harvey would furnish them their beef. What made the deal happen was the fact that Harvey had contracted with a farmer to raise hogs for him. Now the miners could get ham and bacon to go along with the beef without traveling out of the country.

The Taylor family, who Logan met the last time he was there, asked him how their son and brother were getting along as a ranch hand. Logan had forgotten that Rebecca had hired young Jeff Taylor when he showed up at the ranch. Logan told them, "I'll make sure Jeff is along when we deliver the beef so you can see him."

Logan, on his return trip, decided he needed to bring in more young cows to help build the herd faster. Rebecca had brought the first cattle over from the Rafter T. Since then Rafter T riders had delivered three hundred head. This was good cattle country, and with all the winter range along the river, Logan knew they could handle another five hundred head with no problem.

Later that day Logan found Rebecca when she rode in from where the round up crew was working. He told her about buying another five hundred head of young breeding stock. She agreed they could handle it.

"I figured on a trip to Kilgore in the future for winter supplies. I'll ride on over to see if Dad and John have that kind of stock for sale."

Logan nodded, "It would be good if you spent a few days with the folks."

Rebecca left the following week for the Rafter T. Logan told her, "Two of the men from the crew will meet you in two weeks at Jerry's in Kilgore. They will bring all the pack horses with them for the supplies."

Logan had the crew gather the cattle for Harvey Lewis in Spirit Lake. He put Jeff Taylor in charge of delivering them. Crews were busy moving cattle down out of the mountain meadows and pushing them toward the winter range. Time was passing fast, and before Logan knew it, he saw Rebecca and her riders coming across the meadow with the long pack string. As Logan watched them ride in, he knew they should start thinking of clearing a wagon road to the ranch. As big as the ranch was getting, supplies were becoming a big problem. It would be shorter to build down river and over the lower summit to Spirit Lake, but with the steep canyons, the road would have to be built close to the river. Logan had seen how high the river got in the spring and knew the road would be washed out each year. The road out to Kilgore would be the best except the deep snow on the pass was slow melting in the spring. Rebecca rode up and handed Logan some mail from ranger headquarters.

After supper that evening, Logan opened and read his letters from George. George filled him in on all that had been going on with the new rangers. George wrote that Running Wolf had told him about the shootings on the ranch. George said he would try to get up to see Logan come spring. He also said Henry Davis and Becky were moving back east to Washington. He had been appointed by the President to represent the territory during the change over to statehood. George never mentioned who was taking Henry's place as governor of the territory.

Winter passed fast, and Logan thought he should check in at Spirit Lake to see if the miners were behaving. This was kind of put on hold when Logan started having troubles with his back. Ever since he had been shot, there were mornings his back hurt, but now it was a different hurt. He noticed his right arm at times felt somewhat numb. Tug saw him one day flexing his right hand. "What's wrong with your hand?"

Logan shrugged. "At times it feels a little numb."

"Logan, you better ride out and see a doctor."

Little Feather, who had learned much of her mother's knowledge of Indian medicine, told Logan one day. "My mother said after you were shot and started to recover that someday you'd suffer from this wound."

Little Feather told Rebecca about the problems Logan was having. She agreed with Tug; Logan needed to see a doctor. Logan at first said, "Shoshone medicine saved my life, and I'll let Little Feather doctor me."

Logan tried some of her cures, and they did get rid of some of the pain. The numbness would come and go. Logan knew his gun speed with his right hand was something he couldn't count on. Again he was thankful that Claire Matthews had pushed him to use both hands. It still bothered Logan he was losing strength in one side of his body.

The snow finally melted enough that Logan could get over the pass. He headed for the Golden Rose Mine to see if the old doctor was still there. When he got there, the mine was in full production, and the freight wagons from Mill City had been running for two weeks. When he stopped by the office, he found his old friend, Mel Miller, behind the desk in John Griffith's office. Before Logan could comment, Mel grinned. "John has taken his wife to Mill City to catch the stage. She is going east to see her folks, and John is going on to the capital on business. I've been promoted to manager, and John also gave me shares in the mine."

They discussed the winter, and Logan told Mel about the ranch in Raven Basin and invited him to come visit in the summer. Mel told Logan he just might do that as soon as John returned.

Logan headed down the walk to the doctor's office. He found the old saw bones asleep in his chair. When Logan opened the door, he woke up with a grin when he saw who it was. "Who got shot this time, Logan?" the old doctor asked with a short laugh.

Logan smiled. "I've been on the ranch all winter and things were quiet."

Logan explained to the doctor why he stopped by. The doctor motioned Logan to follow him into the next room. He told Logan to remove his shirt. When Logan turned where the doctor could see the huge scare on his side, the old doctor just whistled.

"I heard you were shot one time but I've never seen a scar like that."

Logan explained how Little Feather and her mother had kept him alive. When Logan finished, the old doctor just shook his head. "That shot should have killed you right there. Putting you in a sling between two horses and moving you that far was a feat in itself."

When Doc started poking around, he found some real sore places. He later had Logan put his shirt back on while he sat for a while looking in a book he had taken from the cupboard. He closed the book and looked at Logan with a somber face. "From what I can read, this is probably a kidney problem." Then he added, "It's coming from the old wound. It could be that the bullet hit some of the other organs and they are now shutting down."

This old friend then added. "Logan, I think you should travel down to the capital to see some of the young, new doctors who are up on all the new medicine. Maybe they could operate on you to ease the pain or remove the damaged organ."

They talked for a spell. When Logan turned to leave, he turned back to the doctor. "How about we keep this visit just between you and me?" Doc then nodded.

Logan rode into headquarters three days later. He put his horse in the barn and headed to see if he still had a room in the bunkhouse. He found his room still empty and dropped off his gear before heading for George's office. As Logan walked in, he heard a familiar voice call to him from the back office. When he walked into George's office, he found Ray Johnson sitting at the desk. Ray laughed, "From the look on your face, I guess George hasn't written to you yet. George is the new territorial governor. When Henry went to Washington, the President named George to take his place. George, in turn, made me head of the rangers."

Logan nodded his head and congratulated him on his new job. Ray went on to tell Logan he knew about the deal George had made with Logan. "There'll be no changes on my part."

"I just stopped by on my way to the ranch to see the folks." Logan had decided the less people that knew of his problem the better and that included his new boss. They had supper that evening and Ray filled Logan in on what the other rangers had been doing. The biggest surprise was when Ray said they now numbered over fifty rangers in the territory. After supper Logan headed back to his room to get a good night's sleep.

Logan, the next morning, saddled up and headed uptown and made his way to the Chinese bank to see his old friend, Lu Chung, the banker. He found Lu Chung at his desk and asked if he had time for a meeting on something besides banking. Lu Chung motioned for Logan to follow him, and they went into a private office in the back of the bank. Logan explained to Lu Chung about his problem. "I was wondering if you could recommend a doctor for me to see."

Logan went on to explain he didn't want word out about his problem. Lu Chung thought for a spell. "Do you have a problem seeing a Chinese doctor?" Logan shook his head, "No, I have no problem at all with a Chinese doctor."

Lu Chung smiled and started writing on a pad on the desk. He handed Logan the note. "Go up the street two blocks to a big two-story building on the corner. This note will get you in to see the doctor. This doctor is just out of a medical school back east, and he's also schooled in China to be a doctor."

Logan thanked Lu Chung and headed up the street for the building. When he walked in, an older man sat behind a desk. "What can I do for you," he asked in broken English.

Logan handed him the note. He had noticed on the way over it was written in Chinese. The man looked up, "You're Logan McTier?"

Logan nodded, and the man stood up and offered his hand to Logan. "I'm Min Lin, and you are a friend of my brother, Lo Lin, at the mines in Placer Butte."

Logan nodded. "I have always considered Lo Lin a very good friend."

"Lo Lin always writes you are a good friend to the Chinese, and with your help, we are going to be rich men someday."

The man escorted Logan to a room in the back. "The doctor will be in soon."

A middle aged man walked in and introduced himself as Dr. Burt Chung. He laughed at Logan's look when he had said Burt. "I took an American name while in medical school and have kept it because it's the name on my license."

He had Logan undress and stretch out on a table. He went over the wounded area real careful and checked other parts of his body. "You have what we now call scar tissue building up in the old wound," Dr. Burt said.

He went on to explain to Logan what he would do for him. The problem he thought could be held in check without an operation. Logan spent all morning talking to the doctor. When he got ready to leave, he was glad he had asked Lu Chung's advice on a doctor. Dr. Burt, as he asked Logan to call him, gave Logan some medicine made from herbs and other plants. He gave him a big supply. "If you run out, send word and I'll send you more. You should only use this medicine if you're in pain or your arm feels numb. I don't think your strength will get any worse on the right side, but it may at times affect your grip."

Logan tried to pay Dr. Burt and he just held up his hands. "You have been a great friend of my people and I won't take money from you."

Logan thanked him and headed back to the bank to see Lu Chung. He thanked him for the help and finished some banking business.

Logan rode out toward Benton the next day and headed for the Rafter T. He had talked to Ray during breakfast. Ray told him if they needed him, he would send word. Otherwise, keep ranching. It was a nice sunny day, and Logan decided he didn't need anything in Benton, so when he hit the forks in the trail, he took the old trail to Sheep Creek. This was the trail Hugh and his folks had followed when old Dave, the trapper, led them to the valley. Once they saw the valley, it later became the home of the Rafter T. As Logan looked down upon the place he had called home for a few years, it brought back many memories. Logan was working his way down into the valley when he heard his name called. He turned to look and found Whitey Miller lying in the shade with his head resting on his saddle blanket. Logan started laughing, "What's going on?" His old friend motioned for him to join him.

Whitey had been a hand on the ranch long before Logan took off to see the country. Whitey told Logan, "I'm checking water holes. Rose fixed me a big lunch so I staked out my horse and just finished eating."

Logan grinned as he sat down. "You had a little nap too, didn't you?"

393

Whitey grinned, "Sure, at my age you need to rest during the day."

They visited for a spell then Whitey saddled up. "I'll see you at the ranch this evening," and he rode off.

Logan had supper with his folks. He decided earlier he wouldn't tell them of his problem. Ted and Logan walked out to the porch. "We're gathering a herd for you, and they'll be leaving for Raven Basin in about a week."

"How many head are you sending?"

"I think we'll have about three hundred head of heifers. We're also sending fifteen just weaned bull calves."

"You figure out how much money the Pitchfork brand owed Rafter T and I'll pay you."

Logan had brought his saddle bags in the house with him and reached back for them. He opened them and brought out a bag of gold eagles to pay for the cattle. As Logan counted out the amount, Lottie walked in from the kitchen. When she saw the coins, "Logan, what are you doing carrying that much money in gold?"

Logan turned to his mother and grinned. "If you don't carry money, how do you pay your bills?"

Ted picked up the money and went into his office while Lottie gave her son hell.

The next morning Logan was in the kitchen with Lottie. She walked over and put her hand on his shoulder. "How long has that arm been bothering you?"

Logan could never get over the fact nobody could ever sneak anything past this lady. He grinned, "That's why I'm away from the ranch. I went to see a doctor."

He told her about seeing Dr. Burt. "I can already tell the difference in the pain level."

He assured her he would only take the medicine when needed. After breakfast Logan told the folks he would bring the family and come spend some time before winter.

"You'd better bring them by."

He shook hands with Ted and gave his mother a big hug and headed out.

That evening he sat with Jerry on the trading post porch after supper. Logan told Jerry about the problem and knew it would go no further. Logan then asked Jerry if the old gunsmith was still around. Jerry laughed, "We'll

have to bury old Gabe right here when he dies because he never goes anywhere. He's got a steady business repairing guns. He also has many people
that have him build them custom rifles. You having gun problems?"

"No, I just want the old Sharps worked on. I'll go up and see Gabe in
the morning."

When Logan rode up to the gun shop the next morning, he noticed two
horses tied up at the railing in front. He walked in and two men were giving
him the eye like maybe they didn't want him around. They both wore tied
down holsters. Gabe had their pistols laying on the counter working on
them. Gabe looked up. "Logan, there's coffee on the stove," and nodded
toward the back.

Logan laid the old Sharps down at the end of the counter and smiled at
Gabe. "She needs tuned up."

Logan walked back and poured a cup and found a chair and dropped
into it facing the two nervous men.

Old Gabe was still working on one pistol while the other one was on the
counter. He looked over at Logan and with a smile asked, "How have you
been, Logan? It's been a spell since I seen you. You still with the rangers?"

The two men at the counter both looked toward Logan and then at one
another. Old Gabe started to have a little fun with the two very nervous
young men. "You boys should get to know McTier there. Over the years
he's brought in many a so-called gunfighter."

Gabe laid the pistol he was working with on the counter. "Well, boys,
you can try them, but don't shoot your foot off. I think you're crazy to want
that light of a trigger pull. But you're the one doing the shooting."

They both picked up their guns and asked how much they owed for the
repair. Gabe said, "It's five dollars for both guns."

One threw down a twenty dollar gold piece. "We'll need a couple boxes
of shells too."        Logan knew both pistols were unloaded but watched
in case they tried for a hideout pistol.

After the boys left, Gabe shook his head. "I suppose they'll be back to
try you before long."

Logan just nodded, "You can almost tell when they're just looking to
shoot down someone for bragging rites."

Gabe nodded, "Those two are a little on the crazy side so you'd better be
watching, Logan."

"I see you're still wearing the colts you got from Matthews. I sold them to him when they were new. I've followed your life from the shooting of the Coulter boys through the mines and then as a ranger. I think Claire would be proud of you. He was a gunfighter but never just to see someone die like those two who just walked out. I don't think you remember me the day when you had to shoot the two trappers at the trading post. I was there when it was decided to tell anyone asking about them that they never were around the trading post. Then you rode out before anyone got nosy."

"I remember you with the other men, but I didn't know then you were the gunsmith Claire had spoken of."

Logan had Gabe clean up the trigger and sear on the Sharps. It was getting a little too much pull to suit Logan. When Gabe finished, Logan checked it over. "Now I want a strange pistol built."

Logan went on to tell Gabe about his problem. "I want this gun built to replace my right hand pistol."

When Logan finished explaining what he had in mind, Old Gabe was smiling. "Logan, a pistol like that will kick like a Kentucky mule," and then he started laughing.

They talked for awhile then Gabe reached behind the counter and pulled out a weird looking gun. Logan could tell it had been a shotgun at one time but had been shortened and the stock taken off. Gabe picked up a box of shells from the shelf. "Follow me."

They walked out behind the shop where Gabe had a shooting range set up. There was a hill behind the shop. Logan could see targets set up at different distances with the hill as a back stop. Gabe loaded the cut off shotgun and handed it to Logan. "Now shoot it one-handed. You'd better get a good grip before you pull that trigger."

When Logan fired it, it almost flew up and hit him in the face. Gabe was smiling when Logan handed back the gun. "This is a ten gauge. What you're talking about would be a smaller bore but would still have a mighty kick, both back and in front," he laughed.

They went back inside and Gabe told Logan he needed some time to build the gun. Logan nodded. "Don't worry about the time. If the gun works, I want two of them built."

Gabe and Logan discussed more about the new gun, and before long it was afternoon. "Logan, I got an extra room out back. You're sure welcome to use it for the night."

Logan nodded. "That sounds like a good idea. I'll take you up on the offer."

Gabe smiled. I'm always glad to have company. There's feed in the barn and plenty of water in the corral for your horse.

As Logan neared the barn leading his horse, he heard a sound that meant someone was cocking a gun. Logan dove away from his horse as a bullet hit the door jam sending splinters into Logan's face. He rolled again. Another bullet kicked up dirt where he had just moved from. He then saw the shooter. The man was stepping out for a better shot when Logan fired two fast shots from his left pistol. The man doubled over and fired into the ground. Logan started to move and another bullet hit next to him. It had come from the direction of the hitch rail in front of the gun shop. Logan, by then, was behind the water trough near the corral. Logan worked his way to the end, and he peeked around to find the other shooter. Just when Logan finally could see the other man, a blast came from the shop. The gunman was blown out into the road. Old Gabe stepped out of his shop carrying the shotgun Logan had fired out back.

Logan stood up and moved over to check on the gunman he had shot. He was dead, and Logan recognized him as one of the boys in the gun shop. As he walked over to where Gabe was looking at the other gunman, most of his chest was missing. "I hate back shooters. They thought they had you boxed in, so I joined in," Gabe said as he turned away.

He went in and brought out a couple of blankets to cover the bodies. Logan looked up to see the sheriff and a deputy riding around the corner heading toward the gun shop. As they swung down, he looked at the two covered bodies. "I thought maybe Gabe had started a war down here with all the gunfire. Hearing gunfire down here is common but not hearing so many rounds and with a shotgun added to the noise."

When the sheriff finished checking over the bodies, he sent his deputy for the undertaker. Gabe told his version of the shooting, and Logan agreed with the story. After the bodies had been removed, the sheriff headed back uptown. Logan walked back over to put his horse away. As soon as he was out of sight of Gabe, he started rubbing his right arm and hand. When he dove to the ground, he landed on his right shoulder. Now it was somewhat numb. His hand had a tingling feeling that was slowly going away. He pulled his saddle bags and took out the medicine Dr. Burt had given him. He hadn't taken any that day so he decided maybe it would help get the feeling back in his arm.

Gabe and Logan were eating that evening when Jerry walked in with a serious look on his face. He looked at his old friend. "I thought maybe now young gunnies wouldn't be looking for you to gain a reputation."

Logan smiled. "I don't think those two were looking for anyone special. They just wanted to gun down somebody."

Gabe broke in, "Maybe I was to blame. I mentioned Logan's name. I figured if they knew who he was they wouldn't try anything." Then he added, "I think if Logan hadn't walked in they would have robbed me after I fixed their guns."

Logan nodded. "They were acting very strange when I walked in, like they didn't want anyone around."

Jerry poured a cup of coffee and sat down. "I hope you two are right."

Before Logan rode out the next morning, he had told Gabe more about what he had in mind for this new gun. They had decided it would be a .45 caliber with a short barrel. Logan wanted to be able to also shoot shot shells loaded with balls. Gabe told Logan this would mean a little longer case on the shot shells.

Logan nodded, "I figured that much. I want to be able to reload these cases."

Gabe just grinned at Logan when he stood up to leave. "You know this thing will also handle regular .45 caliber pistol cartridges."

Logan nodded. "I figured as much, and that will come in handy."

Gabe stood on the porch while Logan mounted up. "Stop by in a couple months. Your new gun should be ready to test fire."

Logan made it back to the ranch, and things were busy so he joined right in. They had a good calf crop that year and lost very few. The weather on the river had been good all spring and that always helped during calving time. Logan told Rebecca they should have a herd coming shortly from the Rafter T. Rebecca decided she would ride out and help guide the cattle into the home ranch. Before she left, she rode over where Tug was helping build a new corral. "Do you want to take a couple day's ride?"

He was all smiles as he saddled his horse and tied his gear behind the saddle. Logan laughed when they stopped by the house where he was help-ing Little Feather.

"Don't laugh you big ape. I needed a break from building corrals."

Logan waved as they headed across the meadow toward the trail over the pass.

A week later Fawn, who spent more time aboard a horse than most of the cowhands, came galloping across the meadow toward the house. When she saw her dad working in the blacksmith shop, she rode over, "There's a herd of cattle coming down into the valley. Can I go meet them and help Aunt Rebecca?"

"Go ask your mother, and if she says it's okay, then you can go." Ted Jr., who was helping his dad by pumping the bellows, then asked why he couldn't go. Logan assured him he was needed to help him in the shop and that seemed to satisfy him for now. It was getting so when Logan was home he had a shadow everywhere he went. Ted was getting to be a big boy for his age, and Logan enjoyed his company.

The herd made it into one of the upper pastures that evening. Logan had Boyd send three of his riders up to night herd so the Rafter T hands could sleep in bunks for the night. When they arrived, Logan told them there was a hot water bathhouse up the creek if they wanted to clean up. A couple of the riders had been there before and told him they had been looking forward to that hot tub all day. Later that evening, Logan joined his dad's crew to see how the trail had been. They told Logan the trail was used enough now it was easy to follow and it had been a good trip. Logan told them to stay as long as they wanted to rest the horses before heading back to the Rafter T.

It had been a little over a month as Logan rode into the hitch rail in front of Gabe's gun shop. As he stepped down, he heard Gabe say through the open door, "I figured I'd be seeing you before long."

Logan shook hands with the old gunsmith as they headed into the shop. Gabe reached below the counter and pulled up a short mean-looking pistol. The barrels were on top of each other and one hammer controlled both barrels. Gabe picked up some shells from the counter and motioned Logan to follow him. They stepped out back to the shooting range. Gabe handed Logan two brass cartridges. "One is loaded with shot and the other has four slugs in it. The one with the slugs kinda kicks back," he said with a grin.

Gabe added, "The top barrel will fire the first time you cock the hammer and then re- cock it for the bottom barrel. Logan had put the shot shell on top, and when he pulled the trigger, the short gun came alive with a blast. The target he had pointed it toward was splintered and half blown away. As Logan raised the pistol to fire the bottom barrel, Gabe said, "The slugs give you a lot more distance than the shot does."

Logan picked a target twice as far as the first one he shot at. When he pulled the trigger, the pistol recoiled like something Logan had never fired before. He was able to hang on with his big hands but decided some people may not be able to shoot this piece. The four slugs hit the target still in a tight pattern. There wasn't much left of either target Logan had shot at. As Logan turned, he looked at Gabe, who had a big grin on his face. "How you like them apples?"

Logan grinned. "I do believe you've made just what I wanted."

When they were back inside, Gabe reached under the counter and handed Logan the second pistol. Then he placed two holsters on the counter made for the guns. "My friend next door at the boot shop built the holsters. I told him not to say anything about you having these pistols."

"Where's the bill for all of this?"

Gabe shook his head. "I really don't know. I've never ever built a complete gun like this before."

Logan pulled a leather pouch from his shirt and tossed it on the counter. It hit with a solid thud. Gabe reached for it. "From the sound when it hit, it's way too much."

"It's a thousand dollars, and I don't want any change."

Gabe started to hand it back.

"Gabe, that's what it is worth to me, and I hope you will keep it."

Gabe smiled, "If that's your wish, all I can say is, thank you."

"I think I'll ride up to see Jerry for a spell. This evening the three of us will eat at the hotel, and I'll buy."

Gabe's face became real sober, "Logan, I think it's best if we eat here."

Logan knew something was wrong. "Gabe, why don't you want us to eat uptown?"

Gabe shook his head. "I'll send the neighbor boy with a note to Jerry and invite him to come down here for supper."

Logan was still looking at Gabe. "There's been some young gunslingers in town looking for you the last couple of days. With the war over, there are many young men looking for work. There is also many more who are trying to make it the easy way. With all the gun fights in Dodge City and Tombstone and the cattle wars, we're flooded with men looking for a reputation. If they shoot someone and build a reputation, then they can draw bigger wages in these cattle range wars. "Your reputation is known everywhere, and the man who gets you will be top dog in the gunfighter's world. Since you shot the one here by the corrals, there's been a half dozen here asking about the Pitchfork Ranch. Jerry has had more at the trading post than I've had here. They found out someway that you buy your ranch supplies from him. I know Jerry always tells them you aren't at the ranch very often with your job as a ranger. There's two in town right now watching Jerry's store."

Logan cussed and looked at Gabe. "I really thought that once I was on the ranch and more or less out of sight this would end."

Gabe sent a neighbor kid with a note to Jerry about supper that night. Logan started changing his gun belt so the new gun could be added. He looked over at Gabe. "Is your saddle shop neighbor working today?"

Gabe walked next door. When he came back, he nodded toward the door and said, "Go on over. He isn't busy right now."

Logan went out the back door and into the back door of the saddle shop. Gabe took Logan's horse back to the barn while Logan was in the saddle shop. The saddle maker was an older man with a full head of white hair. He saw Logan looking at his hair and he grinned. "It was black until I tried mining in the Black Hills two years ago. I figured I'd make some of that quick money and then I could forget about repairing saddles. Well, those Sioux Indians changed my mind. I was never so glad to get back to this shop."

Logan showed him how he wanted the holster to hang on his right hip. When that was finished, Logan told him he wanted another holster made for his saddle. While Gus, the saddle maker, was changing the holster, he told Logan to walk to the barn to get his saddle. When Logan carried the saddle into the shop, Gus had him put it on the saddle tree. Then Logan pointed out where he wanted the holster mounted, in front of the horn and out of sight.

Gus grinned. "I've always heard you were a mean man with a firearm. Now I can see why they say that. You know with these young punks looking for you all the time, a little edge is good."

Logan changed his left holster to a cross draw and put the extra pistol in his saddle bag. He thought to himself this would be the first time since he inherited Matthew's guns that he hadn't worn them both. "I hope I'm not making a mistake changing over to this new pistol." Gus looked up from his work and nodded.

When he got the belts adjusted, he walked out back while Gus built the other holster. Gabe, who was just entering the saddle shop, asked Logan, "Where you headed?"

"Outside to see how this gun setup works."

Logan knew the heavier pistol would slow down his draw right handed but that was the hand that sometimes was a problem. After about five minutes of practice, he pulled out the new pistol and loaded it. Gabe, who had been watching, shook his head. "Even with that big pistol, you're still faster than most."

Logan re-holstered the piece. He started to walk over to sit down by Gabe when he heard a voice behind him. The voice said, "You don't look fast to me, and your hands better be full when you turn around."

Gabe, in a low voice, growled, "You've got another one behind the out-house on your right."

Logan spun left pulling the cross draw pistol as he turned. His first shot hit home. The youngster with two tied down pistols was doubled up without firing a shot. The new gun had appeared in Logan's hand as he fired the left pistol. He pulled the trigger. The blast of shot tore into the corner of the outhouse and chips flew. He cocked and pulled the trigger the second time. The slugs blew the side out right out of the building. A torn body was tossed backward behind the building as the sounds died down.

Logan walked over to the first one he shot just as the back door flew open. Old Gus stepped out with a shotgun in hand. The man Logan first shot was still alive; he wouldn't live long enough for the doctor to get there. The fellow whispered, "You don't give a man a chance do you," and he went limp.

Logan asked Gus if he would ride up and get the sheriff. When the sheriff walked back where the bodies were, he looked at Logan and just shook his head. "I guess they'll never learn," as he looked at the bodies." He stood looking down at the body behind the outhouse and turned to Logan. "What kind of gun done this?"

Logan pulled the new gun and handed it to the sheriff. "My god, man, how do you hold on to this thing?"

Later that evening Jerry, Gabe and Logan were eating when Gus walked in to join them.

"My wife's putting on a party for some young girl getting married, and she chased me out of the house."

They were just finishing supper when the sheriff walked in. After supper dishes were done, the conversation turned to all the young men looking to make Logan their target. Logan listened for a spell. "I think I'll retire from the rangers and stay in Raven Basin full-time."

The sheriff shrugged. "They'll just come after you there."

Logan smiled. "There, I'll have the upper hand. Riding out here you can expect a bullet at anytime, and from the looks of the last four, they'll back shoot you just to get the reputation. I thought it would go away, and now I have a family to worry about. I moved away from the Rafter T just to protect my folks, but this time I won't leave the Pitchfork for anybody. The men I've shot were shooting at me or my friends but I've never shot anyone just to watch him die."

As the friends started to leave for the night, Logan asked the sheriff, "If I write a letter to Ray Johnson at headquarters, will you see it's delivered?"

The sheriff nodded. "Just leave it with Gabe, and I'll stop by tomorrow to get it."

"Thanks, I'll be gone before daylight and out of sight before we have another gunfight."

As Jerry was leaving, he shook hands, and with a grim look, asked, "When will I see you again, Logan?"

Logan looked at one of his oldest friends. "I really don't know when I'll be back this way. It seems every trip out now ends up in a gun fight by some young punk wanting a reputation. I think maybe I'll just stay in the basin. At least there I will know if anybody's around and not have to worry about getting shot in the back."

With a nod, Jerry headed back toward the trading post.

It was still dark when Logan saddled his horse and loaded his gear. Gabe was up and had told Logan he would have breakfast by the time he got his horse ready. As they ate neither one had much to say. When Logan started to help clean up, Gabe grabbed his friend's hand. "I'll take care of this. It's best you clear the valley before light in case there's somebody watching for you."

Logan smiled. "Thanks for everything, Gabe. Maybe I'll see you when this all dies down."

Gabe watched as Logan rode off into the dark thinking, "There is one of last of a dying breed of lawmen." He was still a young man, age wise, but he was a lot older than his years. Gabe had noticed a little gray showing in his black hair, and he was only in his early thirties.

Logan rode into the yard at the ranch. It looked deserted. As he dismounted, he heard horses coming toward him. When he turned to look, he found the two McTier kids galloping into the yard. They both came sliding their horses up to Logan. They both bailed off to tell their dad, "We saw you way off but mother wouldn't let us ride out to meet you."

403

About then Little Feather came riding into the yard with a smile on her face. "I think maybe you should talk to Little Hawk about teaching these kids to ride so wild. His boys have been giving these two lessons on trick riding and somebody's going to break their neck."

Logan started laughing. "I think it would be better if you talked to Little Hawk. He's your brother. After lunch I want to ride out and look over the cattle. I'll take them with me."

While they were eating, Fawn told her father the crew was branding up at the third fork corrals. So Logan decided to ride up that way and see if he could help. Logan went to the corrals to pick out another horse. Fawn opened the gate and Logan rode out. She closed the gate and ran for her horse. She grabbed the horn and hollered ,and the little Indian pony broke into a high run. She dropped down on the horses side, and when her feet hit, she bounced up into the saddle. Logan turned just as a blur went flying by, and Ted did the same thing only he had grabbed the saddle strings instead of the horn. Both slowed their horse and rode up alongside their father one on each side. Logan looked back toward the house and could see Little Feather on the porch. Logan could tell from her looks she wasn't happy with her kids. Logan looked away grinning. "Maybe you two should do that type riding out of sight of your mother." Then he added, "Don't tell Little Feather what I just said." They both were grinning at their dad.

As they rode up to the corrals at Third Fork, dust was coming up as the crew was working the calves. Rebecca saw him riding up and tossed her rope to another rider. "Well big brother, what are you doing home so quick? You know there's lots of work to be done around here."

Logan grinned. "I'm just riding to get these kids away from Little Feather for awhile," Fawn and Ted were both grinning.

"I know, they bug me each morning to come along. I tried to get them to help Tug rounding the cattle up but that's not a fast enough pace for them. Tug makes them ride slow and not push the cows hard, and they say that's not any fun," Rebecca laughed.

Logan tied up his horse and spent the afternoon helping in the corral. Logan was real surprised how well his sister could handle a rope; she very seldom missed a calf.

As the crew moved toward the cook wagon, their day done, Logan went over to put his saddle back on his horse. He looked over at Rebecca. "The kids and I are going back to the ranch." Rebecca nodded. "If you'll wait a

404

minute until I talk to Boyd about tomorrow's work, I'll ride back with you."
As the buildings came into view, the two kids were off at full speed with
Dad hollering to the wind to slow down.

Logan stayed busy with ranch work in general. Rebecca suggested he
take over supplying the line camps. This chore had been handled by about
everyone. They needed the same person to take charge full time. They
needed more supplies when crews were working in certain areas. Then each
fall they needed to get them ready for winter. Logan took his new job seri-
ously and had two real helpers, Fawn and Ted. They were real happy when
they had to spend a night at the cabins instead of riding home. Fawn told her
mother after one trip, "Dad sure cooks a lot different than you do."

Little Feather laughed. "You're getting old enough you should be doing
the cooking." This brought a frown from Fawn.

"Oh, I like Dad's cooking alright, and he only makes us wash what
dishes we use."

Logan and the two were returning one afternoon to the ranch after being
out one day. Logan noticed two strange horses in the corral as they rode in.
Then he recognized they were both marked with the ranger brand. When
Logan first started with the rangers, they only marked their horses with a
small mark under the mane. Now they branded with a "T"on the left shoulder. As he dismounted, he saw Ray Johnson walking toward him from the
bunkhouse. The kids finished putting their horses away and went running to
the house. Ray waited until they had left. "I got your message."

Logan told him a little of why he wanted this meeting. Ray shook his
head. "I stopped in Kilgore and talked to Jerry. He told me about your last
trip out. Then he told me you've been having trouble every time you ride
into Kilgore lately. You know, you're not the only one they're after but
you're at the top of the list. We have had a number of other rangers challenged. One was wounded down along the lower boundary last week.
"Logan, I think you retiring will probably help some. You could pick your
own time to leave the ranch and where you're traveling. We had a shooting
in Spirit Lake by two young gunnies. We found later it all happened just to
lure you there. I sent the ranger from Sweetwater over there. He ended up
shooting them both. Before the one died he confessed to the fact they had
shot the fellow on the street just to get you there."

Logan heard Little Feather calling him, and when he looked, she was
motioning from the porch that supper was on. Ray waved to a fellow sitting

on the bunkhouse steps to come join them.  When he walked up, Ray introduced him as Bill Morgan.  "Bill is one of our new rangers.  He'd been a
marshall in a cow town in Kansas before joining the rangers."

Logan sized him up.  He was near Logan's age, and from the way he
wore his pistol, Logan knew he could use it.  Logan noticed Ray looking at
his right hip and he motioned, "Is that the pistol Gabe built for you?"

Logan smiled and pulled it out and handed it to Ray.  "My god, Logan,
it almost takes two hands to lift it," Ray complained.

Ray handed it to Bill, "No wonder the guy in the trading post said both
men had stayed down in that last shoot out.  How bad is the recoil?" They
both asked almost at the same time.

Logan grinned.  "After supper we'll go up on the hill and you both can
shoot it."

After supper Logan and the two rangers walked up to a place where he
practiced sometimes and handed the pistol to Ray.  Ray handed it to Bill,
"Rank has its privileges. You shoot first."  Bill pulled up and shot the top
barrel.  As he lowered it, Logan laughed.  "That' the barrel loaded with shot.
The bottom barrel is loaded with slugs, and it's a little wilder to hang on to."
Bill aimed further up the hill and fired.  He turned toward Logan and
grinned. "Now, that is something else. I shot too quick. Look up there now."

A rock chuck had poked his head up in the rocks close to where Ray had
fired .  A bark of a pistol was heard and the chuck lay dead in the rocks.
Logan shucked the empty from his other pistol.  Bill looked at Logan and
grinned. "I believed the stories, but now I know for sure how fast you really
are."

Ray fired the new pistol.  "That's more gun than I want to carry and
shoot."  As they walked back down to the buildings, Tug came out of the
cookhouse and walked over to join them.

He was grinning as he walked up, "What do you fellows think of that
cannon? My hands are too small to hang onto that beast."

When Ray and Bill rode out the next morning, Logan watched them
until they were out of sight.  Tug, who was going to help Logan clean out a
spring, stood there watching Logan.  "Well, old friend, it looks like now
you're unemployed."

Logan nodded. "It's time to head for that spring that needs cleaning
out." Logan thought to himself that he was glad Ray had chose to let him
keep his badge.  He was no longer an active ranger, but he could still arrest

someone if there was no other way to handle it. He hadn't told any of the family or Tug about the deal he made with Ray.

Time had gone fast, and before he knew it, it was time for Logan to start stocking the line cabins for winter. As he climbed up the trail leading to a line shack on Third Fork, he could smell smoke close by. He finally decided it was coming from up near the ridge top. He tied off the two pack horses he was leading. Then he tied his horse in some willows out of sight of the ridge above. When Logan got to the top, he moved around real quiet like. He finally spotted the smoke. As he got closer, he could see the fire was almost out and no one was around. He walked up and could see where two men had spent the night. You could see the ranch building off out in the valley. The trail Logan had been riding was hidden from these people if they had been watching the ranch. Logan followed the tracks. They headed off away from the ranch and from the line shack where Logan was headed. As Logan walked back to the horses, his thoughts were on the two visitors. A couple of the riders from the ranch had found similar camps almost all around the basin. All day as Logan put the supplies away at the cabin his thoughts were on the campfire that morning.

Back at the ranch that night he told Rebecca and Tug about finding the smoldering fire that morning. Logan was still for a minute. "I'm about through supplying the line cabins. I think maybe I'll spend a few days looking over the hills surrounding the ranch."

Tug nodded. "I think that's a good idea. I know where the other places are, where the riders have seen fresh sign in the last month or so. I'll ride along and show you."

"No, I think it's best we don't change our work pattern. I've been leaving each day by myself, and if we change that, we could scare them off."

Rebecca and Tug both nodded.

Logan loaded up the next morning for a trip to the South Fork upper line camp. This would be a two-day trip. He went and found Tug when he was ready to leave. "I'll meet you in the lower South Fork meadow tomorrow afternoon. You can bring back the pack horses."

They agreed this way if anyone was watching the ranch it would be dark by the time Tug made it back in. That way they wouldn't be able to tell who rode in with the horses. The trip was a long day's ride, and by the time Logan unpacked the horses, it was dark. After fixing supper, Logan turned in for a good night's sleep. Logan had been asleep maybe an hour when something woke him. It had sounded like maybe a rifle shot way off in the distance. After that Logan couldn't get back to sleep. Finally, he got up and cooked breakfast. He finished putting the supplies away in the cellar using a lamp to see. At daylight he saddled up and moved down the trail to the lower meadow. He knew he was way too early to meet Tug, so when he got to the meeting place, he unsaddled the pack horses. He watered and picketed them on a good patch of grass. He wrote Tug a note and put it on the pack saddles where he would find it. The note told Tug, "If you find this note and I'm not back, don't worry and head back for the ranch."

Logan angled off toward where he thought maybe the shot came from last night. He was about ready to ride on when he spotted a movement in the brush. He pulled his rifle and then saw it was a dog hiding in the brush. He stepped down and got on his knee and tried to call the dog. The dog just looked at him. Logan finally sat down and pulled some jerky from his pocket. He ate a piece then tossed a small piece toward the dog. The dog slowly inched its way forward to the meat. When he ate it, Logan tossed another piece over toward the dog. Logan slowly got up and walked over to his horse and opened his saddle bag. He had cooked extra bacon that morning and still had some biscuits from the ranch. He walked back over and sat down and held out a piece of the bacon. He knew the dog could smell it, and he slowly moved toward Logan. When the dog finally got close, he sniffed the bacon and grabbed it. He moved back eating the bacon and watching every move Logan made. Logan held out a biscuit with bacon on it. Again the dog moved up to get it but this time also smelled Logan's hand. He laid down and ate the biscuit watching Logan. He finally stood and walked closer to Logan. Logan reached out real slow and touched the dog's head. The dog then started to wag his tail a little bit and licked Logan's fingers. Soon he was rubbing against Logan's leg. When Logan stood up, the dog moved back a little. Logan patted his leg, and the dog moved back over to him.

When Logan mounted his horse, the dog dashed off into the brush. Then Logan heard a small bark. Logan followed the dog into the brush, and up the trail a few yards could see a pair of boots sticking out of a willow patch. Logan moved over and found the body of a grey haired man who had been shot in the back. He pulled the fellow out where he could turn him over. From the looks of the wound, he was shot from very close range. Logan's horse had its head up looking down the hill off the trail. Logan moved over that way just as a horse whinnied in the trees below him. Logan worked his way down and found a camp with two horses picketed near a spring. There was a full coffee pot next to the cold fire and a bed roll all laid out. Logan walked back and got his horse. He carried the body down by the camp. It looked like the fellow must have heard something up near the trail and went to investigate. Logan walked back up to the trail, and after looking over the area, found a rifle laying in the brush not far from where he found the body. Logan looked through the man's saddle bags and found a letter addressed to a Jay Howe. He found a note with the name Jay at the start so Logan decided this fellow must be Jay Howe. There was fifty dollars on the body and another twenty in the saddle bag. Nothing had been disturbed so Logan figured this fellow just got curious at the wrong time. Logan loaded the body on the saddled horse and the camp gear on the pack horse. He headed back down the trail toward where he had left the pack horses hoping to get there before Tug left. When he got to where he could see the meadow, Tug was just packing up the horses. Logan whistled and watched as Tug turned around to look up the ridge. Logan knew Tug would recognize the whistle because they had used it many times while traveling together.

When Logan rode up, Tug looked at the body. "I didn't shoot this one."

Logan told Tug the story about finding the dog, the body and the cold camp. Logan gave Tug all the stuff he had found on the fellow. "I'll see you back at the ranch in a couple of days. I'm going to try to follow the tracks I spotted while moving the body."

As Logan mounted, the dog looked at Logan then back at its master on the horse. Logan moved off a ways and called the dog. It just sat there watching him as he rode off. Logan called back to Tug, "If he don't follow me, take him back to the ranch."

Logan was just riding into the timber when the dog came running by and moved out ahead of him. With a grin, Logan thought back to the last dog he had found and all the good times they had together. He wondered if old Traveler was still at the livery stable with Wade. Then he remembered about how many years that had been and decided Traveler was in the happy hunting grounds by now.

Logan started following the tracks of two horses from where he found the body. The tracks showed they were traveling like they weren't in any hurry. Usually when you found someone shot, the tracks leaving the area were of someone riding hard to get away. These two riders were moving at a normal pace. This could be because maybe they didn't know the country. It was dark when Logan heard the shot, and there wasn't any moonlight because of the high clouds. This was a good trail, but if it was dark, you won't know that. Logan had traveled for about two hours and decided he should find a camping place before it got dark. He found a small creek crossing the trail and moved upstream until he found a good place away from the trail. Logan wanted to be close enough to hear any traffic on the trail below. This camp was hidden enough so he was out of sight of anyone on the trail.

At first light Logan and his new partner were back following the tracks. It started to look like the people he was following were just circling Raven Basin. Logan found a place where the two men had camped last night. He also found this camp had been used many times. There was a small poled-in area used for a corral, and it looked like it had been there for quite a while. Logan felt the ashes of the cold fire. They still felt warm deep down. This meant they weren't that far ahead of him now. As Logan moved out again, he traveled a short distance when the tracks left the main trail and headed up the mountain. This trail showed use, and Logan was trying to think where it could lead. He had traveled all this area over the years and finally started to figure out where the two riders were headed. This would lead up on the ridge to a peak the Indians called Eagle's Roost. If this was where they were headed, Logan decided he had better change direction. Up the trail another half mile and he would lose the timber cover, and they'd be able to see him following them. Logan decided to circle around and come up on Eagle's Roost from the back side.

It was afternoon by the time Logan worked his way up to the ridge leading to the roost. As he worked his way around afoot to where he could see the peak, he spotted one fellow sitting on the peak looking down into the valley. As he moved to another spot, he saw smoke coming from a flat below the peak and figured that was their camp. Logan had left his horse down the mountain by a spring with good grass. He had unsaddled and made a small camp before heading up. It was getting along in the afternoon when Logan saw the fellow on the peak stand up. He looked around then headed down the trail toward the camp. Logan worked his way where he could see down into the camp. The two men down below started to fix supper so Logan decided he would hurry them up a little. One fellow was stirring something in a frying pan when Logan's first shot with the old Sharps blew up the coffee pot. The hot coffee sprayed both men who jumped back and dove for cover. Logan's second shot hit the frying pan laying in the fire and caused hot coals to fly everywhere. Logan could see two rifles leaning against a tree by the fire. His third shot blew the stock off one rifle. When this happened, the second rifle was knocked into the fire. Logan could see one fellow trying to work his way over to the fire using rocks for cover. He shot into the rock in front to where the fellow was laying. Logan knew that lead bullets would splatter the man hiding there. About then both men jumped up and headed down the mountain through the rocks. Logan smiled when he heard horses running. Then he saw the two riding bare back down the trail. He sent a shot into a tree as they passed just to let them know they were still in range. The rifle in the fire exploded as the rounds in the magazine were going off. Near the timber line, Logan could still see the horses and rider dashing down the trail.

When the rounds stopped going off, Logan worked his way down to the camp. He looked through their belongings for a name or something to tell him who they were. He looked and found their grub sack. He decided they could furnish his supper. They had a slab of bacon, a few spuds and a couple cans of fruit. Logan smiled and decided he and the dog would have a feast. Before he headed back up the trail with the grub sack, he cut the cinches on the saddles the men had left.

Logan moved his camp down the mountain to a place well hidden for the night. As he cooked supper, he wondered if the shots were heard by anyone from the ranch. He doubted if they were heard at the buildings but some of the line riders should have heard them. He and the dog had a good supper. Later on as Logan laid back on his bed roll, he decided he should name his new partner. He laughed to himself when he thought about calling his new partner Bacon because that's the way he finally got close to him. He decided he would let the kids name him and rolled over and went to sleep.

Logan circled the mountain above the basin and found more camps that had been used that summer. They were all situated where they could see the ranch buildings. Logan was stumped on who would be so curious about the Pitch Fork Ranch. If they were after him, they would have tried something by now. As he dropped down into White River near the winter quarters of Little Hawk's group, he spotted a small herd coming toward him. As they got closer, he recognized Boyd, the ranch foreman. When Logan rode up, Boyd told him this bunch was going to Harvey Lewis, the butcher in Spirit Lake. While talking to Boyd he mentioned, "We heard shooting up toward

Eagle's Roost yesterday evening."

Logan grinned. "I was just doing a little practicing."

Boyd laughed. "I kinda doubt that's what you were doing." Then he added, "We're going to make camp for the night at the winter ranch buildings."

Logan had been in the saddle all day. "You know, Boyd, I think I'll join you. It's a long ride to the home from here."

Logan rode into the ranch the next afternoon. Tug and Rebecca were talking to one of the ranch line riders. The line rider was leading two horses with dead men tied on pack saddles. Logan recognized the horses. When he got closer, he recognized the red shirt on one of the bodies. The rider was telling them about the bodies as Logan rode up. Tug turned to Logan, "These two men rode into the Third Fork camp last night plumb crazy. Only one of them had a gun, and they tried to take fresh horses with saddles from the corral. They kept babbling about someone trying to kill them. The boys in camp tried to capture them alive, but when the shooting stopped, they both were dead."

The rider looked at Logan. "They both were riding bareback, and their horses were plumb worn out when they rode into camp."

Logan looked over at Tug, "I guess we should add these two to our outlaw graveyard on the hill."

Rebecca told the rider to spend the night and head back to his camp in the morning. The rider told Rebecca the horses were carrying the pack saddles from the line camp. He used them so he could tie the bodies on the horses. Rebecca nodded. "I'll help you pack up some supplies in the morning to take back to Third Fork camp. When you saddle up your horse in the morning, put these pack saddles on two of our horses." The rider nodded and headed for the barn.

After supper that night, Logan turned to Rebecca. "Whoever makes the next trip to Kilgore for supplies needs to take a letter to ranger headquarters about these men. We'll send all the information on these two men plus the old man I found on the trail."

"I'm going to Kilgore with a big pack string next week. I'll take the letter with me."

Logan had carried in with him that evening the saddle bag with all the gear from the camp on Eagle Roost. When he emptied it out, Tug said, "You know when Shorty was telling us about the two crazy men, my thoughts turned to you."

As Logan told the story Little Feather joined them. Tug was laughing when he finished. "You know all of these used camps I found on the ridge tops were looking into the basin. It doesn't make sense why we're being watched."

The next day Logan asked Rebecca how many riders she was taking on the trip to Kilgore.

She smiled, "Three besides me." Before Logan could say anything, she added, "Little Hawk's taking three riders to shadow me along the trail."

Logan grinned. "Sis, I keep forgetting you think the same way on such things as I do. When you're in Kilgore, you might check with both Jerry and Gabe about these mystery riders. They kinda know what's happening around the area and maybe can help."

As Logan started to walk toward the barn, he turned. "Let's send those men's horses with you. Jerry can keep them until someone claims them."

Rebecca left with her riders the next week. After she was gone, Logan told Tug, "I'm going to take another trip into the hills."

Logan didn't find other tracks or camping areas during his ride. When he was back at the ranch, he started helping get ready for the winter. Wood logs were brought down closer to the ranch to be cut up by the crew when there was nothing else to do. Rebecca and her crew had made good time and were back. It took one day just to put all the winter supplies away. "Ranger Bill Morgan was in Kilgore when I got there so I gave him your letter," said Rebecca to Logan. "I also told him about what you had found around the ranch and the two men you run off. Both Jerry and Gabe said there were many new faces around Kilgore but nobody had asked anything about Pitch Fork Ranch lately."

The cattle were moved down along the river to winter range and the ranch settled in for the snow. Boyd delivered another hundred head of cattle to Spirit Lake for the butcher, Harvey Lewis. While there he picked up all the supplies needed for the winter camps on the river. Logan kept some yearling stock at the ranch to feed from the hay they'd put up last summer. Four riders stayed at the upper place to feed the cattle, and the rest moved down along the river at the different camps. Acel built new buildings at all the locations where the cattle wintered. Rebecca let the riders more or less decide who went where and so far it had worked out well. The four who stayed up to feed the cattle at the home ranch had asked for the job. When

413

not feeding the cattle, they spent their time cutting wood for the house and cook shack. With only the four riders during the winter, they used the small bunkhouse connected to the cook shack. The big bunkhouse was closed up for the winter and that saved a lot of wood cutting. Logan liked the exercise of cutting wood. Tug wasn't about to let Logan outdo him whenever he was at the ranch. Tug traveled back and forth from the winter area to the ranch.

It was the last part of the winter and the sun was feeling warmer each day when Logan got a big surprise. After supper one evening, both Tug and Rebecca walked down to visit at the house. Logan and Little Feather didn't think much about this until Rebecca made her announcement. "Tug and I are getting married. We're going to leave tomorrow and ride into Spirit Lake to find a preacher."

Logan kinda chuckled when Tug looked over at him. "What are you laughing about?"

Logan shook his head, "I wasn't laughing at you two. It's just a big surprise. Don't get me wrong, I'm all in favor of it."

Logan went and got a bottle of wine from the cabinet. "We need a toast to this event." Both Fawn and Ted were listening, and Logan poured them both a small drink of wine. They looked surprised. Logan grinned, "This is a special occasion and you both should join in."

Ted looked at his sister and whispered, "Does this mean we don't have to study anymore?" Rebecca, who had been teaching them the three "R's", heard this.

"No, this don't mean the studies are through."

When they got back from Spirit Lake, Logan found out married life didn't slow Rebecca down a bit. She was still everywhere running the ranch. The grass was getting greener and Logan thought about bringing up some of the horses that needed to be broke to ride and work. Acel and Caddie, on their last trip out, had brought in ten more mares to be bred to Acel's big stud. He also bought ten head of three-year-olds for Rebecca to use for work horses. With time on their hands until the main herds were moved back up, the four riders could break the horses to work. They were still feeding once a day, and they could use the new horses with the old teams for awhile. Tug and Rebecca made plans to head for Kilgore with a big pack string for supplies. Little Hawk had checked and the pass was open. It was decided Fawn and Ted could go on this trip. While in Kilgore, they would make a quick trip over to the Rafter T.

"I need to let the folks know about Tug and me getting married," Rebecca told Logan. "Besides that Lottie, and Ted Sr. need to see their grand kids."

The group took off one early morning. Logan didn't think the kids slept any the last night. As they were going out of sight, Little Feather took Logan's arm, "I hope they don't have any trouble."

"Little Hawk, unknown to them, is going to shadow them over the pass," Logan said to her with a grin.

Rebecca and her party rode into the Rafter T one afternoon and brought the ranch to a standstill. Lottie was everywhere like an old hen with new chicks. Ted laughed at her and told the grand kids she hadn't moved that fast in ten years. Lottie couldn't get over her almost grown up grandchildren. Fawn was a beautiful dark haired girl with her mother's features, and Ted Jr. was built just like his father and grandfather.

Lottie, in her bold way, asked, "Tug, why did you take so long to marry my daughter?"

Before Rebecca could say anything, Tug spoke up, "I guess because she didn't ask me until now." This brought the group into a laughing mood for the rest of the evening.

As the group mounted to leave the next morning, Lottie and Ted had tears in their eyes. The trip back to Kilgore was full of chatter from the youngsters about meeting their grandparents. It was afternoon when they tied up in front of the trading post. Rebecca sent Tug to find the riders who probably had partied all last night. He returned with the four riders, and to Rebecca's surprise, they were in good shape. Loads for each horse were packed and placed near the door for loading the next morning. When this was completed, Rebecca looked over at Tug.

"I'm going to the post office to see if there is any mail for the ranch." The kids wanted to go with her. When they stopped in front of the post office, she looked at her two helpers, "Why don't you wait here, I'll be right back."

Fawn and Ted were watching people on the street. Two men walked out of the nearest saloon and walked toward the McTier kids. Fawn heard one say, "I think we have found us a squaw for the evening."

When she turned to see who was talking, one of the men reached for her horse's rein. Fawn pulled back and her horse backed up away from the man before he could grab the reins. The man started toward her again when Ted said, "Leave her alone."

The second man yelled, "I'll shut that kid up," and reached for his gun.

The first man was also reaching his gun when two shots rang out. Both men crumpled to the ground. The door of the post office flew open, and Rebecca was on the walk. She had a pistol in her hand. Fawn held the small pistol her dad had given her years ago. He had also taught her to shoot it real well. Off to one side Ted was holding a pistol aimed at the two men on the ground. One man hadn't moved while the other one was complaining about his wound. Logan had placed a holster on Ted's saddle in front of the horn. Logan had also spent many hours giving him lessons on shooting.

The man on the ground was yelling, "That damn squaw shot me," as people came running up. The sheriff was one of the first there. "What happened here?"

A lady stepped forward and pointed at the two on the ground. "These two were going to take the Indian girl. The boy there told them to leave her alone. Both men started to draw their pistols when these two kids shot them."

Both Fawn and Ted had put the pistols away. The sheriff turned to the McTier kids. "Do you two have names?"

Before Rebecca could say anything, Fawn nodded, "I'm Fawn and this is my brother, Ted, and our last name is McTier."

The sheriff turned and then recognized Rebecca. "Are these Logan's kids?"

Rebecca nodded, and the sheriff just shook his head. A storekeeper from across the street who had seen the whole show agreed with the lady. The sheriff looked down at the fellow groaning on the ground. "You fellows picked the wrong girl to try to grab."

The wounded man looked up. "Who cares, his days are numbered."

Rebecca heard this but didn't let on. "If you're through with us sheriff, we'll be heading back to the trading post," he nodded.

When they got back to the trading post, Jerry already knew about the shootings. Jerry looked at Fawn, "How long have you been carrying a pistol?"

"Dad gave me this when I wasn't very big. Mom carries one just like it."

She pulled it out and handed it to Jerry. "I've never seen one of these. It's a small caliber like maybe a thirty-two. I guess it would slow a person down if the shot was placed right."

"When Dad finds out, he will be mad. He always said if you have to shoot, aim to kill. I pulled off when I shot that fellow back there. I could have hit him in the heart just as easy."

Ted listened to his sister but didn't say anything. Tug, who was next to Ted, did take note that Ted had done just what his dad had taught him. He shot the guy dead center.

When they were inside, Rebecca pulled Tug aside, "Have you heard what the fellow said to the sheriff about Logan?"

Tug shook his head. Rebecca told him what the wounded man had said.

"I don't like the sound of that. I think something's in the works."

"I'm heading for home tonight. You can bring the pack string."

Tug took hold of her arm. "It's going to be dark before long, and we can't travel that trail after dark with these clouds. We will leave at first light and let the crew bring the pack string. Fawn and Ted can travel with the pack string."

Rebecca shook her head. "I think they should go with us."

Tug nodded, "We'll leave at first light."

The morning broke clear. The clouds and light showers had passed during the night. Logan was up at first light, and he and Little Feather were the only ones at the ranch. One crew took cattle up to the meadows above Third Fork. Another crew moved another herd to the South Fork pastures. Logan had decided he and Little Feather would ride over toward the Indian village to see Little Hawk. Logan saddled up two horses while Little Feather fixed a lunch for them to take along. Logan was as happy as he had ever been that winter and spring. With only ranch work and the family to enjoy, this was the life he had always dreamed of. No more lawman work, and he hadn't drawn a gun other than practice since last year in Kilgore. He walked toward the house, and Little Feather walked out carrying a saddle bag. He tied the saddle bags behind her saddle and boosted her up on her horse. She was laughing about the boost up on her horse. She was always commenting about all the help Logan was these days. With the kids now out of the house most of the time, Little Feather had spent all spring riding with Logan.

They were about half way to the village when Logan noticed horsemen riding toward them. Then he saw three other riders coming in on them from the side. He motioned for Little Feather to stop. Logan turned to tell her to head back toward the ranch. As he spoke, something hit him in the back, and he was knocked from his horse. Little Feather pulled her rifle, spun her horse and dug in her heels. Before the horse was at full speed, it was hit and started to stumble. She kicked her feet free as the horse fell and landed hard away from the horse. She hurt everywhere as she turned to look at the riders bearing down on them. She pulled up the rifle and emptied the saddle of the rider in the lead. She shot again and saw the rider pull up and fall from the saddle. As the jolt hit her, she was knocked over backward. She knew she had been hit. She heard a horse sliding to a halt and heard someone say, "I got me a squaw to play with before she dies." As hands grabbed her and turned her over, a muffled shot rang out. The man grabbed his chest as he fell on top of her. As she rolled him off, she shot once more as two men closed in on her. She hit the one man as the other one had shot her and she fell back not moving. From her lifeless hand fell a small caliber pistol.

Logan had given it to her a few years ago, and she always carried it in the folds of her riding shirt. When she was hit, she pulled the pistol from the hidden holster. She pushed it against the stomach of the first man as he turned her over and pulled the trigger. He was gut shot and was now hollering in pain, dying a very slow death a few yards away. The fellow that had shot her last looked down at the small Indian woman with the pistol in her hand and said out loud, "This squaw was one hell of a fighter."

As he mounted his horse, he saw his boss and his son riding up to the downed man. Another rider was riding toward them. He had been their lookout.

Two other riders stopped to look down at Logan's body laying face down on the green grass of the prairie. The older one said, "I've always looked forward to this day since he shot my brothers when I was just a kid. I see he's still breathing, so now I will be able tell him who's going to kill him," the man laughed as he rolled Logan over. A great roar broke the silence. The man was hurled backward, his whole stomach blown away. The other rider hollered, "Pa!" and as his hand went to his gun, another blast broke the air. The young man was almost blown into by the slugs coming from a big pistol that was falling from Logan's nerveless fingers.

Two other riders slid to a stop looking at the torn bodies, then yelled, "Lets get the hell out of here. I see riders coming over the ridge. Pa and the others are dead. We're the only ones left alive," the other rider said as he spun his horse and sank his spurs. Four riders were coming over the trail from Kilgore. They were all flat on their horses using their reins as whips.

Off toward the Indian village, six other riders appeared. They headed to cut off the two fleeing gunmen. They separated and soon had the two fleeing riders boxed in. As they closed in on the two, the other four riders slid to a halt beside Logan and Little Feather. Rebecca dropped from her saddle and kneeled beside her brother. She knew then he was dead. Tug rolled Little Feather over and shook his head as Fawn walked to his side. As Tug got to his feet, he looked around at Fawn and Ted, "Your folks died fighting like only they could. This lady killed four of them before they could finish her."

Tug walked over to Rebecca, who was still kneeling over her dead brother. He took her by the arm and pulled her to her feet and held her. The six riders were leading the men they had run down up to where Tug and Rebecca were standing. Little Hawk was the leader. When he stopped, he lowered his head when he saw Logan. He then turned his head to look at his sister's body laying in the green grass. Rebecca walked over to the two captives who were looking down from their horses.

She yelled, "Who in the hell are you people?" as she swung the quirt she was holding. The rawhide end of the quirt brought blood on the man's face. When she tried to swing again, Tug grabbed her arm.

The youngest of the two looked down at the body with its stomach missing and at the other body you could hardly recognize. "What kind of gun did that man have? It ripped my dad and brother apart?"

Tug looked up at the kid. "What's your name? Why were you after Logan?"

"My name is Billie Coulter. My dad was Roy Coulter. McTier there," as he pointed to Logan's body, "killed my dad's brothers and some of our cousins years ago."

Rebecca spun around, "You mean the Coulters that tried to rob Hugh Davis outside of Benton twenty years ago? Logan shot them in self defense. They were going to shoot everybody that was with Hugh."

"Dad's hired other men to kill him. None ever came back. So, Dad said we'd take care of him ourselves," the young man sobbed as he looked at the two dead men.

"He sent two of our cousins here last fall. They never did come back so we figured they are dead ,too."

Tug looked at the older rider, "Where do you fit in here?"

"I just worked for Roy Coulter as a hired hand."

Tug turned to Little Hawk. "Would you send one of your men to the ranch and get a wagon?" Little Hawk nodded and walked over to where his men stood near Little Feather's body.

Tug turned back to the two captives. "Both of you step down and load your dead people on their horses."

Rebecca, who hadn't said a word after Tug stopped her from hitting the fellow, now turned to face them. "I'm going to hang you both."

Tug looked at his wife then pulled her aside, "You calm down. We'll handle this the right way. First off, these two are going to bury their kin up at the graveyard. Then we'll talk about what happens to them."

Little Hawk took a bedroll from the back of one of the dead men's horses and used the blankets to cover Logan and Little Feather.

Ted motioned toward the ranch. They could see two wagons coming. "That second wagon is Acel. I can tell by the draft horses pulling the wagon."

When they got closer, they could see two men in the wagon, Acel and Cliff. They loaded Logan and Little Feather in Acel's big wagon.

Cliff walked over too Rebecca, "I'll take charge of burying these outlaws."

Tug turned to Cliff, "Make sure those two prisoners help dig the graves." Old Acel motioned to Fawn. He wanted to talk to her. "Would you ride up to our place and get Caddie to come down to the ranch?" Fawn nodded and rode off.

They laid Logan and Little Feather out in their bedroom. Caddie chased everyone out. I'll get the bodies ready for burial. If I need help, I'll call Acel."

Tug sent Rebecca up to their cabin and told her to take Fawn with her. Tug, Little Hawk and Ted headed up the mountain to dig two more graves. Logan would be buried close to where he had laid wounded until he was found by Little Feather and her brothers. As they finished digging the graves, Tug looked out over the huge Pitch Fork holdings and shook his head. He looked over at Ted. "We've got one hell of a job ahead of us, and Logan will be looking down watching us."

The Coulters were all buried on the hill with others who had tried to kill Logan. This was getting to be a large number of graves. When they finished covering the graves, Cliff walked up to the other grave site. He walked over to Tug, "Acel's just finished that new cellar. We could put the prisoners in there for the night."

Tug nodded, "That's a good idea. Maybe Rebecca will cool down before she does something stupid like hanging them. Little Hawk sent two Indians with Cliff to stand guard for the night.

That evening the house was real quiet. It was decided they would send Little Hawk to the Rafter T to let them know. Little Hawk nodded, "I will take my oldest son with me with extra horses so we can make a faster trip."

"Little Hawk, I want to write letters to my folks and to Jerry at the trading post. I'll ask Jerry to get a message to ranger headquarters and to Running Wolf," Rebecca said as she sat down at the table to write her letters.

Little Hawk and his son spent the night in the bunkhouse. At dawn the next morning, they headed for Kilgore and the Rafter T. They rode two and led four extra horses when they left. Another boy from the village would meet them at the summit and bring back the two horses used on the first leg of the trip.

Tug sent Little Hawk's other son to tell the crews on Third Fork and the South Fork of Logan's death. Another Indian rider headed for Spirit Lake to let Boyd know what had happened. Tug told both riders to tell the men. They're burying Logan and Little Feather that morning. He didn't want to wait for everyone to get back because it would take too long.

A solemn group started up the hill that morning following the wagon carrying the remains of Logan and Little Feather. The Helmicks were there; Acel, Caddie and Cliff. Acel acted as the minister for the services. All the Indians from the village were there. Little Bear spoke over Little Feather's grave before the graves were covered. As they walked back down the hill, Rebecca held on to Tug with her other hand holding Fawn. When they got to the house, Caddie started setting out food she had prepared that morning. Cliff took Tug aside. "I'm going back to our place to make sure the prisoners haven't tried to escape."

As Cliff left, Rebecca looked at Tug. Then in a very stern voice she said, "I'm still going to hang them both."

Tug knew better than to say anything right then but was hoping he could talk her out of it. He wanted to take them to ranger headquarters and let the law take over.

After everyone left for home, Tug, Rebecca, Fawn and Ted sat out on the front porch as the sun started to set. Ted held the big pistol of Logan's and the holster and belt were on his lap. Tug looked over, "Ted when you fire that, remember, it will kick like hell."

Ted nodded, "Dad let me fire it once loaded with shot. He said the slugs kicked a lot harder."

Tug grinned, "I'll show you how to load those shell when you get low."

Later that evening as they were going to bed, Tug thought he heard shots coming from up toward the Helmick place. He ran for the barn to get a horse. Ted was right behind him. As they spurred their horses up the canyon, Tug looked back. Rebecca was running toward the barn. When he rode into the yard, he saw Caddie kneeling over someone laying by the corral. It was Acel, and he was bleeding from the shoulder. Caddie said, "It's only a flesh wound."

"When Cliff went to feed the prisoners, they must have jumped him. They had snuck up on Acel, who was feeding the stock, and jumped him. They had stuck him with a pitch fork, but only one tine poked him. I grabbed the rifle by the door and shot over their heads once to get them away from Acel. When they started my way, I shot in front of them. I think maybe I might have nicked one of them in the leg. He grabbed his leg, and they both turned and headed for the corrals." Then she added, "One was limping as they ran toward the corral."

The only horses in the corral were two of the big draft horses. Tug figured when they saw the big horses, they headed down the canyon on foot toward the ranch. Tug figured he and Ted had ridden right past them. Tug spun his horse, and now it was almost dark as they headed down the canyon. As Tug rounded a corner in the trail, he could see Rebecca's horse across the trail with two people struggling on the hillside. He rode up and jumped off just as a shot sounded and the man struggling with Rebecca fell backwards. Before the man hit the ground, Rebecca fired again. The body didn't move when it hit the ground. Ted spurred his horse down the trail when he heard Fawn holler down by the house. Tug and Rebecca mounted up and dug the spurs heading down to the main house. As they rode into the yard, they heard a pistol shot out back followed by two fast rifle shots. They both ran around the house with guns drawn and found Fawn and Ted looking down at a body laying on the grass. Billie Coulter was dead. Tug kneeled down and saw he was hit three times.

Fawn looked over at Tug. "I started out the door to see where Rebecca had gone when someone grabbed me and tossed me back into the room. He grabbed for a rifle standing in the corner of the room. I pulled my pistol and shot him. He dropped the rifle, and holding his side ran out the door into the yard."

Ted had pulled his rifle from the saddle scabbard as he dismounted. When he rounded the house he saw Billie. Billie had heard the sound of Ted running around the house and turned toward Ted. Ted shot him twice with the rifle from the hip. The two shots almost sounded like one.

Rebecca put her arm around Fawn, "I wish all this killing would stop. You and Ted have been involved in more shooting in your young years than most people have in a lifetime."

Tug looked at the three McTiers. "Now we know why Logan left the Rafter T at a young age. Someway he knew his life would be filled with such people. Now it seems to have passed on down to his kids," Tug added while just shaking his head.

As the crews got back to the ranch, they all paid their respects to the family. Rebecca told them the ranch would go on, and they all still had jobs. She met with Boyd when he got back from Spirit Lake. "Your job has just doubled. I want you to manage all the range work and cattle. You can pick another man to be your foreman and work under you."

As the crews moved out again, only a few hands stayed at the home ranch. Getting all the cattle moved to summer range and branded kept everyone busy. Tug stayed close to help Rebecca with getting the books done.

It was a few days later when Little Hawk rode into the ranch. He handed Rebecca a letter from her mother. His son had turned off when they hit the river and had gone to the village to let everyone know they were home. "Little Hawk, thank you so much for making this trip to the Rafter T for us. Why don't you go home and see your family now."

Rebecca had tears in her eyes as she read the letter to the family from Lottie. Tug just shook his head after she had finished. "That woman is different than anyone I ever knew. She never lets anything get her down and just goes on."

It was a cool day after a good rain the day before. Everything looked so green as far as the eye could see. Rebecca and Tug got ready to ride over to Acel's and Caddie's. Ted was upstairs doing some lesson Rebecca wanted done, and Fawn was up at her cabin washing clothes in the hot spring. Rebecca looked up the valley. She could see six riders cross the meadow toward the house. At the same time Tug noticed two riders coming in from down the valley. Tug looked at Rebecca, "I don't like the looks of this," and he flipped the thong off the hammer of his six gun. As the six riders got closer, neither Tug or Rebecca recognized any of them. They rode with rifles across their saddles. They rode up and stopped near the hitch rail in front of the house.

The bigger man riding in the middle asked, "Is this the Pitchfork headquarters?"

Tug nodded, "It is, what can we do for you?"

The man smiled, "You've got twenty minutes to get your gear and ride out of here."

Rebecca, with her temper rising, yelled, "Why in the hell would we do that?"

The fellow grinned. "Because I'm taking over this ranch. I know the old bull Logan is dead, and this is too much ranch for someone like you two to handle."

The man slowly turned his rifle toward Tug. "Stand easy, ex-ranger and don't get any ideas. Now you're wasting time, and if you don't pack now, you'll leave here with nothing."

Tug looked at Rebecca when a bullet hit the big man dead center and knocked him over the back of his horse. Then the sound of a large bore rifle echoed from the tree line above the barn. Tug drew his pistol and shot the man nearest to the big man as the fellow swung his rifle toward him. Another fellow was knocked backward as the echo of the big rifle in the trees sounded again. A bullet caught Tug below the waist and spun him to the ground. The bullet had come from behind him. About then a rifle opened up from the wash house on the hill. A man with a rifle ran across an opening toward the barn when he stumbled in mid stride. He'd been hit by a bullet from the wash house. Another man jumped out from behind the bunkhouse. As he started to move, the big bore in the trees knocked him down. Rebecca had dove for the porch when the first shot knocked the man from his saddle. At almost the same time, a blast came from the back corner of the house. The horses of the last three riders started bucking. That blast from behind the house was Logan's big pistol loaded with buck shot. All three men hit the ground as the horses ran off. They tried to shoot at Tug and Rebecca from horseback when the blast came from beside the house. When they hit the ground, all three had dropped their guns from the jar of hitting the ground. They scrambled to retrieve their guns when the second blast knocked the nearest gunman backward. The other two grabbed their guns and started toward the house firing as they went. Rebecca finally got to a rifle she had leaned up against the porch. She fired at the two men running across the yard toward the back yard. One stumbled, and at the same time another blast came from beside the house and both men were knocked backward.

There was a stillness over the area. Rebecca ran over to Tug to see how bad he was hit. She found it was a deep flesh wound in his thigh, but it hadn't hit the bone. None of the men moved in the yard as Ted walked out from beside the house. His nose was bleeding and he had a cut above his eyes. He walked over to the downed men. He then walked over to where Rebecca was working on Tug to stop the bleeding. "They're all dead."

Fawn came out from behind the bunkhouse with her rifle in her hands. Tug winced as Rebecca wrapped the bandage. Tug said, "I guess this little show is over thanks to a big bore rifle fired by somebody on that ridge."

Tug looked at Ted's nose and forehead and grinned, "That big pistol really bounces with those slugs, don't it?" Ted grinned and nodded his head.

As Ted looked up toward where the big bore shots had come from, he could see two riders just coming out of the trees. As they got closer, Fawn yelled and started waving, "That's Running Wolf and his wife."

Tug laughed, "You know when I heard the big bore, I thought Logan had raised up from his grave." Then he added, "I knew it had to be one of the Indians that Logan had given the big bore rifles to that was doing the shooting."

Running Wolf swung down from his horse, "Don't you people ever get any peace around here?"

Rebecca had finished wrapping Tug's leg, and they moved him over to the porch steps. He stuck out his hand toward Running Wolf. When Running Wolf took it, he said, "You saved our bacon today. They weren't going to let us go. I knew that was a lie. Anyone would know they weren't going to leave any witnesses to this takeover."

"Who were they?"

Both Tug and Rebecca shrugged their shoulders. "We don't know; we've never seen them before.

Running Wolf put his arm around Fawn, "Young lady, that was some fine shooting you did back there. When I saw the fellow dashing across the yard, I was trying to get a shot when you got him. Then I knew we had those fellows in a cross fire."

Then Running Wolf exclaimed, "What the hell spooked those horses!

That one guy was knocked plumb over backward by the next shot. Those last two were knocked down the same way."

Tug looked at Ted. "Show him."

Ted handed the big pistol over to Running Wolf who started laughing. "Is this the gun Logan had Old Gabe build? From the looks of your forehead and nose, it must kick a little."

Ted grinned. "On that last shot, I had loaded slugs in both barrels. I'm glad it only took one shot."

Running Wolf's wife pointed then said in broken English there were more riders and pointed toward the river trail. Running Wolf shrugged his shoulders. "Well, I guess we better get ready for another bunch." Then he laughed, "I don't think we will have to fight this bunch. I can see reflections from badges on their coats. I think the rangers have arrived." As they watched the riders getting closer, Ted pointed toward the trail from the Indian village. More riders were riding toward them.

Ray Johnson was in the lead as the rangers pulled up in front of the house. He looked down at the dead men, "I guess you people handled this without our help."

The rangers dismounting were Bill Morgan, Ben Tate, Jeff Taylor and two riders Tug didn't know. Tug told the rangers what had happened.

Ray just shook his head. "This has got to stop before more of you get killed."

Little Hawk and his group rode up. Tug again told them what had happened. Bill Morgan walked over to look at the bodies. He turned back toward the group, "Ray, you need to look at this big man."

Tug called to Ray as he walked away, "He was the leader of this bunch; do you know him?" Bill Morgan nodded his head yes.

Ray walked back to where Tug was leaned back on the step and sat down by him. "That fellow is Bob Crawford. There's many wanted posters out on him all over the west. We just got notice he was headed into our area. We also found out he's related to the Coulters. He stole a herd of cattle coming up from Texas. They killed all the riders and then sold the herd at the railhead. The owner had been waiting at the railhead for his cattle, and when he saw them being loaded on cars, he notified the law. The cattle buyer told the sheriff he thought it was suspicious when the herd boss hadn't let his men loose to party and wanted the money in cash. The sheriff sent some riders to back track the herd, and they found the bodies of the real crew scattered all around a night camp. Most of them had been shot in the back. He must have known his cousin, Roy Coulter's, plans to kill Logan and decided to deal himself in."

As he looked at the people around him, Ray added. "These type people will never learn the McTier family is hard to kill."

The Helmick's arrived a little after the rangers did. They were armed and ready to fight. Cliff told Tug his headaches were getting better from the beating he got from the two prisoners in the cellar.

Caddie kicked everyone out of the kitchen as she cooked a meal for the large group. Little Hawk had left earlier with his people and went back to the village. The rangers, with Acel, Cliff and Ted, buried the eight bodies. Ray Johnson stopped and looked back at all the graves and just shook his head. As they walked back toward the house, Ray put his arm around Ted, "I hope you'll get left alone so you can enjoy what your father left you folks."

Bill Morgan, who had been listening, added, "An old ex-ranger and hot tempered lady and two kids. I don't think those fellows ever thought when they rode in this morning that they wouldn't leave alive."

"An Indian agent with a big rifle helped, but I'm sure many would have died even without him. Logan taught this family the art of survival, and the old ranger just fits right in," Ray added.

The ranger group left the next morning. Ray told them he was adding two men to the ranger staff in Spirit Lake. The Pitchfork Ranch could figure on seeing rangers at least once a week for awhile. Tug was walking around by aid of a crutch Acel had made. He walked out on the porch to watch as the rangers left.

Running Wolf had taken his wife back to the village last night so she could visit her folks. He had told Rebecca he was thinking real serious of quitting the job at the reservation. "I know of a nice little valley not far from here that I found while riding with Logan one time. I know I'll have a hard time owning the ground because I'm an Indian, but I still wanted to try. Logan told me he owned the ground and would deed the ground to me whenever I wanted to settle down."

Rebecca nodded, "I know about that valley, and when the family gets title to all this land, I'll honor Logan's promise."

They shook hands, and Running Wolf smiled. "I will make you a good neighbor," Rebecca just grinned at the big Indian.

For another couple of weeks the ranch was back to normal. Acel and Cliff ran the crews as they started putting up hay. Tug got around now with only a small limp. Fawn, who had been helping Caddie in the cook shack one morning, hollered at Tug, who was in the corrals, and pointed across the valley. Tug moved out where he could see across the prairie and saw five riders. As they got closer, Rebecca walked out on the porch. "Oh, my God! That's Mom and Dad."

Tug walked toward the house and said, "Who did you say that is?"

By then the riders had waved, and Rebecca recognized Henry and Becky Davis as the other two riders. As they rode up, Rebecca walked down to grab her mother when she stepped down from her horse. "Mom, that's a long trip. You and Becky rode all this way?"

Lottie stepped back, "I wanted to see my son's grave and the ranch he was so proud of."

Rebecca hugged her dad who said, "That woman has been hell to live with until I agreed to this trip." Rebecca hugged both Henry and Becky. She turned to pull Fawn forward and introduced her.

Becky smiled, "You're one beautiful young lady."

Rebecca nodded, "She looks just like her mother," as she watched Fawn blush.

They were untying their gear as a horse and rider came loping across the pasture toward the house. Tug heard Henry say, "Oh, my God, he's a carbon copy of Logan," as Ted swung down from the saddle.

Ted had his dad's gun rigging on as he walked up to hug his grandparents.

Lottie looked at the guns and shook her head. "I guess you have no choice but to wear a gun."

Tug, in Ted's defense, said, "That boy has paid his dues these last few months, and little sister here is just like him," as he put his arm around Fawn. "Logan taught them well, and they both are great kids."

Henry and Ted Sr. spent a day riding with Tug and young Ted looking over the ranch. Ted Jr. told them as they rode if they wanted to stay a couple weeks he would show them all of the place. Henry laughed, "I'm not used to this riding. The trip back to Kilgore will be enough riding for me."

Henry and Becky had come all the way from Washington just to pay their respects to Lottie and Ted. When they found out Ted and Lottie were going over to the new ranch, they decided to ride along. Lottie and Becky walked up the next morning to look at the graves of Logan and Little Feather. As they stood there, Lottie told Becky, "Rebecca told me this also is where Logan was shot that time. Little Feather and her brothers found him, and she nursed him back to health."

The two women turned to leave, and the grave yard below caught their attention. Lottie shook her head. "Those are all men who have tried to kill some of my family."

Running Wolf had come over to see them yesterday, and he had told them about the battle he had got in on. Caddie had told Lottie about the men who shot Logan and Little Feather and about the two prisoners that tried to escape. Running Wolf told Lottie that her two grand kids were almost unbelievable in there ability to fight any odds. "Fawn is like her father over and over, and Ted Jr. is also like Logan."

Becky smiled. "It's hard to believe that pretty, dark haired girl could handle herself the way everybody says she does."

Running Wolf laughed, "She can do everything her Aunt Rebecca can do, and some things better."

Lottie laughed. "I wouldn't say that too loud."

This was the last evening before the company headed back to the Rafter T. Everyone was in a silent mood. Rebecca hated to see her folks go, and she would probably not see Henry and Becky for a long time. Ted walked in. "We've got more visitors riding in. I think the one rider is Jerry from the trading post."

Tug walked out to meet them and saw then one of the other riders was Old Gabe, the gunsmith. Jerry and Gabe shook hands all the way around. Then Jerry introduced the third rider, Bess Walters. Jerry looked over at Rebecca, "Bess is that new cook you wanted me to find."

Rebecca laughed. "I'm glad to meet you, Bess. I thought Jerry had forgotten about me asking him to find a cook for the ranch."

Bess told all listening, "I was raised on a ranch in Nebraska. When my husband died, I lost the place. I got the place from my parents when they both died of small pox."

Bess was dressed in men's range clothes and with her short hair nobody knew she was a woman until Jerry introduced her. Rebecca told her to bring her horse and gear up to the cookhouse. Caddie greeted them. "I think I know two men who will be glad to meet you."

Caddie had been doing all the cooking for the hay crew, and Acel and

Cliff thought she had forgotten about them. Even though her men had been eating with the hay crew, they missed being pampered by Caddie.

The next morning with everybody hugging and shaking hands, the group finally rode off headed back to the Rafter T. Jerry and Gabe took Tug and Rebecca aside later. "We've got some business to talk over with you people before we leave."

Rebecca nodded. "Lets go up on the porch, and I'll bring out some coffee and we will do it right now."

Jerry started by telling them about the road being built toward the pass leading into Raven Basin. "The people from the other side will build to the top if the McTiers will build down into the valley."

Rebecca looked over at Tug, Ted and Fawn; they all nodded to her. Rebecca smiled. "Jerry, the ranch will be glad to pay the full amount of the cost to build the road. We'll need to find someone with road building know how to do the work."

Jerry nodded, "I know of two different people who'd like the job."

With this all agreed on, Jerry grinned. "Now I can tell you what Gabe and I came for besides paying our respects. Once this road is built, you'll start getting mail service, and you'll need a post office. Gabe and I would like to build a trading post here in the valley and apply for a post office. We think Kilgore is getting too big for us, and we'd like to move here. I'll need to buy ground for a new trading post, and Gabe wants to build a new shop for himself."

"Jerry, Logan would turn over in his grave if I sold you the ground," Rebecca said with a smile on her face. "You and Gabe can have all the ground you need, and there'll be no charge. You've supported us for so many years maybe now we can pay you back."

Jerry and Gabe both laughed, "We can't beat a deal like that."

"I'll apply for the post office as soon as I get back to Kilgore," Jerry added.

With your permission, I want to name it, "The McTier Valley Post Office."

This brought some quick tears to Rebecca's eyes. She turned away to wipe her eyes. Tug looked at the two kids, and they both were grinning. "Jerry, I guess you got a deal."

Jerry and Gabe left the next morning, and Rebecca and Fawn rode with them over to look for a place for the new trading post. Jerry and Gabe had picked out a place when they rode in. It was on a little knoll overlooking the river. Looking back the other way, you could see mountains behind the ranch buildings and the grave site of Logan and Little Feather McTier. Both Fawn and Rebecca, after looking around, told Jerry he'd picked the perfect spot. Jerry told them, "I've already got a buyer for the trading post in Kilgore, so I'll be back in a month to start building the new buildings."

Gabe nodded. "I'll be moving over with Jerry."

"I'll get somebody over to see you about building the road."

Rebecca shook her head. "Jerry you hire the man you think the best and get them to work, and I'll pay the bill."

Ranch work went on and, true to his word, a pack string loaded with supplies arrived at the sight of the new trading post. Jerry and Gabe built a leanto for their supplies and a tent to sleep in and started to work. Little Hawk brought all the able bodied men from the village who weren't helping hay on the ranch to work for Jerry. Little Hawk told Jerry they would like to take part of their wages in supplies next winter. Jerry agreed, and he had a good work force and later hired some of the younger boys from the village to peel logs. Rebecca couldn't believe how fast the main building was going up. Tug and Rebecca rode up the trail and found the road already built half way down the mountain. The contractor was a big Irishman with a true Irish name of O'Leary. He said with a grin, "I won't tell you my given name, but everybody just calls me Pug."

Tug figured that name came from his nose someone had flattened at one time. Pug saw Tug looking at his nose. "In my younger days, I liked to fight. Now I'm older, I've changed my way of life a little and stay away from such things."

Rebecca told him she would like to pay him for the work already done. Pug shook his head, "No, I'd rather finish the job first. If you pay me now, I'd pay the crew and they'd all head for Kilgore to party. It would take me a week to get them all back. Then most of them wouldn't be in shape for work when they did get back."

Rebecca laughed. "Whenever you're finished, just come to the ranch, and I will pay you."

The first wagons with supplies made it into the basin in early fall. Pug O'Leary had done a good job on his part of the road. All the teamsters were bragging about the good road. Jerry told Tug and Rebecca to bring their list of supplies they'd need for the coming winter. He had pushed the teamsters to get all the supplies over the pass they could before the first snow came. Acel and Cliff contracted to build Jerry a big warehouse, and they already had it covered so Jerry could start filling it. Jerry told Rebecca now he knew why all the buildings on the Pitchfork looked so good; he had never seen builders like those two. Rebecca told Jerry that Boyd, her foreman, was Acel's other son, but he liked ranch work better than being a carpenter.

The post office contract was awarded with Jerry named postmaster. Acel made a big sign to hang on the front of the trading post. Jerry invited everyone in the valley for the ceremony. Caddie and Bess took charge of the food. It was Raven Basin's first big party. The crowd that gathered that day stood in silence as the big sign was uncovered. A big roar went up when everyone saw McTier Valley Post Office & Trading Post. The McTier family, Acel's family and Jerry and Gabe were the only ones that knew what Jerry had named the place. Unknown to Rebecca, her family had made the trip over by buggy to be there for the celebration. Ted, Lottie, John and family and Mary and her family were all there. Lottie had insisted that Rose also join the family on this trip. Jerry had made sure Rebecca didn't know it until Lottie stepped out to pull the rope to uncover the sign. Jerry had told Tug, Fawn and Ted, so they all made sure Rebecca didn't find out until the unveiling. A letter from soon-to-be Senator Henry Davis of the new state was read. He apologized that he and Becky couldn't be there but sent his best wishes. The rangers were represented by the head man, Ray Johnson, and Bill Morgan was with him. They handed Rebecca a letter from Governor George Bennett, offering his sorrow in losing a good friend.

After everyone had eaten and before the dancing began, Rebecca stepped up to address the crowd, "Thank you all for coming. I know Logan would've been proud of everything that has happened. My brother was one of the first lawmen of this territory, and he was only a teenager then. In those times, they were forced to try to bring some law into this wilderness. They worked alone much of the time. Logan was a noted fast gun. His gun was on the side of the law, thanks to some men that formed this territory. Logan killed many men, maybe too many, but he never fired unless his life was in danger. When he tried to settle down to this valley to watch his family grow and to watch over this ranch, he was shot down in cold blood. He took his killers to the grave with him. His wife, Little Feather, killed three men that day, and she died alongside Logan. This year after Logan's death, as many of you know, we've had to fight for our lives to keep what Logan

432

started. He and Little Feather left behind two children who didn't have a chance to be children. They were taught well by Logan, and during the troubles this year, they proved they were of Logan McTier's bloodline. They are both fighters and along with Tug and me, will make sure this ranch and this valley survive."

The crowd started clapping, and it grew louder as Rebecca motioned for Tug, Fawn and Ted to join her.

When it was quiet again, she added, "Everyone has made a point to surprise me today including my family from the Rafter T. Well that works two ways; I also have a surprise. This valley will have another McTier come winter. His or her last name will be Higgins, but they will also be half McTier."

Lottie, who was standing up front, said, "Well, I'll be damned, she pulled one over on me," and everyone started laughing.

That evening the entire McTier family walked up the hill to Logan and Little Feather's graves. Ted and Lottie walked in the lead, and behind them came Tug and Rebecca, Fawn and Ted Jr. Next was John and his wife, Beth, and their four children, and Mary with husband Charlie Rote and their three kids. They formed a circle above the graves. Lottie placed flowers she had picked next to the headstones. The headstones were brought over on the first freight wagon into the valley. Ray Johnson had them made. Logan's name was on top; a ranger's badge was molded into the stone in the center. Below that was, "Territorial Ranger, a lawman who helped tame this huge territory. He was one of the best." Little Feather's stone was the same size, and it had her name and below that, "The lady who bore his children, and at the end, was at his side".

Lottie looked over her family then back at Ted, "I can still hear what Hugh Davis said of Logan at a young age, 'That boy will go down in history,' mark my word!"

Ted just nodded and pulled his wife of so many years to him.

As they started to leave, Lottie pointed to a dog laying among the rocks above the graves. Fawn smiled, "Grandmother, that's Bacon. Dad found him alongside a dead man and brought him home. He's my partner, but many times I find him lying up here visiting Dad."

As the group walked down the hill toward the ranch buildings, Bess, the new cook, watched from the cookhouse porch. Many of the crew sat around the porch watching the family walk down the hill. "You know that family owns more land than some of the smaller states back east. A friend of mine once told me she heard from her Chinese cook that Logan keeps his money in a Chinese bank in Capital City. She says Logan bought the Rafter T Ranch years ago from Henry Davis and gave it to his folks. He made big money before he was a lawman packing gold for the Chinese miners up around Butte. He found this area while working for the rangers, then started building the Pitchfork Ranch and took Rebecca in as his partner."

One old cowboy listening to Bess had been on the first cattle delivery from the Rafter T. When given a choice of staying here or going back to the Rafter T, he had decided he'd stay and help build this new ranch. He stood up, "Bess, you really know so little about this family." He walked down the steps and headed for the bunkhouse. As he walked away, he was shaking his head and mumbling, "If you don't know the whole story, don't tell it."

When everyone was getting ready to leave the next morning, Ray Johnson took Rebecca aside, "I received a note from Lu Chung at the Chinese bank in Capital City that he wanted to see me. When I got over there, he told me he had heard about Logan's death, and he needed to see you. He said he knew you were one of the partners in this ranch along with Logan's children. He said Logan had everything in order with the bank but he needed to see you if possible."

Rebecca nodded, "I guess I'd better head that way to see what he needs."

"If you'd like, I can stay another day and ride with you to Capital City."

Rebecca smiled, "Ray, I thank you for the offer but I think I'll get things settled here, then Tug and I will take Fawn and Ted and ride over. Please tell Lu Chung when you get back I'll be there next week sometime."

Ray nodded. "Well, if you're taking that crew with you, I think you'll be safe enough along the trail. Only a damn fool would try to stop you four along the trail."

Rebecca got her company all on their way then settled down to plan her trip to Capital City. When she told Tug and the kids about the trip, they were all excited to see the city. Rebecca told Boyd he was the main man while they were gone. He laughed, "Boss, I hope you know what you're doing leaving me here to run this place."

Rebecca nodded. "You can do it. Just rely on Acel to take care of everything here at the ranch; you just take care of the rest. Little Hawk and his crew will be close by so you shouldn't have any trouble. Ray said two rangers out of Spirit Lake will be here tomorrow. They'll stay over at the trading post until we get back in case you have some unwanted visitors."

As they rode into Capital City, Fawn and Ted about broke their necks trying to see everything. Tug knew his way around, and they stopped at ranger headquarters first. Ray told them he had quarters for them at headquarters. Once they were settled in, they cleaned up from the trail and headed uptown to eat. Tug took them to a small café just outside the ranger compound.

When they finished, it was early afternoon, and Rebecca decided they should go to the bank. As they walked out, a ranger drove up driving a light buggy. He stepped down and handed the reins to Tug, "Ray said to use it as long as you're in Capital City."

Tug drove up in front of the Chinese bank and Rebecca shrugged her shoulders, "I sure wish I knew what this is about."

Tug nodded, "Knowing Logan it's nothing serious, probably just a need for you and the kids to sign some papers."

Rebecca walked up to the front desk, "I'm Rebecca McTier Higgins. I'm here to see Mr. Lu Chung."

The man behind the desk smiled, "Welcome to our bank. My father will be glad to see you."

They were ushered into a big office in back. A gray haired man stood and walked around to take Rebecca's hand. "I'm Lu Chung. I'm glad to meet the family of my dear friend Logan. I was so sorry to hear of his death. He was a great friend to the Chinese people."

Rebecca introduced Tug, Fawn and Ted to Mr. Chung.

Lu Chung motioned to chairs. "Please sit down." The young clerk from out front was still in the room, and Lu Chung turned to him. This is my oldest son, Lin Chung. I would like him to sit in on this business. He will be taking over for me when I retire from the banking business. The reason I sent word for you to come to see me was I need you to sign many papers for you and Logan's children to take over the large account. Logan is one of our largest investors in this bank. I have made a list of his stock in this bank and his money deposited with us." He handed Rebecca a folder.

When she opened the folder and looked over the figures, she looked up at Lu Chung. He smiled. "Logan was a very rich man. He told me to invest his money anyway I thought best, and I have been very fortunate to invest well. I hope you will see fit to let this bank handle your banking."

Tug had been looking at the folder and was staring in disbelief. Rebecca looked at her family and then back at Lu Chung, "I never had any idea my brother had money like this. By all means, Mr. Chung, we will keep banking here."

Lu Chung smiled, "Then I will have Lin Chung start getting all forms ready for you to sign. It will be best if both children sign with you, then any of you can draw from this account without any problems. If you could come back in the morning, we will finish this." Lu Chung stepped around his desk and offered his hand to the four. As he shook Ted's hand, he smiled, "This lad looks and walks like his father; he will go far." As he stepped over to Fawn, "You are a beautiful lady, and you have the eyes of your father. It is no wonder he spoke so well of his family."

When they were back at the quarters, Tug shook his head, "I knew he had made some big money packing that gold, but I had no idea it was like this."

"When he bought the Rafter T for the folks, I couldn't believe he had enough money to pay cash for the place. Then when Dad needed money to build up the herd, he always brought gold. As we've bought cattle for the Pitchfork, he always had the money," said Rebecca.

Lu Chung had everything ready the next morning when they got to the bank. With everything done, Lu Chung again shook hands, "If you ever need anything, feel free to send word, and I'll do whatever you wish. Somewhere in Logan's belongings you should find a disk like this." He held up a broken disk. "Logan had it as proof he was Logan McTier should he need assistance from this bank. As long as I'm alive, and my son Lin Chung, you won't need it. Should something happen to us, it will make your banking easier, if you can find the other piece of this disk. It will also let you get money from any Chinese bank in the west."

Fawn walked up and looked at the broken disk, "I know where the other piece is at the ranch. Mom showed it to me one time and told me what it was for."

Lu Chung smiled, "It is well, you'll find it. It will let you be with friends whenever you are with Chinese people."

With business done, they thanked Ray for his help and headed back to Raven Basin.

When they topped the pass looking down on Raven Basin and their home, they stopped. Rebecca, with tears in her eyes, looked at her family, "He built it for us, and it will never belong to anyone other than his kin!"

## THE END

# CHARACTERS

Hugh Davis, Owner of the Rafter T

Henry Davis, Son and future owner of Rafter T.

Becky Davis, Henry's wife

Alice Davis, Henry and Becky's daughter

Ted McTier, Foreman

Lottie McTier, Ted's wife

Logan and Rebecca, Oldest two McTier children

Mary and John, Younger two McTier children

Beth Mc Tier, young John's wife

Dave Bowman, Mountain man and friend of the Rafter T

Ike, Lottie's dad

Joe and Elsie Philips, Owners of the Lazy P

Rose Miller, Ranch Cook

Ed and James Benton, Store owners and namesake of town site
    of Benton

Doctor McCrea, Benton Doctor

Sutter Creek Trading Post, Supply point

Yates Horse Ranch, Horse ranch south of Sutter's Trading Post

Little Bear, Leader of small Shoshone tribe

Hawk, Leader of small group over on the winter range

Little Hawk, Oldest son of Hawk

Running Wolf, Another son of Hawk

Little Feather, Daughter of Hawk

Clair Matthews, Gunfighter and gambler

Kilgore, Small town a half day's ride from the winter cabin

Jerry Crawford, Owner of trading post in Kilgore

Del Rogers, Sheriff of Benton

Jeff Rogers, Sheriff of Sweetwater, brother of Del

Laura Benton, Daughter of Ed Benton

Whitey Miller, Rider from the Rafter T

Jerry Miller, Whitey's brother

Dave Olson, Rider for Rafter T

Coulter bothers, Ollie and Thad

Willie Coulter, Cousin of Ollie and Thad

Del Wilson, Another cousin of Thad, Ollie and Willie

Tiny Lang, Owner of road house and gang leader.

Ling, Chinese store owner in Butte

Lo Lin, Chinese miner and Logan's friend

Lin Wa, Sun Lee and Ah Toy, All Chinese miners.

Dr. Burt Chung, Doctor in China town in Capital City

Wade, Manager of livery in Butte

Fred, Foreman at Ling's ranch

Frank, Fred's brother

Tug Higgins, Territorial Ranger

George Bennett, Captain of the Rangers

Clover, A small town

Lenny Cook, Sheriff in Clover

Chip Brown, Man shot by Logan in Clover

Wes Miller, Territorial Ranger

Rex Taylor, Ranger missing in Rapid River area

John and Frank Griffith, Owners of Golden Rose Mine

Bill and son, Charlie Milford, Owners of Milford Mine

Fred Hitt, Ranger

Lee Taylor, Ranger

Mel Miller, Golden Rose mine handyman

Acel Helmick, wife, Caddie, & sons, Boyd and Cliff, Carpenters.

Merryville

Marshall Cromwell, Capital City

Mollie and Dave Mc Intire, Moved to Mrs Tidwells mine.

Rachel & Gail, Placer Butte Trading Post.

Blue Bird Mine

Jeff Milner, Store Kilgore

Cliff Stroup

Spirit Lake

Jeff Taylor, Miner from lower White River

Ben Tate, Undercover ranger Milford Mine

Slim, Horse handler for Golden Rose Mine

Skip Bolen, Undercover ranger, blacksmith for Golden Rose

Ray Johnson, Ranger

Roger Stills, Ranger

Harvey Lewis, Butcher in Spirit Lake

Bill Morgan, Ranger

ISBN 0-9763421-5-4

90000

9 780976 342151